ANNE McCAFFREY was educated at Radcliffe College, Massachusetts, and has a degree cum laude in Slavonic Languages and Literature. She is a past winner of both the Hugo and Nebula Awards, and has written many novels, short stories and novellas, and various articles. Her most celebrated series is the world-famous *Dragonriders of Pern* saga. She now lives in Ireland and enjoys riding, cooking and knitting.

MARGARET BALL is the American author of the acclaimed fantasy novels, *Flameweaver* and *The Shadow Gate*.

**ANNE McCAFFREY and
MARGARET BALL**

Partnership

ORBIT

An *Orbit* Book

First published in Great Britain in 1994 by Orbit
This paperback edition published in 1994 by Orbit
Reprinted 1994 (twice), 1995, 1997

A CIP catalogue record for this book
is available from the British Library.

ISBN 1 85723 204 6

Printed in England by Clays Ltd, St Ives plc

Orbit
A Division of
Little, Brown and Company (UK)
Brettenham House
Lancaster Place
London WC2E 7EN

• CHAPTER ONE

To ordinary human ears the slight crackle of the speaker being activated would have been almost inaudible. To Nancia, all her sensors fine-tuned for this signal, it sounded like a trumpet call. Newly graduated and commissioned, ready for service — and apprehensive that she would not be able to live up to her family's high Service traditions — she'd had little to do but wait.

He's coming aboard now, she thought in the split second of waiting for the incoming call. And then, as the unmistakable gravelly voice of CenCom's third-shift operator rasped across her sensors, disappointment flooded her synapses and left her dull and heavy on the launching pad. She'd been so sure that Daddy would find time to visit her, even if he hadn't been able to attend the formal graduation of her class from Laboratory Schools.

"XN-935, how soon can you be ready to lift?"

"I completed my test flight patterns yesterday," Nancia replied. She was careful to keep her voice level, monitoring each output band to make sure that no hint of her disappointment showed in the upper frequencies. CenCom could perfectly well have communicated with her directly, via the electronic network that linked Nancia's ship computers with all other computers in this subspace — and via the surgically installed synaptic connectors that linked Nancia's physical body, safe behind its titanium shell, with the ship's computer — but it was a point of etiquette among most of the operators to address brainships just as they would any other human being. It would have been rude to send only electronic instructions, as if the

brainships were no more human than the AI-control-
led drones carrying the bulk of Central Worlds'
regular traffic.

Or so the operators claimed. Nancia privately
thought that their insistence on voice-controlled traffic
was merely a way to avoid the embarrassing comparison between their sense-limited communication
system and a brainship's capabilities of multi-channel
communication and instantaneous response.

In any case, it was equally a point of pride among
shellpersons to demonstrate the control over their
"voices" and all other external comm devices that Helva
had shown to be possible, nearly two hundred years ago.
Nancia knew herself to lack the fine sense of musical
timing and emphasis that had made Helva famous
throughout the galaxy as "The Ship Who Sang," but this
much, at least, she could do; she could conceal her disappointment at hearing CenCom instead of a direct
transmission from Daddy to congratulate her on her
commissioning, and she could maintain a perfectly
professional facade throughout the ensuing discussion
of supplies and loading and singularity points.

"It's a short flight," CenCom told her, and then paused
for a moment. "Short for *you*, that is. By normal FTL drive,
Nyota ya Jaha is at the far end of the galaxy. Fortunately,
there's a singularity point a week from Central that will flip
you into local space."

"I *do* have full access to my charts of known decomposition spaces," Nancia reminded CenCom, allowing
a tinge of impatience to color her voice.

"Yes, and you can read them in simulated 4-D, can't
you, you lucky stiff!" CenCom's voice showed only
cheerful resignation at the limitations of a body that
forced him to page through bulky books of graphs and
charts to verify the mapping Nancia had already
created as an internal display: a sequence of three-
dimensional spaces collapsing and contorting about

the singularity point where local subspace could be defined as intersecting with the subspace sector of Nyota ya Jaha. At that point Nancia would be able to create a rapid physical decomposition and restructuring of the local spaces, projecting herself and her passengers from one subspace to the other. Decomposition space theory allowed brainships like Nancia, or a very few expensive AI drones equipped with metachip processors, to condense the major part of a long journey into the few seconds they spent in Singularity. Less fortunate ships, lacking the metachips or dependent upon the slow responses of a human pilot who lacked Nancia's direct synaptic connections to the computer, still had to go through long weeks or even months of conventional FTL travel to cover the same distance; the massive parallel computations required in Singularity were difficult even for a brainship and impossible for most conventional ships.

"Tell me about the passengers," Nancia requested. When they came aboard, presumably one of her passengers would have the datahedron from Central specifying her destination and instructions, but who knew how much longer she would have to wait before the passengers boarded? She hadn't even been invited to choose a brawn yet; that would surely take a day or two. Besides, picking CenCom's brains for information on her assignment was better than waiting in tense expectation of her family's visit. They would certainly come to see her off . . . wouldn't they? All through her schooling she had received regular visits from one family member or another — mostly from her father, who made a point of how much time he was taking from his busy schedule to visit her. But Jinevra and Flix, her sister and brother, had come too, now and then; Jinevra less often, as college and her new career in Planetary Aid administration took up more and more of her time.

None of them had attended Nancia's formal graduation, though; no one from the entire, far-flung, wealthy House of Perez y De Gras had been there to hear the lengthy list of honors and awards and prizes she'd gained in the final, grueling year of her training as a brainship.

It wasn't enough, Nancia thought. *I was only third in my class. If I'd placed first, if I'd won the Daleth Prize. . . .* No good would come of brooding over the past. She knew that Jinevra and Flix had grown up and had their own lives to lead, that Daddy's crowded schedule of business and diplomatic meetings didn't leave him much time for minor matters like school events. It really wasn't important that he hadn't come to see her graduate. He would surely make time for a personal visit before liftoff; that was what really counted. And when he did come, he should find her happy and busy and engaged in the work for which she had trained. "About the passengers?" she reminded CenCom.

"Oh, you probably know more about them than I do," the CenCom operator said with a laugh. "They're more your sort of people than mine. High Families," he clarified. "New graduates, I gather, off to their first jobs."

That was nice, anyway. Nancia had been feeling just a bit apprehensive at the thought of having to deal with some experienced, high-ranking diplomatic or military passengers on her first flight. It would be pleasant to carry a group of young people just like her — well, not *just* like her, Nancia corrected with a trace of internal amusement. They would be a few years older, maybe nineteen or twenty to her sixteen; everybody knew that softpersons suffered from so many hormonal changes and sensory distractions that their schooling took several years longer to complete. And they would be softpersons, with limited sensory and processing capability. Still, they'd all be heading off to start their careers together; that was a significant bond.

She absently recorded CenCom's continuing instructions while she mused on the pleasant trip ahead. "Nyota ya Jaha's a long way off by FTL," he told her unnecessarily. "I expect somebody pulled some strings to get them a Courier Service ship. But it happens to be convenient for us too, being in the same subspace as Vega, so that's all right."

Nancia vaguely remembered something about Vega subspace in the news. Computer malfunctions . . . why would that make the newsbeams? There must have been something important about it, but she'd received only the first bits of the newsbyte before a teacher canceled the beam, saying something severe about the inadvisability of listening to upsetting newsbytes and the danger of getting the younger shellpeople upset over nothing. Oh, well, Nancia thought, now that she was her own ship she could scan the beams for herself and pick up whatever it had been about Vega later. For now, she was more interested in finding out what Cen-Com knew about her newly assigned passengers.

"Overton-Glaxely, del Parma y Polo, Armontillado-Perez y Medoc, de Gras-Waldheim, Hezra-Fong," CenCom read off the list of illustrious High Family names. "See what I mean?"

"Umm, yes," Nancia said. "We're a cadet branch of Armontillado-Perez y Medoc, and the de Gras-Waldheims come in somewhere on my mother's side. But you forget, CenCom, I didn't exactly grow up in those circles myself."

"Yes, well, your visitor will probably be able to give you all the latest gossip," CenCom said cheerfully.

"Visitor!" *Of course he came to see me off. I never doubted it for an instant.*

"Request just came in while I was looking up the passenger list. Sorry, I forgot to route it to you. Name of Perez y de Gras. Being a family member, they told him to go right on out to the field. He'll be at the launching pad in a minute."

Nancia activated her outside sensors and realized that it was almost night . . . not that the darkness made any difference to her, but her infrared sensors picked up only the outline of a human form approaching the ship; she couldn't see Daddy's face at all. And it would be rude to turn on a spotlight. Oh, well, he'd be there any minute. She opened her lower doors in silent welcome.

CenCom's voice was an irritation now, not a welcome distraction. "XN? I asked if you can lift off within two hours. Your provision list is more than adequate for a short voyage, and these pampered brats are kvetching about having to wait around on base."

"Two hours?" Nancia repeated. That wouldn't give her much time for a visit — well, be realistic; it was probably more time than Daddy could spare. But there were other problems with leaving so soon. "Are you out of your mind? I haven't even picked a brawn yet!" She intended to get to know the available brawns over the next few days before choosing a partner. The selection process was not something to be rushed through, and she certainly didn't want to waste the precious minutes of Daddy's visit choosing a brawn!

"Don't you young ships ever catch the newsbeams? I told you Vega. Remember what happened to the CR-899? Her brawn's stranded on his home planet — Vega 3.3."

"What a dreary way to name their planets," Nancia commented. "Can't they think of any nice names?"

"Vegans are . . . very logical," CenCom said. "The original group of settlers were, anyway — the ones who went out by slowship, before FTL. I gather the culture evolved to an extremely rigid form during the generations born on shipboard. They don't make a lot of allowances for human frailty, little things like names being easier to remember than strings of numbers."

"Makes no difference to *me*," Nancia said smugly.

Her memory banks could encode and store any form of information she needed.

"You should get along just great with the Vegans," CenCom told her. "Anyway, this brawn is out in Vegan subspace, no ship, nothing in the vicinity but a couple of old FTL drones. OG Shipping ought to be able to divert their metachip drone from Nyota, but as usual, we can't contact the manager. So it's either waste months of Caleb's service term by sending him home FTL, or provide our own transport. You're it. You can drop off your friends and relations on the planets around Nyota ya Jaha — I'll transmit a databurst of your orders after we get through chatting — and then proceed to Vega 3.3 to pick up your first brawn. Very neat organization. Psych records suggest the two of you ought to make a great team."

"Oh, they do, do they?" said Nancia. She had her own opinion of the Psych branch of Central and the intrusive tests and questionnaires with which they bombarded shellpersons, and she had no intention of being hustled by Central into forgoing her right to choose a brawn just because some shelltapper in a white coat thought they knew how to pick a man for her — and because she was a convenient free ride for a brawn who'd already lost one ship. Nancia was about to turn up her beam to CenCom and favor the operator with a few choice words on the subject when she felt her visitor stepping aboard. Well, there'd be time for that argument later; she could think about it on the way out. Agreeing to transport the CR-899's stranded brawn back to Central wouldn't commit her to a permanent partnership, and when she returned from this voyage she'd have plenty of time to choose her next brawn . . . and to tell Psych what they could do with their personality profiles.

Meanwhile, her visitor had ignored the open lift doors in favor of climbing the stairs to the central cabin, taking the last steps two at a time; Daddy made a point of keeping in shape. Nancia activated her stairway sensors and speakers simultaneously.

"Daddy, how nice of you —"

But the visitor was Flix, not Daddy. At least, from what Nancia could see of his face behind the enormous basket of flowers and fruit, she assumed it was her little brother: spiky red hair in an old-fashioned punk crown, one long peacock's feather dangling from the right earlobe, fingertips callused from hours of synthcom play. It was her little brother, all right.

"Flix." She could keep her vocal registers level, to conceal her disappointment; but she couldn't for the life of her think of any words to add.

" 'S'okay," Flix said, his voice coming slightly muffled from the stack of Calixtan orchids and orange Juba apfruits that threatened to topple over him from the insecurely stacked basket. Nancia slid out a tray from a waist-level cabinet just in time. Flix staggered into the tray, dropped the basket on it and sat backwards on the floor with a look of mild surprise. Two glowing orange apfruits fell off the towering display and rolled towards Nancia's command console, revealing a bottle of Sparkling Hereot in the center of the basket. "Know you'd rather have Daddy. Or Jinevra. Somebody worthy of the honor you do House Perez y de Gras. You deserve 'em, too," he added after a sprawling dive to retrieve the Juba apfruits. "Deserve a brass marching band and a red carpet instead of this thing." He brushed one hand across the soft nap of the sand-colored, standard-issue synthorug with which Nancia's internal living areas were carpeted.

"You — you really think I didn't disgrace the House?" Nancia asked. She *had* been wondering if that was why nobody had come to see her graduated and commissioned. Daddy had always spoken of her graduation with the words, "When you win the Daleth. . . . " And she hadn't done that.

Flix turned his head toward the titanium column and gave Nancia the same disbelieving, slightly contemptuous look he'd bestowed on the beige synthorug. "Stupid," he mourned. "Only member of the family I can stand to talk to, our Nancia; only one who doesn't give me hours of grief about giving up my synthcomposing for a Real Career, and it turns out she has worse problems than a few little malfunctioning organs. If you hadn't been popped into your shell at birth I'd suspect you were dropped on your head as a baby. Of *course* you've done the House proud, Nancia, what do you think? Third in academics and first in Decom Theory and taking so many special awards they had to restructure the graduation ceremony to make time for your presentations — "

"How did you know about that?" Nancia interrupted.

Flix looked away from the titanium column. Of course she could still see his expression perfectly well from her floor-level sensors, but it would have been rude to remind him of that. He looked embarrassed enough as it was. "Had a copy of the program," he mumbled. "Meant to show up, as long as I happened to be on Central anyway, but . . . well, I met these two girls when I was doing a synthcom gig in the Pleasure Palace, and they taught me how to mix Rigellian stemjuice with Benedictine to make this wonderful fizzy drink, and . . . well, anyway, I didn't wake up until the graduation ceremony was about over."

He scowled at the carpet for a moment longer, then brightened up. "Another thing I like about you, Nancia, you're the only relative I've got who won't burst into a long diatribe about how I could lower myself by playing synthcom at the Pleasure Palace. Of course, I don't suppose you have any idea what those places are like. Still, neither does Great Aunt Mendocia, and that doesn't stop *her* from sounding off."

He got to his feet and began pulling things out of the basket. "So . . . since I was unavoidably detained at the Pleasure Palace . . . and Jinevra's off at the tail end of nowhere investigating a Planetary Aid fraud, and Daddy's in a meeting, I thought I'd just drop by while you were waiting for assignment and we'd have a little private party."

"What meeting?" Nancia asked before she could stop herself. "Where?"

Flix looked up from the basket, surprised. "Huh?"

"You said our father was in a meeting."

"Yes, well, isn't he always? *No*, I don't know where; it's just a logical deduction. You know how full his dayplanner program is. Y'know, I often wondered," Flix rattled on as he unpacked the basket, "just how the three of us got born. Well, conceived, anyway. Do you suppose he sent Mother a memo? *Please come by my office this morning. Can work you in between ten and ten-fifteen. Bring sheets and pillow.*" He reached the bottom of the basket and pulled out two scratched and faded datahedra. "There! I know you think I'm a selfish bastard, bringing fruit and champagne to somebody who doesn't eat or drink, but actually I have covered all contingencies. These are my latest synthcompositions — here, I'll drop them in your reader. Background music for the party, and you can play them on the trip to entertain yourself.

As the jangling sounds of Flix's latest experimental composition rang out in the cabin, he held up a third datahedron and smiled. Unlike the first two well-worn hedra, this was a glittering shape with a slick commercial laser-cut finish that spattered rainbows of light across the cabin. "And here — "

"Let me guess," Nancia interrupted. "You've finally found somebody to make a commercial cut of your synthcompositions."

Flix's smile dimmed perceptibly. "Well, no. Not exactly. Although," he said, brightening, "I do know this girl who knows a chap who used to date a girl who did temporary office work for the second VP of Sound Studios, so there *are* distinct possibilities in the offing. But this is something quite different. This," he said, sounding almost reverent, "is the new, improved, vastly more sophisticated version of SPACED OUT, not due for public release until the middle of next month, and I won't tell you what I had to do to get it."

Nancia waited for him to tell her what the thing was about, but Flix paused and beamed as if he was expecting some immediate reaction from *her*.

"Well?" he said after a few seconds. His spiky red hair began to droop around the edges.

"I'm sorry," Nancia confessed, "but I have no idea what you're talking about."

Flix shook his head mournfully. "Never heard of SPACED OUT? What *do* they teach them at these academies? No, no, don't tell me." He held up one hand in protest. "I know. Decomposition theory and subspace astrogation and metachip design and a lot of other things that make my head hurt. But I do think they could have let you have a little time off to play games."

"We *did* play," Nancia told him. "It was in the schedule. Two thirty-minute periods daily of free play to improve synapse/tool coordination and gross propulsion skills. Why, I used to love playing Stall and PowerSeek when I was in my baby shell!"

Flix shook his head again. "All very improving, I'm sure. Well, *this* game" — he grinned — "is absolutely, one hundred per cent guaranteed *not* to improve your mind. In fact, Jinevra claims playing SPACED OUT can cause irreversible brain damage!"

"It can?" Nancia slid her reader slots shut with a click as Flix approached. "Look, Flix, I'm not sure —"

"Consider our big sister," Flix said with his sunniest smile. "Go ahead, just call up an image from her last visit. Don't you think anything she disapproves of must be worth a try?"

Nancia projected a lifesize Jinevra on the screen that filled the center wall of the cabin. Her sister might have been standing beside Flix. Trim and perfect as ever, from the hem of her navy blue Planetary Technical Aid uniform to the smooth dark hair that fell perfectly straight to just the regulation 1/4 inch distance from her starched white collar, she was the pattern of reproach to every disorderly element in the universe. Nancia couldn't remember just what had caused the disapproving glint in Jinevra's eyes or the tight, pinched look at the corners of her mouth at the moment this image had been stored, but in this projection she seemed to be glaring right at Flix. One of the red spikes of his retro-punk hair crown wilted under the withering gaze of the projection.

Nancia felt sorry for him. Jinevra had never bothered to conceal her opinion that their little brother was a wastrel and a disgrace to the family. Daddy, she suspected, felt much the same way. The weight of the Perez y de Gras clan's disapproval would have been crushing to her. How could she join them in condemning Flix? She'd heard stories enough about his wild tricks — there were times when Jinevra and Daddy seemed to have nothing else to discuss on their brief visits — but to her he was still the tousle-headed toddler who'd hugged her titanium shell every time he came for a visit, who'd waved and yelled as enthusiastically as if she were a real flesh-and-blood sister who could cuddle him on her lap, who'd screamed with glee when she carried him around the school track for a quick round of PowerSeek with her classmates.

And what harm could it do her to try the stupid game?

"You'd like it, Nancia," Flix said hopefully as the

projected image of Jinevra faded into a blank screen. "Really. It's the best version SpaceGamers has ever released. It's got sixty-four levels of hidden tunnels, and simulated Singularity space, and holodwarfs. . . . "

"*Holodwarfs?*"

"Just look." Flix dropped the glittering datahedron into the nearest reader slit — funny, Nancia couldn't remember having decided to open that reader, but she must have done so. There was a soft whirring noise as the contents of the datahedron were read into computer memory, then Flix said, "Level 6, holo!" and a red-bearded dwarf appeared in the middle of the cabin, brandishing a curved broadsword whose hilt glittered with a shower of refracted colored light. Flix dropped to one knee as the dwarf's broadsword slashed through the space where his head had been, rolled towards a control panel and shouted, "Space Ten laser armor!"

A shape of light beams bent into impossible curved paths around him. The dwarf bent and thrust his sword through a gap between the rapidly weaving lights —

And vanished.

So did the lights.

Flix got to his feet, aggrieved. "You cut the game off! And I was winning!"

"I, umm, I don't think I'm quite ready for the holo-dwarfs," Nancia apologized. "I have this automatic reaction to seeing people I love attacked."

Flix nodded. "Sorry. I guess we'll have to bring you up to speed slowly. Want to start at Level 1, no holos?"

"That sounds . . . better."

And it was better. In fact, after a few rounds, Nancia found herself actually enjoying the silly game, although she still had trouble making sense of the rules.

"What am I supposed to do with the Laser Staff?"

"It helps you walk uphill through the gravity well."

"That's dumb. Lasers don't have anything to do with gravity."

"Nancia. It's a *game*. Now, be sure to ask the simugrif for the answers to the Three Toroid Triples; you'll need them after you reach the trolls' bridge. . . . "

As Flix instructed her in the rudiments of the game, Nancia discovered that the actual game program used very little of her computing power. She was easily able to scan CenCom's databurst about her coming passengers while they played. At the same time she activated the ship's enhanced graphics mode to fill the three wall-size screens in the central cabin with color images of the game and of their play icons. Flix had chosen to be, of all things, a brainship, careening through imaginary asteroid belts in search of the Mystic Rings of Daleen. Nancia preferred to imagine herself as Troll Slayer, the long-limbed, bold explorer who strode through gravity wells and over mountain ranges with laser staff and backblasters.

"Nancia, you can't slay that troll yet!"

"Why not?"

"Because he's in ambush behind the rocks. I can see him, but you can't."

"I can so. I can see *everything* in this game. It's part of my main memory now, remember?"

"Well, your play icon can't. He's just a man. He hasn't got multi-D vision. And you see that blinking blue light? The program rules are warning you that he's going to die of hypothermia if you don't get him into some kind of shelter soon."

"Why doesn't he just increase his fuel — oh. I remember. You softpersons certainly are limited in your fuel allocation capabilities." Nancia went ahead and bent her laserstaff to take out the hiding troll, as well as three of his fellows, then sent her play icon under the trolls' snow bridge. Behind three hidden doors and through a labyrinth there was a nice warm cave, now uninhabited, where Troll Slayer could rest and refuel.

"Nancia, you're cheating!" Flix accused. "How did you find that place so quickly, without making any mistakes?"

"How could I *not* find it? The game maps are in my main memory too, remember? All I had to do is look."

"Well, couldn't you *not* look? To be fair?"

"No, I could not," Nancia said in a tone that should have effectively closed off further discussion. Cut off her consciousness from a part of the ship's computer memory? The single worst experience of her entire life had been the partial anesthesia required while experts completed her synaptic connections to the ship. There was nothing, absolutely nothing a shellperson hated more than losing connections! Flix ought to understand that without her telling him.

"Just shut down that memory node for a little while," Flix wheedled.

He never did know when to stop. And the idea of shutting down her own nodes made Nancia so uncomfortable that she couldn't bear to discuss it with him.

"Listen, softshell, I'd have to cut off more than one node to bring myself down to your computational level!"

"Oh, yeah? Come outside and say that again!"

"Sure, I'll come outside. I'll take you right up to the Singularity point and let you find your own way out of the decomposition!"

"Aah, relying on brute force again. It's not fair." Flix appealed to the ceiling. "Two big sisters, and they both pick on me all the time!"

"We had to do *something* to keep you under control — " Nancia shut down her vocal transmissions abruptly. There was an incoming beam from Central.

"XN? Message relay from Rigellian subspace." A brief pause, then the image of Nancia's father appeared on the central screen opposite her pillar. On the left-hand screen Flix's brainship icon flipped and rotated in an endless, mindless loop against the glittering stars of deep space; on the right, Troll Slayer stood frozen with one foot lifted to step across the threshold of the hidden cave. Between them, a tired man in a conservative green and blue pinstripe tunic smiled at Nancia.

"Sorry I couldn't come to your graduation, Nancia dear. This meeting on Rigel IV is vital to keeping Central's economy on the planned graph for the next sixteen quarters. I couldn't let them down. Knew you'd understand. Hey, congratulations on all those awards! I didn't have time to read the program in detail yet, but I'm sure you've done House Perez y de Gras proud, as always. And I think you'll like your first assignment. It'll be a chance for you to get to know some of the younger members of the High Families — a very fitting start for our own Courier Service star. Eh? What's that?" He turned towards his left, so that he seemed to be speaking to the frozen Troll Slayer icon. "The Secretary-Particular? Oh, very well, send him in. I'll need to brief him before the next session."

Eyes front again. "You heard that, I suppose, Nancia? Sorry, I have to go now. Good luck!"

"Daddy, wait — " Nancia began, but the screen went blank for a moment. The old image of the snow bridge and the trolls reappeared and she heard the voice of the CenCom operator.

"Sorry, XN. That was a canned message beam. There's no more. And your passengers are ready to board now."

"Thank you, Central." Nancia discovered to her horror that she had lost all control over her vocal channels; the trembling overtones that surrounded her speech made her emotional state all too apparent. *A Perez y de Gras does not weep*. And a brainship *could not* weep. And Nancia had been well trained to repress the sort of unseemly emotional displays that softpersons indulged in. All the same, she very much did not want to talk to anybody just now.

Flix seemed to have sensed her mood; he silently packed up the basket of fruit and sparkling wine and patted Nancia's titanium column as if he thought that she could feel the warmth of his hand. For a moment she had the illusion that she did feel it.

"I'd better get out of the way now," he said. "Can't have a Perez y de Gras brainship caught *partying* on her maiden voyage, can we?"

He paused on the stairs. "Y'know, Nancia, there's no regulation says you have to greet your passengers the minute they step aboard. Let 'em find their cabins and unpack on their own. There'll be plenty of time for social chitchat on the way out."

Then he was gone, a redheaded blur vanishing into the darkness, a whistled melody lingering on the night air outside; and moments later, the bright lights of a spacepad transport shone in Nancia's ground-level sensors and a party of young people tumbled out, laughing and talking all at once and waving glasses in the air. One of them stumbled and spilled the liquid over Nancia's gleaming outer shell; from a fin sensor she could see the snail-trail of something green and viscous defacing her side. The boy swore and shouted, "Hey, Alpha, we need a refill on the Stemerald over here!"

"Wait till we're inside, can't you?" called back a tall girl with ebony skin and features sharp and precise as an antique cameo. Right now her handsome face was etched with lines of anger and dissatisfaction, but as the fair-haired boy looked back over his shoulder at her she gave him a bright smile that wouldn't have deceived Nancia for a minute.

They were all still talking — and drinking that sticky green stuff — as they crowded into the airlock lift without even asking permission to board. Well, she *had* left the entry port open after Flix's departure; maybe they considered that an implied welcome. And Nancia had heard that softpersons — at least those outside the Academy — didn't observe the formality that governed greetings and official exchanges in the Courier Service and other branches of Central's far-flung bureaucracy. She wasn't one to take offense yet, not when she herself was hardly ready for introductions to this bunch of strangers.

As they trooped out of the airlock and into the central cabin, Nancia played a game of matching faces to the names Central had given her. The short red-haired boy with a face like a friendly gargoyle had Flix's coloring and the flashing smile that reeled girls in to Flix like trout on a hook; he must be one of the two related to Nancia's family. "Blaize?" the black girl called. "Blaize, I can't *open* this." She held out a plastic pouch full of shimmering green liquid, and Nancia winced in anticipation as the redhead tore off the sealstrip with two short, strong fingers. But not a drop spilled on her new, official-issue beige carpeting — not now, anyway.

"Here you are, Alpha," the boy said as he handed it back, and Nancia matched their faces with the names and descriptions that had come in CenCom's databurst. The red-haired boy must be Blaize Armontillado-Perez y Medoc, of a family so high that they barely deigned to recognize the Perez y de Gras connection. And for some puzzling reason his first posting was to a lonely Planetary Technical Aid position on the remote planet of Angalia; she would have expected anybody from a three-name Family to start off somewhere near the top of whatever Central bureaucracy he chose. As for the ebony princess, with her sharp clever face that would have been beautiful if not for the discontented expression, she had to be Alpha bint Hezra-Fong. The short burst transmitted from CenCom identified her as a native of the warm, semi-desert world of Takla, with high marks in her medical research program, and no hint as to why she'd chosen to take a five-year sabbatical in the midst of training to run the Summerlands Clinic on Bahati.

As they passed the pouch of Stemerald back and forth, Nancia was able to identify the other three from their casual conversation without having to introduce herself. The slightly pudgy boy with a halo of overlong brown curls clustering around his red face was Darnell Overton-Glaxely, going to Bahati to take charge of OG Shipping from the cousin who'd been administering the business during Darnell's minority. The other girl, the sleek black-haired beauty whose delicate bones and slightly tilted eyes suggested a family connection with the Han Parma branch of the family, would be Fassa del Parma y Polo. The del Parma y Polo clan controlled all the major space construction in this subspace, and now it appeared they were sending this delicate little thing out to establish the family's rights in Vega subspace as well. The girl was probably, Nancia reflected, stronger than she looked. At any rate she was the only one refusing the pouch of Stemerald as it went around the circle, and that was a good sign.

And the last one — Nancia let her sensors take in the full glory of Polyon de Gras-Waldheim, the cousin she'd never met. From the crown of his smoothly cropped yellow hair to the gleaming toes of his black regulation-issue shoes, he was the epitome of the perfect Space Academy graduate: standing straight but not stiff, eyes moving in full awareness of what each of his companions was doing, even in this moment of repose conveying a sense of dangerous alertness. Like Nancia, he was newly graduated and commissioned. And like her, he'd ranked high in his class but not first; first in technical grades, the databurst said, but only second overall because of an inexplicable low mark in Officer Fitness — whatever that might be.

When she'd first scanned the databurst, during Flix's

silly computer game, Nancia had been looking forward to meeting her cousin Polyon. He was the only one of the group with whom she felt that she had much in common. As two High Families members trained for a life of service to Central, just setting out to meet their destinies, they should have felt an instant sense of kinship. Now, though, she felt strangely reluctant to introduce herself to Polyon. He was so tense, so watchful, as though he considered even this laughing group of other young people in the light of potential enemies.

And, she reminded herself, he had personally consumed at least two-thirds of the recently opened pouch of Stemerald, plus Central only knew what else before coming on board. No, it wasn't a good time to introduce herself and tell Polyon of their family connections. She would just have to wait.

"Hey, guys, look at the welcoming committee!" Blaize interrupted the chatter. He was staring past Nancia's titanium column, at the triple-screen display of the SPACED OUT game that Nancia had absentmindedly left up after Flix's abrupt departure. The concealed visual sensors between the screens showed Blaize's freckled, snub-nosed face alight with pure, uncomplicated joy.

Blaize moved slowly across the soft carpet until he sank into the empty pilot's chair that should have been reserved for Nancia's brawn. "This," he said reverently, "has got to be the biggest, best SPACED OUT I've ever seen. Two weeks will go like nothing with this setup to play with." The game control channels were still open, and as Blaize identified himself and took control of the brainship icon, Nancia let the underlying game program alter the brainship's course to zoom in on Troll Slayer's world. The brilliance of the graphic display drew the other passengers to look over Blaize's shoulder, and one by one, with half-ashamed comments, they let themselves be drawn into the game.

"Well, it beats watching a bunch of painbrains dose themselves silly in the clinic," Alpha murmured as she took a seat beside Blaize.

Nancia had hardly recovered from the shock of this callous comment when Darnell, too, joined the game. "I'll have to copy the mastergraphics off this program and have somebody install it on all OG Shipping's drones," he said, animating Troll Slayer. "Anybody know how to break the code protection?"

"I," said Polyon de Gras-Waldheim, "can break any computer security system ever installed." He favored Darnell with a slanting, enigmatic side glance. "If it's worth my while . . ."

Oh, you can, can you? thought Nancia. *We'll see about that.* Software game piracy wasn't exactly a major crime, but a newly commissioned Space Academy officer ought to have a stronger ethical sense than some commoner who hadn't had the benefit of a High Families upbringing and an Academy training. She felt distinctly less eager than she had been to introduce herself to her handsome cousin.

Polyon turned his head and treated Fassa del Parma y Polo, still lingering beside the door, to a brilliant smile. "Now you, little one, could make just about anything worth my while."

Fassa moved towards the game controls with a sinuous, gliding motion that riveted Blaize and Darnell's attention as well as Polyon's. "Forget it, yellowtop," she said in a voice as sweet as her words were stinging. "A second-rate Academy officer with a prison-planet posting doesn't have enough to keep me interested. I'm saving it for where it'll do me some good."

Nancia briefly shut down all the cabin's sensors. How had she gotten stuck with these greedy, amoral, spoiled brats? She had a good mind to put off introducing herself indefinitely. From the freedom of their comments, they must be assuming she was only a drone ship with no power to understand or act on anything but a limited set of direct commands.

But she would still need to know what they were up to. She opened one auditory channel and heard Blaize leading Darnell and Polyon in a raucous chorus of, "She never sold it, she just gave it away!" while Fassa glowered and slithered off to her cabin.

Nancia had the feeling this would be one of the longest two-week voyages any brainship had ever endured.

● CHAPTER TWO

Polyon

Nancia watched curiously as Polyon de Gras-Waldheim sauntered into the central cabin. The other passengers were still sleeping off their departure-night Stemerald party, snoring and thrashing as the last doses of the stimulant worked its way out of their exhausted bodies. Polyon had recovered remarkably early. Like any good Academy graduate, he'd been up at 0600 ship's time, washed in the shower cubicle and dressed in his neatly pressed undress grays before presenting himself in public. Nancia had shut down visual sensors in the cabins to allow her passengers the privacy they would be expecting, but the auditory sensors brought her enough small sounds to enable her to follow Polyon through his early-morning routine.

Nancia caught her first glimpse of Polyon as he swung down the passageway to the central cabin. This was public space; she had no compunction about leaving all sensors activated here. And Polyon de Gras-Waldheim was certainly a treat for the sensors. Just a shade under two meters tall, with his golden hair ruthlessly cropped in the Academy bristle cut, he was a happy blend of the best in the Waldheim and de Gras family lines: Waldheim height and rugged strength, de Gras refinement and quick awareness. Nancia felt a moment of regret. Polyon was a Space Academy graduate; he might have been her brawn.

A de Gras-Waldheim? jeered an inner voice. *What are you dreaming of, girl?* A young man who combined those two bloodlines could look far higher than command of a single brainship. He should have been destined for a staff position somewhere, being groomed for high command.

The short databurst of information about her passengers and their destinations didn't explain why, instead of joining a Fleet General staff, Polyon was headed out to be the technical overseer for a prison metachip plant in a remote subspace. *Oh, well, there must be some good reason for the assignment. Maybe there's more going on in Vega subspace than I realized.* Nancia remembered that interrupted newsbyte about Vega and her resolve to study it in depth, now that she was her own ship. *I'm Courier Service now; I'd better start keeping up with public affairs.* But just at the moment, watching her cousin was more interesting than pulling up files of old newsbeams.

Polyon glanced about the cabin and his body relaxed imperceptibly as he scanned the area; a human observer might not have noticed the slight change, but Nancia — by now scanning for muscle tension and autonomic nervous system response as well as for the usual visual and auditory cues — was immediately aware of his relaxation. That must be Academy training, that alertness upon entering any unfamiliar territory. She should have expected no less of one trained in the High Families' tradition of service; just as she should not have been surprised that Polyon wakened at a regulation hour, no matter what he'd been indulging in the night before. The other passengers might be soft and self-indulgent, but this one, at least, was a credit to his training. *That's the de Gras blood in him,* she thought with a trace of smugness; Daddy had always stressed the value of Nancia's connection, through her mother, with the House of de Gras.

Polyon glanced once more around the room — if he hadn't been a de Gras-Waldheim, Nancia would have described his second look as *furtive* — and then sat down, not in the pilot's chair facing the central console, but in one of the spectator seats to the side of the room. He nodded once, sharply, as if to say, "That's all right, then," and spoke in a low voice that no softperson could have heard.

"Computer, open master file, pass 47321-Aleithos-Hex242."

The automatic security system that guarded the ship's main computer acknowledged Polyon's command. Hardly believing what she observed, Nancia let the computer act without overriding it. How had Polyon learned the master file password? Perhaps there was a secret side to her mission, something only another member of the High Families could be trusted to know and to reveal at the proper time. That would explain Polyon's near-furtive way of approaching the cabin. It would also explain his crude behavior last night; naturally, as an undercover agent, he'd have to be sure to blend in with his fellow passengers.

Or . . . there might be no such explanation forthcoming. Now that he had master file access, Polyon was typing, moving the touchscreen icons, and issuing verbal commands in a rapid low stream that rivaled even a shellperson's multi-channel capacity. And he still hadn't acknowledged her as anything more than a droneship. What *was* going on? Nancia waited and watched, following Polyon's maneuverings through her computer system while her external sensors kept track of his bodily movements.

Piece of cake, Polyon thought as his fingers darted from keyboard to touch-screen, setting up his user account with system privileges that would allow him access to any data in the ship's computer. *Easy as debugging a kid's first program.* Now for the tricky stuff — persuading the security system to treat him as a privileged user on the Net. Once linked to that subspace-wide communications system, he would be able to find out anything he wanted to know about anybody who'd ever linked into the Net.

Voice commands wouldn't work here; just as well, he didn't want to be overheard by any of those small-time snoops he was stuck with on this voyage. His fingers flashed over the keys, rattling out commands as fast as his excellent brain could analyze the results. Hmm, security block here . . . but having already granted himself user privileges on the ship's system, he could take a look at the object code in the blocking program itself. He could even "fix" it. "Here a patch, there a patch," Polyon hummed as he entered a slightly revised version of the object code, "everywhere a trapdoor, dum-de-dum-de-dum." As the system accepted and ran the revised program, Polyon's humming switched to a triumphant version of, "I'm the man who broke the bank at Monte Carlo!"

Not quite accurate, of course; he intended to win far, far more than the proceeds of a single night's old-Earth-style gambling. He would show them — all of them. Starting with — but definitely not finishing with — the lamebrains who'd shipped out with him. Polyon knew why *he* was being posted to a second-rate assignment in a third-rate solar system — his memories skittered like frightened mice over the surface of that ugly scene with the Dean — but there must be some reasons why all these other pampered darlings of the High Families were going into semi-exile. He would start by finding those little secrets, and then . . . well, then maybe even these rich brats could be useful in the Grand Plan.

And after them . . . the Nyota system. All of Vega subspace. *Central.* Why not? Polyon thought, dazzled by the grandeur of his own desires. If there was one thing he'd learned while he was growing up, it was that you could get away with nearly anything if you did most of it while people weren't watching and used your charm when they did watch.

And where charm didn't work . . . there were other means of persuasion. Polyon smiled grimly and tapped into Alpha bint Hezra-Fong's med school files.

What *could* Polyon be doing? Nancia watched and waited as he redefined the ship's security system, reached out to the Net, scanned his fellow-passengers' files. Ought she to stop him? Discretion was the first thing a Courier Service brainship learned, the first and last component of duty. She hadn't been briefed on what to do with a passenger who started manipulating the Net as if it were part of his personal comsystem. He was redefining the security parameters now . . . no matter, she could change those back whenever she chose. So far he hadn't touched her personal data areas, didn't show any signs of knowing that her synaptic connections to the ship's computer allowed her to follow everything he was doing.

Could it be that he really thought her a drone ship? Maybe not. At least, he wasn't sure. Now that he was through playing with the Net, Polyon sent out an exploratory tendril of code to report on other activities linked into the ship's computer . . . a patch that would reveal the exact location and extent of Nancia's connections within the ship.

A little late to check that, my lad! Didn't the Space Academy teach you to look for ambushes before you started maneuvers? Self-protection was an automatic response, more deeply ingrained even than discretion. Nancia closed down pathways and redefined access codes in a single, instinctive wave of activity that left Polyon staring at a blank screen and touching a keyboard that no longer responded to his search commands.

Darnell

Darnell Overton-Glaxely moaned gently as he caught

sight of his puffy face, a distorted reflection in the polished curve of synthalloy along the ship's central corridor. It was too early in the morning to face mirrors, especially curving ones that made his reflection swell and shrink and ripple like waves on the damned ocean. Darnell moaned again and reminded himself that the artificial gravity of space was practically like being on Earth; it was only his imagination making him feel sick. This was really nothing like being aboard one of the old-style oceangoing vessels that had been the start of OG Shipping, back when they were still a planetbound local corporation. His old man had made him go on one of those monsters once, with some crap about remembering the family's roots. Darnell had taken a lot more crap from the old man when he puked his guts out before the ship left harbor.

Well, there wouldn't be any more of *that*! Dear Papa was history now, and so was the unexplained space-station collapse that had killed him and left OG Shipping in the hands of its directors until Darnell finished school. And last night's Stemerald debauch was also history — if only he could convince his queasy stomach and pounding head of that!

It wasn't fair that he should suffer like this after what had only been a perfectly reasonable indulgence to celebrate the end of schooling and the start of his new career. A pity neither of the girls had seen fit to continue the celebration in the logical manner. Well, they had two weeks to planetfall; they'd come around and see his attractions soon enough. After all, it wasn't as if he had any serious competition on this droneship. De Gras-Waldheim was handsome enough, but a cold fish if Darnell had ever seen one. Something frightening about him, with those intense blue eyes burning like dry ice under the stiff Academy haircut. As for the Medoc boy, Blass or Blaze or whatever his name was, no girl was going to waste time on a kid with a face like a friendly gargoyle. No, it would be old Darnell to the rescue again, the only man on board with the social skills to entertain two lovely ladies all the way to their destination planets around Nyota ya Jaha.

And he could hear sounds in the central cabin. Was one of the girls up and about already? Darnell sucked in his gut, threw his shoulders as far back as they would go, and glanced at his reflection in the synth-alloy wall once again. His face wasn't really soft and puffy like that, he told himself; it was a trick of the distorted reflection. Made him look middle-aged and flabby and tired. Nonsense. He was the handsome young heir to OG shipping and he was fit to take on anybody or anything. . . .

But not, maybe, that cold fish, Polyon de Gras-Waldheim. Darnell clutched at the doorway and tried to stop his impulsive movement into the central cabin. His legs kept going while his arms tried to haul him back.

"Oh, come on in, OG," Polyon said impatiently, his back to the door. "Don't just cling to the doorframe waving your tentacles like a seasick jellyfish."

Seasick.

Jellyfish.

Darnell gulped down a wave of nausea and reminded himself again that space travel on a grav-enhanced drone was *not* like being on an actual moving, swaying, shifting oldstyle sea vessel.

"What are you doing?"

Polyon released the chair controls and spun slowly round to face Darnell, long limbs relaxed as if to emphasize his comfort in this environment. "Just . . . playing games," he said with a queer smile. "Just a few little games to pass the time."

"What'd you do, crash the SPACED OUT gameset so badly you lost the screens?"

"Something like that," Polyon agreed. "You can help me start it up again, if you like."

It was the closest thing to a friendly overture Darnell had heard from Polyon since they met the previous night. Maybe, he thought forgivingly, maybe the poor guy didn't know *how* to make friends. Coming from a stiff-backed upper-crust lot like the de Gras-Waldheims, spending his life at military boarding schools, you couldn't expect him to have the *savoir vivre* and easy social manners that Darnell prided himself on displaying. Well, he'd help old Polyon out, be his friend on this little jaunt.

"Sure thing," he said, walking on into the room with a careful soft step that didn't jar his aching head. He sank into one of the cushioned passenger chairs. "Nothing to it, I used to play this stuff all the time in prep school. Tell you what — if I help you get into the computer, maybe you'll help me get into something else?" He winked laboriously at Polyon.

"What exactly did you have in mind?" The man didn't have a clue how to make light conversation.

"Two of us," Darnell explained cheerfully, tapping away at the console keys. "Two of them. The black one is more your size. But I need a strategy to get into the del Parma skirt's pants. Tactics, maneuvers, advance and retreat — Got any suggestions?" Not, Darnell thought, that he really needed any help, but there was nothing like a round of good, bawdy male-to-male bonding talk to cement a friendship. And since Polyon evidently wanted to be friends, Darnell was more than ready to meet him halfway.

"I'm afraid you're on your own there," Polyon said distantly. "I've . . . never had occasion to study the problem." He flicked an invisible speck of dust off his pressed sleeve and affected to study the SPACED OUT screens as Darnell brought them back to fill the walls of the cabin.

The implication was clear; he'd never *needed* to work out tactics with the ladies. Well, of course not. With the de Gras-Waldheim name and fortune behind him —

and that muscle-bound, oversized physique — still, he had no call to sneer at somebody who was just trying to be friendly. Darnell glowered at the console and tapped the commands that would set the game at — hmm, not Level 10, his reflexes weren't quite up to the interactive holowarriors just yet. Level 6. That should be high enough to scramble Polyon's moves and let him see what it was like dealing with an expert.

"It's a new version," Polyon said in surprise. "I don't remember that asteroid belt."

"I'll bet five credits there's a clue to the Hidden Horrors of Holmdale somewhere in the new asteroids," Darnell offered.

"No bet on that. But I'll lay you five credits that *if* it's there, I'll find it first. Choose your icon!"

Darnell chose one of the play icons displayed along the bottom of the central screen. He always liked to be Bonecrush, the cyborg monster who stalked the lower tunnels of the labyrinth but occasionally blasted out into space with his secretly installed jetpacks and personal force shield. Polyon, he noticed with pleasure, was taking the icon for Thingberry the Martian Mage, a wimp of a character if there ever was one. This game should be over in no time.

"So what brings you out to the Nyota system?" Polyon asked after a few minutes of seemingly idle maneuvering and pointless commands.

Darnell scowled at the screen. How had Thingberry managed to surround two-thirds of the asteroid belt with a charm of impenetrability? Very well, he would let Bonecrush turn around and use his internal jetpacks as a weapon; that should blast through sneaky Thingberry's magic. "Taking up the old inheritance," he replied as he tapped in the commands that would give Bonecrush maximum blasting power. "OG Shipping, you know. Can't think why old Cousin Wigran moved the firm's headquarters out to Vega subspace, but I'm sure he'll explain everything when I get there."

"If he can," Polyon agreed. "You have that much faith in him?"

Darnell stealthily maneuvered Bonecrush into range. That idiot Polyon was looking at him, not at the screen; he could get away with murder if he could keep Polyon's attention away from the game for a few more seconds.

"What d'you mean?" he asked, not really listening for the answer. "Why shouldn't I have faith in Wigran?"

Polyon looked shocked, and for a moment Darnell was afraid he'd noticed Bonecrush's moves on the central game screen. "My dear chap! You mean you haven't heard? *Decom* it," he cursed in a low vicious tone. "I didn't realize — Look, Darnell, I shouldn't be the one to tell you this. Haven't you been paying attention to the newsbytes from Vega?"

"Management bores me," Darnell told him. "I'll be perfectly happy to draw the profits from the company and let Cousin Wigran keep running the store." His hands were resting on the key that would activate Bonecrush's jet packs. Any minute now he'd execute a controlled power surge that should blast a hole right through Thingberry's defenses. But he wanted Polyon to be watching in the moment of defeat, not babbling on about some boring accountant's trial in the Vega system.

"Well, I suppose you'd have to know pretty soon anyway," Polyon was saying now. "I hate like hell to be the one to tell you, though." He was watching Darnell's face more closely than he'd ever looked at the game screens.

"Tell me what?" For the first time Darnell felt a chill of apprehension creep over him.

"It's all been coming out in the trial," Polyon said. "That accountant who was skimming his clients' credits to play Lotto-Roids? OG Shipping was one of his biggest accounts. And your cousin Wigran knew exactly what the fellow was doing. He even helped him — for a share in the cash. Together, they've gambled away more than ninety per cent of OG Shipping's assets. I'm afraid all you're going to inherit on Bahati is one over-age AI drone and a bunch of debts."

Darnell's sweaty fingers slipped and punched the power key harder than he'd intended. Bonecrush's jet packs released their maximum thrust. The blast rebounded harmlessly off Thingberry's invisible charm-shield and propelled Bonecrush, too depleted of power to activate his personal force-shield, into the blackness of deep space. His cyborg body exploded into a million stars of synthalloy debris.

"Wow," Polyon said, finally glancing at the dazzling light effects on the screen. "This *is* a great game! Will you look at those graphics? What is it, a supernova?"

"Me," said Darnell Overton-Glaxely. A gentleman knew when to bite the bullet. "I owe you five credits."

Blaize

Oh, no, not another one!

Nancia briefly shut down all her internal sensors as Blaize Armontillado-Perez y Medoc stirred in his cabin. She had come to the conclusion that her passengers were most bearable when they were sleeping it off. If only she could flood all their cabins with sleepgas and keep them unconscious until they reached the Nyota ya Jaha system. . . . Nancia caught herself in mid-thought. She was becoming as bad as they were! How could she even think such a thing? Hadn't she made perfect marks in all her Integrity and Shell Ethics classes? She should have been doubly guarded, by family heritage and Academy training, against even imagining such a betrayal of her ideals.

There was nothing to stop her from leaving her internal sensors inactive until they reached Nyota ya Jaha, though. Nancia considered this briefly before deciding against it. True, her passengers wouldn't notice anything, since they already assumed she was a droneship programmed to carry them in privacy to their destination. And it was also true that she would rather perform the Singularity transformations that carried them through decomposition space without the irritating distraction of these . . . *brats*. But she shrank from the idea of spending days, more than a week, in the isolation of space, with nothing to see but the wheeling stars, no other brain to communicate with — for if she opened a beam to Central, her cousin Polyon, with his propensity for snooping through the ship's computer systems, would be bound to notice the comm activity. Brainships were as human as any softpersons; Nancia knew that it would be unwise to expose herself for so long to the strain of partial sensory deprivation.

Besides, she wanted to know what her passengers were up to.

When Nancia reactivated the central cabin's sensors, Darnell was already stalking down the hall to his cabin and Polyon, lips taut with rage, was about to follow him. "I don't care for that name," he told Blaize.

Nancia hastily scanned the cabin's automatic recording system. Blaize had been teasing his cousin by calling him "Polly." Academy records on Polyon de Gras-Waldheim mentioned this nickname as the basis for several vicious fights that had occurred during Polyon's Academy training, including one in which Polyon's opponent was so badly injured that he had to drop out of the officer training program. Witnesses had attested that Polyon went on twisting the boy's bones and listening to them splinter long after his opponent was begging for mercy.

Following that incident, Polyon's file had been flagged with warning signals that would forever preclude his being assigned to a responsible military post . . . and he had been verbally notified of this decision in an interview with retired General Mack Erricott, Dean of the Space Academy—

What was she doing? Nancia closed down all her information channels momentarily. Where had all this private information come from? She reopened her channels and traced the dataflow. It came through the Net, and she shouldn't have had access to any of this material; it came from the Space Academy's private personnel files. Somehow the Net had responded to her momentary curiosity by opening up material that should have been shielded under the Dean's personal password.

After a moment's confusion, Nancia realized what had happened. Polyon's meddling with the ship's security system had extended to some very sophisticated tampering in the Net itself. He had, in effect, defined Nancia as the node of origin for a system controller with unlimited powers to access and change files and codes in any computer on the Net. Nancia's instinctive intervention had then made the "System Controller" identity unavailable to Polyon himself . . . but had left the node definition in place, allowing her access to all the files he had scanned, and a great deal more besides.

Nancia felt as embarrassed as if she'd been caught peeking into an anesthetized classmate's open shell during synaptic remodeling . . . the invasion of privacy was that great. *I didn't realize what I was doing!* She defended herself, and hastily erased the super-user node definition before she could be tempted into looking at anybody else's private files.

But she couldn't forget the shocking and disturbing things she'd just read about Polyon. And she was relieved that he'd left the central cabin to Blaize, stalking back to his own cabin in a pose of offended dignity far more impressive than Darnell's pout.

Blaize looked directly at Nancia's titanium column and winked. "Bet you thought he was going to beat me up, didn't you?"

Nancia responded without thinking to this, the first direct address she'd received since her passengers boarded and she lifted off from Central. "I hope you weren't counting on me to protect you!"

Blaize gave a soft, satisfied chuckle. "Not at all, dear lady. Until this moment I wasn't even sure what — or who — you were." He lifted an imaginary cap and mimed an extravagant bow. "Allow me to introduce myself," he murmured as he straightened again. "Blaize Armontillado-Perez y Medoc. And you?"

It was too late to retreat into the silence that had protected her so far. Nancia gave a mental shrug — no more than a quick flashing of connectors — and decided that she might as well converse with the brat. She'd been starting to get lonely, anyway; the isolation of deep space was too great a contrast after her years of comfortable, constant multi-channel input and output with her classmates in Laboratory Schools. "XN-935," Nancia said grudgingly. And then, because the call letters seemed inadequate, "Nancia Perez y de Gras."

"A cousin, a veritable cousin!" Blaize crowed with unabashed delight. "So tell me, cousin, what's a nice girl like you doing convoying a rabble of riffraff like us?"

The question was uncomfortably close to Nancia's own opinion of her passengers. "How did you know I was a brainship?" she countered.

"The liftoff procedures *could* have been performed by an AI drone. But somehow I didn't really think the Medoc clan and the rest of our loving families would have sent us off to jaunt through Singularity on automatic. Wouldn't be fitting to the dignity of the High Families, y'know, to have a packet of metachips responsible for our safety instead of a human brain."

"You don't have much respect for your family, do you? No wonder they're sending you off to a fringe world. They're probably afraid you'll embarrass them."

For a moment Blaize's freckled face looked cold and hard and infinitely sad. Then, so quickly that a human eye would hardly have recognized the brief betrayal, he grinned and flashed a salute at Nancia's column. "Absolutely. Just one minor correction. They're not *afraid* I'll embarrass them. They're bloody sure of it!" Pulling out one of the padded chairs, he seated himself cross-legged in the middle of the cabin, arms folded, and beamed at Nancia's column as though he hadn't a care in the world. She retrieved the image of his face a moment earlier and projected it on interior space, comparing the bleak-eyed young man of the recording with the smiling boy in the cabin. What could be hurting him so deeply? Against her will, she felt a twinge of sympathy for this spoiled scion, this disgrace to the High Families.

"And do you intend to?" she asked in carefully neutral tones.

"What? Oh — disgrace them?" Blaize shrugged a little too gracefully. Nancia began to wonder how many of his seemingly casual gestures were rehearsed. "No, it's too late now. Sure, I had fantasies when I was a kid. But I'm a little old for running away now, don't you think?"

"What — to join the circus?"

For another split second, the mobile face before her matched the bleak image she'd stored. "No. The Space Academy. Actually," Blaize said in a voice as carefully neutral as Nancia's own, "I used to think I'd train as a brawn — Don't laugh; it was a kid's idea. But I never could imagine anything better than working with a brainship. To fly between the stars, saving lives and worlds, partnered with a living ship to learn the dance of space. . . . " His voice cracked on the last word. "I told you. Kids have dumb ideas."

"It doesn't seem like such a dumb idea to me," Nancia told him. "Why did you give it up? Did somebody tell you brawns have to be six feet tall and built like . . . like Polyon de Gras-Waldheim?"

"Give it up!" Blaize echoed. "I didn't give it up. I ran away three times. The first time I actually got into the Space Academy, too. Took the open tests, forged papers saying I was a war orphan, won a scholarship. It was three weeks before my tutor found me." The momentary, unguarded joy in his face as he remembered those weeks wrenched at Nancia's heart. "The second and third times they knew where I'd go; there was a squad of House Medoc private guards waiting for me at the Academy."

"Your family seems to have been rather violently against the idea."

Blaize's mobile, ugly face twisted into a sneer. "Wouldn't do for folks in our position, y'know. Not quite the thing. My cousin Jillia is in line to be the next Planetary Governor of Kaza-uri, and my buddy Henequin — m'father's best friend's son," Blaize explained parenthetically, "is already in charge of the Vega branch of Planetary Technical Aid. A son who's in brawn training doesn't quite match up with those stellar accomplishments for after-dinner bragging."

"I wonder if my family feels that way," Nancia said. Was that why Daddy hadn't made time for her graduation?

"Shouldn't think so. They sent you to Laboratory Schools, didn't they?"

"They didn't," Nancia said, "have many options. I would not have survived a normal birth."

"Oh. Well. Anyway," Blaize said carefully, "I don't think your branch of the family is *quite* as snobbish as ours. And neither one can beat the de Gras-Waldheims for exclusiveness. Polly got to go to the Academy, but he was supposed to turn into a general, not a lowly space jockey; I can't imagine what he's doing on his way to administer a metachip plant on Shemali. Must have been some scandal at the Academy. I thought I knew all the family gossip, but whatever he got into, they hushed it up exceedingly well. *You* probably have access to the files, though — or — anyway, I bet you could find out if you wanted to."

"I imagine," Nancia said, "they are in need of his technical expertise." She felt no impulse whatever to share the details of Polyon's Academy problems with this gossipy boy. Didn't the High Families train their softperson children in any kind of discretion? First Polyon, using his computer expertise to hack through security checks and find out the other passengers' secrets, and now Blaize, turning his charm on her to the same end.

"You don't approve of gossip, do you?" Blaize guessed. "All right. Have it your way. You will be a suitably discreet Courier Service brainship and a credit to the family, and I'll be a nice little PTA administrator on Angalia and try not to disgrace my side of the family, and we can all drift on in boredom forever."

"Planetary Technical Aid isn't so bad," Nancia told him. "My sister Jinevra is an area administrator, and she's only twenty-nine. You could rise rapidly —"

"From *Angalia*?" Blaize's eyebrows shot up like red exclamation marks, giving his face a look of comical astonishment. "Dear Cousin Nancia, you really *don't* pry, do you? If you'd read my file you would know better than to try and stir up my ambitions for Angalia. The sum total of civilization there consists of one PTA office, one corycium mine, and a bunch of humanoid natives with the collective IQ of a zucchini. A *small* zucchini. It's amazing they even qualify for Planetary Aid; somebody must have filled out the FCF wrong, and whoever later determined that they didn't have ISS forgot to correct the PTA data. The wheels of the bureaucracy grind on and on. . . . So here I go to Angalia, less than the dust beneath old Henequin's chariot wheels."

"You should do well enough," Nancia said. "You've certainly got the jargon of the bureaucracy down pat." She scanned her data files for translations of the initials Blaize had used. PTA was Planetary Technical Aid, of course, and FCF turned out to be a First Contact Form, and ISS — ah. Intelligent Sentient Status. Nancia had learned all the regulations for dealing with alien sentients in Basic Courier Diplomacy and Development 101, but she wasn't used to hearing the abbreviations tossed about so casually. Daddy, when he visited and told her about his work, was always careful to give each bureaucratic office its full name, each official his full title.

It was possible, Nancia thought, involuntarily contrasting Blaize's darting, hummingbird speech patterns with Daddy's measured delivery — it was possible that her father, Javier Perez y de Gras, was just a bit stuffy. No. That was ridiculous. She was getting corrupted by her passengers, straying into non-regulation and non-approved ways of thinking. Heaven knew what indiscretions Blaize would lure her into if they continued this conversation.

"Do you play SPACED OUT?" She filled the three wall-size screens with the displays that had tempted Polyon and Darnell into the game. "It'll have to be solitaire, I'm afraid."

"Why?"

"I can't *not* know the underlying structure," Nancia

apologized. "You see, the game's part of my memory banks now. And I've never learned your softperson trick of selectively turning off awareness." She wasn't about to try, either. But she could, she told Blaize, make the solitaire game a little more challenging by redefining the maze of tunnels and Singularity nodes that connected one part of the SPACED OUT galaxy with another.

"Rules that change as you play?" Blaize hummed in delight. "Great idea. Polly will hate it, too."

That thought seemed to increase his pleasure in the game. And while he happily manipulated a solitary play icon through the traps and surprises set up by the designer, Nancia contemplated the vast loneliness of the stars around them and the distance she must travel before she could make private contact with another shellperson.

● CHAPTER THREE

Alpha

When she awoke after the graduation "party," Alpha bint Hezra-Fong made her way to the main cabin and found her traveling companions engaged in one of those silly role-playing games. Medical school and a demanding research program had never given her the time to waste on such frivolities. *But there might be plenty of time where she was going*. Alpha pushed that thought to the back of her mind. She would find something productive to do; she always did. She might even find a way to continue her research.

For the present, her companions watched the game screens, and Alpha watched them. They were considerably more amusing than the game; especially Blaize and Polyon, stalking one another in an ongoing verbal battle. Blaize was obviously dying to know why someone like Polyon, destined by family and training for a high command post, was being sent out to start his career on a remote planet of no real military importance.

Alpha rather wanted to know the answer to that little puzzle herself. As part of the powerful and high-ranking de Gras-Waldheim clan, Polyon would seem like a good person to cultivate. And in some ways, Alpha thought, it would be a pleasure to make friends with Polyon. He was certainly the most attractive man on this ship, the only one worth her time. But if he'd disgraced himself at the Academy and been disowned by his family, she couldn't afford the risk of getting close to him. Some of that scandal — whatever it could have been — might rub off on her. And she couldn't afford any more blots on her record, not after the way the medical school had overreacted to that trivial business about her research protocols. No, she'd wait and find out a little more about Polyon before she moved on him. And she'd let Blaize Armontillado-Perez y Medoc, a born gadfly if ever there was one, do the finding out.

"Shemali's such an *obscure* spot," Blaize hinted, "for a brilliant young man on his way up."

Polyon stared into the display of distant mountain peaks for a moment before he answered. Alpha could see a muscle twitching in his jaw. *As well as all the muscles everywhere else . . . those Academy undress grays don't leave much to the imagination! Why doesn't he just break the little pest in half?* But Polyon retained his control. "Yes, it's nearly as godforsaken as Angalia, isn't it? My brilliant little cousin-on-his-way-up," he added remotely.

"Ah, but we all know I'm the black sheep of the family," Blaize countered, "a modern-day remittance man. You, on the other hand, are supposed to be the pride of the de Gras-Waldheims, the last and finest flower of those entwined family trees, bursting with military potential and — umm — hybrid vigor."

"At least the Academy taught me not to mix my metaphors," Polyon said.

"It must be some super-secret military base," Blaize decided aloud. "Nothing less would suit for a de Gras-Waldheim's first posting. So classified even the droneship doesn't know why you're going there."

Alpha noticed that his eyes flicked towards the central titanium column as though he expected an answer through the ship's speakers. Well, she conceded, it was as likely that the drone would take part in the conversation as that Polyon would tell his cousin anything he didn't want to. Likelier.

She yawned and fiddled with the joyball, rolling the

SPACED OUT display from the Mountains of Momentum to Asteroid Hall and back. This conversation was *boring*. Polyon wasn't going to tell them anything. He wasn't even going to smash his cousin into the wall. No information, no amusement. Alpha was about ready to go back to her cabin and take a nap. There was little enough else to do on this stupid droneship.

"No secret military plans," Polyon said. "No secrets at all, Blaize, sorry to disappoint you. But if it'll shut you up, I'll try to explain what I'm going to do in terms you'll be able to understand. . . . Leaving out the technical terms, let's just say that I'm going to manage the metachip plant attached to the Shemali prison. Governor Lyautey is out of his depth. He knows how to run a prison. He doesn't know anything about metachip manufacturing. And the productivity record shows it. I'm going to set things straight, that's all."

Alpha sighed. The man's discretion was so perfect, she almost believed him; except that Blaize was right, it didn't compute for a de Gras-Waldheim to take a job as a factory manager.

"Ahh, *now* I understand," Blaize almost purred. "The governor is to take lessons from you in the finer points of chip manufacture, and you're to take lessons from him in the finer points of . . . ahhh . . . torture and degradation of prisoners? Or do I have it wrong? Maybe it's the other way round."

Polyon smiled. "If the governor wants an expert in nagging prisoners to death, I'll advise him to send for you."

"What a pity, though," Blaize prodded. "All that military training going to waste. Seems the family could have arranged something a little better for you. Unless there's something you're not telling us about your Academy record. . . ."

Polyon's perfectly shaped ears turned red and Alpha raised her head, suddenly alert. The flush of rage didn't improve Polyon's looks, but that was all right with her; if anything, his face in repose was a little too perfect. And now he looked ready to kill somebody — or tell something. Alpha mentally applauded. Blaize had finally hit on a nerve!

"And what better position might the family have arranged for *you*, dear cousin?" Polyon inquired. "Save a little of that pity for yourself. When your posting at Angalia is finished — if you ever do get off that godforsaken planet — you'll have nothing but your savings. Granted, they should be considerable, since there's nothing to spend money on there, but how much can a PTA-17's monthly salary add up to?"

"About as much as a factory supervisor's, I should imagine. Face the facts, Polyon. We've both been screwed over by our respective families. For once you're in the same boat I'm in, regardless of that pretty face and stiff back. I know why I'm here. What I'd dearly like to know is why they did it to you."

Alpha, too. She leaned forward, tensing slightly in anticipation of the answer, but Polyon chose to answer the first part of Blaize's goading speech rather than the second. "Oh, but I've no intention of trying to make it on my savings, dear coz."

"What, then?"

"Metachips," Polyon said meditatively, "are very expensive. Not to mention that they're in short supply."

"Tell me something I don't know," Blaize invited him.

"I plan," said Polyon, "to . . . improve on the current rationing system."

Unnoticed in her corner, Alpha nodded thoughtfully. Polyon had a good point. Metachips were exceedingly scarce and costly, and for good reason. The metachip manufacturing process involved at least three different acids so hazardous to the environment that most planets refused to harbor the plants, despite the unquestioned financial benefits. Shemali, inhospitable, cursed with the perpetual biting north wind that had given the planet its name, with its one land mass dedicated to a maximum-security prison, was the only major metachip manufacturing site in existence; Shemali, where nothing you did could make the environment much worse, and where the workers bought their lives one day at a time by laboring in the metachip plant.

Because who else could you use, in the final analysis, but convicts already under sentence of death? One of the acids involved, when used in the quantities required for manufacturing, released a gas whose effects on human tissue were slow, painful, deadly . . . and so far, irreversible. Alpha was an expert on those effects; her research at Central Med had been devoted to trying various drug therapies to reverse the effects of Ganglicide. She might have had a major paper out of the work if the school's Ethics Committee hadn't got so upset about her testing methods . . . Alpha clamped her lips down on the flare of anger that possessed her. That was all in the past. The present was Polyon and his plan, which he was explaining to Blaize with a wealth of patronizing detail about the adverse effects on the economy of the present rationing system.

"It's ridiculous to have metachips distributed by a committee of old men and do-gooders," he declared. "Sure, the military is entitled to first cut at the chips, but after our applications have been satisfied, the remaining chips ought to go where they'll do the most good."

"I thought that was the object of the rationing system," Blaize remarked. "Companies get Social Utility Marks for their intended use of the metachips, and the chips are distributed in proportion to the SUM. What's wrong with that?"

"Unrealistic," Polyon said promptly. "They're using chips for single-body operations like repairing kidneys or replacing damaged spinal nerves, when the same chips could go into, oh, applications that thousands of people could use at once. Dorg Jesen would pay *millions* for a handful of metas and a promise of steady supply."

Blaize began to laugh. "*Dorg Jesen?* The feelieporn king? *That's* your idea of a SUM?"

"Millions," Polyon repeated himself. "And if you don't believe I can think of a socially useful function for all that cash—"

"That," said Blaize, "I can believe. But just how do you think you'll sneak the feelieporn application past the advisory board?"

"I see no reason why the matter should ever come before the board. QA testing for the metachips is one of the areas Governor Lyautey asked me to supervise. Disposal of the chips that fail QA will presumably also fall within my duties." He looked so smug that Alpha felt the need to puncture his self-satisfaction.

"I wouldn't plan on selling defective chips to Dorg Jesen if I were you," she interrupted Polyon's gloating. "He's been known to rearrange the features of people who interfered with his business." Her shiver wasn't assumed; one of her first tasks in med research had been to diagram the facial injuries on a girl who'd refused Jesen's offer of employment. Alpha had eventually made a complete inventory of the damage, together with holosims of the girl's face before the attack and as she would look after plastifilm had replaced what used to be living flesh.

Eventually.

After she rushed out of the lab theater and threw up in front of the senior surgical advisor.

At the time, she'd thought it would be the most humiliating thing that could ever happen to her in med school.

Remembering, she barely heard Polyon's bland reply that he had no intention of selling defective chips to anybody.

Blaize gave a low, admiring whistle. "Of course. Fiddle the QA parameters one way for Governor Lyautey's reports, the other way for sales, and who knows what happens to the metachips in between? You could make a fortune in five years!"

"I intend to," said Polyon.

He was really *much* too self-satisfied, especially for a man who'd left the Academy under some kind of a cloud that he was afraid or ashamed to discuss. Alpha decided that it would be doing humanity a favor to wipe that smug smile off Lieutenant de Gras-Waldheim's face. He really shouldn't smirk like that. Spoiled his looks.

"I do hope you'll still be able to enjoy your fortune by then," she cooed sweetly at Polyon. "Better stay out of the way of your convict laborers, though. Nasty accidents are *so* easy to arrange in a D-class facility, aren't they? But don't let it worry you. Even if you do get a little spot of Ganglicide on your precious skin, I'm sure Governor Lyautey will rush you to Bahati for medical treatment. And you're lucky to have an expert in Ganglicide therapy right there at the Summerlands clinic."

"You." Polyon nodded stiffly. "That was to be your thesis topic, wasn't it?"

Alpha suppressed a start. How had Polyon known of her research? Oh, well, the High Families were such an inbred group. Probably her aunt Leona had been gossiping over the chai tables. But Polyon wouldn't know much more than the title of her projected paper; the symptoms of Ganglicide exposure were hardly fit material for chai-table gossip. She relaxed and prepared to enjoy her project of wiping that superior smirk off Polyon's face.

"I had some success with chemical treatments for the skin decay," she told him. "Halted the disintegrating process, anyway. I'm afraid we couldn't do much to reverse the effects, though. The skin shreds like paper and turns sort of blue-green. And it spreads very rapidly. If you get a drop of Ganglicide on one finger while you're on Shemali, your arm will look like it's been through a paper shredder by the time the shuttle delivers you to Bahati. *Do* try to keep it away from your pretty face."

Polyon's handsome features betrayed only slight uneasiness, but there was a knowing look in his eyes. "You — had to interrupt your research rather suddenly, didn't you?"

Alpha silently cursed all interfering, gossiping old relatives and friends. Never mind. "More's the pity," she sighed. "I was just getting into the most *interesting* cases. You know, when Ganglicide goes into its gaseous form it attacks nerves and brain synapses. Has much the same effects on them that it has on the skin; we dissected a really fascinating case, a senior assembly tech from Shemali, as it happens. The inside of his head looked like a wet blue sponge. Of course, by the time the Ganglicide got that far he was too far gone to know or care what was happening to him. A mercy, really. Not that we'll ever really know how long he felt the pain. Ganglicide goes straight to the pain receptors, you know; we can't block the effects with drugs. And towards the end he was screaming continuously. Like an animal dying under torture." She licked her lips and regarded Polyon. He was standing quite still, two fingers beating a nervous tattoo on the command panel behind him. The dance of his fingertips on the sensitive pressure pads made the SPACED OUT screen on the far side of the room shift back and forth jerkily, displaying alternate images of deep space and of a flaming labyrinth where molten lava menaced the hapless play icons.

"If you're nice to me," Alpha added, "I'll promise to kill you before the Ganglicide eats out your brains. No human being should have to die like that."

"Oh, I'll be nice to you," Polyon said. His voice was still even; he thrust off from the control panel with two fingers and floated across the room. As he came closer, Alpha recognized the look in his eyes. Not frightened. Wary. Like a hunter waiting for his quarry to burst from cover. And as he reached out to encircle her wrist with strong, blunt fingers, the look changed to a light of triumph. "I think we can be *very* nice to one another, lovely Alpha. It's so kind of you to take an interest in my career." His voice changed on the last words, mocking, savagely amused. "But enough about me. Tell us about yourself, why don't you?" He gestured towards Darnell and Fassa, floating through the open door to join them. "We'd all like to hear about your interrupted research. And why one of the school's brightest young medical researchers chose to donate five years of public service to an obscure clinic on Bahati. You're too modest, Alpha."

Alpha tossed her head and tried to pull away from Polyon, but he was too strong for her. "There's nothing to tell, really. I was tired — wanted a change of scene. That's all."

"*Is* it?" Polyon murmured. "Funny. The way I heard it, there were some other people who wanted to change your scene. The newsnibblers never beamed the story, did they? Can't have scandals about a High Families girl going out as entertainment bytes. But I fancy our friends on board here would find the story *very* entertaining."

Alpha stared up at Polyon, looking for a hint of compassion in the sharp planes of his face and the ice-blue eyes that had seemed so attractive a moment ago. "I did nothing to be ashamed of," she whispered. "The tradition of scientific experiments — "

"Does *not* include testing Ganglicide on unwitting subjects." His voice was so low the others could not hear it.

"Charity cases," Alpha defended herself. "Street bums. Some of them were so far gone on Blissto they didn't even know what was happening to them. They were incurable — nothing but an expense to the state as long as they lived. I did them a favor, making sure their lives ended for some purpose."

"Somehow," Polyon murmured, "I don't think the court would have seen it that way. But then, you never did come to trial, did you? Hezra clan and Fong tribe wouldn't let that happen. Private settlement in the med school offices, records sealed."

"How — did you find out?" Alpha gasped. He was very close to her now, his voice the subtlest vibration of sound from lips that almost brushed her cheek. The raw power of his will and his anger wrapped about her. She felt weak from the spine out. His smile made her shiver.

"That's my little secret," he told her, still smiling. His face and gestures might have been those of a courtship; Alpha realized that the others in the room might imagine they were flirting. That was a relief. Anything was preferable to having her humiliation made public before these people who were to be her constant companions for the next two weeks — having them see her as the disgraced failure she was, instead of the successful young researcher with a social conscience she pretended to be. "You were lucky to get off with five years of community service on Bahati, weren't you?" Polyon commented, stroking her cheek with his free hand. "A commoner would have been doing time. *Hard* time. Who knows, gorgeous, you might even have wound up on Shemali — getting a chance to check out Ganglicide at first hand, so to speak. Wouldn't our innocent little friends love to hear the story?"

But he was still speaking in a low voice, head partially turned away from Fassa and Blaize and Darnell, who had grouped together in the far corner of the cabin and were pretending deep interest in a round of SPACED OUT.

"What — do you want?"

"Cooperation," Polyon said. "Only a little — cooperation."

Blindly, drowning in a sea of air that somehow gave her nothing to breathe, Alpha turned her face up to meet Polyon's parted lips.

"Not that sort of cooperation," Polyon told her, laughing gently, "not yet." His eyes measured her with a cold glance that made her more afraid than ever — and, somehow, more excited too. "Maybe later, if you're a good girl. You were too uppity before, you know that, Alpha? Now you're the way I like my women. Quiet. And respectful. Stay that way, and we won't have to discuss any — ah — painful subjects with the others. Come with me and follow my lead. That's all I expect of you — for now."

Submissive, head bowed, Alpha drifted towards the three SPACED OUT gamers in Polyon's wake. They were still pretending to be totally involved in the game, but she felt sure they had avidly witnessed her humiliation.

She would pay them back. That was certain, she vowed. Fassa, Darnell, Blaize — they would all learn not to laugh at her.

She didn't even think of retaliating against Polyon.

Nancia quietly transferred the recording of the scene she'd just witnessed to an offline storage hedron. Having those bits in her system made her feel . . . dirty. As if *she* were somehow implicated in Polyon's sadistic games.

Perhaps she should have interfered. But how . . . and why? Alpha was just as bad as Polyon, worse even, to judge from what he'd revealed of her unauthorized medical experiments. The two of them deserved each other. Blaize was the only one of the bunch she would care to talk to. The little redhead reminded her of Flix — and unlike the others, he didn't seem to have anything wrong with him that a few years away from family pressures wouldn't cure.

And what, exactly, will you say if you do interrupt? Nancia couldn't answer her own question. She was a Courier Service Ship, not a diplomat! She wasn't supposed to interfere with her passengers! She should have had a brawn on board — an *experienced* brawn — to break up nasty scenes like the one she'd just witnessed, to keep these spoiled young passengers happy and away from one another's throats for the two weeks of the trip. *It's not fair! Not on my very first voyage!*

But there was nobody to hear her plaint. They were still five days away from Singularity and the decomposition into Vega subspace.

At least I can keep evidence recordings going, Nancia thought grimly. *If one of the little brats drives another over the edge, there'll be plenty of datahedra to show what happened.* But at the moment, the five passengers seemed to be getting along reasonably well. Perhaps his sadistic games with Alpha had momentarily satiated Polyon's need for command and control; he had taken a play icon and seemed absorbed in that silly role-playing game. Nancia relaxed . . . but she kept her datacorders running.

● CHAPTER FOUR

"Why can't I get past the Wingdrake of Wisdom?" Darnell griped. He had chosen Bonecrush again, but his mighty-thewed play icon was backed into a corner where a winged serpent hissed menacingly at him every time he tried to move.

"You should have bought some intelligence for Bonecrush at the Little Shop of Spiritual Enlightenment," Polyon commented. His fingers flicked carelessly at the screen as he spoke, sending Thingberry the Martian Mage to spin an apparently pointless web in the night sky above Asteroid 66.

"I didn't know you *could* buy intelligence." Darnell's lower lip protruded in a definite pout. "That wasn't in the rule book."

"A lot of things aren't in the rule book," Polyon said, "including most of what you need to survive. And information is always for sale . . . if you know the right price. Anything from the secrets of Singularity to the origins of planet names."

"Oh. Encyclopedias. Libraries. Anybody can buy the Galactic Datasource on fast-hedra," Darnell whined. "But who has time to read all that crud?"

"The price of some kinds of information," Polyon said, "is more than the cost of a book and the time to read it. I could print out the rules of Singularity math for you, but you haven't paid the price of understanding it — the years of space transformation algebra and the intelligence to move the theories into multiple dimensions."

"Oh, come on," Blaize challenged him. "It's not that

complicated. Even I know Baykowski's Theorem."

"A continuum C is said to be locally shrinkable in M if, and only if, for each epsilon greater than zero and each open set D containing C, there is a homeomorphism h of M onto M which takes C onto a set of diameter less than epsilon and which is the identity on M — D," Polyon recited rapidly. "And it's not a theorem, it's a definition."

Nancia quietly followed the discussion with mild interest. The mathematics of Singularity was nothing new to her, but at least when her brat passengers were talking mathematics they weren't trying to drive each other crazy. And she was impressed that Polyon had retained enough Singularity theory to be able to recite Baykowski's Definition from memory; common gossip among the brainships in training was that no softperson could *really* understand multidimensional decompositions.

"The real basis for decom theory," Polyon lectured his audience, "is what follows that definition. Namely, Zerlion's Lemma: that our universe can be considered as a collection of locally shrinkable continua each containing at least one non-degenerating element."

Fassa del Parma pouted and jabbed her play icon across the display screen in a series of short, jerky moves. "Very useful information, I'm sure," she said in a sarcastic voice, "but do the rest of us have to pay the price of listening to it? All this theoretical mathematics makes my head hurt. And it's not as if it were good for anything, like stress analysis or materials testing."

"It's good for getting us to the Nyota system in two weeks instead of six months, my dove," Polyon told her. "And it's really quite simple. In layman's terms, Singularity theory just shows us how to decompose two widely separated subspace areas into a sequence of compacted dimensionalities sharing one non-degenerating element. When the subspaces become singular they will appear to intersect at that element — and when we expand from the decomposition, pop! out of Central subspace and into Vega space we go."

Nancia felt grateful that she'd resisted her impulse to join in the conversation. Her Lab Schools classmates had been right about softpersons. Polyon knew all the right words for Singularity mathematics, but he'd gotten the basic theory hopelessly scrambled. And clearly he didn't understand the computational problems underlying that theory. Pure topological theory might prove the existence of a decomposition series, but actually forcing a ship through that series required massive linear programming optimizations, all performed in realtime with no second chances for mistakes. No wonder softpersons weren't trusted to pilot a ship through Singularity!

"I agree with you," Alpha told Fassa. "Bo-ring. Even the history of Nyota is better than studying mathematics."

"You'd think so, of course," Fassa said, "seeing that it was discovered and named by your people." The small grin on her face told Nancia that this was a jab of some sort at Alpha. Hastily she scanned her data notes on the Nyota system, but nothing there explained why the Hezra-Fong family should take a particular interest in it.

"Swahili is a slave language," Alpha said haughtily. "It has nothing to do with the Fong tribe. My people come from the other side of the continent — and we were *never* enslaved!"

"Will somebody give me a map of this conversation?" Darnell said plaintively. "I'm more lost than I was during Polyon's math lecture."

"This particular information," Alpha told him, "is free." She drew herself up to her full height, several inches taller than Fassa, and favored the top of her sleek, dark head with a withering glare. "The system we're going to was discovered by a Black descendant of the American slaves. In a burst of misguided enthusiasm, he decided to give the star and all the planets names from an African language. Unfortunately, he was so poorly educated that the only such language he knew was Swahili, a trade language spread along the east coast of Africa by Arab slavers. He called the sun Nyota ya Jaha — Lucky Star. The planets' names are fairly accurate descriptions, too. Bahati means Fortune, and it's a reasonably decent place to live — green, mild climate, lots of nice scenery that stays put. Shemali means North Wind."

Polyon groaned appreciatively. "I know. Unlike some of us, I did read up on my destination. The place is called North Wind because that's what you get for thirteen months out of the year."

"*Thirteen* months you have in the year? Oh — I get it! Longer rotation period, right?" Darnell beamed with pride at his own cleverness.

"Shorter, as it happens," Polyon said. His voice sounded remarkably hollow. "Shemali has a year of three hundred days, divided into ten months for convenience. I was being sarcastic about the fact that there is *no* good season."

"Never mind," Alpha told him almost kindly, "it's better than Angalia. Actually the full name is Angalia! with an exclamation point at the end. It means Watch out!"

"Dare I ask what *that* means?" Blaize inquired.

"It means," Alpha told him, "that the scenery — unlike that of Bahati — doesn't stay put."

Blaize and Polyon stared at one another, briefly companions in misery.

Polyon was the first to recover himself. "Oh, well," he said, turning back to the game screen, "you see the value of information, Darnell — and the fact that it isn't always in the Galactic Datasource. And some of the information that isn't — ah — publicly available — is the most valuable of all." With delicate gestures he nudged the joyball while the fingers of his left hand tapped out codes to enlarge and strengthen Thingberry's magical net. "You need to think of ways to trade for that kind of information. For instance, your shipping company — such as it is — could offer discreet transport for parcels that *don't* get on the cargo list, or that go by a slightly misleading name — in some cases, disinformation or the lack of information is as valuable as actual data."

"Who'd want that?" Darnell objected. "And who cares, anyway? Can't we just play the game?"

Polyon favored him with a dazzling smile. "Dear boy, this *is* the game — and a far more rewarding one than SPACED OUT. Why, I can think of any number of people who might want a — suitably discreet — cargo carrier service. Myself, for starters."

"Why you?"

"Let's just say that not all the metachips going off Shemali are going to be in the SUM rationing board's records," Polyon said.

"So? What's it worth to me to oblige you?"

"I could pay you back with Net contacts. I can work the Net like no hacker since the days of the first virus breeders. It's an unsecured hedron to me. How soon could you rebuild OG Shipping if you knew ahead of time about every big contract about to be let in Vega subspace . . . and what your opponents' sealed bids were?"

Darnell's pout vanished to be replaced by a look of stunned calculation. "I could be rich again in five years!"

"But not, I fancy, as rich as I could be from selling metachips," Polyon murmured. Thingberry's web glistened on the screen above him, strings of jeweled light looping and floating above the play icons on the surface of Asteroid 66. "What would you say to a friendly wager? The five of us to meet and compare notes, once a year — to see how we're each doing at making lemonade out of the lemons of assignments our dear families have landed us with? Winner to take a twenty-five percent share in each of the losers' operations — business, goods, or cold credits?"

"When do we decide to stop and make the final evaluation?" Darnell asked.

"Five years — that's the end of most of our tours of duty, isn't it?"

"You know it is," said Alpha quickly. "Standard tour. And," she went on under Polyon's firm gaze, "I think it's a marvelous idea. I've got my own plans, you know."

"What?" Darnell demanded.

Alpha gave him a slow, lazy smile. "Wouldn't you like to know?"

"I'm sure we would *all* like to know," Polyon put in. A deft twist of the joyball set Thingberry's jeweled web spinning over the top half of the display screen. "Will you enlighten them, Alpha, or shall I — er — contribute my own scraps of information?" He crooked his finger, beckoning to her, and she moved closer to his control chair.

"Nothing much," Alpha said. "But . . . Summerlands is a double clinic. One side for the paying customers — mostly VIPs — and one side for charity cases, to improve their SUM rating. I've got some ideas for an improvement on Blissto — something we can give addicts in controlled doses. They won't get locked into a cycle of craving and ever-increasing hits of street drugs."

"Hey, *I* like Blissto," Darnell protested, "and I don't get into that cycle."

"Good," Alpha told him. "You're not an addictive personality. Some people aren't that lucky. You've seen Blissed-Out cases? Big enough doses, over a long enough period of time, until their nervous systems look like shredded wheat? *My* version won't do that. We'll be able to take Blissed-Out cases out of the hospital and send them out to do useful work as long as they stay on their meds. And I'm the one who did all the preliminary design work on this drug. Actually, it was a side-effect of my work on — well, there's no need to discuss all the boring details of my research," she concluded with a sidelong glance at Polyon. "What matters is that I've got the formulas and all the lab notes on hedra."

"But won't Central Meds hold the patent, if you did the work there?"

"When — and if — it's patented," Alpha agreed.

"And you can't sell it until it's passed the trials and been patented — so it's no good to you!"

Alpha's eyes met Polyon's over Darnell's head. "Quite true," she agreed gravely, "but I think I may find a way to profit from the situation anyway."

"What about you, Fassa?" Polyon asked. The girl had been very quiet since her jab about the slave names of the Nyota system. "You going to take this boondocks construction company Daddy handed you *lying down?*" His tone invested the question with a wealth of obscene possibilities.

"Double profit on every job," Fassa announced calmly. "I've got a degree in accounting. I can fix the books in ways an auditor will never catch."

Darnell whistled appreciatively. "But if you *are* caught — "

Fassa coiled herself on the other side of Polyon's chair in a series of languorous, sinuous movements that drew all eyes to her. "I think," she said dreamily, "that I can distract any auditors who *may* think about checking the books. Or any building inspectors who need to sign off on materials quality." Her slow, dreamy smile promised a world of secret delights. "There's a lot of money in construction . . . if you go about it the right way."

The four of them made a tight grouping now: Polyon in the control chair, Darnell standing behind him, Fassa and Alpha seated on either side of him. Four pairs of eyes gazed expectantly at Blaize.

"Well," he said, swallowed, and started over again. "Ah — PTA doesn't offer quite as much scope for creativity as the rest of your outfits, does it now?"

"You're with us or against us," said Polyon. "Which is it to be, little cousin?"

"Ah — neutrality?"

"Not good enough." Polyon glanced around at the other three. "He's heard our plans. If he doesn't join us, he could have some idea of informing. . . . "

Alpha leaned forward, smiling sweetly. Her teeth looked long and very white against her dark skin. "Oh, you wouldn't do that, would you, Blaize dear?"

"I wouldn't even think about it," Darnell put in, tapping one pudgy fist against his open palm.

Fassa licked her lips and smiled like a child anticipating a treat. "This could be *interesting*," she murmured to no one in particular.

Blaize glanced around the circle of faces, then looked towards Nancia's titanium column. She kept her silence. Nothing had actually happened yet; if these brats attempted violence, she could stop it in seconds with a flood of sleepgas. And Blaize knew that as well as she did. Nancia saw no reason to give up her anonymity just to reassure him. He'd been brave enough when he was picking on Polyon alone; why, for heaven's sake, couldn't he stand up to the rest of them?

"But then, Blaize never did have the guts to do something as decisive as *telling*," Polyon dismissed his cousin with a brief nod. "We'll let him think it over . . . all the way to Angalia. It'll be a long couple of weeks, little cousin, with nobody to talk to. And a much longer five years on Angalia. Hope you enjoy life among the veggie-heads. I shouldn't think anybody else in the Nyota system will have much to do with you." He swiveled to face the SPACED OUT display, and the other three turned with him.

"Oh — don't leap to assumptions so fast. I'm with

you, definitely with," Blaize babbled. "There *are* possibilities — I just haven't had time to think them over yet. The corycium mine, for instance — it hasn't been properly developed — maybe I could get a part interest in that. And PTA makes regular food drops to Angalia, who's to say how much of the food gets distributed to the natives and how much gets transshipped to some place that can pay for it . . . " He spread his hands and shrugged jerkily. "I'll think of something. You'll see. I'll do as well as any of you!"

Polyon nodded again. His fist closed over the joyball and Thingberry's jeweled web spiraled down to enclose Asteroidland, trapping the others' play icons in a tissue of glittering strands. "Done, then. Five of us together. Here, we'd better each have a record." He drew a handful of minihedra from the pocket of his Academy grays and dropped them into the datareader. One by one, Alpha, Fassa, Darnell and Blaize identified themselves by hand and retina print and spoke aloud the terms and conditions of the wager they'd agreed to. Polyon retrieved the minihedra after the recording was over and handed one faceted black polyhedron to each of them, keeping the last for himself. "Better store them someplace safe," he suggested.

Fassa clipped her minihedron inside a silver wire cage that hung from her charm bracelet among tinkling bells and glittering bits of carved prismawood. She alone seemed in no particular hurry to escape Polyon's influence; while the others jostled to reach the exit door, Fassa fiddled with her charm bracelet and tried out the shining black minihedron in various places, as if her only concern was to see where it would show to best advantage.

As Alpha, Darnell and Blaize left the central cabin, Nancia wondered whether Polyon's quick actions and mesmerizing personality had made them forget that he alone, of the five, had not recorded his intentions on the minihedra. Or were they simply afraid to challenge him?

Not that it mattered. She had the entire scene recorded. From several angles.

"You'll see," Blaize repeated over his shoulder as he left. "I'll do better than any of you."

"Small time, little man," Alpha sneered on her way down the corridor, "small-time plans for a small person. You'll be the loser, but who cares? *Somebody* has to lose."

"She's wrong, you know," Polyon commented to Fassa. "*Four* of you have to lose. There'll be only one winner in this game." And he too left, twiddling his black minihedron between two fingers and humming quietly to himself.

Fassa

The gleaming black surfaces of the minihedron flashed in the central cabin lights as Fassa turned her arm this way and that, admiring the effect of the stark blackness against the jumble of silver and prismawood trinkets. The hedron was as black as Fassa's own sleek hair and tip-tilted eyes, an admirable contrast to the whiteness of her creamed and pampered skin. In its hard glossy perfection she saw a miniature of herself ... beautiful, impenetrable ...

A shell full of dangerous secrets.

Fassa stared at the mirror-smooth surfaces of the minihedron and saw her face reflected and distorted in half a dozen directions at once, a shattered self looking out, trapped in the black mirrors that distorted her lovely features to a mask of pain and a silent scream.

No! That's not me — that can't be me. She dropped her arm; the jingling silver bells on the bracelet tinkled a single discordant peal. Pushing off from the strange titanium column that wasted so much cabin space, Fassa floated into a corner between display screens and a storage locker. "Blank screens," she ordered the ship.

The dazzling display of SPACED OUT graphics faded away, to be replaced by a black emptiness like the surfaces of the minihedron. Fassa stared into the flat screen, lips parted, until the reflection of her own beauty reassured her. Yes, she was still as lovely as she'd always believed. The distorted reflections from the minihedron had been an illusion like the dreams that troubled her sleep, dreams in which her lovely face and perfect body peeled away to reveal the shrunken, miserable creature underneath.

Reassured, she stroked the charm bracelet with two fingers until she touched the sharp faceted surface of the minihedron. *I keep my secrets, and you keep yours, little sister.* As long as she had the shield of her perfect beauty between herself and the world, Fassa felt safe. Nobody could see beyond that to the worthless thing inside. Very few tried; they were all too mesmerized by the outer facade. Men were rutting fools, and they deserved no better than to have their own folly turned back on them. If she could use their desire for her to enrich herself, so much the better. Gods knew her beauty had cost her too much in the past!

Mama, mama, make him stop, wailed a child's voice from the recesses of her mind. Fassa laughed sourly at the memory of that folly. How old had she been then? Eight, nine? Young enough to think her mother could stand up to a man like Faul del Parma y Polo, could make him give up anything he really wanted — like his daughter. Mama had closed her eyes and turned her head away. She didn't want to know what Faul was doing to their lovely little girl.

Ugly little girl. Dirty little girl, whispered another of the voices.

All the same, it had been Mama who stopped it, in a way. Too late, but still — her spectacular and public suicide had ended Faul's private games with his daughter. Jumping from the forty-second story balcony, Mama had shattered herself on the terraces of the Regis Galactic Hotel in the middle of Faul del Parma's annual company extravaganza, the one *all* the gossipbyters attended. And the news and gossip and rumor and innuendo that surrounded the suicide of del Parma's wife had been splashed all over the newsbeams for weeks thereafter. Why should she kill herself? Faul del Parma could give a woman everything. There was no history of mental instability. And everyone knew Faul del Parma never so much as looked at another woman, he only cared for his wife — well, one didn't hear so much about the wife, did one? A homebody type. But he went everywhere with that lovely little daughter at his side, only thirteen but a heartbreaker in the making. . . .

It occurred to a dozen gossipbyters at once that the daughter should be interviewed. And *that* had stopped it. Faul del Parma had whisked his daughter into a very exclusive, very private boarding school where no gossipbyters could find her and ask inconvenient questions.

Fassa twisted the minihedron on its clasp. *Thank you, Mama.* Even now, six years later, the story of the del Parma wife's suicide still made an occasional gossipbyte. Even now, Faul del Parma didn't want to risk having Fassa anywhere near him. So now that she was graduated from the expensive, exclusive school, he'd found a position for her with the least of his companies, Polo Construction, based on a planet in Vega subspace. And Fassa had practiced her bargaining skills for the first time.

"I'll take it. But not as your subordinate. Make over Polo Construction to me, and I'll go out to Bahati and manage the company and never trouble you again. Call it a graduation present."

Call it a bribe for going into exile, Fassa thought, twisting the minihedron back and forth until the sharp angles of the facets bit into her thumb and forefinger. Because when Faul had balked at giving her complete ownership of the company, Fassa had leaned elegantly on his desk and speculated aloud about her chances of getting a position with one of the major newsbeamers. "They're all *very* interested in me," she teased her father.

"Interested in picking up sleazy gossip about our family," Faul snapped. "They've no interest in you for your own abilities."

Fassa smoothed her gleaming black hair back from her face. "*Some* of my abilities are very interesting," she told him. She let her voice drop down into the husky lower register that seemed to produce such an effect on her male teachers. "And the del Parma y Polo family is always news. I bet some of the major newsbeam companies would just love to serialize a book by me. I could tell them all the secrets I learned from my father. . . . "

"All right. It's yours!" Faul del Parma y Polo slapped his hand on the palmscanner beside his deskcomp, jabbed the hardcopy pad with his free thumb and ejected the finished minihedron with a glare for his daughter.

"You won't object if I scan it first?"

"Use a public scanner. You can't be sure of mine," Faul pointed out. "I might have programmed it to give a false readout. You'd better start thinking smarter if you want to make a success of this business, Fassa. But don't worry — it's all there. Ownership transfer and my palmprint to back it up. I wouldn't cheat you. I don't want you coming back to this office."

"*Don't* you, Daddy dear?" Fassa twisted forward over the desk, sinuous and flowing in her formfitting sheath of Rigellian spiderspin. She leaned close enough to let Faul breathe in the warmth and subtle perfume of her skin . . . and was rewarded by a flash of pain and desire in his eyes.

"Ta-ta, Daddy dearest." She slid from the desk and

clasped the minihedron inside a corycium heart that
dangled from her charm bracelet. "See you around . . .
I *don't* think."

"I wonder," Faul said hoarsely, "how many of those
little charms contain men's hearts and souls."

"Not many — yet." Fassa paused at the door and
gave him a sparkling smile. "I'm starting the collection
with you."

Now, three days out from Central, she had already
added a second hedron to the collection. Fassa jingled
the charm bracelet reflectively. Each of the sparkling
bits of jewelry was a clasp or a cage or an empty locket,
waiting to receive some trinket. She'd collected the
charms over those lonely years at boarding school,
spending the lavish birthday and Christmas checks
from Faul on expensive custom-made baubles. One
for each time that Faul had come to her room at night.
Only twenty-three in all; strange, she thought, that
less than two dozen carefully chosen nights over a
period of four or five years could make you rot away
from the inside. Twenty-three shining jewels, each as
perfect and beautiful in its own way as Fassa was in
hers; each as empty inside as she was.

No, not any more. Two of them are filled. Fassa pushed
off from the wall with the tips of her fingers and floated
gently through the main cabin, twirling the charms
around her wrist. Before she was done, she'd fill every
charm with something. . . appropriate.

And then what?

No answers to that, no conceivable end to the future
she'd mapped out for herself.

Blaize

The central cabin was empty; Polyon's buddies had
all slunk off to their cabins to think over their wager
and its probable consequences. Good. Blaize knew he
could perfectly well have talked to Nancia from the

privacy of his own cabin, but somehow it seemed more real to come here and speak directly to the titanium column that contained her shell.

Besides, she wasn't answering him from the cabin. He thought maybe she'd turned off the cabin sensors to give her passengers privacy.

He cleared his throat tentatively. Now that he was here, and not so confident of his welcome, it seemed rather strange to be talking to the walls. Sort of thing that got you shipped off for a nice rest in a place like Summerlands Care, Inc. Blaize shivered. Not for him, thank you. If he ever *did* need medical treatment, he'd make sure to go to a clinic where that snake Alpha bint Hezra-Fong was *not* operating.

"Nancia? Can you hear me?"

The silence was as absolute as that of the empty, black space outside the brainship's thin skin.

"I know you're listening," Blaize said desperately. "Watching, too. You *have* to be. *I* wouldn't close my eyes or turn my back on somebody like Cousin Polyon, and I don't believe you'd risk letting him sneak into your control cabin unobserved."

His wild gestures as he made the last statement almost overbalanced him in the ship's light grav field. He grabbed at a handrail and made a dancer's turn into the center of the cabin, recovering from the near-stumble as gracefully as a cat correcting a mis-timed jump. Nancia's titanium column coruscated in rainbow reflections of the cabin lights, sparkling and dancing around him. And she did not reply.

"Look, I know what you're thinking, but it's not like that. Really." Blaize grasped a chair back to steady himself. "I mean, what could I do? Did you expect me to call them all criminals and wrap myself in my own integrity? They could've *spaced* me before we got to Angalia, and called it an unfortunate accident."

Silence.

"All right," Blaize conceded. "They probably wouldn't have spaced me. Especially if I told them you were a brainship and could bear witness against them."

Silence.

This was worse than the time he'd been locked in his room for a month.

"But that would have meant telling on *you*," Blaize pointed out, "and you didn't really want them to know you've been listening, did you?"

Silence.

"Well, what did you expect me to do, anyway? They'd all have hated me." Blaize's voice cracked. "Isn't it bad enough I have to go out to Angalia and spend the next five years handing out PTA boxes to some walking veggies? Do I have to start by losing my only friends in the whole star system?"

Nancia answered at last. "They are not your friends, and you know it."

Blaize shrugged. "Best imitations I've got. Look, I've spent my whole life being the family black sheep, the one nobody bothers with, the one nobody likes much, nobody respects. Can you blame me for wanting to change that? Just once in my life I want to *belong*."

"You do," Nancia told him. "As far as I'm concerned, you do indeed belong with the rest of this amoral bratpack. And as for respect . . . you can add me to the list of people who don't respect you. I don't believe you ran away from home three times, either. You haven't got the gumption to cross the street without somebody holding your hand."

"I did so!"

Silence.

"Once, anyway. And if I *had* run away again, it would've been just like I said. They'd have been waiting for me at the Academy. So what was the point? And what difference does it make? Worked out the same as if I'd actually done it, didn't it?"

Silence.

Blaize decided to go back to his cabin before somebody drifted in here and caught him talking to the walls.

"One more thing," he called as he pushed off for the return. "I *did* win that scholarship. Under the name of Blaize Docem. You can check Academy records on that!"

Nancia maintained her silence. All the way to Angalia.

CHAPTER FIVE

Singularity

The neighborhood of the brainship collapsed inward on itself, spiraling down tornado-like to the Singularity point where Central Worlds subspace could momentarily be defined as intersecting Vega subspace. The ship's metachip-augmented parallel processors solved and optimized the set of equations represented in a thousand-square matrix of subspace points, dropped out of that subspace into Decomposition, rode the collapsing funnel of spaces with a new optimization problem to choose and resolve every tenth of a second. To Nancia, Singularity was how she envisioned the ancient Earth sport called "surfing"; balanced at the non-degrading point where decomposing subspaces met, she recognized and evaluated local paths so quickly that the massive optimization problems blurred together into a sense of skimming over a wave that was always just about to crash beneath her.

The Singularity field test she'd taken at the Academy had been simpler than this. There, she'd had to deal with only one set of parallel equations; here, the sequence of equations and diminishing subspaces streamed past her in an incessant flow. It was challenge, danger, joy: it was what she had been trained for. She swept over matrices of data and guided them to the ship's processors, choosing and resolving the ever-changing paths to Singularity with an athlete's single-minded concentration.

The same newsbeam that showed Nancia the sport of "surfing" had also had a section on a diving competition. The clean lines of the divers' movements, the seconds during which they hurtled through the air as though they could give their bodies the lift and freedom of brainships, fascinated Nancia; she'd viewed the beam over a dozen times, marveling at what softpersons would go through for a few seconds of physical freedom. "Didja see how he ripped that dive!" the newsbyter had jabbered after one athlete's performance, then explaining that the term referred to the clean way the diver had entered the water without a single splash.

Nancia ripped a perfect dive through Singularity and came out into Vega subspace.

For her passengers, with nothing to do during Singularity and no way to filter the barrage of sensory data, the transition was markedly less pleasant. The few seconds of decomposition and reformation seemed like hours of wading through air gone viscous, picking their way among shapes distorted out of all recognition, in a place where colors hummed on the air and light bent around corners.

They gasped with relief when the ship broke through into normal space again.

Nancia watched them staggering and rubbing their eyes and ears. She was rather surprised by the intensity of their reactions; the trainer who'd accompanied her through her Singularity test had not seemed to be bothered by the few seconds of sensory distortion. Perhaps practice made a difference to how softpersons took Decomposition. Polyon's first words after the return to normal space suggested this might be the case.

"Well, *mes enfants*," said Polyon, "how did you like your first Decomposition? It's been so long since *my* first training flights that I've forgotten how it affects newcomers."

"Once is enough," said Darnell with feeling. "If I

ever go home again, I'll *take* the six months of travel by FTL. Or better yet, I'll *walk*."

Fassa nodded vigorous agreement, then winced as if she wished she hadn't moved her head so soon.

"Have a Blissto," Alpha offered. "Works on hangovers — ought to help with Singularity headaches too."

Darnell snatched the small blue pills out of her hand and downed six of them in a single desperate gulp. Fassa started to shake her head and then obviously thought better of it. She waved Alpha's hand away with a languid gesture. "Never touch drugs."

"More fool you," said Alpha. "I know more about side effects than any of you, and I promise you a few blues won't do any harm. Just wish I'd thought of it before we entered Singularity. Blaize?"

"Excellent idea," Blaize said hollowly, accepting the offered pills. Unlike Darnell, he made his way to the far side of the cabin and found a half-empty bottle of Stemerald to help him choke down the pills. "Almost as good an idea as walking. Don't think I ever really *appreciated* Earth before." His skin was pale green under the spattering of freckles.

Polyon chuckled. "May have been a blessing in disguise that you weren't allowed to go in for brawn training, little one. Apparently you haven't the stomach for it. Now when you imagine combining frequent Decom hops with Mil Spec meals of boiled synthoprot and anonymous vitacaps that all smell like cabbage—"

Fassa clapped a hand over her mouth and ran for the door. Darnell swallowed convulsively two or three times. "Would you mind very much not mentioning food just now?" His last words were slurred and relaxed; the Blissto was already taking effect.

"At least not till I've had my own blues," Alpha added, pouring a handful of the shiny blue pills down her throat.

Fassa didn't quite make it to the privacy of her cabin. Silently, Nancia extruded probes that captured and vaporized the resulting mess. She activated the release latch on Fassa's cabin door so that it irised open in front of the girl.

"T-thank you," Fassa hiccuped into the wet cloth Nancia's second probe held out. "I mean — I know you're just a droneship, so this is silly, but — oh, thank you anyway." She collapsed on her bunk, a huddle of misery. Nancia closed down the cabin sensors, transmitted a shut command to the door iris, and left Fassa to recover on her own. At least, she thought, the girl had the strength of character to abstain from mind-rotting drugs. And the manners to thank whoever helped her, even a supposedly inanimate droneship. Her stated intention of using sex to get concessions for her company was appalling, as were her manners in general; but maybe she was a shade less repellent than the rest of Nancia's young passengers.

They had completely ignored Fassa's distress, Nancia noted. Polyon was playing a solitaire round of SPACED OUT and the other three were giggling over a new bottle of Stemerald. Nancia wondered uneasily what the mix of stimulants and depressants was likely to do to a softperson's nervous system — and what else Alpha might have smuggled aboard. Maybe it had been a mistake to turn off the cabin sensors; these people didn't *deserve* privacy.

But then, what business was it of hers if they wanted to drug themselves into a stupor? They'd be much nicer that way, after all. Nancia herself could conceive of nothing more horrible than voluntarily scrambling one's synapses, but softpersons did, by all reports, have very strange tastes.

Besides, they were much easier to put up with now that they were too doped to do anything but giggle softly and spill their Stemerald. Nancia's housekeeping probes mopped up the green puddles on the cabin floor; her passengers ignored the probes and their cleanup activity, and she, as far as possible, ignored the passengers.

Because now, at last, there was somebody else to talk to.

Within seconds of her emergence from Singularity, Nancia had initiated a tightbeam contact with Vega Base. By the time Fassa was cleaned up in her cabin and the other passengers busy with their own peculiar amusements, she had gone through the recognition sequences and the official messages and was happily chatting with Simeon, the managing brain of Vega Base.

"So how did you like your first voyage?" Simeon inquired.

"Singularity was . . . " Nancia couldn't find words for it; instead she transmitted a short visual burst of colors melting and expanding like soap bubbles, iridescent trails of light joyously spiraling around one another. "I can't wait to jump again."

Simeon chuckled. "You're one of the lucky ones, then. From all I hear, it doesn't take everyone that way."

"My passengers didn't seem to enjoy it much," Nancia conceded, "but who cares?"

"Even brainships don't always get such a kick out of Singularity," Simeon told her.

Nancia found that hard to believe, but she remembered that Simeon was a stationary brain. Embedded in the heart of Vega Base, his only experience of travel would have been the jump that brought him here from Laboratory Schools — as a passenger, like any softperson. Perhaps she shouldn't go on about the joys of Singularity to someone who could never experience the thrill of managing his own jumps.

Besides, Simeon wanted to pursue something else.

"You don't seem to care much for your passengers' comfort."

Again words failed Nancia. She damped the colors of her visual burst to a muddy swirl of greenish browns and grays. "They're not . . . very nice people," she finally answered. "Some of the things I overheard them discussing on the trip . . . Simeon, could I ask you a hypothetical question? Suppose a brainship happened to learn that some people had unethical plans. Should she report them?"

"You mean, like a plot to murder somebody? Or high treason — an attempt to overthrow Central?"

"Oh, goodness, no, nothing like *that*!" How could Simeon sound so calm while discussing such dreadful things? "At least, I don't think — I mean, suppose they weren't planning to hurt anybody, but what they meant to do was morally wrong? Even illegal?" Alpha's plans to profit from a drug that should have been credited to Central Meds, Polyon's idea of creating a black market in metachips — no, Nancia assured herself, her passengers were nasty and corrupt as all get-out, but at least they weren't violent.

"Hmm. And how might this brainship have found out about her passengers' plans?"

"I — they thought she was a droneship," Nancia said, "and they discussed everything quite freely. She has datacordings of it all, too."

"I *see*." Simeon sounded quite disapproving, and for a moment Nancia thought he shared her shock at her passengers' plans. "And has it occurred to you, young XN-935, that masquerading as a droneship in order to eavesdrop on High Families' conversations is a form of entrapment? In fact, given that the passengers involved *are* High Families and very close to CenCom, the act of taking surreptitious datacordings could even be interpreted as treason. What if they'd been discussing vital military secrets?"

"But they weren't — I didn't — Listen, VS-895, *they're* the criminals, not me!" Nancia shouted.

"Ouch."

Simeon's reply was almost an electronic whisper.

"Turn down your waveforms, would you? That nearly jolted me out of my shell."

"Sorry." Nancia controlled her impulses and channeled a clean, tight beam at Simeon. "But I don't see what you're accusing *me* of."

"Me? Nothing, XN, I assure you. I'm just trying to warn you that the courts may see things rather differently. Now, I don't know what your young passengers have been up to, and I don't particularly care to know. You haven't seen much of the world yet, or you'd realize that most softpersons have some way or other to get a little extra out of every situation in which they find themselves."

Nancia mulled that over. "You mean — are they *all* corrupt, then?"

Simeon chuckled. "Not all, Nancia, just enough to make it interesting. You have to understand the poor things. Short lifespan, limited to five senses, single-channel comm system. I expect they feel cheated when they compare themselves with us. And some of them translate that feeling into trying to get extra goodies for themselves."

Nancia had to agree that what Simeon said made a lot of sense. She tried to emulate his attitude of lofty detachment while she went about the business of landing her passengers at their assigned stations in the Nyota ya Jaha system. Since four of them still thought her a droneship and the fifth knew she wasn't speaking to him, it was easy enough to remain aloof.

Nancia made each planetary landfall an exercise in split-second timing and perfect orbit-matching. It was good practice, it kept her concentrating on her own business and not on that of her passengers, and if the rapid maneuvers involved gave them a bumpy ride — well, so much the worse. She took pride in making the actual moments of touchdown as gentle as the landing of a feather. At least, Bahati and Shemali went that way. When she reached Angalia, she couldn't quite restrain her impulse to give Blaize a good shaking on the way down. He was pale and sweating by the time they came to a bumpy halt on the mesa that served as Angalia's spacefield.

"That," he said as he collected his baggage, "was not necessary."

Nancia preserved an icy silence — literally. Each moment that Blaize delayed, she lowered her internal temperature by several degrees.

"You could at least send a housekeeping probe to help me with all this stuff," he complained, gripping a box of novelhedra with fingers that were rapidly turning blue with cold.

"You're not my mother, you know," he said while leaning on the button to the lift. "Nobody asked *you* to pass judgment on my moral standards. Just like nobody asked *me* if I wanted to come out to this godforsaken place."

"I guess it would be too much to expect anybody to have a little sympathy," he said as the lift sped downward.

Nancia tilted the hatchway floor so that Blaize's carefully stacked boxes of supplies tumbled out as soon as he stepped onto the surface of Angalia.

"I know what you're thinking," he shouted from the red dust of the mesa top, "but you're wrong about me! You're all wrong! I'll show you!"

Nancia was pleased that her assignment made no mention of collecting the previous PTA administrator, the one whom Blaize had been sent to relieve. Apparently, not being a member of the High Families, he was expected to wait for the regularly scheduled PTA transport rather than taking advantage of a brainship for the Courier Service. Hard on him, Nancia thought, but quite appropriate. She would proceed directly to Vega 3.3, collect this stranded brawn, and return to Central for a *real* assignment — with a brawn of her own choosing. Thank goodness she was through being used as a substitute droneship for the convenience of the rich and powerful!

She discovered her error when she was halfway from Nyota ya Jaha to Vega 3.

"What do you *mean*, another little errand?" she blasted poor Simeon.

"Turn it down," came Simeon's low-intensity reminder. "It wasn't my idea and you don't have to shout like that. Anyway, what difference does it make? you were going to Vega 3 anyway."

"I was going to 3.3, not 4.2," Nancia pointed out, and this reminded her of another grievance. "Why can't these people give their suns and planets real names, anyway? This Vega numbering system makes me feel like a machine."

"They're great believers in efficiency," Simeon said. "And logic. You'll see what I mean when you pair up with Caleb."

"Hmph. You mean, when I transport the man — for that's all I've agreed to. Efficiency!" Nancia grumbled. "That's a new word for misuse of the Courier Service. Why, it's a whole different solar system and an extra stop to pick up this governor Thrixtopple and his family, not to mention having to feed them all the way back to Central. Time and fuel and ship's stores wasted. My fuel belongs to the Courier Service," she said, "and so does my time."

"What about your soul?" inquired Simeon, returning to a normal-intensity beam. "Oh, never mind. I keep forgetting how new you are, XN. Wait till you've been around the subspaces a few hundred years. You'll start understanding how the rules have to be bent to accommodate people."

"You mean, to accommodate *softpersons*," Nancia corrected proudly. "I've never asked for an exception or a favor in my life, and I'm not about to start now."

Simeon's responding burst of discordant waves and clashing colors was the electronic equivalent of an extremely rude word. "I can see why Psych thought you and Caleb would be a good match," he said. Infuriatingly, he shut down transmissions on that comment, leaving Nancia to wonder all the way to Vega 3.3. Why *did* Psych see fit to match her with a brawn whose major accomplishment so far had been the loss of his first brainship? Was there something wrong in her profile, some instability that made it appropriate to assign her an incompetent brawn? This Caleb softperson was probably going to be stuck doing interplanetary hops and minor errands — like picking up Governor Thrixtopple — for the rest of his Service. And Central Psych wanted to stick *her* with *him* and his flawed record! It wasn't *fair*. Nancia brooded about it all the way to Vega 3.3.

Her first sight of Caleb did nothing to restore her confidence in this assignment. Courier Service records said that he was only twenty-eight — young for a softperson — but he walked slowly and carefully, as if he were already old and tired. His Service uniform looked as if it had been designed for a larger man; the tunic hung loosely from broad but bony shoulders, the trousers flapped about his shins. *Short, scrawny and sour-faced*, Nancia mentally catalogued as he made his halting way up the stairs. *And why couldn't he use the lift, if he's too out of shape to walk up one flight of stairs?*

His greeting to her was correct but lifeless. Nancia responded in the same tone. Listlessly, they went through the Service formulas until Nancia displayed the orders beamed from Vega Base.

Caleb exploded. "Detouring to pick up that lard-bottomed junketer and his family? *That's* not a Courier

Service job. Why can't Thrixtopple wait for the next scheduled passenger transport like anyone else?"

Nancia sent a ripple of muddy brown rings across the screen where their orders were displayed. "Nobody told me anything," she responded verbally for Caleb's benefit. "Stop here, go there, take these kids to the Nyota system, collect a stranded brawn on Vega 3.3, pick up the governor of 4.2 and take him back to Central. *I* don't know why he rates a special deal; he's not even High Families."

"No, but he's been working this subspace for a long time," Caleb told her. "Probably has more pull than half a dozen empty-headed aristos with their double-barreled names."

"We are not all," Nancia said, "empty-headed. Perhaps you failed to read your orders in detail?" She flashed her full name on the screen to get his attention.

"Oh, well, you can't help your birth," Caleb said absent-mindedly, "and I suppose a good Lab Schools training will make up for a lot. Are you ready for liftoff? We can't waste time gossiping if we have to fit this extra stop into the itinerary."

I give him ten minutes after we reach Central to get himself and his bags off me and make room for a brawn with some manners, Nancia vowed to herself as she drove her engines through a harder and faster takeoff than she would normally have imposed on a softperson passenger. *No, that's too generous. Five minutes.*

She felt slightly regretful when she peeked through Caleb's cabin sensors and saw him struggling to sit up after the takeoff, white and shaken. But she wasn't sorry enough to change her basic position on brawn assignments.

"There's one thing we should have settled before liftoff," she announced without preamble.

"Yes?" Caleb didn't bother turning his head to look at the cabin speaker. Of course, he was an experienced

— if incompetent — brawn; he would know that she would be able to pick up his words from any direction. Still, Nancia felt vaguely ruffled — as if she were being ignored even as he replied to her.

"Transporting you back to Central Worlds is my official assignment, and I cannot refuse it. But I do not wish you to construe this as formal acceptance of you as my brawn. I have no intention of waiving my rights to free choice of my own brawn just because this match is convenient for Central."

Now what ailed the man? He had just begun to regain some color after the high-G lift-off; now his face was drained again, still as a mask — or a corpse. Nancia began to wonder if this brawn would live to see Central. *If he wasn't fit enough to make the journey, somebody should have warned me.*

"Of course," said Caleb in a voice so level and drained of meaning that it could have issued from any housekeeping drone, "no one would expect you to waive that right. Particularly for me." He turned his head and for the first time looked directly at the sensor. "Shut down sensors to this cabin, please, XN. I wish to rest. In privacy," he emphasized. He lay down again with one arm flung over his face. After a moment he rolled over and lay facedown on the bunk, as if he didn't trust Nancia not to peek at him.

"Simeon? Shellcrack, Simeon, I know you're picking up my beams. TALK TO ME!"

"You're an excessively demanding young thing, XN-935, and you're shouting again."

"Sorry." Nancia was so glad to have got some response from the Vega Base brain that she immediately lowered the intensity of her beam to match Simeon's almost inaudible burst. "Simeon, I need to know about this brawn they've saddled me with."

"So scan the newsbeam files."

"I did. There's nothing in them. Not what I need to know, anyway." The files had been enlightening in their own way, with their lurid stories of a ship and a man almost destroyed by a sudden radiation burst, the brawn's limping, months-long journey homeward in his crippled, brainless ship and the hero's welcome he had received when he arrived at Vega 3.3 with the survey data he'd been sent to gather. The tale of what Caleb had gone through, the months of solitude and deprivation and the lingering effects of radiation poisoning, had done much to reshape Nancia's feelings towards the pallid brawn who'd boarded her on Vega 3.3. She felt a grudging respect for the man she saw spending hours in her exercise facility, working out with gyroweights and spring resistors to restore wasted muscles.

The man who had accepted her initial hostile attitude as no more than his due, who'd shut her out of his mind at once and had not spoken a word to her since. They had traveled in silence through the three days it took to move between the suns of Vega 3 and Vega 4, while Nancia waited impatiently for Simeon to resume communications so that she could ask what she wanted to know. Finally she'd begun battering at the Vega Base brain's frequencies with ever-increasing bursts of communication that must have given him the equivalent of a softperson's "headache."

Nancia condensed the newsbytes she'd read and transmitted them in three short bursts to Simeon, just to convince him she'd done her homework.

"So what else do you want to know?"

"How. Did. He. Lose. His. Ship?" Nancia punctuated each word with a burst of irritated static.

"You read the newsbytes."

"WE'RE SHIELDED AGAINST — sorry." She started over at normal intensity. "We're shielded against radiation. He shouldn't have been harmed, unless he was being careless — leaving the ship without checking radiation levels? And there's no way his ship could have been affected. What could have got through her column?"

"*His* column, in this case," Simeon corrected, as if that mattered.

Unless Caleb used the access code to open his brainship's shell. That was the nightmare, that was what she wanted reassurance about. No brawn was supposed to know both the syllables and the musical tones that comprised his brainship's access codes. One sequence was given to the brawn on assignment, the other deeply classified in CenCom's codes. But Polyon's casual dabbling in the Net had left Nancia deeply suspicious of computer security systems. Any code invented could be broken . . . and how else could the CL-740 have been lost to something as minor as a radiation burst?

"Nothing did get through the column," Simeon told her. "The CL-740 was one of the first Courier Service ships commissioned, though. Three hundred years ago they didn't know as much as we do about shielding the synapse connectors. The radiation burst they were subjected to wasn't enough to harm the major ship's systems, but it fried the connections to the shell, leaving CL-740 in total isolation — unable to communicate or to receive signals, completely unable to control the ship. Caleb brought the ship back on manual controls, but by the time they got to Vega the CL-740 had gone mad from sensory deprivation."

"But the Helva System — " Nancia protested. It had been a long, long time since any brainship had been subjected to sensory deprivation; shell-internal metachips, named for the legendary brainship who'd survived the ordeal and suggested the modification, should have been invulnerable to any outside interference.

"The Helva modifications are not universal, though

God knows they should be." Simeon sounded very tired. "It's a traumatizing procedure for those of us who aren't lucky enough to have it built into our first design, young'un. Some of the older brainships, those who'd paid off and continued in the Courier Service as free agents, had a right to refuse retrofitting. CL . . . exercised that right."

"Oh." It was a brain's worst nightmare, that being cut off from the world with a thoroughness no softperson could even imagine. Nancia closed down all her sensors for a moment, imagining that absolute blackness. How long would *she* be able to bear it? No wonder her supervisor at Lab Schools had canceled the first newsbyte about the CL-740. No wonder the newsbyte files made available to her now had been censored. No one wanted a brainship to start thinking about the worst that could happen. Nancia didn't want to think about it any longer. With an internal shudder she threw open all her sensors and comm channels at once.

The minor clatter of everyday life was a warm, reassuring tide about her, connecting her with the rest of humanity, the rest of all sentient life. Nancia catalogued the details with surprise and gratitude. *How strange and wonderful all this is . . . to see, hear, feel, think, know . . . and I have been taking it all for granted!* For a moment, the smallest input was precious to her, a gift of life. Caleb was hanging between two spring-resistors in the gym, the display screens in the central cabin were dancing with their elegant geometric screen-saver patterns, the stars outside burned with their distant fire, Vega 4 was a ruddy glow before her, someone was chattering between Vega 4.3 and 4.2 about Central synthsilk fashions. Someone else was crying into a satellite link. . . .

And Simeon was still talking. "Levin." The databits transmitted like a whisper. "His name wasn't CL-740. His name was Levin, and he was my friend."

*   *   *

At Vega 4.2, Governor Thrixtopple and his family spilled aboard Nancia like a pack of cruise passengers, dropping their luggage anywhere for the patient servants who followed to pick up, commenting loudly on any feature of Nancia's interior that caught their attention.

"Hey! Look at these display screens!" The youngest Thrixtopple, a weasel-faced brat in his early teens, lit up on sight of the three wall-size display screens in the central cabin. "Sis, where's my SPACED OUT hedron? I could play all the way home — "

"*I* don't have to keep track of where you drop all your junk," his older sister whined. "Mama, there's only one storage bin in my cabin. My Antarxian ruffs will get all wrinkled!"

"Who cares? They still won't make any difference to your ugly face!" Thrixtopple Junior stuck out his tongue at his sister. She hurled a globe of something pink and slushy at him; he ducked out of the way and Caleb caught the globe in a neat one-handed catch.

"Now, kiddies," Thrixtopple Senior mumbled, "mustn't upset your mother or the servants." He held out one skinny hand to receive the pink globe his daughter had thrown; glance and gesture included Caleb among those "servants." Nancia bristled. He might not be her official brawn, she might still have her reservations about the way Psych was trying to throw the two of them together for the convenience of CenCom, but Caleb was still a trained brawn and deserving of more respect than that!

"Governor Thrixtopple, I'm afraid I will have to ask all of you to enter your personal cabins and strap down for lift-off now," Caleb said tonelessly.

"*Already*? Why, these clumsy servants haven't begun to unpack for me yet! I'm not nearly ready to send them away!" Trixia Thrixtopple complained without a word of gratitude or farewell to the servants who had, presumably, waited on her through the twenty years of Governor Thrixtopple's service. It was clear where her daughter had learned that penetrating whine.

"My apologies, ma'am," Caleb said, still without any inflection that they could react to, "but I am bound by regulations. Section 4, subsection 4.5, paragraphs ii to iv. Courier Service ships are not permitted to dally for any reason; a prolonged stop here could upset urgently needed communications elsewhere."

He personally escorted the Thrixtopple family to their bunks and made sure each of them was secured against the high-grav stresses of lift-off. Nancia kept the cabin sensors open to double-check every move, but Caleb made no mistakes.

Once the passengers were strapped down and their luggage stowed, Caleb returned to the central cabin and waved one hand towards the door. "Would you close us off, please, XN?" He sighed with exaggerated relief. "If only we could keep them out of here for the entire flight. People like that are a disgrace to Vega. Why, they didn't even have the manners to greet you!"

"Neither did the passengers I took on the way out," Nancia told him. "I was beginning to feel invisible."

"Not to me," Caleb told her. His eyes scanned the entire cabin with a look of longing that surprised Nancia. "Never to me. . . . If I don't get a new assignment, this could be my last voyage on a brainship. And we had to be saddled with these, these . . . " He threw up his hands as though words failed him.

"It is a pity," Nancia agreed, "but there's no reason *we* can't be professional about doing our jobs, is there?" While she made conversation with Caleb, she was rapidly reviewing the volumes of Courier Service regulations with which her data banks had been loaded upon commissioning. There should have been something in the third megahedron. . . . Ah, there it was. Precisely what the situation called for. But she wouldn't mention it now. Caleb was eager to escape the surface of Vega 4.2 before the Thrixtopple family started complaining about their restraints, and she couldn't blame him.

In deference to Caleb's weakened condition, Nancia made this lift-off as slow and gentle as she could. After all, it wasn't his fault that Psych Central was practically forcing their personal codes into one datastream. And she didn't want to kill the man on the way home.

When they entered freefall again, Caleb unlatched himself from the support chair and moved about the cabin with none of the languor he'd shown after the previous lift-off. "Being gentle with the civilians?" he inquired. "I seem to recall that you can lift considerably faster than that when you're so inclined, XN."

"I . . . um . . . I didn't see any need to hurry," Nancia muttered. Damn the man! Too stiff-necked to admit that he, too, could benefit from a slightly gentler takeoff!

Caleb looked faintly amused. "No. Considering that now there's no excuse to keep them strapped in, and we'll probably have the brats in our laps until you reach Singularity. . . . I wouldn't have wanted to hurry, either."

As if on cue, the Thrixtopple boy punched through the iris-opening of the door. Nancia winced at the damage to her flexible membranes. She left the door iris open so that Governor Thrixtopple, proceeding down the corridor at a stately pace behind his son, wouldn't inflict further violence on her.

"Ok, we're in space now, lemme play with the computer!" the boy demanded.

Nancia slid her datareaders shut as the boy approached and deliberately blanked her screens. "I'm sorry, young sir. Courier Service Regulations, volume XVIII, section 1522, subsection 6.2, paragraph mcmlii, strictly prohibit allowing unauthorized passengers access to the ship's computer or free movement within the central cabin. The prohibition is intended as a protection against illegal interference with Courier Service property."

"Hear now, you — you talking shell, that's not meant to apply to people like us!" Governor Thrixtopple blustered as he entered the cabin.

"The official orders which were transmitted to me by CenCom at the beginning of this voyage make no reference to your family, Governor Thrixtopple," Nancia replied. She paused slightly between words and gave her voice a slight metallic overtone to make the Thrixtopples feel they were talking to a machine that could not be threatened or bribed. "I am not myself authorized to change such orders save on direct beam from Central Command."

"But Vega Base *told* you to ferry us to Central!"

"And I am always happy to do my good friends at Vega Base a favor," Nancia replied. "Nevertheless, it is not in my power to change regulations. Should Central Command retroactively authorize you to access my computers, I will — retroactively — permit you to have done so. In the meantime, I must request that you return to your personal cabin areas. I should be reluctant to enforce the order, but you must know that I retain the power to flood all life support areas with sleepgas."

Governor Thrixtopple grabbed his son's collar and dragged him out of the central cabin. The iris of the door membrane slid together.

"That," said Caleb reverently, "was brilliant, XN. Positively brilliant. Ah — I suppose there *is* such a regulation?"

"Of course there is! You don't think I'd *lie*?"

"My deepest apologies, ma'am. It was only that I had no personal recollection of the paragraph in question — "

"I understand that softperson brains are quite limited in their storage and retrieval powers," Nancia said loftily. Then she relented. "It took me several minutes of scanning to find something applicable, actually. And I never would have thought of it if you hadn't quoted regulations to get them out of here before lift-off."

"If it weren't for meals," Caleb reflected aloud, "we wouldn't have to speak to them again all the way back to Central. . . . "

"I have the capacity to serve meals from any room in the living quarters," Nancia informed him. *Unlike the older models* . . . She cut that thought off before voicing it. It would be sheer cruelty to remind Caleb of what he had lost.

"Okay, XN, try this one." Caleb manipulated the joyball to bring up a display of a double torus containing two simple closed curves. Three disks labeled A1, B, and A2 contained sections of the torus. "You're in A1; A2 is your target space. Find the Singularity points and compute the decompositions required."

"No fair," Nancia protested. "It's never even been proved that there *is* a decom sequence that'll navigate that structure. Satyajohi's Conjecture." She quoted from her memory banks, "If h is a homeomorphism of E3 onto itself that is fixed on E3 — T, need one of h(J1), h(j2) contain an arc with four points of A + B such that no two of these points which are adjacent on the arc belong to the same one of A and B? If so, the decomposition space H does not yield E3. And in this application," she reminded Caleb, "E3 is equivalent to normal space."

Caleb blinked twice. "I didn't expect you to know Satyajohi's Conjecture, actually. Still — let me point out, XN, it's only a conjecture, not a theorem."

"In one hundred and twenty-five years of deep-space mathematics it's never been disproved," Nancia grumbled.

"So? Perhaps you'll be the first to find a counter-example."

Nancia didn't think there was much point in even trying, but she set an automatic string-development program to race through the display, illuminating various possible Singularity paths as lines of brilliant blue light, then letting them fade out as the impossibility of one after the other was proved. There was something else on which she very much wanted Caleb's advice, and now — with the Thrixtopple family intimidated into staying in their cabins, and Caleb in as good a mood as she'd ever seen him after his demonstration of Satyajohi's Conjecture — now was the best time she could have to bring it up.

"I haven't been commissioned very long, you know, Caleb," she began.

"No, but you're going to be one of the best," Caleb told her. "I can see it in the way you handle little things. I wouldn't have thought of finding a regulation to get the Thrixtopples out of our hair. And I don't think I'd have tested Satyajohi's Conjecture the way you're going about it right now, either." Two possible Singularity lines flashed bright blue and then vanished from the screen as he spoke, while a third snaked through A1 and into the B disk around the double torus.

"Some things," Nancia said carefully, "get more complicated than that. In mathematics a conjecture either is or isn't true."

"The same is true of Courier Service Regulations," Caleb pointed out.

"Yes, well . . . not everything. They don't tell you what to do if a brainship happens to hear her passengers making illegal plans."

"If you've been eavesdropping on Governor Thrixtopple in his cabin," Caleb said sternly, "that's a dishonorable action and I hereby formally request you to stop it immediately."

"Oh, I haven't," Nancia assured him. "But what if—if a brainship had some passengers who didn't *know* she was sentient, and they liked to sit in the central cabin and play SPACED OUT, and they just happened to discuss some possibly illegal plans while they were doing it?"

"Oh — a hypothetical case?" Caleb sounded relieved, and Nancia felt the same way. At least he hadn't guessed immediately, as Simeon had, that she was talking about her own previous experience. Everything Nancia had learned or seen of Caleb — the newsbeams of his heroic solo return to Vega, the dedication with which he put himself through a grueling exercise program, his respect for Courier Service regulations — made her think of him as a man of supreme integrity, one whose word she could trust under any circumstances. She would not have wanted to hear him laugh at her as Simeon had done, or suggest — as Simeon had done — that her own actions in this instance had been morally culpable.

"Well, in such a case — if it ever arises — you should remember that a sentient ship is morally obliged to identify herself as such to her passengers at the first opportunity."

"That's not in the regulations," Nancia defended herself against a charge Caleb didn't know he had made.

"No, but it's common sense. Anything else would be like — like me hiding in a closet to catch Governor Thrixtopple counting his ill-gotten gains from bribes while in public office." Caleb said this with so much disgust in his voice that Nancia shrank from pursuing the subject.

So, evidently, did Caleb. He looked up at the central display screen, where a network of dim gray lines showed Nancia's repeated attempts to compute a path of Singularity points through the topological configuration he'd defined.

"Let's just take it that Satyajohi's Conjecture is upheld in this particular case," he suggested, "and now it's your turn to put up a problem. I don't know why we're discussing hypothetical ethical problems that are never likely to arise when we could both be improving our Decom Math skills. Nor do I understand why — " He bit his lip and blanked out the screen with a swift roll of the joyball.

"Why what?" Nancia asked.

"Your turn to pose a problem," Caleb reminded her.

"Not until you finish that sentence."

"All *right*! I don't understand why you're asking for ethical guidance from a brawn whose greatest achievement to date has been the loss of his first ship!" Caleb bit out the words with a frustrated savagery that aroused Nancia's sympathy. She remembered Simeon's grief for his lost friend Levin, the CL-740. How stupid she had been.

"I'm sorry," she told Caleb. "I should have realized that discussing such issues would remind you of Levin. Do you miss him so very much?"

Caleb sighed. "It's not that, XN. Levin was a good, competent brainship, and he trained me when I was a new brawn, and I'll always owe a debt of gratitude to him. But we weren't — we never just talked, like this, you know? Five years I served with him, and I don't feel I ever really got to know him. No, I'm not in mourning for Levin. But he had a right to look forward to hundreds more years of service, and I lost him that time. And I myself had rather hoped to spend more than five years as a brawn."

"You may yet," Nancia pointed out. "Just because you haven't got a ship assignment yet — "

"And what brainship is going to accept the brawn

who let the CL-740 die?" Caleb snapped back. "You yourself have made that little point tolerably clear, XN. Now *drop* it. Next problem, please!"

Nancia started transmitting to CenCom — on a private beam — the moment she exited Singularity and entered Central Worlds subspace. She wanted to have everything arranged, with no possibility of argument, before Caleb was ready to leave the ship.

All proceeded as planned. Dahlen Rahilly, her Service Supervisor, requested permission to enter even before the Thrixtopple family had gathered their numerous items of luggage and departed.

"Arrogant snit," Rahilly commented as they watched the last of Governor Thrixtopple's bony shoulders through Nancia's ground viewport. "He could at least have credited you with a bonus for doing him the favor of this quick transport home."

"I didn't expect it," Nancia replied with perfect truth. The only bonus she expected — or wanted — was still in his cabin, using the cabin comm board to enter a job application letter that somehow kept getting wiped from his personal file storage area. This was his third attempt, and Nancia could tell by the emphatic way Caleb's voice snapped out the words for the dictaboard that he was losing patience. If she didn't get matters settled soon, he would quit trying to use the ship's comm system and make his application personally, at CenCom offices. And that wouldn't suit her at all.

"Well . . . there will have to be a few changes. Paperwork," Rahilly said. "We . . . weren't expecting this, you know, XN. In fact, VS at Vega seemed quite certain that you had formally refused the assignment."

"He . . . may have misinterpreted my words," Nancia said demurely. "How soon can it be arranged?" Shellcrack! While she was talking to Rahilly, Caleb had managed to dictate the complete text of his application letter. He was getting ready to transmit it to CenCom. That mustn't happen . . . not yet. Nancia shut down all outgoing beams at once.

"Oh, we can finish the paperwork in a day. If you're sure that's what you want?"

"I am," Nancia said firmly. There was another party to be consulted, but Rahilly didn't seem to think that would be necessary.

Caleb stalked into the central cabin, brows drawn together. "XN, what do you mean by shutting down my beam to CenCom?"

"*Your* beam?" Nancia replied. "Oh, dear. All my external beams seem to have lost power for a moment."

"We'll have a tech out to fix the malfunction immediately," Rahilly promised.

"Oh . . . I don't think that will be necessary," Nancia told him. "I've been investigating while we talk, and I believe I have found the source of the problem. It should be easy enough to correct internally." All she needed to do was reopen the power gate. . . .

"Very well, CN-935." Rahilly sketched a Service salute in the general direction of Nancia's titanium column. "The remaining paperwork will be completed within the day, and then you and Brawn Caleb will be requested to hold yourselves ready for a new assignment — there was one pending, actually; Central will be happy not to have to wait while you choose a brawn."

He left as soon as the last word was snapped out, and Nancia was grateful for that. Caleb was staring around the cabin with an expression she could not read. If he was going to be angry with her for going behind his back, she'd just as soon have it out in private.

"I . . . don't understand," he said slowly. "You aren't waiting to choose a new brawn? You're going to go out solo again?"

"Hardly that," Nancia told him. "I've had enough of solo voyages, thank you very much; I find that I much prefer to travel with a partner."

"Then . . . "

"Didn't you hear the man? From now on I'm the CN-935. I've decided that Psych Central was right," Nancia said. It was a struggle to keep her voice projections calm and even. "We make a very good team."

Caleb was still speechless, and Nancia felt her one fear approaching.

"If . . . if that's all right with you?"

"All right, all *right*, *all right*!" Caleb exploded. "The woman gives me back my life — and with the perfect brain partner — and she wants to know if it's *all right*? I — Nancia — oh, wait a minute, would you? There's something I've got to take care of before you restore external beam transmissions."

He hurried off to his cabin, presumably to erase the job application letter that had taken so long to create, and Nancia permitted herself a small coruscating display of stars and comets across her three wide screens. It was going to be all right.

More than all right. "Nancia," she repeated to herself. "He finally called me Nancia."

• CHAPTER SIX

Angalia, Central Date 2750:
Blaize

Blaize Armontillado-Perez y Medoc stared in disbelief at his new home as the exit port of the XN-935 slid shut behind him. The mesa top that had served Nancia as a landing field was the only level bit of solid ground in sight. Behind the mesa was a wall of crumbly, near-vertical rock that rose in jagged peaks to block out the morning sun. The long black shadows of the mountains fell across the mesa and down into a sea of oozing *glop* that looked like the Quagmire of Despair as displayed in the latest version of SPACED OUT. The only variation in the brownish sea was that at a few locations large, lazy bubbles rose from the glop and burst with a sulfurous stink.

At the very edge of the mesa, cantilevered precariously out over the Quagmire of Despair, was a gray plastifilm prefab storage facility. Bulging brown sacks stenciled with the initials of Planetary Technical Aid hung from hooks on one side of the shack, dangling right out over the sea of glop. On the side of the shanty nearest Blaize, the plastifilm roof had been extended with some sort of woven fronds to create a sagging awning. Beneath this awning lounged an immensely fat man wearing only a pair of sweat-stained briefs.

Blaize sighed and picked up the nearest two pieces of his kit. Staggering slightly under a gravity considerably higher than ship's norm, he made his way towards the obese guardian of Angalia.

"PTA tech-trainee Armontillado-Perez y Medoc, sir," he introduced himself. *Who is this guy? He's got to be one of the corycium miners. They're the only humans on Angalia — except, of course . . .*

"And the top of the morning to you, Sherry, me lad," said the sweating man-mountain cordially. "Never was so glad to see anybody in m'life. Hope you enjoy the next five years here."

"Ah — PTA Grade Eleven Supervisor Harmon?" Blaize hazarded. *Except my new boss.*

A richly alcoholic wheeze almost knocked him off his feet. "You see anybody else around here, kid? Who d'you *think* I am?"

"The corycium mine — "

"Dead. Defunct. Abandoned. *Kaput*, all gone splash, stinko," Grade 11 Supervisor Harmon said with relish. "Went bust. Owner sold the mine to me for a case of spirits before he pulled out."

"What went wrong?"

"Labor. Company couldn't keep miners here for love nor money. Not that they offered much love — even a corycium miner ain't desperate enough to try and get it on with a Loosie, heh, heh, heh." Another wave of alcohol-flavored breath washed over Blaize.

"Loosie?"

"*Homosimilis Lucilla Angalii* to you, m'boy. The veg-heads Lucilla Sharif discovered, damn her soul, and reported as possibly intelligent on the FCF, double-damn her, and for her sins we're stuck administering Planetary Technical Aid to a bunch of walking zucchini. All the company I've had since they closed the mine. And all *you'll* have for the next five years. Next PTA transport comes by here is taking me off-planet." Harmon looked enviously at the sleek length of the XN-935, her tip now gleaming in the sun that peeked over the jagged mountains. "Nice perks you High

Families kids get, transport like that. I don't suppose you could persuade that brainship — "

"I doubt it," Blaize said.

Harmon chortled. "No, didn't much sound like it, way you come out yelling and screaming over your shoulder, with it dumping your luggage after you. You musta pissed it off real handsome. No matter. Next PTA shipment oughta be along any day now. And when it comes, my new assignment should be ready." He stretched luxuriously, took a deep drink from the bottle beside him, and sighed with anticipated contentment. "Reckon I've earned myself a nice long tour of duty on Central, in a nice office tower with air conditioning and servos and no need to pay any bloody attention to bloody nature unless you happen to feel like looking out the window. Sit down, Madeira-y-Perez, and don't look so miserable. Do your five years and maybe they'll post you back in civilization. You're in luck, coming when you did."

"I am?" The sun was over the mountain by now, and it was *hot* on the mesa. Blaize pulled his largest grip under the shade of the awning and sat down on it.

"Sure. Today's feeding time at the zoo. Put on a real show for you, the Loosies will." Harmon waved again, this time as if beckoning the cliff that towered above them to come on down. Blaize stared in shock as craggy bits of mountain broke loose and trickled down to the mesa top, shambling like crazy puppets made of rocks and wire. Strange costumes — no, they were naked; that was their *skin* he was looking at.

"Yaohoo! Feeding time! Whoee!" Harmon yodeled, simultaneously jerking the cord that ran along the side of the PTA prefab. One of the sacks overhanging the muddy basin opened and brownish-gray ration bricks spilled out in a torrent, piling up in the mud below the mesa.

The Loosies scurried to the edge of the mesa and let themselves down into the muddy sea, fingers and toes clinging to crevices in the rocks. The first ones down threw themselves on the ration bricks as if they were greeting a long-lost lover; the later arrivals piled on top of them, swinging uncoordinated limbs and wriggling to burrow into the muddy heap of rations.

Blaize felt a rumbling vibration coming up through the soles of his feet.

"Look out!" Harmon roared.

Blaize jumped and Harmon chuckled. "Sorry to startle you, kid. You wouldn't want to miss the other big show of Angalia." He pointed to the western horizon.

It seemed to be moving.

It was a wall of water. No, mud. No — Blaize struggled for the right word and could only find the one that had first occurred to him: *glop*.

The "Loosies" had ignored Harmon's shout as if they were deaf, but something — perhaps the rumbling vibration that Blaize felt — alerted those still at the bottom of the quagmire. They swarmed up the sides of the mesa, clutching their ration bricks in teeth and fingers. The last one got out of the way just before the advancing tide of glop struck the mesa.

The whole desperate, squirming consumption of ration bricks had taken place in total silence. Now, less than three minutes later, it was over and the mesa was surrounded by a sucking, slimy tide of glop. As Blaize watched, the tide receded, sliding back down the sides of the mesa until the new mud melted into the same soggy configuration of puddles and bubbles that had greeted him on arrival.

"That was a small one," Harmon said with regret. "Oh, well, there'll likely be some better ones before you go. Bound to be, in fact."

In response to Blaize's questions he explained, without much interest, that the erratic climatic pattern of Angalia produced a constantly moving band of thundershowers in the mountains which surrounded this central basin. Whenever the storms stayed in the same place for a while, the rainfall built up into a flash flood which raced across the plain, picking up mud as it went, and sweeping away anything that might be foolish enough to remain in its path.

"Terraforming," Blaize mused. "Dams to catch the rainfall and release it slowly . . ."

"Expensive, and who'd bother? Nothing here to repay the investment. Besides," Harmon explained, "it's *fun*. Damn sure ain't much else to watch out here!"

Blaize gathered that one of Harmon's amusements was trying to predict the times of the mud-floods so that he could feed the natives just before one, forcing them to scramble first for ration bricks and then to save themselves from the tide of mud.

"Ain't it the damnedest thing?" he demanded as the rock-like natives climbed back to their mountain heights, some clutching a few ration bricks for later consumption, some still chewing the last mouthfuls of their haul. "You ever see anything like it?"

"Never," Blaize admitted. *Are the — the Loosies starving? Is that why their skin hangs loose like that? Or is that their normal appearance? And how does this fat creep get away with putting them through such a degrading performance?*

"I know what you're thinking, Port-Wine-y-Medoc," the fat man said, "but wait'll you've done six months out here, you'll forget all the PTA regs about respecting the natives' dignity and all that crapola. Damned Loosies don't have any dignity to respect, anyway. They're a bunch of animals. Never developed agriculture — or clothing — or even language."

"Or lies," commented Blaize.

"What?" For a moment Harmon looked startled, then he chuckled and wheezed with amusement. "Righto. No language, no lies — gotta say that for them, anyway! But they're not *people*, young Claret-Medoc. Waste of resources, this whole operation — some paperpusher's mistake. Only encourages the veg-heads to breed more little veggies. We oughta pull outa here and let 'em starve on their own, y'ask me."

"Maybe they could be trained to work the mine," Blaize suggested.

Harmon snorted. "Yeah, sure. I did hear about some prisoners in olden times who amused themselves trying to train their pet rats to run errands. You could do that sooner'n you could teach a Loosie anything, kid. I tell you, there's just three amusements on Angalia: feedin' time for the Loosies, drinkin' time for me, and playing computer games. And I've mapped every damn level of the Maze of the Minotaur so many times I can't stand to look at it no more."

Blaize felt in his pocket. The datahedron recording the wager wasn't the only item he'd copied from Nancia's computer. "Does your computer — "

"Yours now, Sake-Armontillado," Harmon interrupted with a cheerful belch. "PTA issue."

"Does it have enough memory and display graphics to run SPACED OUT? Because," Blaize said, "I just happen to have a copy of the latest version here. Pre-release — it's not even on sale at Central yet." He winked at Harmon.

"Is that so!" Harmon oozed to his feet. "C'mon inside, Burgundy-Champagne. Pass the time in a li'l friendly game until my transport gets here." He scratched his bare chest, squinting at Blaize with the rudiments of a thoughtful expression on his face. "Have to name some stakes, of course. No fun playing for nothing."

"My sentiments exactly," Blaize agreed. "Lead the way."

Five days later, exactly as scheduled, the PTA transport touched down to deliver new supplies and to pick up Supervisor Grade 11 Harmon for the months-long FTL journey to his new assignment. Blaize remained behind with the Loosies and his winnings: two partially depleted cases of Sapphire Ruin, Supervisor Grade 11 Harmon's hand-woven palm-frond sun hat, and the title to an abandoned corycium mine.

Deneb Subspace, Central Date 2750: Nancia and Caleb

"That," said Caleb as he and Nancia left Deneb Spacebase, "was one of our more satisfying assignments."

"Out of a grand total of two?" Nancia teased him. But she agreed. Their first scheduled run out of Central, delivering medical supplies to a newly settled planet, had been worthwhile but hardly challenging. And they had both been apprehensive about this assignment: transporting some semi-retired general, another High Families representative, into the middle of a particularly nasty conflict between Central Worlds settlers and Capellan traders. But General Micaya Questar-Benn had proved completely different from the spoilt High Families children Nancia had taken out to Vega subspace on her first assignment. Short, competent, unassuming, the general had won Caleb's heart at once with her in-depth knowledge of Vega's complex history. She'd proceeded to spend much of the short run to Deneb subspace talking shop with Nancia; half the general's body parts and several major organs were cyborg replacements, and she was interested in the possibility of improving her liver functions with one of the newer metachip implants such as kept Nancia's physical body healthy within its shell. Nancia had never envisioned herself discussing something so personal with anybody, let alone a high-ranking army officer, but something about General Questar-Benn's unassuming manner made intimate talk unthreatening and easy.

Nancia wasn't too surprised to learn that before she and Caleb had even prepared for the return journey, General Questar-Benn had drawn human and Capellan antagonists into negotiations and worked out a settlement that would allow each side to feel they had "won."

"And here I thought we were warmongering, delivering somebody with authority to send in the heavy armored divisions!" Caleb went on.

Nancia chuckled. "The galaxy could do with a few more 'warmongers' like Micaya Questar-Benn. Ready for Singularity, partner? Central should have a new assignment for us by now."

Bahati, Central Date 2751:
Alpha

Alpha bint Hezra-Fong stared down in distaste at the writhing body of her experimental subject. What had gone wrong? The molecular variations of Blissto which she'd been preparing should have rendered the patient calm and tractable. Instead he was contorting his limbs and moaning uncontrollably, trying to break the restraint straps on his stretcher.

Alpha tightened the straps until the patient stopped thrashing and passed a medscanner over his forehead. She frowned at the results. Instead of generating soothing hormones, Blissto.Rev.2 was invading and replicating itself within the man's nervous system like a cancer gone wild.

"Damn! I haven't got *time* for this," she muttered. Quickly she considered her options. If she could keep the patient alive and in isolation for a few days, perhaps she would be able to find out what was causing this invasive replication and find a way to stop it. But if anybody questioned her work —

The man's convulsions increased. One leg broke the reinforced restraint strap and kicked out wildly.

"Too dangerous," Alpha decided. She pressed a hypospray to the man's neck and watched his body sag back against the stretcher. His eyes rolled upwards and the thrashing stopped.

So did all other movement.

Alpha had papers prepared for just such an emergency. The clinic director was an old fool, too lazy to check her reports; nobody else would dare to question her. Charity Patient B.342.iv would be listed as having died of heart failure brought on by a preexisting medical condition which the clinic had not had time to reverse.

The only trouble was, that made the third such death in the year since Alpha had begun testing her improved version of Blissto. Sooner or later, if she didn't get the drug dosage right, somebody was going to notice the string of identical sudden-death reports and ask questions.

Alpha seriously considered returning to experimenting on rabbits. But rabbit cages stank, and taking care of the beasts was a lot of work, and there was even more probability that somebody would question her sudden interest in raising pets.

She'd just have to think up a few more excuses for sudden deaths on the charity wing. A little variation in the paperwork would help disguise these unfortunate accidents.

Procyon Subspace, Central Date 2751: Caleb and Nancia

"This is boring," Nancia complained as she watched workers on Szatmar II unload the cases of vaccine she and Caleb had transported there.

"It is important to see that children's vaccinations are kept up regularly," Caleb told her.

"Yes, but it's hardly an emergency. At least, it wouldn't have been one if PTA would keep its records up to date." A horrified bureaucrat had discovered that some incompetent named Harmon, working out of PTA on Central Worlds, had forgotten to ship last year's supplies of vaccine to any PTA client planets in the Procyon subsystem. In consequence, Nancia and Caleb were getting an extended tour of that subsystem, delivering measles and whooping-cough vaccine to several dozen settlements on widely scattered planets. "I've got a good mind to speak to my sister about this idiot Harmon," Nancia grumbled. "Jinevra would never tolerate such inefficiency in her own branch of PTA; maybe she can get Central to transfer Harmon to a spot where he can't do any harm."

"Nancia, you wouldn't seriously consider using your family connections for personal interest!"

Caleb sounded shocked. Nancia apologized immediately. She hadn't realized that trying to get an incompetent bureaucrat ousted came under the heading of "personal interests." But Caleb was doubtless right; he always was. And she felt quite guilty as he lectured her about the consequences of being flighty and expecting glamorous assignments. He was right about that, too. Service loyalty demanded not only that she go where she was needed, but that she do so willingly and cheerfully.

Nancia closed her loading dock and tried to lift off for their next vaccine delivery with a willing and cheerful heart.

Bahati, Central Date 2752:
Darnell

Darnell leaned back in his upholstered stimuchair and activated the interoffice transmitter. "You may send Hopkirk in now, Julitta m'lovely."

"Oh, Mr. Overton-Glaxely!" Julitta's delighted giggles came clearly through the transmitter. Darnell activated the double display screens as well and enjoyed two views of his secretary. The top screen showed her tossing her pretty yellow curls and preening with delight at his compliment; the lower screen displayed her shapely legs, crossing and recrossing restlessly beneath the desk. Darnell noted with pleasure that Julitta's petiskirt had ridden up almost to her waist. *Such a delightful, twitchy little girl*.

Darnell considered Julitta, like the second display screen and the vibrostim units in his executive chair and the view of Bahati from his glass-walled executive office, to be one of the perks appropriate to a Man Who Had Made It. He let Hopkirk wait awkwardly in front of his desk while he contemplated with equal delight his own rapid success, his immediate plans for Julitta, the view of her legs in the lower display screen, and the fact that Julitta didn't know about the second screen.

"Hopkirk, I've got a job for you," Darnell ordered. "Productivity in the glimware plant dropped by three thousandths of a percent last month. I want you to get out there and send me a full report of any contributing factors."

"Yes, Mr. Overton-Glaxely," the man called Hopkirk murmured.

"It's probably cumulative worker fatigue due to the poor design of the assembly line," Darnell continued. Ah, that was better; a flash of pain crossed Hopkirk's features. Six months ago the man had owned, designed, and managed Hopkirk Glimware, producers of fine novelty prismaglasses for the luxury trade. And managed it damn poorly, too, Darnell thought; the place would have gone bankrupt soon enough anyway, even without his interference. Now it was a profitable, if small, addition to Darnell's revitalized OG Shipping (and other) Enterprises.

"Questions, Hopkirk?" Darnell snapped as the man remained standing instead of speeding to his task.

"I was just wondering why you did it this way," Hopkirk said.

"Did it what way?"

Hopkirk shrugged. "You know and I know that Hopkirk Glimware would have done all right if you hadn't manipulated the Net to bring my stock prices down and cut off my credit."

"That's a matter of opinion," Darnell told him. "Admit it, Hopkirk. You're an engineer, not a manager, and you didn't know how to run the company. It would have crashed eventually in any case. All I did was help it along."

"But why do it this way? Why ruin me when you could have bought the company for a fair price and still made your profit?"

Darnell was pleased that the man didn't argue the basic point. He'd been an incompetent manager and he knew it.

"You're a brilliant businessman," Hopkirk went on. "Look at how you turned OG Shipping around in just a year!"

With a little help from my friends . . . Darnell quashed that thought. Sure, Polyon's ability to hack into the Net and get advance information had been useful. But it was also true that Darnell had discovered within himself a true talent for efficiency. Cut out the deadwood! Fire the incompetent, the lazy, and those who've merely failed to get results! And know everything! Those were Darnell's new mottoes. Those who'd been fired talked about the Reign of Terror. Those who hadn't been fired yet didn't dare to talk. And OG Shipping prospered . . . leaving Darnell free to amuse himself again.

There was Julitta, of course. There were an infinite number of Julittas. But Darnell had discovered that no number of willing girls could give him quite the thrill of victory that his business manipulations brought.

He regarded Hopkirk thoughtfully. The man seemed to intend no offense; perhaps he honestly wanted to understand the workings of Darnell Overton-Glaxely's brilliant mind. A laudable impulse; he deserved an honest answer.

"Sure, I could have done it straight," he said at last. "Would have taken a little longer. No prob. But," he winked at Hopkirk, "it wouldn't have been as much fun . . . and that way I wouldn't have had you working for me, would I? Get on with the job, Hopkirk. I've got another assignment for you when you get back."

Now that he'd as good as admitted his illegal use of the Net to Hopkirk, Darnell thought, the man had to go. It had been fun to keep him around for a little while, using him as a clerk and gofer, but one couldn't risk disgruntled victims getting together to compare notes. Once OG Glimware was taken care of, Darnell would "reward" Hopkirk with a free vacation at Summerlands Clinic. The Net revealed, among other things, that Alpha bint Hezra-Fong's patients on the charity side of Summerlands had an unusually high death rate. He'd "suggest" to Alpha that it would be convenient for both of them if Hopkirk never came back from Summerlands. That way nobody would talk about Darnell's use of the Net; and in return, he'd get Polyon to fix the Net records so that nobody would raise inconvenient questions about the number of charity patients Alpha had lost.

Achernar Subspace, Central Date 2752: Caleb and Nancia

"I wonder if he'll really be able to resolve anything," Nancia said thoughtfully as she and Caleb watched their latest delivery being greeted at Achernar Base on Charon. The short, spare man whom they'd brought halfway across the galaxy wasn't doing much to take control of his first meeting with the Charonese officials. He was just standing there on the landing field, listening to the speeches of welcome and accepting bouquets of flowers.

"None of our business," Caleb reminded her. "Central said, take Unattached Diplomatic Agent Forister to Charon, and do it fast. They didn't say to evaluate his job performance. And we've got another assignment waiting."

"Don't we always?" But the little group of pompous Charonese officials that surrounded Forister was moving off now, leaving the spacefield clear for Nancia's liftoff.

"It's just that I like to feel we've accomplished something," she lamented as Caleb strapped down for liftoff, "and I do feel this Charonese situation calls for somebody a bit more . . . more forceful." Somebody like Daddy, for instance. With his brisk, no-nonsense manner and willingness to enforce his decisions, Javier Perez y de Gras would have made short work of Charon's seven feuding factions, the continual war between the Tran Phon guerrillas and all seven provisional governments, and the consequent destruction of Charon's vital quinobark forests. He'd have been using Nancia's comm facilities and working the Net every minute they weren't in Singularity, preparing for his descent on the Charonese, arming himself with every last detail of the conflict, softening up the principal offenders with stern warning messages.

This Forister had spent the three days of the voyage reading ancient books — not even disks, but some account of an Old Earth war too minor to have been transcribed to computer-readable format. And when he wasn't reading about this place called Viet Nam, he wasted his time in relaxed, casual conversation with her and Caleb, chatting about their families and upbringing, their hopes and dreams. Too soft to stop a war, Nancia thought contemptuously. Oh, well, Caleb was right — the results were none of their business. They were Courier Service; they went where they were sent, quickly and efficiently. Sticking around to report on the failure of the resulting mission was not in the CS job description.

Bahati, Central Date 2753:
Fassa

"You can't just leave me like this!"

Fassa del Parma y Polo paused at the door and blew a mocking kiss at the gray-faced, potbellied man who was looking at her with such pain in his eyes. "Watch me, darling. Just watch me." She touched her left index finger to the charm bracelet on her wrist. There'd been an empty prismawood heart there, just the right size to hold the minihedron recording this stupid bureaucrat's sign-off on the Nyota ya Jaha Space Station contract. "Our business is done." *All* their business, including those boring maneuvers on the man's synthofur rug. At least it hadn't taken too long. These old guys had dreams of grandeur, but they really couldn't do much when they did get the chance. *You're past it, sweetheart, and the future belongs to me.* Something uncomfortable writhed under the triumphant thought, some question as to why she exulted so much in the moral destruction of a small-time civil servant old enough to be her father; but Fassa pushed the question away with the ease of long practice. She had got what she wanted. It was as simple as that.

"But we were going to live together. You were going to quit this messy, unfeminine job, now that you've got enough money to pay for your sister's metachip prosthesis, and we were going to retire to Summerlands . . . "

Fassa laughed out loud. "What, me? Spend my last hundred years tending to some old man in a Summerlands retirement cottage? You've been popping too much Blissto, my friend." She paused to let the rejection sink in before delivering her final warning. "And don't even think about blowing the whistle on me.

Remember, you've got more to lose than I have." She always set it up that way.

There was an unwelcome surprise waiting for her when she reached her offices. Two, in fact. One was minor; some kid was slumped in the corner sackback chair in the outer office, fiddling with forms. Employment applications were supposed to be handled in a different office; the kid should have been sent there to begin with.

Before she had time to point this out, her secretary lowered his head and apologetically informed her that Bahati CreditLin insisted on one more palmprint before they would release the final payment for the space station construction into her Net account. Just a formality, the secretary quoted the CreditLin officials.

Fassa's brows snapped together as the man assured her there was nothing to worry about. "Inspection? What inspection? Everything's been passed and signed by Vega Base." Or rather, by the befuddled old fool she'd just left, who hadn't even bothered to take a transport up to the station and walk its corridors in person, much less assign a qualified engineer to the task of a detailed structural inspection.

"That's what I told them," the secretary said, "and I'm sure this will take no time at all, since Vega's engineering division has already signed off on all the main structural elements. Just a formality," he repeated. "It seems there's been a new law passed; CreditLin is obliged to send one of its own independent inspectors to verify that our construction meets standards before they can transfer the credits."

A new law . . . Damn! I thought all the Bahati Senators had been paid off. Do I have to do everything myself?

Fassa suppressed the thought with a quick frown. She'd deal with the legislature later. For now — so there was one more fool of a man to deal with, to wheedle and distract and please into forgetting the obvious checks that would reveal her substandard materials. Annoying, that was all. She didn't like surprises. But it would, after all, be one more minihedron to fill her charm bracelet.

Fassa caught a flicker of movement in the corner, just enough to distract her for a moment. The kid in the sack-back was stretching, rising out of the enveloping chair. *Not now. Go away. I have other things to think about.*

"Miss del Parma y Polo?"

Not such a kid; a man grown, older than she was herself — but not by so very much. Fassa took in his appearance with growing appreciation. Broad shoulders, legs long enough to carry off his out-rageously psychepainted Capellan stretchpants, black hair and eyes whose blue was set off by slashing streaks of ochre face paint. *A pretty peacock of a man. Maybe I'll hire him after all, even if he did bypass the employment office. Who cares whether he can do anything? Keep him around just to look at.*

"I should introduce myself now, I guess." He smiled down at her and enveloped her hand in his. "Sev Bryley, chief inspector for Bahati CreditLin. I reckon it'll be a pleasure working with you, Miss del Parma."

Cor Caroli Subspace, Central Date 2753: Caleb and Nancia

Caleb slammed one fist into the opposite palm and paced the width of the central cabin, growling deep in his throat. He paused opposite a purple metalloy bulkhead with silver-gilt stenciled borders and raised his fist again.

"Don't even think about it," Nancia warned him. "You'll only hurt your hand and damage my nice new paint job."

Caleb lowered his fist. A reluctant smile twitched at the corners of his lips. "Don't tell me you *like* the paint job?"

"No. But it seemed suitable for our role. And I don't wish to return to Central looking as if I'd been through a clawing match with some of Dorg Jesen's popsies, thank you very much."

They had been undercover for this mission, Caleb posing as a debauched young High Families scion who wanted a cut of Dorg Jesen's secret metachip supply. In return, he was to have offered the feelieporn king secret information on certain of his High Families customers.

"Could be dangerous," Rahilly had warned them, back on Central Base. "Jesen doesn't like awkward questions. Try to keep the meetings on shipboard. Nancia, you'll have to protect yourself and Caleb if Jesen tries anything."

But they hadn't even lured Jesen into one shipboard meeting. He'd taken one look at Caleb's vidcom image, listened to Caleb's stiff delivery of the speech he'd been assigned to make, and burst out laughing. "Pull the other one, it's got bells on," he taunted Caleb. "And next time Central decides to send someone to investigate me, tell them not to make it an Academy boy with a Vega accent you could cut with a knife, in a brainship with a tarted-up central cabin. If you're High Families, I'll eat my . . . "

Nancia cut the sound transmission at that point.

"Perhaps," she said now, "undercover work is not our *metier*."

"I hate lies and spying," Caleb confirmed moodily. "We should have refused this mission." He looked up with a glimmer of hope in his eyes. "Unless . . . did you get anything?"

Nancia had used the brief minutes of the vidcom link to insert feelers into Jesen's private computer system, so private that it didn't even have a Net connection. Central had surmised he might have such a system in addition to the open accounts he maintained via Net, but nothing could be checked until they arrived planetside.

"Nothing," she told him. "I did get into his supply acquisition database, but all the metachips in the records there show perfectly legitimate Shemali Base control numbers."

Caleb made a fist again. "Then you didn't get into the right records. Somebody's counterfeiting metachips, and Jesen could lead us to the source . . . could have led us. He must be keeping *three* sets of books. Do you think if I got him on vidcom again . . . "

An incoming transmission reached Nancia, and she activated her central display screen. Dorg Jesen's narrow face appeared. "Been doing a little research of my own," he announced, almost pleasantly. "Got your Central ID now to add in to my report. CN-935, lift your Courier Service tailfins offplanet in fifteen minutes and we'll forget this episode ever happened. Otherwise I'll file a formal complaint with CS, charging you and your brawn with entrapment."

"You can't win them all," Nancia tried to soothe Caleb when they were offplanet and on their way back to Central. "We do many things well. Lying doesn't happen to be among them, that's all." *But I'm lying, right now, by saying nothing.* Nancia made an internal playback of the datacordings she'd made four years earlier, on her maiden voyage. There was Polyon, cheerfully announcing his plan to slip metachips past the SUM board and sell them to unauthorized operations like Dorg Jesen's feelieporn empire. If only Caleb knew what she knew, he could make a report to Central that would send them straight to Shemali.

Except . . . he wouldn't do it. In the four years of their partnership, Caleb had never once wavered or compromised his moral principles. He would never stoop to using a datacording made without the knowledge or consent of the passengers. And he would never respect Nancia again, once he knew what she'd done on that first voyage.

Sadly, Nancia ended the replay and slapped five more levels of security classifications on the datacording. Caleb must never know. But there must be some way to point Central's investigations towards Shemali, to stop them thinking in terms of counterfeit metachips and start them thinking about the prison factory.

Shemali, Central Date 2754:
Polyon

Polyon slapped the palmboard built into his armchair and activated a vidcom link with Bahati.

"Summerlands Clinic, Alpha bint Hezra-Fong, private transmission, code CX22." That would scramble his message so that only someone with the CX22 decoding hedron would be able to see and hear anything but gibberish. "Alpha, my sweet, you were just a tad premature in announcing that you'd finished your Seductron research. The free sample you sent up has one of my key techs too blissed-out to do any useful work. I've no idea when he'll stop contemplating his toenails, so you'd better find out — and fast. Unless you want to be the next test subject." He smiled sweetly into the vidcom unit. "I *can* arrange it, you know."

The next message went to Darnell, using a similar scrambling technique. In a few words Polyon informed Darnell that IntraManager, the small commlink manufacturing company Darnell was presently trying to take over, was not to be touched. "It's one of mine," he said pleasantly. "I'm sure you wouldn't have made a takeover move if you'd known that, would you now? By the way — did I show you the latest vids of the metachip line?" A tap of his fingers on the palmboard called up a datacording from the lowest circles of Hell: suited and masked workers toiling amid clouds of poisonous green steam. This was the last and most dangerous phase of metachip assembly, when the blocks between the polyprinted connection patterns were burned off with a quick dip into vats of acid.

The burn-off process released a gaseous form of Ganglicide into the atmosphere. Before Polyon's time, this phase had been handled — rather badly — by automated servos that misjudged the depth and timing of the burnoff phase, dropped metachip boards, and quickly self-destructed in the poisonous atmosphere. Expensive and wasteful. By contrast, prison workers in protective suits could process more than three times as many metachips in a session, and only a few of them were lost each year to leaks in the suit sealing.

"See the third man from the left, Darnell?" Polyon spoke into the vidcom while the images unreeled. "He used to be High Families. Now he's a Shemali assembly worker. How are the mighty fallen, eh?"

He cut the connection on that — an implied threat was ever so much more effective than a specific one. Actually, Polyon had no idea who the masked workers on the line might be. They were the scum of the prison system, the expendables who had neither tech training nor business sense to justify keeping them in the safer areas of design and preprocessing. And while there was indeed a High Families convict on Shemali, the man had been sent there for a particularly revolting series of crimes involving the torture of small children. Polyon didn't really think he could frame Darnell for something like that and make it stick; anybody would see the rich boy didn't have the guts to torture anybody.

But I won't need to, will I? The threat will be enough to keep old Darnell in line.

The last call was to Fassa. He was lucky enough to catch her in person. Polyon enjoyed the sight of Fassa's eyes widening while he explained in detail just how unhappy he felt about the collapse of his new metachip assembly building, how personally hurt he was to discover that Polo Construction had supplied the substandard materials used in the building, and exactly what he might do to assuage his sense of loss and betrayal. The only trouble with the live connection, Polyon thought, was that he didn't get to finish outlining the list of things he could do to Polo Construction as a company and to Fassa personally. Before he was half through, she was stammering apologies and practically begging to be allowed to rebuild the assembly facility. Free of charge, naturally.

Polyon graciously accepted the offer.

Just one more item of business to clear up. "Send in 4987832," he commanded.

A few minutes later, a pale-faced man in the prison uniform of green coveralls came into the office. He gave Polyon a confident smile. "Thought it over, have you?"

"I most certainly have," Polyon agreed. He smiled and shrugged with palms outspread. "Can't say I'm altogether happy about the idea — but I see you leave me no choice. You're a clever fellow, 4987832. Who were you, before?"

"James Masson," the prisoner said. "Head of research for Zectronics — you've heard of them? No? Well, it's a large galaxy. But it so happens I personally directed the metachip design effort there. That's how I happened to recognize the changes you've introduced in the chips."

"My hyperchips will be faster and more powerful than the old metachips by at least two orders of magnitude," Polyon said. "They'll revolutionize the industry. It didn't take any genius to recognize that. The genius was in figuring out how to do it."

"And that's not all the hyperchips will do, is it, de Gras-Waldheim? Industry isn't the only thing about to suffer a . . . revolution."

Polyon inclined his head slightly. "You'll have a glass of Stemerald with me, to celebrate our arrangement?"

Masson's eyes widened and he licked his lips. "Why, I haven't tasted Stemerald in — in — well, it must be ten years! Not since I came here! I must say, de Gras-Waldheim, I didn't think you'd take our little arrangement so well."

Polyon's back was to Masson as he poured out the Stemerald into two sparkling globes from OG Glimware.

"A lot of men would be petty about cutting me in on the profits," Masson babbled on, accepting his globe and draining it between words, "but that's you High Families type, you know how to accept defeat graciously. And after all, giving me a small cut isn't much when you think of what it would do to your plans if I told Governor Lyautey about *all* the hyperchips' programming." He swallowed the last drops of Stemerald, ran his tongue round his lips once more to savor the taste, then sat back with the slightly dazed expression of a man who'd just had his first strong drink in ten years.

"As I said," Polyon repeated, "you leave me no choice in the matter." He frowned quickly. "You have honored your end of the agreement, haven't you, Masson? No word to anyone else?"

"No word," Masson agreed. He spoke more slowly now. "I wouldn't . . . want . . . anyone else . . . cutting in . . . " His eyes glazed over and he sat staring into space with a blissful smile on his face.

"Very good. Now, Masson, I have a special task for you." Polyon leaned forward. "Hear and repeat! You will go to the dip chambers."

"I . . . will . . . go . . . to . . . the . . . dip . . . chambers," Masson droned.

"I want you to make a surprise inspection. You will not announce yourself."

" . . . not . . . announce . . . 'self."

"You do not need a protective suit."

Masson nodded and smiled. All the intelligence had

left his face now. Polyon felt a twinge of regret. The man had been brilliant; would be again, if the Seductron wore off. He could have been a useful subordinate if he hadn't made the mistake of trying to blackmail Polyon. But as it was . . . well, there was no point in waiting, was there? Damn Alpha. If she'd only developed the controlled Seductron she kept promising, with doses ranging from ten-minute zaps to a state of mindless, permanent bliss, there would be no need for this last distasteful step.

Polyon finished his orders to Masson and snapped a dismissal. "Go. Now!"

Masson stood unsteadily and left Polyon's inner office. Polyon sat back and began sketching a metachip linkage plan with one forefinger, tracing glowing paths across the design screen.

Five minutes later, his vidcomm lit up to show the face of the afternoon shift supervisor. "Lieutenant de Gras-Waldheim? Sir? There's been a terrible accident. One of your designers just . . . the man must have gone mad, he walked right into the dip room without a suit . . . if only he'd knocked they could have kept him waiting in the outer lock until the gases were cleared out . . . they didn't even know he was there. . . . The room was filled with Ganglicide in gaseous form, he didn't have a chance. . . . " Screams sounded in the background. "Oh, sir, it's terrible!"

"A most distressing accident," Polyon agreed. "Begin the paperwork, 567934. And don't blame yourself. Sometimes it just takes them like that, you know, the lifers. Better any death than a lifetime on Shemali, they think, and who knows? Perhaps they're right. Oh, sorry, I forgot — you're a lifer too, aren't you?"

He didn't start laughing until the connection was broken.

CHAPTER SEVEN

**Spica Base, Central Date 2754:
Caleb and Nancia**

Nancia limped into Spica Base on half power, dependent on Caleb for reports on the lower deck damage where her sensors had self-destructed to preserve her from shock when the asteroid struck them.

"Freak accident," commented the Tech Grade 7 who came out to survey the damage in person.

Nancia mourned the sleek gloss of her exterior finish, now pitted and gouged around the torn metal shreds of the entrance hole. "I should have taken a different route."

"Freak ship." The tech snapped his IR-Sensor goggles down, hiding his eyes behind a band of black plastifilm. "Ain't natural. Ship talks, pilot don't."

"The correct terms, as I'm sure you are aware, are 'brainship' and 'brawn,' " Nancia said frostily. "Caleb is . . . it's none of your business. Just leave him alone, okay?" She'd seen him plunged into these unreasoning depressions before, whenever one of their missions was less than one hundred percent successful. He'd retreated into himself without speaking for a week after the disastrous undercover assignment with Dorg Jesen, while Nancia tried to tempt his appetite with fancy dishes from the galley and interesting tidbits of news picked up from the gossipbeams.

"I'll need somebody at the other end to help me link the hyperchips into the ship's system," the tech protested. "Somebody who knows the ship. My guys are good, but this is a small base. They ain't never worked on a talking ship before. And nobody's got that much experience with hyperchips. They might not interface with these sensor setups just like the old metachips did."

"Then," said Nancia, "perhaps you should explain to them that a talking ship can, in fact, *talk*. There's no need to trouble my brawn for information; I'll manage the installation myself." She didn't feel nearly so cheerful and carefree as she tried to sound; the thought of some dolt like this tech fooling around with her synaptic connectors made her feel sick and weak. But she did *not* want him bothering Caleb. One thing she'd learned in the last four years of partnership was that Caleb only stayed depressed longer if he was forced to talk to people before he was ready to.

The tech grunted acquiescence and twiddled something she couldn't see. "Sensor connection to OP-N1.15, testing."

"If you mean can I see what you're doing," Nancia responded, "the answer is no."

The tech gaped but recovered himself quickly. "Hah! OP-N1 series . . . optic nerve connections? Sorry, lady — ship — whatever you are. What I'm looking at, see, it's just schematics. I didn't think . . . " His voice trailed off for a moment. "Awesome, really, when you think about it that way. That there's a *person* somewhere inside this steel and titanium."

"Correction," Nancia said. She was becoming used to this tendency among softpersons; they insisted on equating her with the body curled inside the titanium column, as if that was all there was to her. "I *am* a person. That's my lower deck vision you're twiddling with now, and I'd very much like to have it — Thank you!" A partial visual field opened as she spoke. Now she could see the tech again, and one gloved hand reaching up into the tangle of fused metal and wires that had been her lower deck sensory system.

"OP-N1.15 restored," the tech noted. "Now if — say,

this is going to be easy. Don't need this stuff." He clipped a test meter to his belt and used both hands to rejoin severed wires. "OP-N1.16 functioning now? Good. 17?" He worked through the full series rapidly, while Nancia kept him informed of the status of each repair.

"Thank you," she said again when he'd restored her full optic series for the lower deck. "It's . . . most troubling, being unable to look at a part of myself."

"Imagine it would be," the tech agreed. "Glad to help a lady, any time."

Nancia noted that in the course of one short repair session she had advanced from "unnatural talking ship," to "person" to, apparently, "lady in distress." *By the time the repairs are finished, he'll be wanting to sign up for brawn training . . . and most distressed to learn he's over age.*

"And this is just the beginning," the tech promised. "We'll have you fixed up good as new in a day or so. *Better* than new, really. You had any hyperchips installed before? Thought not. They're — I dunno — about a thousand times better than the old line metachips. You're gonna like this, ma'am." His fingers twisted, seating one of the new chips. It felt strange to see the movements without feeling the slight pressure and hearing the click as the chip slid into place.

"Can you feel anything when I do this?"

"No — yes. Oh!"

"Hurt you?"

"No. Just — surprised." Nancia felt as if her sensors had been turned up to full volume, without sacrificing the slightest accuracy. Every movement was clear; the world sparkled like crystal around her. "How many more of those do you have? Can you replace my upper deck sensor chips too?"

The tech shook his head regretfully. "Sorry, ma'am. It's a new design out of Shemali. There's not enough hyperchips out yet to go around to all the folks who need them for repairs, let alone bringing in functional equipment and retrofitting it. Shemali Plant estimates it'll be a good three-four years before they can produce enough to retrofit all the Fleet ships."

"Oh. Of course." Nancia remembered the plan Polyon had described on her maiden voyage. "I suppose," she said, feeling very crafty, "I suppose a lot of the chips are failing QA tests? It being a new design, and all," she added hastily.

The tech shook his head. "No, ma'am. Actually, these new chips don't fail in testing near as often as the old design. Pretty near the full production run is being cleared for distribution, most times. It's just that even a year's full production runs out of Shemali don't amount to that much when you consider all the places the chips have to go these days. It's not just the Fleet, y'know. Hospitals, Base brains, cyborg replacements, defense systems — seems like we just about couldn't run the galaxy without 'em!"

Nancia felt first disappointed, then relieved. She had expected to hear that the new design somehow caused a great many metachips to fail in the QA phase and that nobody knew what became of the substandard chips rejected by the SUM ration board. That would have been evidence she could mention to Caleb, something to steer his mind in the direction of Polyon's illicit activities without revealing that she already knew about the plan.

Instead, it seemed that Polyon had given up his plan altogether. He *was* brilliant. Perhaps the hyperchip design was his idea; and perhaps, Nancia thought optimistically, he had forgotten his original notion of stealing metachips in favor of the honest pleasure of seeing his design accepted and used galaxy-wide.

Angalia, Central Date 2754

The third annual progress meeting of the Nyota Five was held on Angalia, an arrangement which pleased no one — least of all the host.

"It was *your* idea to rotate the annual meetings," Alpha bint Hezra-Fong pointed out, somewhat snappishly, when Blaize apologized for the primitive accommodations. "We could have been comfortably settled in a Summerlands conference room, but nooo, you and Polyon had to fuss that it wouldn't be fair if you two had to travel to Bahati every time just to suit the three of us who had the good luck to be stationed there. So we have to rotate. Two nice meetings on Bahati, now this godforsaken dump, and next time, stars help us, Shemali. You and your bright ideas! Send someone to unpack for me — you must have *some* help around the place, surely?"

" 'Fraid not," Blaize said with a sunny smile. He was beginning to enjoy the prospect of Alpha's discomfort on Angalia. Rotating the meeting sites had really been Polyon's idea, not his, but Alpha was obviously afraid to take out her bad temper on Lieutenant de Gras-Waldheim. Blaize glanced sidelong at Polyon, very straight and correct in his Academy dress blacks, and admitted to himself that he didn't blame Alpha. Given a choice of tongue-lashing the enigmatic technical manager of Shemali MetaPlant, or the little red-haired runt from PTA, who wouldn't choose to lash out at the PTA wimp?

But this understanding didn't make him love Alpha — or the rest of the Nyota Five, including himself — any better.

"Welcome," Blaize said with a sweeping bow that included all four of his guests, "to the Angalia Tourist Center. A modest facility, as you can see — "

Darnell's snort of laughter testified to the truth of that statement.

" — but vastly improved from its humble beginnings," Blaize finished. "If the winner were to be chosen on the basis of progress rather than of absolute wealth, I'd have no doubt of succeeding next year."

And that, by God, was the absolute and unvarnished truth! The rest of them might sneer at Blaize's long, low bungalow with its thatched roof and thatch-shaded balcony, the garden of native ferns and grasses and the paved path leading from there to the corycium mine. Never mind. *He* knew what it had taken to create these amenities from the mud-hole that Supervisor Harmon had left him with.

"All done with native labor?" Fassa interrupted his explanation. "But everybody knows the Loosies are too stupid to do anything useful."

Blaize put one finger to the side of his nose and winked, a gesture borrowed from an old tri-D show called *Fagin and His Gang*. "Amazing what even a veg-head can do with the proper . . . incentive," he drawled.

"Where d'you store the whips and spiked sticks?" That was pudgy Darnell, bright-eyed as if he actually expected Blaize to produce a panoply of torture instruments and demonstrate their use.

"You've no subtlety, Overton-Glaxely," Blaize reproved the man. "Think. The — er — Loosies were starving when I came here, kept alive only by PTA ration bricks. The task of distributing the ration bricks, naturally, belonged to the PTA representative on Angalia. Me."

"So?" Darnell really was amazingly slow. Not for the first time, Blaize wondered how he'd made such a success out of OG Shipping and the smaller corporations that OG Enterprises had swallowed up over the years.

"So," Blaize drawled, "I saw no reason to *give* away PTA ration supplements when they could perfectly well be used to train the natives. We have a simple rule of life now on Angalia, my friends — no work, no eat." He pointed towards the entrance to the corycium mine. "And it's not just applied to building the master's bungalow. I hold the title to that mine. United Spacetec abandoned it because they couldn't keep human miners on Angalia. *I* use the native resources to mine the native resources, so to speak — you'll see the day shift coming out in a few minutes."

"And you pay them with ration bricks, which come free via PTA?" Alpha gave Blaize an approving smile that chilled him to the bone. "I must admit, Blaize, you're not as stupid as you look. Anything you make from the corycium mine is profit, free and clear."

Blaize opened his mouth wide in simulated shock. "Dr. Hezra-Fong! Please! I am deeply shocked and disillusioned that you should think such a thing of me. Any profits accruing from the corycium mine naturally belong to the natives of Angalia." He waited a beat before continuing. "Of course, since the natives of Angalia do not have Intelligent Sentient Status, they can't have bank accounts — so the credits do, perforce, go into a Net account in my name. But held in trust for the Loosies — you understand?"

The others chuckled knowingly and all agreed that they did indeed understand, and that Blaize was a clever lad to have found such a good way of covering his tail in the event of a PTA inspection. All but Polyon de Gras-Waldheim, who was tapping one finger against the seam of his black trousers and staring at the thunderclouds on the horizon.

"You've done pretty well, considering," Darnell admitted, "but with creatures as dumb as these, surely you have — er — discipline problems?" He was getting that whips-and-chains expression again.

"If he does, maybe regulated doses of Seductron would be the answer," cooed Alpha. "I've just about got the bugs worked out of the dosage schedule now, and it might be interesting to test it on non-humans."

Blaize forced himself to smile. Time for his demonstration. He'd planned it beforehand, in case there was need to make an additional impression on the others, but had hoped it wouldn't be necessary.

Messy, it would be. And wasteful. But apparently they still weren't convinced of his firm control over the Loosies.

"Thanks, Alpha, but Seductron wouldn't quite do the trick; the Loosies are passive and malleable enough already. What they need is occasional stimulation, and that," he said with a low laugh, "that I can arrange for myself." He raised one hand in the air and brought it down with a swift chopping motion.

Two of the tall rock pillars beside the garden wall moved forward in the shambling, awkward gait characteristic of the Loosies. With movement, their features and humanoid shapes could be clearly seen, although until a moment earlier they had blended in with the real stones making up the rest of the wall. Between them they hauled a third "rock," a native whose double-jointed legs sagged under him and whose flapping liplike folds of skin opened and closed with a mimed display of silent terror.

"They may not talk," said Blaize, "but they've learned to understand simple sign commands quite well. Most of them have, anyway. This fellow in the middle dropped a serving dish when he was waiting on me at dinner yesterday. I've been saving him to make an example of in front of the miners, but since there's an audience here already" — he allowed his eyes to roam lazily over his four co-conspirators — "why wait any longer for the pleasure?"

He pointed over the side of the mesa with a deliberate downward motion, three times repeated. The two Loosie guards bobbed their square heads and half carried, half dragged their prisoner over the edge.

"You make 'em throw themselves over the cliff?"

"Not at all," Blaize cackled. "Too fast, that'd be. Come and watch!"

By the time everybody had crowded around the low wall at the mesa's edge, the three Loosies were already down on the mud flats, approaching one of the areas where bubbles rose and burst in the glop with a stench of sulfur. The two guards hauled the prisoner to the edge of this bubbling area and thrust him into the soft mud. As he writhed and struggled to escape, they picked up the long sticks that had marked the site of the bubbles and used them to thrust him back into the steaming mud.

"Natural hot springs under there," Blaize explained. "Very hot. Takes a couple of hours to cook 'em through. Fortunately, the Loosies are real patient. Those two I use as guards will keep pushing him down until he quits trying to get out, even if it takes most of the evening."

He turned away from the spectacle of torture and bowed once again to his guests. "Well, ladies and gentlemen," he inquired with a benign smile, "shall we begin the business meeting?"

Even Polyon, Blaize noted, was pale against the dead black of his uniform; while the other three were shocked into silence. So much the better. It would be a while, he thought, before any of them underestimated little Blaize again.

After the shocking scene Blaize had just provided, the third annual progress meeting began more quietly than the previous meetings had gone. The underlying tensions in the group were still present, however, and all the sharper for another year's fermenting.

As host, Blaize claimed the honor of giving the initial report. While Polyon gazed over his head in unfeigned boredom and the two girls sat pale and silent, he began reciting facts and figures to back up his earlier assertions. In earlier years he'd had little to report. This year he was at last coming into his own. He fancied a glimmer of respect in Polyon's eyes as Blaize explained how he was using the first profits from the corycium mine to finance the purchase of heavy mining equipment that would open up even more of the planet for exploitation. Darnell twitched and muttered to himself during this part of the report, but he didn't explode until Polyon pointedly inquired as to how Blaize had financed the initial startup costs of the mine.

"Reselling surplus PTA shipments," Blaize replied promptly.

"Dear me," commented Polyon, "I thought the — ah — 'Loosies' were starving. Didn't this move reduce your potential worker population somewhat?"

"Waste not, want not," Blaize waved his hand in vague circles. "There's a lot of surplus in any bureaucracy. I just — as you might say — cut the fat out."

It was perhaps unfortunate that his eyes met Darnell's at this moment, and that the airy circles his hand was sketching could have been taken for an indication of Darnell's growing paunch.

"The hell you did!" Darnell exploded, surging to his feet on a wave of red-faced fury. "Cut it right out of *my* hide, you mean!" He turned to the others as if appealing for their sympathy. "Little bastard blackmailed me to ship extra food here — *free* — while he was selling the supplies that ought to've gone to the natives!"

This accusation did not have quite the effect he might have been hoping for.

"Really, Darnell?" asked Polyon with bright-eyed interest. "And what were you doing that he could blackmail you for, I wonder?"

Darnell puffed and stammered and Alpha interrupted him. "Who cares? I'm delighted *somebody* finally nailed you. Ever since you took over Pair-a-Dice I've wanted to pay you back!"

"What do you care whether I buy out a crummy casino?"

"That 'crummy casino,' " Alpha informed him, "just

happened to be my primary outlet for Seductron at street prices. The gambling was only a front — once you pay the Bahati cops off for a gambling operation, they're too dumb to check and see if that's really where all the money is coming from. Pair-a-Dice — Paradise — get it, stupid? That's the street name for Seductron."

"I thought you didn't have the dosage schedules worked out yet!" Fassa sounded appalled.

Alpha shrugged thin, elegant shoulders. Her face was sharp as a knife under the elaborate Nueva Estrella style of tight braids piled high in a prismawood spiral frame. "So a few Blissto addicts go out happy. Who cares? I've got to start making something off Seductron before next year. Even if I work around all the side effects, it's too late to patent it now. So it's street deals or nothing." This reminded her of her grievance. "And since *you* took over my best outlet, Pudge-face, it's been nothing. You owe me!"

"So do you," Fassa told Blaize. "Del Parma was low bidder on the corycium processing plant. By government regulations you ought to've given us the job. How much did the winning contractor slip you under the table?"

"That," Blaize replied stiffly, "is between the two of us, and nothing to do with you, Fassa! Besides, knowing what I do about del Parma's construction methods, what made you think I'd be fool enough to let you build a latrine trench on Angalia?"

"Huh! Angalia already *is* a latrine trench! Ha-ha-ha!"

Nobody except Fassa paid the least attention to Darnell's lame jest. She whirled and stabbed a long iridescent corycium-sheathed fingernail at his chest. "And you! Remember the Procyon run? That's the last time OG Shipping gets any del Parma business!"

Darnell smoothed down his green synthofur jacket

and smirked. "Can't see what you're complaining about," he replied. "Switching good construction materials for substandard ones is standard practice for del Parma."

"Only," Fassa said, "when *I* keep the profit. I'm not running a charitable association for the benefit of OG Shipping."

"Can't see why not," Darnell leered. "The word is you've been charitable to enough of Bahati's male population already."

Fassa sat down abruptly, holding her head in her hands. "Don't remind me," she wailed, "as if you and everybody else cheating me weren't enough, can't I at least forget about that inspector from CreditLin for a little while? I gave him what he wanted, the space station's paid for, I can't understand why he won't go *away*."

"I can," suggested Blaize helpfully. "Fraudulent QA records, shoddy materials, slipshod building practices, non-union workers . . . "

"Cheat!"

"Bloodsucker!"

"Shark!"

The meeting dissolved into the usual chaos while Polyon sat back, arms crossed, and murmured, "Naughty children."

● CHAPTER EIGHT

Kailas, Procyon Subspace, Central Date 2754

The Central Diplomatic Services office tower was a lacework of steel and titanium needles, wrapped in translucent green synthofilm that trapped and redistributed natural light in a soft, unchanging glow. Midnight or noon, the CDS offices on Kailas were lit by a gentle, slightly green-tinged light that was energy-efficient, situation-appropriate, and psychologically proven to be simultaneously soothing and inspirational.

It made Sev Bryley feel as if he was about to suffer a recurrence of the jungle rot that had attacked his skin on Capella Four. He tried not to think about the light. It was a minor matter, not worth wasting the precious minutes this important man had granted him.

"You hate this, too, don't you?" the important man said.

"Sir?"

An impatient grunt. "The blasted light. Something Psych and EcoTech dreamed up between them. Makes me feel as if I were back on Capella Six."

"For me it was Four," Sev confessed.

Another grunt. "Different war, same jungle. I'd open a window if this place *had* windows. Can't peel plastifilm open, more's the pity."

"It's very good of you to make time to see me at all, sir," Sev said cautiously. So they had a common background — service in the Capellan Wars? Was that why this highly placed diplomat had given a mere private investigator ten minutes out of his crowded schedule?

"Not at all. Do the same for any friend of the family

who needed help. So. What's your problem, d'Aquino?"

Sev stiffened. "I didn't intend to call on family connections, sir —"

"Then you're a damned young fool," said the gray-haired man in the conservative blue tunic. "I've been checking your Net records. Your full name is Sevareid Bryley-Sorensen d'Aquino — why didn't you use it when you requested this appointment? You could have gotten in to see me three days sooner. And why me, if you didn't mean to call on High Families connections?"

"I was not aware that there was a relationship between our families. Sir," Sev said stiffly. "I came to Kailas because it was the nearest world with any CDS representatives high-ranking enough to deal with my problem. And I approached you because you have the reputation of being one of the two Central Worlds officials on this planet who cannot be bribed, threatened, or suborned."

"So you found two honest men, my Diogenes? I'm flattered."

"Sir. My name is Bryley, not Dio — whatever."

"A classical reference. No matter. What *do* they teach them in University these days? But then, you didn't finish your schooling. Why didn't you cash in your veteran's benefits after Capella IV to complete your education at Central's expense?"

Sev tried without success to conceal his surprise.

"The Net can supply — um — rather a lot of detail," his interlocutor explained gently. "Even about a rather obscure private investigator who's recently lost his position with Bahati CreditLin — yes, I found out about that too. Something about a gambling scandal at the Pair-a-Dice, wasn't it?"

"It was a lie!" Sev leaned forward, burning with indignation at the memory. "My supervisor — he had anonymous letters about me. I know who sent them, but I can't prove it."

"And who might that be?"

"The same man who transferred credits into my Net account and played under my name at Pair-a-Dice — or maybe he sent one of his flunkies to play the part. When I went to the casino, they wouldn't tell me anything about the man who used my name."

"No. They beat you — rather badly — and threw you out into the ecocycler in the back alley." The gray-eyed man surveyed Sev with eyes that took in every faint mark of healing bruises and scraped skin. "Lucky you didn't wind up being recycled into somebody's rose garden; we suspect that's what has happened to a few other people who annoyed the proprietor of that particular establishment. So. You came to your senses, crawled out of the ecocycler before it began its chop sequence, got treatment for your more obvious wounds from some shady blacklisted ex-doctor among your underworld friends, and . . . came halfway across the galaxy to wait three days for an interview with me. Want me to get you reinstated with Bahati CreditLin, is that it? Favor for a friend? Teach them not to act on anonymous accusations against a High Families lad — even one who's rebelled against his background and is working incognito?"

"Sir!"

"It can be arranged, you know," said the gray-eyed man, watching Sev closely. "A word from this office, and Bahati CreditLin will reinstate you, full back pay, no questions asked. If that's what you want . . . "

"No, sir."

The gray-eyed man nodded briskly. "Good. I didn't think so, but one has to be sure. You want to track down the people who framed you, then."

"More than that." Sev dropped his eyes. "I think I know who framed me. And why. But it's a long story, and there are High Families involved. That's why I came to you, sir. Somebody without that background might be tempted to shove everything under the carpet for fear of offending someone powerful. And of those in Central Administration who are High Families — well — " He spread his hands helplessly. "I don't know the lineages and their reputations. The only two people whose integrity everyone is absolutely sure of are you and General Questar-Benn — and she's on some kind of secret assignment, nobody would tell me where."

"How flattering," purred the gray-eyed man.

Belatedly, Sev realized the implications of his words. "Sir. I didn't mean — I am most grateful that you agreed to see me, truly I am."

"Take that as read. Now why don't you tell me what's going on?"

Sev's cheekbones reddened. His tongue felt like a wad of cotton in his mouth. Where could he begin? In this cool green-lit office, the madness that had seized him on Bahati seemed like a dream.

"There was — a girl."

"Ahh. You know, there quite often is, in such cases. And you — made a fool of yourself?" He looked at Sev sympathetically. "You know, I *can* remember the urge to make a fool of oneself over a young lady. I'm not so old and dried-up as all that. But if this story is going to be personal, perhaps you'd feel easier continuing it in a less formal environment? Sometimes I go across town for lunch — there's a cafe in Darkside. Nothing fancy. But at least it gets one out of this damned jungle light."

Fifteen minutes later, feeling somewhat as if he'd actually been through the ecocycler's processing sequence, Sev and the man he'd come to see were seated at a table in the back of a cavernous, dimly lit cafe. The one window that might have admitted a little sunlight was curtained by dusty streamers of glitzribbon and prismawood light-dangles. In one corner of the room, a weedy boy with long red hair tied in a black velvet bow tinkered with his synthocom set, producing occasional bursts of strident sound that grated on Sev's eardrums.

Even his sleazy story seemed no more than normal, here. He wondered if that was why they'd come to this dingy place. It seemed an odd setting for a man who spent his working life meeting with presidents and kings and generals.

"It's quiet here," said the only honest man on Kailas, "and more to the point, I know there won't be any un-authorized datacordings made of our conversation; I'm acquainted with the proprietor of this place. She has quite a number of visitors who don't want their discussions overheard or recorded."

"I can believe it," said Sev with feeling.

"So. If that answers your curiosity about why we came here — why don't you tell me about this girl?"

"She was — " Sev stopped, swallowed, searched again for a place to begin. "She is head of a construction company based on Bahati. Their most recent contract was for a space station to catch Net signals and route small-package traffic between Vega subspace and Central. As part of my routine duties for Bahati CreditLin, I was asked to do a final walk-through inspection of the station. It was — it should have been just a formality; the head of Contracts Administration had already signed off on the work."

"I take it," murmured the gray-eyed man, "there were, in fact, some deficiencies in the construction methods?"

"It was a *joke*." Sev's hands moved freely and he forgot his nervousness as he sketched the discoveries he'd made. "Oh, everything looked good enough on the outside. Fresh new permalloy surface skin. Interior corridors painted and glowlit, shiny new sensor screens to scan the exteriors. But once I opened up a few panels and started looking at what was behind the fresh paint—" He shook his head, remembering. "She tried to distract me. No. That's not fair. She . . . did distract me. For a while." Three days and nights in Fassa del Parma's private cubicle on her personal transport ship, wheeling around the space station, watching the blazing dance of the stars through the clear walls above and below and around their own dance . . .

Sev felt himself on fire again, remembering. And regretting. Even now, some part of him wanted nothing better than to be back on the *Xanadu* with Fassa del Parma y Polo. Whatever the cost.

"She was . . . annoyed," he said slowly, "when I told her I'd have to complete the inspection according to form." He looked up at the man seated across the table, searching for a hint of condemnation in the level gray eyes. "I should have done the inspection immediately. I'd given her three days." *No, she gave them to me. Three days I'll never forget.* "She'd had her people working overtime to conceal their cheap work. Panels behind panels. Fake safety numbers stenciled on the recycled supporting beams. Warning signs about chemical danger areas in front of the rats' nests they called an electronic system — as though that would've stopped me!" Sev snorted.

"If *I* had put up signs warning of chemical dangers," the other man commented, "I would have made sure that you did indeed run into such dangers the first time you removed a panel. Nothing fatal, of course. Certainly nothing really nasty, like gaseous Ganglicide. Maybe a little sinoidal stimulant. Or Capellan fungus spores."

"She thought of that," said Sev grimly. "So, unfortunately for her, did I . . . I wore a chem-pro suit and gas mask while I checked out the electronics."

"And?"

"The place never should have passed the most cursory inspection," Sev said tonelessly. "It *didn't* pass mine. I transmitted a full report via the Net — enough to stop payment on the space station and put Polo Construction under investigation. The lady was, ummm — not pleased when I told her what I'd done." A reminiscent smile tugged at one corner of his mouth and he rubbed absentmindedly at the four parallel scratches under his right ear. Nothing more than the faint memory of scars now, but the lines still tingled whenever he thought of Fassa. Being clawed by Fassa del Parma wasn't nearly as much fun as the things they'd done on the *Xanadu*, but it was still a remarkably stimulating experience. Even now, Sev reckoned he would rather have a fight with Fassa than party with any six other girls of his acquaintance.

Not that the opportunity was likely to come his way again....

"You said your report should have shut down the space station," his companion prompted gently. "Instead ... ?"

"Damned if I know." Sev spread his hands. "When I got back planetside, my report was gone. All my files had been erased by some freak computer malfunction, and nobody had bothered to copy it to a datahedron first ... or so they said. And I was up on charges of sexual harassment. Specifically, failing to complete a scheduled inspection, and threatening Fassa del Parma y Polo with a bad inspection report if she didn't comply with my perverted desires."

"She got there first," the other man murmured.

"She's fast," Sev admitted grudgingly. "And smart. And ... well, it doesn't matter. Not now." *I'll never get back on the* Xanadu *now. And if I did, she'd nail me to a wall and flay me. Slowly.*

"It was her word against mine, no evidence on either side. Or so my supervisor told me. A second inspection, a second *honest* inspection, would have found the same flaws I detailed in my report. But they weren't going to send me, not after her complaints. And while they were waffling around looking for somebody else with the technical background to do the inspection, Senator Cenevix pushed a special bill through his committee. He's in charge of the Ethics Committee," Sev explained. "This bill made second inspections in the same class as trying a man twice for the same crime — placed a construction company under the protection of the old double jeopardy rule. So we weren't allowed to go back and collect the evidence. *Then* the letters started coming — about me gambling at the Pair-a-Dice — and, well, you know the rest of it."

"What I don't know, though, is what you expect me to do about it. You've said you don't want me to get you reinstated at Bahati CreditLin — and I think that's a good idea; if you went back to the Nyota ya Jaha system, I don't think your life would be worth much. And you must know Central doesn't interfere with other worlds' internal legislative affairs. If this young lady has bribed a senator, that's most deplorable, but we must wait for the people of Bahati to recognize the fact and remove him by due electoral process."

"Not," said Sev grimly, "if I can get incontrovertible evidence of what she's been up to."

"My dear boy, you'll never get close to a Polo Construction job again. From what you've told me, I'm quite sure she's too bright to let you anywhere near her operations."

"True," Sev agreed. "*I* haven't a chance of catching her now. And there aren't many investigators — male or female — whom I'd guarantee to be immune to Fassa's, umm, methods of distraction." He paused for a moment of brief, intense, almost painful memory. "Maybe none," he concluded, opening his eyes again. "But a brainship would be safe enough, don't you think?"

"Tell me," said the gray-eyed man, "exactly what you have in mind." He hadn't moved by so much as the flicker of an eyelash, but Sev could sense the suddenly heightened interest. He outlined his plan, accepted several corrections and emendations to the basic strategy, and all but held his breath with hope and excitement. It had been a long shot, coming to this man, and one he hadn't really expected to pay off.

"I think it can be done," was the final verdict. "I think it should be done. And I do believe I can arrange it."

"Then it only remains to find a brainship capable of carrying out the plan."

"Any Courier Service ship would be *capable*." There was a hint of reproof in the level, passionless voice. "But we can do better than that. You want integrity, brains, diplomatic skills, and the ability to pass as a droneship. There's one ship fairly recently commissioned — about five years — that should suit your purposes. I can guarantee her personal integrity, you see, and that's what is most important in this operation. For the rest — " a brief, ironic smile that puzzled Sev — "well, let's just say I've been following this particular ship's career with some interest."

He stood, and Sev followed suit. As they passed the music platform, the synthocommer broke into a raucous burst of primitive melody — annoying, far too loud, but with a compelling rhythm behind the raw sounds. Sev rather liked it, but his companion closed his eyes and shuddered faintly.

"I apologize," he said as the door closed behind them, "for the music. It's not one of the cafe's attractions, in my opinion. Still, it is the other reason why I come here."

Sev frowned in puzzlement.

"You'd think a young man of High Families stock, with a good education and a family eager to help him get started in a worthwhile profession, could find some better career than playing synthocom in a dusty bar on the wrong side of town, wouldn't you?"

It was clearly a rhetorical question. Sev nodded his head in agreement.

"So," said the only honest man on Kailas, "so would I. But evidently my son is of a different opinion."

CHAPTER NINE

Rahilly, Nancia's CS supervisor, ordered her to take it easy while she was getting used to the hyperchip implants. "Cruise back to Central and take your time about it," he ordered her. "You'll have several assignments to pick from when you get here, but there's nothing urgent and no reason for you to strain yourself with too many Singularity transitions while you're getting up to speed with your new capabilities." So Nancia chose a lengthy return route that required only one very small transition through Singularity, while she reveled in the enhanced clarity and speed of thought she enjoyed wherever the hyperchips had been installed.

After the jump she was inclined to grumble at the caution displayed by the Courier Service.

"That was the best jump I've ever made," she told Caleb. "Did you feel how cleanly I ripped that dive into Central subspace?"

"Ripped a dive?" Caleb inquired.

Nancia realized that in all their time together, she'd never discussed how she felt about Singularity, or mentioned the Old Earth-style athletic metaphors that came to her when she was diving through decomposing three-space. "It's . . . a term athletes use," she explained. "There were some newsbytes of the Earth Olympics once . . . anyway. I just meant it was a perfectly wonderful jump. Don't you think so?"

"It was over faster than most," Caleb allowed. "Let's see what our next assignment is."

They had a choice of three, but as soon as Nancia scanned the beam she knew there was only one she wanted to take. A brainship was needed for an under-cover assignment investigating the methods of BLEEP Construction Company on planet in the star system CENSORED. The matter must be handled with extreme discretion; details would be available only to the brainship accepting the assignment.

"Two weeks travel. One major Singularity point. I bet I know where it is," Nancia said.

"That could describe any number of routes," Caleb pointed out.

"Yes, but . . . " Nancia created a pattern of dancing lightstrings on her central panel. She would have been willing to bet her four years' accumulated pay and bonuses that at least one of the spoiled brats she'd carried out to the Nyota ya Jaha system was implementing the plans she'd discussed. Fassa del Parma y Polo. Polo Construction. Bahati. Hadn't there been something on the newsbytes about a delay in financing the new space station off Bahati, some question about the inspection? . . . It had to be Fassa's company. And here, at last, was Nancia's chance to stop one of the unethical little beasts. "Caleb, let's take this one. I like it."

Caleb sniffed disapprovingly. "Well, I don't. Under-cover — that's next door to espionage. Vega Ethical Code considers it the same thing, in fact. I didn't sign on to Courier Service to become a dirty, sneaking *spy*." He made the word sound obscene. "And look at this." He overrode Nancia's pattern of dancing lights to display a copy of the assignment description on the central screen. A laser pointer highlighted the wait-code inconspicuously marked on the top left corner of the message header. "See that? Somebody specifically routed this assignment to us, even if it meant waiting three weeks for us to come back from Spica subspace by the longest route. With a little checking the Net we could probably find out who — no, that would be unethical," Caleb conceded with a small sigh. "But I don't like it, Nancia. Smells of High

Families meddling and pulling strings. I think we ought to take one of the other two assignments. Something that's presented in a straightforward manner, something we can do without compromising our integrity."

But even Caleb couldn't work up much enthusiasm for their other two choices.

The first, they were warned, might be a relatively long-term assignment. A ship was required to transport the Planetary Technical Aid inspection committee on its five-yearly rounds, remaining at each planet while the committee inspected the situation and prepared a report.

"I guess there are worse chores," he said. "And maybe it wouldn't take so long. If they do this trip every five years, the last inspection ship should have been coming back just before you were commissioned. Want to check the records and find out how long the round trip took?"

Nancia began checking the Courier Service's open records while Caleb studied the third assignment choice. "Taking a bull to Cor Caroli subspace? This is a Courier Service assignment?"

"Improving agriculture," Nancia suggested, and then, "but they can't be serious. Surely all we'd have to take out is a sperm sample."

But it turned out, when they checked, that nobody had ever successfully taken a sperm sample from Thunderbolt III, the prize bull buffalo of the Central Worlds Zoo. And since the only surviving cow buffalo was on Cor Caroli VI, and since the zoo keeper there claimed Shaddupa suffered from terrible Singularity stress and couldn't possibly handle spaceflight, the preservation of the species required that Thunderbolt III be transported to Cor Caroli VI.

"I think even a PTA committee would be better company than Thunderbolt Three," Caleb commented. "Nancia, isn't there any CS record of how long the previous inspection tour lasted?"

"I just found it," Nancia told him. She'd had to check through more years of records than she anticipated.

"And?"

"And they should be returning some time next year. They're still out in Deneb subspace. I've been reading the interim reports. It seems the PTA bylaws prohibit the inspection committee from leaving any planet until they have all agreed to and signed the report for that planet."

"And?'

This time Nancia did sigh. "Caleb, it's a *committee*."

Three hours later Sevareid Bryley-Sorensen d'Aquino came aboard to explain his plan in detail.

"I don't like the paint job," Nancia complained when the retrofitting was done.

Caleb glared at her control panel. She wished he would turn around and look at her central column, now hidden behind fake bulkheads. "It was your idea to travel under false colors. Don't complain now."

"It's not being disguised as an OG Shipping droneship I mind," Nancia said. "It's Darnell's choice of colors. Puce and mauve, ugh!"

That wasn't quite true. She did mind the OG Shipping logos stenciled on her sides; it gave her a creepy feeling to know that strangers would look at her and see part of Darnell Overton-Glaxely's rapidly growing empire. But she wasn't about to admit that to Caleb, not after arguing so hard to convince him that they should take the assignment.

Sev Bryley's plan had been simplicity itself. Fassa del Parma seduced men when she needed to, but she was economical with herself as with all Polo Construction's resources: very few strangers were allowed close enough to the construction company's operations to become any sort of a threat. Her workers were fanatically loyal to her—

"Let's not discuss that part," Caleb had interrupted Sev at this point. "It's not fit for Nancia to hear."

"I believe," Sev said carefully, "that their loyalty is purchased by stock options and high financial bonuses. Not to mention the fact that a number of them are rumored to be wanted by Central under other IDs; somebody seems to be doing a fine business in supplying Fassa with fake Net identities for her workers."

Polyon. Nancia remembered the ease and dexterity with which he'd hacked into the Net accounts via her own computer. And that had been five years before. He was probably much, much better at it now. She could tell Sev Bryley where to look for the Net forger . . . or just drop him a hint. A hint might be enough for this determined young man; look how quickly he'd dredged up the connection between Polo Construction and OG Shipping, the very basis for their hastily executed plan.

Fassa's business required heavy transport facilities. For the most part Polo Construction ran their own ships, but when she had too many contracts Fassa rented droneships from OG Shipping. The drones were the safest way for her to transport illicitly acquired materials; there would be no witnesses except her own men, loading materials at one end, and the customer's men unloading at the other end of the run. Neither would be inclined to bear witness against a system that brought them so much profit.

Sev had worked out all this from a combination of studying partial Net records, interviewing anybody with even casual interest in Polo Construction, and putting the bits together with his own flashes of brilliant insight. He lacked just one thing: the testimony of an unimpeachable eyewitness to confirm his deductions. Somebody needed to *see* the substitution of materials going on . . . somebody whose integrity could not be questioned . . . somebody who could get close to operations without warning Fassa.

The integrity of Courier Service brainships was beyond question. And Fassa, accustomed to the services of the patient, silent, brainless OG droneships, would hardly suspect that behind painted bulkheads and empty loading docks there resided a human brain with the sensor capacity to hear and see all that went on aboard the ship ... and the intelligence to testify about it later.

"It's a brilliant plan," Nancia declared when Sev first explained it.

"I don't like it," Caleb glowered. "Sending Nancia out alone — without me to tell her how to do things? What if she panics?"

"I won't panic." Nancia made her voice as calm and soothing as possible.

"And I'll be with her," Sev pointed out. "I won't risk coming out where they can see me, but I'll track everything via Nancia's sensor screens and send her cues if she needs help."

Caleb folded his arms. "That," he said grimly, "is not a satisfactory solution. Why can't I go too? I'm her brawn. I should be wherever she is."

"Minimizing the risks," Sev said briefly. Actually, his original plan had called for the brainship to go completely unattended, just like a drone. But he was damned if he would miss out on the culmination of his careful plans. He trusted himself to have the self-control to stay out of sight until Fassa had completely incriminated herself; he didn't trust Caleb to display the same good sense. But explaining all that would hardly mollify the brawn.

Caleb appealed directly to Nancia. "You're too young," he said. "You're too innocent. You won't recognize their dirty tricks until too late. You — "

"*Caleb.*" Sev Bryley's voice cracked like a gunshot. The brawn stopped his compulsive pacing around the narrow perimeter of the remodeled cabin. "You aren't helping Nancia," Sev said once he had Caleb's attention. "Don't make her nervous. Why don't you go to the spaceport bar and have a drink? I'll join you as soon as Nancia and I have run through her final checklist of instructions."

Caleb opened his mouth for an angry retort and then shut it again. Nancia wished she had a sensor that could report on the rapid ticking of his brain. He was thinking something behind that quiet, tight-lipped exterior — but what?

"Consumption of intoxicating beverages is against the Vega Ethical Code," Caleb said at last, and Nancia relaxed connections that she hadn't realized were so tight. Whatever Caleb's thoughts, they weren't leading him into a fight with Sev that would very likely abort the mission at this late date. "I'll, I'll, I could have a vegosqueeze, though."

"You do that, then," Sev agreed. "See you in a few minutes."

He leaned against a fake bulkhead, arms folded. The temporary wall squeaked in protest and Sev straightened up quickly. "Crummy construction job they did on your interior," he remarked as Caleb's footsteps echoed down the central stairs.

"Then it should m-match the rest of the work around P-Polo Construction." Where had that stammer come from? Nancia ordered her vocal circuits to relax. They only tightened up farther, making the next sentence come out in a squeak. "What final checklist?"

"What? Hmm? Oh, there isn't one. I just wanted to get Caleb out of the way. He was making you nervous, wasn't he?"

"I'm fine," Nancia said, this time more gruffly than she had intended.

"You'll need to get better control over your vocal registers if you want to sound like a dronetalker," Sev warned. "Drones' synthesized voices don't wobble."

He sank to the cabin floor, long legs folding under him with no apparent strain, and gazed at the fake wall concealing Nancia's titanium column. "Undercover work is always a strain," he confided. "I used to do half an hour of yoga meditation before taking on a false identity."

Nancia rapidly scanned her data banks. Apparently *yoga* was an old-style Earth exercise designed to induce tranquility and spiritual enlightenment.

"Too bad you can't do the same thing," Sev commented.

"A brainship can do anything you softpersons can," Nancia snapped, "only better! Tell me about this *yoga*."

Sev grinned. "Well. Maybe you can. It just requires a little translation. Let's see, start with regular breathing . . . Not heavy," he said reprovingly as Nancia flushed clean air in and out through her ventilation ports, "just regular. Even. Smooth. That's the idea. Now close your . . . umm, deactivate your visual sensors."

Usually Nancia hated the blackness that accompanied temporary loss of visual sensor connections. But this time it was voluntary. And Sev's voice continued, low and soothing . . . and it *was* restful not to be scanning her remodeled interior.

Caleb must be exiting her lower entry port now; if she opened an external sensor she'd be able to see him walking across the landing field towards the spaceport central building . . . *no*. She wouldn't break the concentration of the exercise now; Sev's patient instructions were working. She felt perceptibly less nervous as she followed his suggestions to feel the energy in her lower engines and let it flow through her propulsion units without actually releasing it. A warm glowing sensation bathed her fins and exterior shell. Caleb's near-quarrel with Sev, the approaching confrontation off Bahati, even the exciting suspicion that Daddy had personally recommended her for this assignment . . . all these doubts and fears and hopes seemed very small and far away. Nancia contemplated herself, a tiny speck in the universe; as was the planet on which she sat, the sun that lit the sky around them. All little floating dots in an infinite pattern; dots winked out or came into existence, but the pattern swirled on and on forever. . . .

"Restore full sensor connections." Sev's calm order was like a gentle wake-up call. Nancia opened her sensors one by one, feeling anew the wonder of existence. The gritty spaceport floor beneath her landing gear, the smell of engine oil in the air outside, the sights and sounds of an ordinary working spaceport were all bright and trembling with new meaning.

"I think you'll do now," Sev said with satisfaction.

"I think so, too," Nancia agreed.

Out of habit, Nancia lifted off as gently as if she were carrying a full committee of Central Worlds diplomats. Just because she was decked out in the revolting colors of OG Shipping didn't mean she had to slam on-and off-world like a mindless drone. Besides, rapid movement would destroy the trance of peace in which she was still floating. And, she thought guiltily, it would also bounce Sev around. If Caleb had been aboard, his comfort would have been her first thought; Sev deserved the same consideration.

The work of outfitting her as an OG drone had been done at Razmak Base in Bellatrix subspace. Razmak possessed the very useful quality of being located just one hour's spaceflight away from a Singularity zone opening directly onto Vega subspace near Nyota ya Jaha; Nancia would not have to risk a long flight during which some authentic OG Shipping employee might notice and report her presence. She arced through the sky like a silver rainbow and made one sleek rolling dive into Singularity.

The disadvantage of this particular transition, from a softperson's point of view, was that the transition through Singularity was subjectively longer than usual. Sev had considered this a reasonable tradeoff for the advantages of Razmak Base; Nancia hoped he would feel the same way when they exited into Vega subspace.

For herself, Nancia had been looking forward to the

jump. She skimmed the rolling waves of collapsing subspace, dove and surfaced and spiraled through the spaces until the decomposition funnel drew her whirling into its shrinking space. Systems of linear equations followed their orderly dance; space shrank and expanded about Nancia, colors sang to her and the inexorable regularity of the mathematical transformations unfolded with the beauty of a Bach fugue. She came out into Vega subspace with an exuberant shout of joy, the golden notes of a Purcell trumpet voluntary echoing through concealed passages and empty loading bays.

"CUT THAT OUT!"

The outraged shout, echoing where no human voice should have sounded, was like a spattering of high-frequency power along Nancia's synaptic connectors.

She opened all sensor connections at once. The world was a faceted diamond of images: painted bulkheads, pseudosteel corridors, Sev still strapped to his bunk for the Singularity transition, the central cabin viewed from three angles at once: all framed by the external sensor views of blackness spattered by the fire of distant suns.

And Caleb, coming from one of the angles where temporary walls blocked Nancia's sensor view of her own interior, resplendent in his Courier Service full-dress uniform and still green in the face from the extended period in Singularity. Nancia closed down all the other sensors and expanded the image of Caleb. Her brawn wasn't usually inclined to Service fripperies; she had forgotten just how fine a man could look in the uncomfortable full-dress black and silver of the Courier Service, with the stiff collar forcing his jaw up and the silver-and-corycium braid winking in rainbow lightfires every time he drew a deep breath.

"You've developed a distaste for classical music?" It was the only thing she could think of to say — the only thing that was even remotely safe to say.

"You were half a tone flat on the high notes," Caleb informed her, using the same carefully remote voice that Nancia had employed. "And *much* too loud."

"I suppose I should apologize for the unintended assault on your delicate sensors," Nancia said. "I had turned off the cabin speakers, and I wasn't aware that there was another softshell aboard."

"A *what*?"

Had Caleb really spent four and a half years as her brawn without ever once hearing the slang term that shellpersons used for mobile humans? Nancia rapidly reviewed a selection of their communications. It was indeed possible. She had never realized how much of her communication she censored for Caleb's benefit, how careful she'd been to avoid offending against his standards of speech and action.

Maybe she'd been too careful, if he thought he could get away with a stunt like this.

"I think you can figure out what the term means," Nancia told him. Then, as she absorbed the emotional impact of what Caleb's action meant, her hard-won control cracked like a faulty shell. "Caleb, you idiot, you could have been *killed*! What if I'd lifted off at full speed? Hiding in that corner, you'd have been bounced around like three dice in a cup!"

"You never do bruising takeoffs or landings," Caleb pointed out. "Too fond of showing off your land-on-an-eggshell, turn-on-a-dime navigational skills."

Nancia was momentarily distracted. "What's a dime?"

"I'm not sure," Caleb admitted. "It's an Old Earth phrase. I think it refers to some kind of small insect. Want to check your thesaurus? We could call up the Old English language files via the Net, too. Something to pass the time."

"Stop trying to change the subject! *Why* didn't you tell me you were going to be aboard?"

"Would you have let me come?"

"Well . . . no," Nancia admitted. "I'd have had to tell Bryley. Your presence could compromise the mission, Caleb, don't you realize that? I'm supposed to be an unmanned droneship, remember?"

"I know," Caleb said. "Don't worry. I won't compromise the bloody mission. But I couldn't let you face this gang of thieves alone, Nancia. Don't you see that?"

She wasn't alone; she had Sev, who knew all about investigative work and undercover missions. But she couldn't very well berate Caleb for wanting to protect her, could she?

"Just keep out of sight," Nancia said finally. "Please, Caleb?" *Oh-oh. Sev is using his cabin. He isn't going to like that.* "Work it out with Sev. If one of you can hide, I guess two of you can. But — he's in charge for this mission. I agreed to that, and you'll have to do the same."

She took the set of his jaw and the brief upward jerk of his head for all the assent she was going to get.

"Oh. One other thing."

"Yes?"

"Why," Nancia inquired, "did you choose to wear full Service uniform for this little jaunt? Not that it isn't becoming, but I'd have thought something a little less conspicuous. . . . "

Caleb explained, patiently and at length, about traditions of honor on Vega. There seemed to be some connection in his mind between wearing uniform and being taken for a spy. Or not taken for a spy. Nancia couldn't quite follow the argument, and when he went from Vega history to Old Earth stories about somebody called Major André, she quit trying. Caleb was Caleb. His sense of honor wouldn't let him send his brainship without him into what he considered a dangerous and morally ambiguous situation. Apparently his sense of honor also wouldn't let him dress sensibly for the occasion. His sense of honor was a royal pain in the synapses at times, but it was part of Caleb. Part of what she respected in him.

While Caleb discussed the laws of war, the concept of a just war, the Truce of God, and the Geneva Conventions, Nancia found and activated her files of baroque brass music. With all speakers off, she ran the Purcell trumpet voluntary through her comm channels three times and was going on for a fourth before Caleb finally ran out of things to say.

Fassa del Parma paced the loading dock of Bahati SpaceBase II, biting her lip. Ever since that near-debacle over SpaceBase I, she had been unwilling to delegate the ambiguous details of her business. That had been a near thing. Who'd have thought Sev Bryley would be so persistent? She'd taken him aboard the *Xanadu* and given him what he wanted, hadn't she? And when that hadn't proved sufficient to shut the man up — Fassa stopped pacing and bit her lip. All she'd wanted from Darnell was to fake a minor gambling and embezzling record that would discredit Sev with his employers. There'd been no need to go as far as he had, even if Sev had come sniffing around the Pair-a-Dice to find out who was framing him. There were other ways to discourage people besides dumping their unconscious bodies in a recycling bin. She should have recognized Darnell's sadistic tendencies, she should have remembered the whispers about mysterious disappearances from the Pair-a-Dice.

Oblivious to the soft thump and the vibration through the base walls that announced the docking of Darnell's OG Shipping drone, Fassa leaned her head against the wall for a moment. It gave slightly where her forehead pressed against it; that was what happened when you replaced the contracted synthosteel with steel-painted plastiflim. Not that she cared. Not that anybody cared about anything. That was how the world was, and nobody bothered to stop any of the corruption. Why should she trouble herself about one man caught up in the general unfeeling way of the world? Nobody had ever cared about *her*, had they?

Certainly not Sev Bryley. All he'd been after was a scandalous case that would build up his career. He'd taken what she offered and then attacked her again as if none of it meant anything. Well, it didn't.

Did it?

Fassa blinked rapidly and activated the series of locks that would automatically check on the seal between an attached ship and the spacebase itself, equalize pressures and open the spacebase for loading and unloading. She hadn't economized on that part of the work. She was clever enough to keep well above standards on any part of a contract that might jeopardize her personal safety. Clever enough, she thought as the spacebase doors irised open, to handle any problem that came up . . . except, maybe, her own memories.

Which were no problem!

She was about to call the loading crew to shift the permasteel beams and other expensive materials onto Darnell's drone when a thought stopped her. You couldn't be too careful these days. She walked through the spaceport iris, through the extruded pressure chambers and into the empty loading bays of the OG Shipping droneship.

Everything seemed to be as it should. The loading layout was rather strange, but Darnell had a habit of taking ships from the other companies he acquired and retrofitting them to suit his own needs. Certainly there was plenty of space. And everywhere she looked, on columns and walls and internal panels, Fassa saw the puce-and-mauve logo of OG Shipping stenciled. Rather sloppily stenciled, in some cases: lines wobbled and droplets of paint spattered the borders of the stencils. Looked like a rush job. Darnell didn't take the trouble to oversee his people personally as she did hers, she thought, and the difference showed.

"Droneship, are you prepared to accept cargo?" she queried the air.

"Prepared. To accept. Cargo. Begin. Transfer." The answer came back from a speaker somewhere behind her, metallic and uninflected like all AI speech. Fassa remembered reading that AI linguists were perfectly capable of designing a more human-sounding speech system, especially with the help of the sophisticated metachips of Shemali design, but that marketing forces wouldn't let them release it. Drones and other AI devices weren't supposed to sound too human; it made people nervous.

"Credit transfer, please," Fassa requested briskly. Darnell had stiffed her on one load of supplies, reselling it and pocketing the profit himself and blandly denying that any of his drones had been anywhere near SpaceBase I. And her own excessive caution, her own refusal to leave any records behind, had given her no way to fight him. Now she demanded payment in advance before a single roll of synthosteel made it onto one of the bastard's drones.

"Your credit transfer will be. Approved. As soon as the. Loading is complete."

Fassa grinned to herself. That speech had sounded considerably more like human inflections than most dronetalk did. She wouldn't put it past Darnell to have diverted some of the new metachips for frivolous applications like improving dronetalk. He hadn't got it quite right, though. She could still tell she was talking to a machine.

And she wasn't about to let a damned droneship cheat her out of the rights to this expensive shipment!

"Credit transfer to be produced when loading is twenty-five percent complete," she said, "as by usual agreement. Or I stop loading there and you don't leave SpaceBase until the credit slip is approved."

"Agreed." The last word from the droneship had a very human sound of resignation to it. Darnell *had* been fooling with the Shemali metachips in his ships; Fassa was now willing to bet on it.

She still felt a vague unease about the operation, but brushed it off. She was just brooding over the Sev Bryley fiasco, that was all. No reason to suppose anything like that would happen again — not with the number of senators and bankers and inspectors Fassa now had personally dedicated to her welfare. Fassa activated the spacebase's comm link and called her hand-picked loading crew to complete the transfer.

With drone-powered lifters and other automated devices, loading the construction materials was a quick job, calling for no more than three men, all of them bound to Fassa by personal loyalty — and by the stock which they had vested in Polo Construction. Those stock options were an expense Fassa regretted, but it was necessary to ensure the absolute silence of her assistants. Once again, while the men went about their business, she cursed the underlying chauvinism of contractors who insisted on building their lifters to the specifications of a six-foot, muscular male body. There was no reason the lifters couldn't be designed so that their controls were within the reach and strength of a smallish woman; the real muscle involved here came from the machines, not from the men. But Fassa was too small to operate the machines. When she calculated what this one fact was costing her in stocks and bonuses to keep her loading crews silent, she was tempted to start her own heavy machinery factory, with lifters and forks and cranes all built so that anybody could operate them at the touch of a button.

Someday, she promised herself. *When I have enough money. When I feel strong enough . . . and secure enough . . . when I am enough.*

Somehow she felt that such a day would never arrive.

But the twenty-five percent mark on transfer had arrived . . . and it was time to claim her credit slip. Fassa motioned to the loading crew to stop. While they waited in position, lifters frozen in mid-arc, she walked back into the partially filled cargo bays of the droneship.

"Credit transfer," she rapped out. "Now!"

"Regret that I do not have facilities to issue credit slips in loading bay area," the droneship replied. "Request that del Parma unit transfer self to cabin area to receive payment."

The inflections were almost human, but the awkward wording was pure dronespeak. Smiling as she waved her hand before the lift-door sensors, Fassa reflected that she would have to recommend some better linguists to Darnell.

The lift-door irised open and Fassa, wrapped in her satisfied thoughts, took one step forward before she took in the glitter of silver and corycium braid against the deep-space black of a Courier Service uniform.

Startled, she flung herself backwards, but the uniformed man grabbed her sleeve just before she was out of reach. Fassa fell back onto the loading dock floor, dragging her assailant with her. He landed heavily on her midsection, knocking the breath out of her. Where were the damned loading crew? Couldn't they see something had gone wrong?

"Fassa del Parma — I arrest you — in the name of Central Worlds — for embezzlement of SpaceBase — construction and supplies," the bastard wheezed. Both his hands were around her wrists now, pinning her to the floor. Fassa gasped for breath, brought up a knee into the brute's crotch, and wriggled free in one movement. Her brain had never stopped working. So there was a witness! Darnell had double-crossed her? All right; dispose of the witness, that was the new problem, then she would deal with the rest.

"Kill that man!" she screamed at the dumbstruck idiots on her loading crew. She raced towards the safety of the spacebase.

The droneship's loading doors slammed shut. How had the bastard managed to transmit the command? He should still be writhing in agony.

He was. But as Fassa looked, he rose to his knees. "Under — arrest," he panted.

"That's what you think," Fassa said with her sweetest smile. What did this fool think, that she was too weak and sentimental to kill a man face to face? He was still on his knees, and she was standing, and the needler in her left sleeve slid into the palm of her hand with the cool solid feel of revenge. Time slowed and the air shimmered about her. The Courier Service brawn was lunging forward now, but he'd never reach her in time. Fassa aimed the needler until she saw a face neatly framed in the viewfinder. Who was he? It didn't matter. He was a total stranger, he was Sev, he was Senator Cenevix, he was Faul del Parma. All turning green around her, and her fingers almost too weak to squeeze the needler; what was happening? Fassa swayed on her feet, squeezed the needler handle and saw an arc of darts ripping wildly through the thick green clouds that surrounded them now. So dizzy . . . her eyes wouldn't stay open to track the darts to their target . . . but she'd been too close to miss. So close . . .

Fassa collapsed in the cloud of sleepgas with which Nancia had, just too late, flooded the closed loading bays. So did Caleb, going down just in front of Fassa with his black and silver uniform all spoiled by blood.

CHAPTER TEN

"Don't gas the lift! Don't gas the lift!"

The shouted commands, coming from a closed-off area behind the fake walls, startled Nancia. She shifted views rapidly, cursing the quick and dirty remodeling job that had left large areas of her own interior cut off from her visual sensors.

Sev Bryley, white-faced, appeared from behind one of the puce-and-mauve pseudoboard walls. "I'll get him out of the loading bay," he snapped without so much as a glance towards Nancia's sensor unit. "You can keep the sleepgas confined to that area?"

"Yes, but —"

"Don't have time for a mask." Bryley was in the lift now, and Nancia could watch him on the agonizingly slow passage down to the loading dock. His chest rose and fell rapidly as he took the deep, rapid breaths of clean air that would keep him going in the loading bay.

Nancia kept the lift door on three-quarter pressure, just enough to let Bryley squeeze through the flexible opening that shut behind him. At the same time she flushed the loading bay with the ventilation system on high power, replacing as much sleepgas as she could with clean air.

Sev's back and shoulders bulged awkwardly half through the lift door. Nancia released the flexible membrane just long enough to let him drag Caleb through into the lift. She kept the ventilation system on high for the long seconds of the ride back. By the time the lift was at cabin level, she could find no measurable trace of sleepgas in the air. But Sev had inhaled enough to make him slump against the wall, too woozy to carry himself and Caleb farther.

"Antidote . . . ?"

"In the corridor," Nancia told him. "*In the corridor!*" She had no housekeeping servos within the lift itself. Sev had to stagger forward, out of the lift, fetching up against the freshly painted corridor wall with a thump. At least it was one of Nancia's true walls; only a few steps away from Sev was an opening from which the servos could dispense stimulants and medical aids. Sev took two gasping breaths of the clean air, reached into the shallow dish presented by the opening in the wall, grabbed a handful of ampules and crushed them under his nose.

"More," he commanded.

"You've already exceeded the recommended dosage."

"I need a clear head *now*," Sev growled.

Was there more blood on Caleb's uniform? Impossible to tell what he'd been hit with, or how bad the damage was. Nancia sent another set of stim ampules to the servo tray. Sev broke these more cautiously, one at a time. After the third deep breath of pungent stimulant, he dropped the rest back in the tray. "Medical supplies!"

"What?"

"I'll tell you when I know." He was on his knees, blocking Nancia's view as he peeled back the front of Caleb's spoiled uniform. "Something to stop bleeding . . . there shouldn't be so much from a needler . . . ahh. The . . . " he used a Vega slang term that was not in any of Nancia's vocabulary hedra. "She loaded it with anticoagulant. And . . . other things, I think. Analyze?" He dropped a torn and bloody strip of cloth into the servo tray. Nancia transferred it to the medical lab and replaced it with ampules of HyperClot which Sev injected directly into Caleb's veins.

"That's stopped the bleeding," he said finally, rising

to his feet. "But I'm not happy about his color. Does that look like normal sleepgas pallor to you?"

"No." The one word was all Nancia could manage.

"Me neither. Can you analyze what else was in the needler?"

"No. Organics of some sort, but it's too complex for me." Concentrating on the technical problem helped to steady her voice. "I haven't the facilities here. I am contacting Murasaki Base for Net access to medtechs."

But Murasaki Base could suggest only that she transport Caleb to the nearest planet-based clinic as quickly as possible. If Fassa's needler had been loaded with Ganglicide—

"It wasn't Ganglicide," Nancia said quickly. "He'd be dead by now. Besides, no one would do such a thing."

"You might be surprised," said the infuriatingly calm managing brain of Murasaki Base. "But I agree, probably not Ganglicide. There are, however, slower-acting nerve poisons which, untreated, can be just as fatal. From what you report of his convulsive reaction, I would suggest immediate medical treatment by someone experienced with nerve poisons and their antidotes."

"Thanks very much," Nancia snapped. Sev had wrapped Caleb in all the blankets he could collect, but nothing stopped Caleb's incessant nervous shivering. And every once in a while his spine arched backward while he cried out in delirium. "We came from Raz-mak Base in Bellatrix subspace. You're not seriously suggesting I take a man in this condition through Singularity, are you?"

"There happens to be an excellent clinic on Bahati," the Murasaki Base brain replied. "If you were calm enough to check the Net records I'm transmitting, CN, you'd see that the assistant director there has a strong background in nerve poison research. With your permission, I will alert the Summerlands clinic to receive an emergency patient for the direct care of Dr. Alpha bint Hezra-Fong."

Time stopped. Snatches of conversation forgotten for nearly four years echoed in Nancia's memory. *An expert in Ganglicide therapy right there at the Summerlands clinic . . . testing Ganglicide on unwitting subjects . . . so far gone on Blissto they didn't even know what was happening to them. . . .*

She had the full conversations recorded and safely stored away. She didn't need them. Her own human memory was mercilessly replaying words she'd tried to forget.

Did she dare put Caleb in Alpha bint Hezra-Fong's hands?

Did she dare *not* take him to the clinic?

There was really no choice.

They were only a few minutes from Bahati, but the time seemed like hours to Nancia. She blessed the multiprocessing capability that allowed her to perform multiple tasks at once. While one bank of processors controlled the landing computations, Nancia assigned two more to maintaining the comm link with Murasaki and opening a new link with Bahati. She reached the director of Summerlands and explained her requirements while simultaneously assimilating Murasaki Base's calm instructions.

The combination of Fassa's arrest and Caleb's wounds presented a complex political problem. Nancia was almost grateful for the complications; they gave her something to think about during the endless minutes before touchdown.

Courier Service policy strictly prohibited the transport of prisoners on a brainship with no brawn. Nancia thought it was a silly policy, born of fears that were decades out of date. Earlier, less cleverly designed brainships might have been vulnerable to passenger takeover, but she was well protected against any little tricks that Fassa might come up with. The auxiliary synaptic circuits known as the Helva Modification would prevent any attempt to close off her sensory contact with her own ship-body.

All the same, Murasaki Base informed Nancia, the regulations existed for good reason and it was not up to a brainship to pick and choose which Service regs she would obey.

"All right, all *right*." Had Caleb twitched again? Summerlands Clinic personnel were standing by to collect him as soon as they landed. Bahati Spaceport was issuing final landing instructions. "I'll hand Fassa del Parma over to Bahati authorities."

"That you will not," the Murasaki Base brain informed her. "I've been in contact with CenDip while you were fussing over your brawn. The young lady is a political hot potato."

"A what?"

"Sorry. Old Earth slang. Never thought about the literal meaning . . . let's see, I think a potato is some kind of tuber, but why anybody would try to ignite one . . . oh, well." Murasaki Base dismissed the intriguing linguistic question for later consideration. "What it means is that nobody really wants to handle her trial. Well, you can see for yourself, can't you, Nancia? If you're going to try a High Families brat and send her to prison, you don't do it out on some nowhere world at the edge of the galaxy. You bring her back to Central and you are very, very careful that all procedures are followed. To the letter. CenDip has strict instructions that *nothing* is to go wrong with this case; there's a certain highly placed authority who has taken a personal interest in stopping High Families corruption."

"You can tell your highly placed authority to — " Nancia transmitted a burst of muddy tones and discordant high-pitched sounds.

"Can't," said Murasaki Base rather smugly.

"Softshells can't receive that kind of input. Fortunately for them, I might add. Where did a nice brainship like you pick up that kind of language?"

Nancia landed at Bahati Spacefield as gently as a feather floating in the breeze. She opened her upper-level cabin doors and waited for the spaceport workers to bring a floatube. They'd already been informed of the reason why she didn't want to open the lower doors; the equipment should have been ready and waiting — ah! There it was now.

"Well, then, just inform your 'highly placed authority,' that a few little things have *already* gone wrong with this operation," Nancia told Murasaki Base. "And if I can't transport del Parma without a brawn, and I can't hand her over to Bahati, what am I supposed to do with her?"

"Wait for your new brawn, of course," Murasaki Base informed her.

"And just how long will *that* take?" They were loading Caleb onto a stretcher now.

"About half an hour, if he can pack as quickly as he should."

"What?"

In answer, Murasaki Base transmitted the CenDip instruction bytes directly. "Senior Central Diplomatic service person Armontillado-y-Medoc, Forister, currently R&R at Summerlands Clinic, previous brawn status inactivated upon joining CenDip Central Date 2732, reactivated 2754 for single duty tour returning prisoner del Parma y Polo, Fassa, to Central Worlds jurisdiction."

Before taking Caleb away, the Summerlands med-techs were running tests and dosing him with all-purpose antidotes. Alpha bint Hezra-Fong had come personally to oversee the operation. Nancia's sensors caught her dark, sharp-featured face from several angles while she leaned over Caleb. Her expression showed nothing but keen professional

interest: no hint of any evil plans to use Caleb as an unwitting experimental subject.

And no compassion.

And now he was going into the floatube, beyond
Nancia's sensor range... beyond her help. *Where was Sev?*
Nancia scanned the sensor banks until she located him in
one of the passenger cabins that had been concealed behind her fake paneling. He was guarding a groggy Fassa
who had just begun to come out of the sleepgas.

"Sev, I need you to go with Caleb," Nancia
announced.

"CN-935, please acknowledge receipt of formal orders," Murasaki Base input on another channel.

"Can't," Sev answered without looking round.
"Have to guard the prisoner. Check regulations."

Nancia knew he was right. The same stupid CS regs
that forbade her to transport Fassa without a brawn
would also forbid her to take sole charge of a prisoner.
"Are regulations more important than Caleb's life?"

"Nancia, he's getting the best possible medical care.
What are you *worried* about?"

"CN-935 RESPOND!" Murasaki Base shouted.

The floatube was a speck on the horizon. They weren't
stopping at the spaceport; they were taking Caleb directly to Summerlands. Where Alpha bint Hezra-Fong could
do anything, anything at all, to him, and Nancia wouldn't
even know until it was too late....

"Instructions received and accepted," she transmitted to Murasaki Base in one short burst. "Now
GET THAT BRAWN ON BOARD!" Forister Armontillado-y-Medoc? Nancia remembered the short, quiet
man she'd transported somewhere, years earlier, to
solve some crisis. The one who'd spent all his time on
board reading. No matter what his records said, he
wasn't her idea of a brawn. But who cared? The sooner
he was here, the sooner Sev could be released from
guard duty to go watch over Caleb.

*   *   *

Fassa was choking on the bottom of a lake. Weeds twined around her ankles, and the clear air was impossibly far away, miles above the green water that pressed her down and pushed at her mouth and ears and nose with gentle, implacable persistence. She tried to kick free of the weeds; they clung tighter, reaching up past ankle and calf and knee with green slimy fingers that pressed close against her thighs. When she looked down, the weeds shaped themselves into pale green faces with open mouths and closed eyes. All the men who'd given her their hearts and their integrity and pieces of their souls were there on the bottom of the lake, and they wanted to keep her there with them. Her chest was bursting with the need to breathe. If she gave back their souls, would they let her go?

She tried to strip off the charm bracelet on her left wrist, but the catch was stuck; tried to break the chain, but it was too strong. Green lake water seeped into her mouth with a bitter taste, and black spots danced before her eyes. She tugged the chain over her hand, scraping a knuckle raw, and flung it at the hungry ghosts. The sparkling charms of corycium and iridium floated lazily down among the muddy weeds, and Fassa was released to rise through rings of ever-lightening water until she broke the surface and breathed in the air that hurt like fire in her lungs.

She was lying on a bunk in a spaceship cabin. Sev Bryley was seated cross-legged on the opposite bunk, watching her with unsmiling attention. And the burning in her lungs was real, as was the throbbing pain in her head; sleepgas hangover. Now she remembered: surprise and violence and a fool who'd been where he had no business, and the gas flooding the cargo bay while she tried to hold her breath.

It all added up to a failure so crushing she could not bear to think about it yet. And Sev, the man who'd never given her a piece of his soul to keep in her charm bracelet — was he the one who'd engineered this disaster?

"What are you doing here?" she croaked.

"Making sure you came out of the sleepgas without complications," Sev said. His voice sounded thin and strained, as if he were trying to reach her from a great distance. "Some people have a convulsive reaction. It looked for a while like you were going to be one of them."

And that had worried him? Perhaps he still cared for her a little, then. Perhaps her experiment of taking him aboard the *Xanadu* hadn't been a total failure, after all. Fassa stretched, experimentally, and saw the way his eyes followed her movements. Perhaps something could yet be salvaged from this catastrophe. After all, they were alone on the droneship . . .

"Not convulsions," she said, languorously wriggling her toes and proceeding upward, muscle by muscle, to make certain that every inch of her own amazing body was back under her command again. "Just bad dreams."

"What sort of dreams?" Sev inquired.

Fassa sat up, rather more quickly than she had intended, and fell back against the cabin wall. "The sort that make you afraid to die."

"Thus conscience doth make cowards of us all," Sev agreed with no change of tone, and Fassa felt a stab of regret. She could have liked this man who so quickly picked up on her thoughts, capping her unvoiced quotations. If only he weren't so obstinately on the wrong side! Ah, well, perhaps that could be changed. It would damn well *have* to be changed if she hoped to get out of this, she reminded herself.

"Speak for yourself," she told him. "My conscience isn't all that troubled; I've done nothing more than what everybody does, just trying to get ahead by my own efforts." Wrong tone, wrong tone. She didn't want to argue with Bryley; she wanted to seduce him. No. Needed to seduce him. That was all.

And she wasn't going to get anywhere in her present condition. Fassa pushed sweaty, matted dark hair away from her forehead with a genuine moan of pain. "God, I must look like hell," she said. "Would you mind very much getting out of here so I can clean up?"

"Yes," said Sev, "I would. You're not to be left unguarded until we return to Central. Orders from CenDip."

Fassa moaned again. If CenDip was interesting itself in her case, she was worse off than she'd thought. Never mind. Central was a long way off. For the present she was alone on a droneship with this gorgeous hunk, and with any luck at all she'd make him change his allegiances before the official transports arrived to carry her to trial.

After only a little pouting and posing she managed to persuade Sev that propping himself against the wall outside her cabin would be adequate to fulfill his guard duty. It was, Fassa thought with satisfaction, a beginning. Now he would feel that this cabin was her territory. When he came in again, it would be at her invitation . . . and invitations could lead to all sorts of interesting things. She washed from head to foot, kicked her stained and crumpled clothes in a corner under the bunk, splashed a little extra cool water over her face, and wrapped a sheet around herself in lieu of fresh clothes. This would be a real test of her abilities. No cosmetics, hair combed straight with no styling, a scratchy Service-issue sheet instead of a clinging gown, and this bare cabin for a romantic setting!

"Fassa baby, you're so sweet, I just can't resist you," Faul del Parma used to moan when he came into her room and buried himself in her. And she'd been an awkward, sullen little girl then, with her black hair in thin tight braids. She'd worn the ugliest, plainest

clothes she could find, but that didn't put Faul off.

For the first time Fassa deliberately summoned up the memories she'd tried for so long to bury, seeking the confidence she needed to go on. She really was irresistible to men. Faul del Parma had proved that, hadn't he? Even knowing it was wrong, even knowing she hated it, he'd still refused to let her alone.

"It's everything about you, the way you walk, the way you smile up at me with those big sooty lashes half covering your eyes."

Instead of giving her confidence, the memories made Fassa feel grimy. She must have invited him, not with words, but with something about the way she walked and looked at him. Somehow she'd made Daddy want her without even knowing it. She was a bad little girl and if Mama ever found out . . .

Somewhere in the back of her mind, Mama screamed and fell endlessly through the glittering interior atrium of the hotel, tumbling in a cloud of gauzy draperies. And it was all her fault. Fassa cried out once and threw something across the cabin with all her might, and Sev Bryley burst through the unlatched door.

"What's the matter? What happened?"

His arms went around her and Fassa rested against the fresh starched fabric of his shirt, feeling the strong beat of his heart beneath her face. For some reason she was crying; she couldn't stop crying for long minutes while Sev just held her. Not easing her backwards towards the bunk, not letting his hands slide artfully downward in a disguised caress. Just holding her.

"Well," Fassa said finally, gulping down the last of her sobs, "I told you; I have bad dreams."

"You seemed wide awake when I left you."

Fassa drew a shaky deep breath. "I — I'm afraid to be alone just now," she said. It happened to be true. "Could you stay with me?"

"As it happens," Sev told her, "I was going to anyway." He released her, as if sensing that she was recovered for the moment, and moved a step backward. Fassa sighed again, with a little more forethought this time, and watched his eyes. Yes, he was aware of what those deep breaths were doing to the sliding knot that held the sheet together between her breasts, and he couldn't take his eyes off the creamy skin that contrasted with the stark white of the sheet. Good. She had a job to do, here; she had best think about that and nothing else, or she'd never win this man to her side before she was taken away for trial.

"Oh, that's right," she said, allowing a tear to creep into the corner of one eye; not difficult, in her present shaky mood. "I forgot; you're my jailer, aren't you?"

Sev looked uncomfortable at this assessment, as she'd wanted him to. "I wouldn't put it quite like that. But someone does have to stay with you until . . . "

"Until the end," Fassa finished for him. "What sort of sentences are in favor these days? Will it be hard labor, do you think?" She tossed her head and gave him her Christian-facing-the-lions look, all nobility and virgin defiance. At the same time she moved slightly so that the sheet molded over one thigh, giving him (she hoped) visions of what sort of *hard labor* she might be good for.

"You'll have a fair trial," Sev told her, "and a chance to speak in your own defense."

"*Will* I?" Fassa challenged him. "Look at me. Don't you think there'll be some old judge who'd just love to see me mindwiped? They'll be thinking what a pity it is to waste such a beautiful body, keep the body, just wipe out the personality and start over."

"Oh, I'm sure they won't do that," Sev said, but he sounded less righteously certain than he'd been a moment before. Fassa mentally applauded her own cleverness. There wasn't much point in trying to convince Sev that she was innocent of the charges against her, not when he was Central's prime witness. Much better to switch the topic to the corruption at all levels of government. Sev knew something about that. Let him stew over the assertion that she couldn't possibly get a fair trial, let him think — as he must be thinking now — about the danger that she'd end up as the mindwiped toy of some corrupt official.

"You know it happens," Fassa said in a low voice. "You know how much cheating there is in the government. Everybody wants something for himself. One of them will want *me*, and then — " She blew a kiss into the air with a mocking smile. "Bye-bye, Fassa del Parma!" Time to let the sheet fall to the ground, giving Sev a good look about what some dirty old man would get if he didn't get there first. She moved towards him, inch by inch, watching the color rise in his sharp features, watching the blue eyes darken with desire. "You could at least say good-bye properly, Sev, my love," she whispered.

She paused, eyes closed, awaiting the warmth of his arms about her and his mouth on hers.

"I think not," said Sev Bryley, and while Fassa's eyes flew open in shocked disbelief he took the two steps that brought him to the cabin door.

Once outside the cabin, Sev reactivated the guardlock mechanism that would prevent Fassa from leaving. He leaned against the wall and wiped his forehead with the back of one hand. It wasn't much help; he still felt as hot as if he'd just done a ten-mile run in the Capellan jungle. He needed a cold shower. And that ten-mile run might not be a bad idea, either, except he couldn't leave Nancia alone to guard Fassa.

He could get some extra help, though — and some insurance against temptation. "Nancia?" he said in a low voice, looking upward at the angle between ceiling and roof where her auditory sensors were installed. "Nancia, I think you'd better activate full sensors within Fassa's cabin. I know it's a breach of the prisoner's privacy, but this is a very dangerous woman. And, Nancia? You'd better keep the sensors on at all times. Even when I'm with Ms. del Parma."

Sev thought that over and decided he hadn't worded that last request strongly enough. "*Especially* when I'm with Fassa," he rephrased.

"I'd already done that, Sev," Nancia responded from the wall speaker. "Don't worry. Everything has been observed and recorded."

"Excellent," said Sev between his teeth. "I'm sure that little scene will be vastly amusing to somebody who's not troubled by hormonal urges. Now, if you don't mind, just keep watching Fassa and let me know if she tries anything. I'll be in the ship's exercise room."

"What for?"

"Taking care of my hormones," Sev said. He stamped off to improve his weight-lifting record.

"FN-935, Forister Armontillado-y-Medoc requests permission to come aboard."

"Permission granted."

Even to her own ears, Nancia sounded brusque. After a grudging nanosecond's thought she added formally, "Welcome aboard, Forister Armontillado-y-Medoc."

The short, spare man whom she'd last seen heading into the tangled planetary conflicts of the Tran Phon guerrillas on Charon dropped three heavy pieces of baggage onto the lift with a grunt of relief. *I'm getting an old man who can't even carry his own luggage without getting out of breath.* But as if to contradict the unspoken criticism, Forister waved the lift upwards with his luggage and took the circular stairs. Nancia watched his progress from sensor to sensor. He moved with quick, neat steps, economical of his motions. You couldn't say he was bounding up the stairs, but he did get to the top more quickly than she'd expected; and there wasn't a gray hair out of place or a drop of sweat on his forehead when he entered the central cabin.

"Greetings, Nancia," Forister said. Unlike Caleb, he looked directly at the titanium bulkhead that housed Nancia's human body and brain. His direct gaze was rather disconcerting to Nancia, who'd been used to Caleb wandering round the ship and addressing her without turning his head, counting on her efficient sensor system to pick up his words wherever he might be. She took a moment to look over this strange elderly brawn and prepare her response. Light eyes in a tanned face, with a network of crinkles around the eyes as if he were accustomed to looking deeply at whatever he saw; hints of red and ginger in the graying hair; a light, erect, relaxed stance, as if he were prepared to move in any direction at a moment's notice. *He may do. But he's not Caleb!*

"You seem remarkably fit for someone who's just been recuperating at Summerlands," Nancia said at last.

Forister grimaced. "Oh, I'm fit enough, if that's what's been worrying you, FN. The stay at Summerlands was not for any medical reasons."

"Then what? The orders I received said you were there for R&R."

"Um. Yes. Well, they would, wouldn't they?" Forister said, maddeningly, while Nancia wondered if the man ever gave a straight answer to anything. Maybe that was trained out of you in the diplomatic service.

At last he vouchsafed one more sentence that could be considered an explanation. "My last posting for CenDip was . . . shall we say, stressful, and things didn't work out as well as I'd hoped."

"Charon?" Nancia asked.

The brawn blinked once, surprised. "Why, no. Why — oh, I remember. I had the honor of being transported to Charon by you, didn't I? Some years ago — you were the CN-935 then, as I recall. My condolences on the loss of your partner."

"It's only temporary," Nancia said. "Which reminds me. I wouldn't wish to hurry your unpacking, but as soon as you're ready, I'd like you to take over guarding the prisoner. Sev Bryley is needed at Summerlands to look after my brawn."

"As you wish." Forister did not quite click his heels together as he executed a perfect bow in the direction of the titanium column. He wheeled, collected his bags from the open lift and marched down the hall to the brawn's cabin — *Caleb's cabin* — leaving Nancia with the feeling that she had been unpleasantly brusque. She opened a speaker in the cabin.

"If you don't object, we could continue our conversation while you unpack."

"No objection," said Forister. He was slightly out of breath now, after lifting the heavy bags to his bunk. What on Earth *did* the man travel with? A fortune in Corycium bars buried beneath his underwear? The first things he drew out of the bags were commonplace enough: CenDip formal dress and spare shirts, toiletries and a handful of laser-printed datahedra.

He might not object, but he wasn't being very helpful either. Well, she hadn't been as friendly as she might; it was up to her to make the first move. "What was your last posting, then, if it wasn't Charon? And why did you pick Summerlands?"

"Summerlands has a very good reputation as a rest facility," Forister said. "I expect you're unduly worried about your former brawn; the medical staff there is top-quality."

"It's not their technical skills I'm worried about," Nancia told him. There was movement in Fassa's cabin. She had been keeping the sensors there down to monitor level; now she activated full pick-up and saw that Sev had gone in to talk to Fassa. The girl was fully dressed this time, and they were sitting on opposite bunks; she didn't think Sev would encounter any real problem. All the same, she captured their quiet conversation and listened to it with one ear while she watched Forister and wished he would hurry up with his unpacking. Now he had got to the bottom layer of the first bag, and she saw what had weighed his luggage down so: nothing but a lot of antiques. One antique book after another, kilos and kilos of them, and doubtless no more information in the lot of them than could be stored in a few facets of a datahedron! There was no accounting for tastes.

"Isn't Summerlands rather remote for a man of your importance?" Nancia probed. She knew she was being pushy, but she didn't care. If Forister was in with Alpha and her criminal friends, she didn't dare set him to guard Fassa — nor did she dare send him back to the clinic to watch over Caleb. She would have to get on the datastream to Murasaki Base at once.

"I've family in the Nyota system," Forister told her. "I was hoping to make a brief visit after I left Summerlands. And I'd a friend at the clinic."

"Alpha bint Hezra-Fong," Nancia surmised. She might as well face all the bad news at once.

"Good God, no!" Forister seemed genuinely startled. "If that's what you think of the company I keep, no wonder you've been so hostile. Somebody else entirely, I assure you."

"Who?"

"I'm not at liberty to say just now. If all goes well — " Forister broke off and rather fussily adjusted the portable folding shelf where he had stowed his books, tightening the spring-bindings that would keep them in place in case of any rapid ship's movements. "But whether it comes off or not," he said, more slowly, "I won't be here to help. *And* I won't have any free time afterwards to visit in this system. I'll be on my way back to Central with you, and once I land there, God knows what six urgent assignments will be waiting." He looked up, directly into Nancia's primary cabin sensor. "So you see, dear lady, this assignment is no more to my liking than it is to yours. I hope we can sink our differences for the duration — "

"*Hush.*" The conversation in Fassa's cabin had suddenly become very interesting; Nancia didn't want to have to wait and replay it, she wanted to know what was going on right now.

It appeared that Fassa was trying to plea bargain with information on some of the other young people who'd been involved in that vicious wager. She began by hinting to Sev that she might be able to inform on a whole gang of criminals in the Nyota system if doing so would get her a reduced sentence. Sev, quite properly, told her that he wasn't authorized to make such promises.

"Oh, what the hell," Fassa said wearily at last. "If I'm going down, I won't go alone. You might as well know everything. At least then you'll see that I'm not the worst of the bunch by a long shot."

She began telling Sev all she knew about Darnell Overton-Glaxely and the ways in which he'd worked his illegal Net access, first to bring in shipping bids that were always just a shade lower than those of his competitors, then to destroy the credit and acquire the stock of any small businesses he felt like adding to his empire.

"All very interesting," Sev told her. "But if Overton-Glaxely is as clever as you say at accessing private Net datastreams, he'll have been clever enough to leave no traces of his taps."

"Oh, he's not clever at all," Fassa said. "He was taught how to tap into the datastream — "

"By?" Sev prompted gently.

Fassa shook her head. She had gone rather white about the lips. "It doesn't matter. Nobody you're likely to catch up with. Not me, if that's what you're thinking; I haven't got that kind of brains."

"I never suspected you had," Sev said, rather too

solemnly. Fassa gave him a suspicious glance. His lips were twitching. She aimed a mock blow at him.

"That's right, insult my intelligence!"

Sev caught her wrist and held it for a long moment while Nancia wondered if it was time to interrupt. At last his fingers relaxed. Fassa subsided onto her bunk. There was a white ring about her wrist where Sev had held her; she rubbed it absently while she went on talking. "Never mind about the Net, then. There's other ways to prove it. One of the men Darnell ruined found out a little too much about his methods, and Darnell sent him to Summerlands."

At that point Nancia decided that Forister had better hear this too. Whatever she thought of the man as a replacement for her Caleb, he *was* a trusted CenDip senior civil servant. He had friends in Summerlands. And he seemed to share her opinion of Dr. bint Hezra-Fong. She piped the input from Fassa's cabin through her speakers in Forister's cabin. After a moment's stunned silence, Forister sat down amid the piles of antiques on his bunk and listened carefully.

"Darnell thought Alpha would kill the man for him. She'd had a bunch of accidents with the tests she ran on her charity patients; she was getting quite good at faking death certificates with innocent-seeming causes of death. She used to boast about it at our annual meetings. One more wouldn't have been any problem for her. But she didn't kill him. She keeps him so full of Seductron that he doesn't know who he is, and whenever she wants Darnell to do her a favor, she threatens to cut the man's Seductron dosage."

"His name?" Sev demanded.

Fassa looked down. "I'd like some assurances that you'll see my sentence reduced."

"You know I can't do that," Sev told her.

She twisted her fingers together. "You could lose the records of this last trip, though. Without your testimony and the recordings, there wouldn't be any hard evidence against me." She looked up, eyes brilliant with unshed tears. "*Please*, Sev? I thought you cared for me a little."

"You were wrong," said Sev in a voice as dead and even as any droneship's artificially generated speech.

"Then what do I have? Why should I give you a damned thing?" Fassa pounded on the yielding surface of the bunk in frustration. Her fists sank into the plasmaform and left momentary dents that smoothed out as soon as she lifted her hands. "Oh, all right. Go ahead and see me mindwiped, or sent to prison until I'm too old to care," she said wearily. "Why should the others get away with it when my life is ruined? The man's name is Valden Allen Hopkirk, and he used to own Hopkirk Glimware right here on Bahati. Is that enough for you, or would you like his Central Citizen Code as well?"

"Any little thing you can tell us would be much appreciated," said Sev carefully.

"Well, I don't happen to know his CCC, so you're out of luck!" Fassa snapped. "Wait — wait — there's more."

"There is?"

"Find Hopkirk, and you'll have evidence on Alpha and Darnell both," Fassa said rapidly. "But there's another one you ought to get. His name's Blaize. . . . "

In the brawn's cabin, Forister lowered his head to rest on his clenched hands. "Blaize Armontillado-Perez y Medoc," he whispered. "No. No."

I've family in the Nyota system . . . I was going to visit after I left Summerlands . . .

Nancia cut off the audio transmission to Forister's cabin and shut down her own sensors there. She listened alone while Fassa babbled out the details of Blaize's felonious career on Angalia; the diverting of PTA shipments, the slave labor and torture of the native population he was supposed to be guarding.

Some day Forister would have to know and face those details, but not yet. She would leave him alone until he requested the recordings of this conversation, and then she would let him listen in privacy.

And so Nancia was the only witness when Fassa's confessional came to an abrupt ending. After she finished the tale of Blaize's misdeeds, Sev probed her.

"I've looked up the records of that first voyage," he said, almost casually. "There were five of you in it together, weren't there? You, Dr. bint Hezra-Fong, Overton-Glaxely, Armontillado-Perez y Medoc, and one other. Polyon de Gras-Waldheim, newly commissioned from the Academy. What was his part in the wager?"

Fassa clamped her lips shut and slowly shook her head. "I can't tell you any more," she whispered. "Only — don't let them send me to Shemali. Kill me first. I know you never cared for me, but as one human being to another — kill me first. Please."

"You're wrong in thinking I never cared for you," Sev said after a long silence.

"You said so yourself."

"You asked if I liked you a little," he corrected her. "And I don't. You're vain and self-centered and you may have killed a good man and you've yet to show any interest at all in Caleb's fate. I don't much like you at all."

"Yes, I know."

"Unfortunately," he went on with no change of expression, "like it or not — and believe me, I'm not at all happy about the situation — I do seem to love you. Not," he said almost gently, "that it'll do either of us much good, under the circumstances. But I did think you ought to know."

● CHAPTER ELEVEN

Caleb recovered with amazing speed. Two hours after his arrival at the clinic, forty minutes after Alpha bint Hezra-Fong had analyzed the poisons in his blood and slapped on stimpatches of the appropriate antidotes, the nervous convulsions had stopped. Nancia knew exactly when that happened, because by then she had thought to send Sev Bryley to Summerlands with a contact button discreetly replacing the top stud in his dress tunic and a second contact button to clip onto Caleb's hospital gown. While Forister remained on board as a nominal guard for Fassa, Sev lounged about the public rooms at Summerlands trying to look like a worried friend-or-relative and chatting up the recuperating VIPs. Nancia watched the clinic from two angles: the convulsive shuddering view of a cracked white ceiling, emanating from Caleb's contact button, and the repetitive views of artificial potted palms and doddering old celebrities to whom Sev talked. On the whole, the potted palms were more valuable than the celebrities; at least they didn't waste Sev's time with their reminiscences of events a century past.

"None of these people know anything about Hopkirk," she whispered through Sev's contact button.

"I've noticed," he replied as the senile director emeritus of the Bahati Musical College, aged one hundred seventy-five Standard Central Years, tottered away for his noon meds.

"Can't you do something more productive?"

"Give me time. We don't want to be obvious. And stop hissing at me. They'll think I'm talking to myself and hearing voices."

"From what I've seen of these befuddled gentry, that'll make you fit right in."

"Only," said Sev grimly, "if they don't hear the voices too."

Nancia hated to leave him with the last word in an argument, but she was distracted at that moment. Something had happened — or stopped happening. Caleb's sensor button was no longer transmitting a jiggling view of the cracks on the ceiling; the image was still and perfectly clear.

Not quite still. A regular, gentle motion assured her that he still breathed.

A moment later, two aides exchanged a flurry of rapid, low-voiced but mainly cheerful comments over Caleb's bed. Nancia gathered that the news was good; his (three-syllable Greek root) was up, his (four-syllable Latin derivation) was down, they were putting him on a regular dosage of (two-word Denebian form), and as soon as he was conscious they were to start him on a physical therapy routine.

She complained to Forister about the jargon.

"Now you know how the rest of the world feels about brains and brawns," he said soothingly. "You know, there are people who think decomposition theory is just a little hard to follow. They accuse us of mystifying the mathematics on purpose."

"Huh. There's nothing mystical about mathematics," Nancia grumbled. "This medical stuff is something else again."

"Why don't you translate the terms and find out what they mean?"

"I didn't have a classical education," Nancia told him. "I'm going to buy one when we get back to civilization, though. I want full datahedra of Latin, Greek, and medical terminology. With these new hyperchips I should be able to access the terms almost as fast as a native speaker."

Somebody shouted just out of visual range of Caleb's sensor button. The view of the hospital ceiling swayed, blurred, and was replaced by glass windows, green fields, and a white-clothed arm coming from the left. "Here," said a calm, competent voice just before Caleb bent over the permalloy bowl before him and gave up the contents of his last meal.

The contact button gave Nancia a very clear, sharply detailed close-up view of the results.

After that, though, he recovered his strength with amazing speed. Throughout the day Nancia followed his sessions with the physical therapist. At the same time she tracked Sev while he prowled the hallways of Summerlands Clinic and listened for any scrap of information about a patient named Valden Allen Hopkirk.

By mid-afternoon a new aide was able to assure Caleb that there would be no permanent nerve damage as a result of the attack.

"You're weak, though, and we'll need to retrain some of the nerve pathways; the stuff your space pirate used was a neural scrambler. Damage is reversible," the aide said briskly, "but I'd advise a prolonged course of therapy. You certainly won't be cleared to act as a brawn for some time. Has your ship been notified?"

"She knows everything that goes on here," said Caleb, placing one finger briefly on the edge of the contact button.

Nancia got a good look at the aide's face. The man looked thoughtful, perhaps worried. "I . . . see. And, um, I suppose the button has a dead-man switch? Some alarm if it's inactivated or removed?"

"Absolutely," Nancia responded through the contact button before Caleb could tell the truth. Some such arrangement would be a great safeguard for Caleb, and she wished Central had thought of it. But failing that, the illusion of the arrangement might give him some protection. She went on through the tiny speaker, ignoring Caleb's attempts to interrupt her. "Please notify all staff concerned of the arrangement. I would be sorry to have to sound a general alarm just because some ignorant staff member accidentally interfered with my monitoring system."

"That would indeed be . . . unfortunate," said the aide thoughtfully.

After he left, Caleb said quietly into the contact button, "That was a lie, Nancia."

"Was it?" Nancia parried. "Do you think you know *all* my capabilities? Who's the 'brain' of this partnership?"

"I see!"

Nancia rather hoped he didn't. At least she'd avoided lying directly to Caleb. That was something . . . but not enough.

She had never before minded her inability to move about freely on planetary surfaces. Psych Department's testing before she entered brainship training showed that she valued the ability to fly between the stars far more than the limited mobility of planet-bound creatures. "I could have told them that," Nancia responded when the test results were reported to her. "Who wants to roll about on surface when they could have all of deep space to play in? If I want anything planetside, they can bring it to me at the spaceport."

But they couldn't bring her Caleb. And she couldn't go to the Summerlands clinic to watch over him. Nancia could see and hear everything that passed within range of those buttons. She could even send instructions to the wearers. But she could not *act*. She was reduced to fretting over the slow progress they were making and worrying about the medications being inserted into Caleb's blood stream.

"Haven't you found anything yet?" she demanded of Forister. Since Fassa had spent the day crying quietly in her cabin, Forister interpreted his "guard" duties

rather liberally. He was on board and available in case
of any escape attempt, but he told Nancia that he saw
no reason to waste his time sitting on a hard bench outside Fassa's cabin door. Instead, he sat before a
touchscreen in the central cabin, inserting delicate
computer linkages into Alpha's clinic records and
scanning for some hint of where she'd put the witness
they needed.

Forister straightened and sighed. "I have found," he
told her, "four hundred gigamegs of patient charts,
containing detailed records of all their medications,
treatments, and data readouts."

"Well, then, why don't you just look up Hopkirk
and find out what she's done with him?" Nancia
demanded.

In response, Forister tapped one finger on the
touchscreen and slapped his palm over Nancia's
analog input. The data he had retrieved was shunted
directly into Nancia's conscious memory stores. It felt
like having the contents of a medical library injected
directly into her skull. Nancia winced, shut down her
instinctive read-responses, and opened a minuscule
slit of awareness onto a tiny portion of the data.

It was an incomprehensible jumble of medical terminology, packed without regard for paragraphing or
spacing, with peculiar symbolic codes punctuating the
strings of jargon.

She opened another slit and "saw" the same tightly-
packed gibberish.

"It's not indexed by patient name," Forister explained. "Names are encoded — for privacy reasons, I
suppose. If the data is indexed by anything, it might be
on type of treatment. Or it might be based on a hashed
list of meds. I really can't find any organizing principle
yet. Also," he added, unnecessarily, "it's compressed."

"We know he's being kept quiet by controlled over-
doses of Seductron," Nancia said. "Why not . . . oh." As

she spoke, she had been scanning the datastream. There was no mention of Seductron. "Illicit drug," she groaned. "Officially, there's no such treatment. She'll have encoded it as something else."

"I should have taken Latin," Forister nodded. "Capellan seemed so much more useful for a diplomat . . . Ah, well."

"Can you keep hacking into the records?" Nancia asked. "There might be a clue somewhere else."

Forister looked mildly offended. "Please, dear lady. 'Hacking' is a criminal offense."

"But isn't that what you're doing?"

"I may be temporarily on brawn service," Forister said, "but I am a permanent member of the Central Diplomatic Service. Code G, if that means anything to you. As such, I have diplomatic immunity. Hacking is illegal; whatever I do is not illegal; hence, it's not hacking." He smiled benignly and traced a spiraling path inward from the boundaries of the touchscreen, wiping the previous search and opening a new way into the labyrinth of the Summerlands Clinic records.

"*I* should have taken *logic*," Nancia muttered. "I think there's something wrong with your syllogism. Code G. That means you're a *spy*?" Caleb would never forgive her for this. Consorting with spies, breaking into private records . . . The fact that she was working as much to save him as to track down criminals wouldn't palliate her offense in his eyes.

"Mmm. You may call me X-39 if you like." Humming to himself, Forister smoothed out the path he had begun and traced a new, more complex pattern on the touchscreen.

"Isn't that rather pointless," Nancia inquired, "seeing that I already know your name?"

"Hmm? Ah, yes — there we go!" Forister chuckled with satisfaction as he opened his access to a new segment of Summerlands Clinic's computer system.

"Supremely pointless, like most espionage. Most diplomacy, too, come to think of it. No, we don't use code names. But I've always thought it would be rather fun to be known as X-39."

"Have you indeed, fungus-brain?" Alpha bint Hezra-Fong muttered from the security of her inner office. "How'd you like to be known as Seductron Test Failure 106 Mark 7? If I'd known who you were — " She bit off the empty threats. She knew now. And if Forister made the mistake of coming back to Summerlands for any reason, she'd have her revenge.

Neither Forister nor Nancia had thought to check Nancia's decks for transmitters — and even if they had, they might not have recognized Alpha's personal spyder, a sliver-thin enhanced metachip device that clung to any permalloy wall and, chameleon-like, mimicked the colors of its surroundings. In all the fuss attendant on getting the wounded brawn into the floatube, Alpha had found it easy enough to leave one of the spyders attached to Nancia's central corridor. From there it picked up any conversation in the cabins, although the voices were distorted by distance and interference.

At the time, Alpha hadn't been exactly sure what instinct prompted her to plant the spyder; she had just felt that the amount of Net communications traffic concerning this particular brainship and brawn suggested they were more important than they looked. Infuriatingly, the datastreams coming from Central over the Net were in a code Alpha had not yet succeeded in breaking, so the spyder was her only source of information.

So far, though, it had proved a remarkably effective tool. Alpha preened herself on her cleverness in dropping one of the expensive spyders where it was most needed. She drummed her fingers on the palmpad of the workstation while she mentally reviewed what she'd done so far and the steps she'd taken to counteract the danger. The rhythm of her fingertips was repeated on the screen as a jagged display of colored lines, breaking and recombining in a hypnotic jazzy dance.

First had come the surprising sound of Fassa del Parma's voice. While admiring the dramatic range Fassa put into pleading with her captor, Alpha hadn't been too surprised when the girl rapidly broke down and began spilling what she knew about her competitors. She'd always felt the del Parma kid didn't have what it took to make it in the big time. Too emotional. She cried in her sleep and then she gloated over her victims. Real success came from being like Alpha or Polyon, cool, unmoved, above feeling triumph or fear, concentrating always on the desired goal.

Fortunately, Fassa didn't know much; she'd been too stupid to think much beyond her personal concerns. Alpha was willing to bet the little snip had never thought of compiling a dossier on each of her competitors, with good hard data that could be traded in emergency. All she had were gossip and innuendo and stories from the annual meetings. Blaize was nasty to the natives, Alpha had developed an illicit drug, Darnell was less than totally ethical in his business takeovers.

Hearsay! Without hard evidence to back up the stories, Central would never make charges like these stick, and they were too smart to try. Alpha grinned and slapped her open hand down on the palmpad, jolting the computer into a random display of medical jargon and meaningless symbols mixed with sentences pulled at random from patient reports. She'd prepared that program years ago, as protection against a computer attack like the one Forister was trying now. And to judge from the snippets of conversation between him and Nancia, it was working. They would waste all their energy trying to decipher a code that had no meaning.

And while they worked, Alpha would take steps to deal with the one piece of hard evidence Fassa had pointed out to them. Her fingers drummed faster; she slapped the palmpad again to enter voice mode.

"Send Baynes and Moss to my office — no, to Test Room Four," she said. Baynes could safely be pulled off the task of watching that brawn for a while; Caleb was too weak to be any danger, and anyway he was protected by his brainship's monitor button.

Alpha didn't think her office was infested with spyders; she was absolutely certain about Test Room 4, a gleaming permalloy shell with no crack in the walls, no furnishings but the permalloy benches and table. Alpha had commissioned the building of this room out of her profits from the first illicit street sales of Seductron. The official purpose of the lab room was for Alpha's experiments on bioactive agents; the extreme simplicity of its design was to aid in complete sterilization of the chamber after experiments were completed.

It served well enough for these purposes. And the contractor who'd installed nets of electronic impulse chargers behind the permalloy skin, making the room impervious to any known external monitors, had suffered a fatal overdose of Blissto shortly after the completion of the room. Alpha shook her head and sighed with everyone else that she'd never have guessed the man was an addict. And the secret of the room was safe.

Baynes and Moss really were addicts. Alpha had "cured" their Blissto addiction, found them jobs at the clinic, and then explained to them that the Blissto addiction had only been replaced by a much more serious drug, a variant of Seductron with the unfortunate side effect of causing complete nervous collapse in victims who were suddenly cut off from their regular dosage. Alpha had been experimenting with a mildly addictive form of Seductron that would create a captive market in anyone who ever tried the stuff; Seductron-B4 was an overresponse to the problem. She was afraid to release the stuff to street markets. But it was incredibly useful in creating willing servants. It had only taken one or two delicately timed delays in the Seductron-B4 doses to convince Baynes and Moss that their only hope of life lay in total loyalty to her. She had picked her tools carefully; they had enough medical background to be genuinely useful as aides in the clinic, but were far too stupid to replicate her work on Seductron. If she died or were incapacitated, Baynes and Moss would die too: inevitably, slowly, and painfully.

She felt quiet satisfaction, as always, at seeing two men to whom her life was, literally, as valuable as their own. *And for all that little snip Fassa vaunts her sex appeal, no man who's rutted after her cares about her life the way these two care about mine.*

She gave her instructions quickly and confidently, expecting nothing but instant obedience. The patient carried on Summerlands' lists as Varian Alexander was to be removed to the charity side of the clinic at once. There was an empty bed in Ward 6, where the recovering Blissto addicts and alcoholics were housed; he would do very well there for the moment.

"Excuse me, Doctor, but are you sure — " Baynes began.

"He'll stand the move," Alpha said.

"Yes, but — "

"It's simple enough even for your drug-logged brain, I should think!"

"It's not Alexander that worries him, Doctor," said the quicker Moss. "It's that half-cyborg freak in Ward

6. Qualia Benton. Been asking a lot of questions, she has. Too many."

Alpha drummed her fingers on the permalloy table. Benton. Qualia Benton. Ah, yes. An interesting case. Presented as an alcoholic veteran of the Capellan Wars who was too shaky and brain-damaged to keep up her own periodic maintenance on her cyborg limb and organ replacements. All parts had appeared to be in good working order, but Alpha had approved the series of tests and maintenance anyway; Veterans' Aid would pay for the work, and if Qualia Benton was too far out of it to do her own maintenance, she'd never think to question whether the work the clinic charged was absolutely necessary—or whether it had even been done.

"What sort of questions?"

Baynes shrugged. "Anything. Everything. How do we like our jobs. How did we get our jobs. How many rooms are there in this wonderful big building, and what all goes on here besides taking care of poor old freaks like her. Supposing she wanted to get work at a nice clean place like this, would we put in a good word for her."

"No harm in all that."

"Yeah, but . . . " Baynes shifted his weight from one foot to the other and fell silent.

Moss took up the story. "Last Friday she was rolling about in her bed, claiming she had nervous pains something awful in her left foot, which it isn't there any more, Doctor, and nothing wrong with the prosthesis connections, I checked 'em out twice. Wouldn't go out for exercise with the rest of the winos, so I left her while we shoved the others out for their healthful walk around the park. Only thing is, I had to come back early on account of old Charlie Blissed-Out collapsed with chest pains and I wanted a floatube to bring him back. And I found her on the floor outside the staff room. She claimed she'd been trying to work the prosthesis and it collapsed on her."

"Possibly true," said Alpha.

"Yeah. But . . . the staff room door was unlocked. I swear I locked up like always, Doctor, but it was open then."

Alpha considered Moss's sweating face for a long moment. He could be trying to cover up his own carelessness in leaving the staff room door unlocked and a patient alone in the ward. But he hadn't had to tell her about the incident in the first place. He would only be risking her anger if he were afraid of something even worse — like a threat to her position at the clinic, something that would take her away and end his supply of Seductron-B4.

"Put the two of them in a private room," Alpha ordered.

"Aren't any on the charity side," Baynes objected glumly.

Moss rolled his eyes. "God give me strength," he pleaded. "Doctor *knows* that, Baynes. Forget about moving Victor Alexander to the charity side. We're to put Qualia Benton in a private room with him on the V.I.P. side, and don't worry about the fact that Veterans Aid won't pay; I reckon she won't be there long enough to run up much of a bill. Right, Doctor?"

He gave Alpha a conspiratorial smile which she did not return.

"Benton's is an interesting case," Alpha said neutrally. "I wish to investigate this prosthesis trouble myself. Any charges incurred will be billed to the experimental lab. Meanwhile, I wish you to keep an eye on the visitor Bryley. He's supposed to be here as escort to that brawn, but he's been spending entirely too much time talking to too many people in the public rooms."

Bryley might not be an immediate threat, but it wouldn't do any harm to have Baynes and Moss keep an eye on him. As for the other two, Alpha had no intention of leaving the disposal of her problems to this pair of bunglers, one stupid and the other trying to wriggle himself into her good graces. Nor did she intend to risk their being able to give direct evidence against her, if worst came to the worst.

Qualia Benton might be no more than an alcoholic old fool who couldn't keep from snooping into other people's business, or she might be considerably more than that. If the first, she would be no loss; if the second, she had to be disposed of immediately. As for Valden Allen Hopkirk — Alpha hated to waste a potential tool like Hopkirk, especially after going to the trouble of keeping him lightly drugged and available for all this time, but she prided herself on the ability to face facts and cut her losses. There were suddenly too many people asking too many questions around Summerlands.

Alpha dismissed Baynes and Moss and went back into her private storage room to prepare. "If you want a thing done well, do it yourself," she murmured as she prepared two stimpads, each loaded with a massive overdose of Seductron-B4.

The woman known as Qualia Benton knew something was wrong when the two aides who were Doctor Hezra-Fong's shadows came to transfer her from the charity side of the clinic. She'd been ready to act then, fingers tensed against the side of her left-leg prosthesis, adrenalin keeping her unnaturally aware of every shadow and change of intonation.

And nothing happened. "You're moving to a private room," the big one called Baynes said.

"Who'll pay?" Qualia Benton demanded in the fretful, shrill tone to be expected from an old soak whose nerves were jangling for just one more drink.

"Doctor's interested in your case," said the little black-haired one, Moss. "She wants to run some special tests. On the clinic, if Veteran's Aid won't cover it.

You could get into the next issue of the Medical Research Journal."

"I'm honored," said Qualia Benton politely. She let the men transfer her to a wheelchair and rode quietly down the long silent corridors of Summerlands clinic, watching the myriad reflections of herself and the aides in the polished tiles of floor and walls and ceiling, ready for the slightest move that would warn her it was time to act.

It won't happen in the halls. They'll move when I'm in a room alone, she told herself. But what if they expected her to count on that, and took her by surprise in one of these long empty hallways? She dared not relax.

Even when they wheeled her into a room with two beds, the one nearest the window already occupied, she was tense with expectation.

"Here now, you said I was getting a private room!" she whined. Qualia Benton would whine; what's more, she would be suspicious and distrustful like most recovering addicts, almost paranoid. God knew, it wasn't hard to fake that part.

"Might as well be private," said the one called Moss. "*He* won't bother you much. Will you, Varian?"

The patient in the other bed nodded and shook his head alternately, smiling with a loose, open-lipped grin that chilled her spirits. *Blissto addict. Or worse . . . if there is anything worse? And they're maintaining him in that condition, instead of trying to break the addiction. That's criminal!*

Qualia Benton, chronic alcoholic, too woozy to take proper care of her own prostheses and replacement organs, wouldn't care about somebody else's problems. She said nothing.

The aides helped her into the free bed.

"Here you go," said the small black-haired man cheerfully. He slapped a stimpad downwards; she recoiled but could not quite escape the stinging contact against her shoulder. "Just a little relaxation med before the tests," he said.

"Don't wanna relax," she muttered. The thickness in her speech was natural. She was suddenly finding it hard to think. Something was infiltrating her bloodstream, something soft as a cloud and warm as sunshine, floating her away to the Isles of the Blest — bless — bliss — Blissto! That was it!

The man in the other bed — was he really a Blissto addict, or had he been drugged in the same manner? Foolish, foolish not to have anticipated this. Once the aides had caught her out of bed and snooping where she had no business, she should have known her time at the clinic was limited.

She set her will to resisting the power of the drug. And not only her will. One thing about being under-estimated, being seen as an old lush without the sense to care for her own artificial organs: Dr. Hezra-Fong hadn't, apparently, run any serious tests on those hy-perchip-enhanced organs. The Blissto was carrying her away; but if she could only gain an hour or two, all might yet be well.

Did she have that hour's grace? No way to tell; she could only watch and wait, and that not very effective-ly. The hard hospital pillow beneath her head was soft as a Denebian flufftuff. Her left hand still rested against the smooth hard prosthesis, but she could barely feel the permaskin; the Blissto was interposing a fluffy cloud of blissful illusion between her and reality.

Doctor wants to run some tests . . . Was that truly all this meant? Surely not. So important a person as Dr. Hezra-Fong, assistant director of Summerlands, wouldn't go to all this trouble to prove that an old lush was faking dis-ability. There had to be more going on here.

By late afternoon Sev noticed that the same two aides kept walking through the public visiting rooms. They were both rather striking in their appearance —

one a burly, blue-chinned man with a lumbering walk, the other neat and quick and given to slicking down his black hair with short nervous strokes. And they would have looked more natural at a portside bar than in a luxury medical clinic.

Sev reckoned he was supposed to notice them and to be scared off. That was annoying. The doddering old CenDip widow he was talking to had finally mentioned a patient named Varian Alexander, a Blissto addict. That could be an alias for Valden Allen Hopkirk; the information that Alexander had just been moved to a semi-private room supported the theory. He was ready to get back to Nancia and check out the records on this Alexander, and he hated like hell to let these two petty thugs think they'd frightened him.

"You will *not* start anything with those two," Nancia instructed him when he muttered his complaints into the contact button. "They're minor. You get back and watch Caleb. I'll send Forister to take care of our friend Hopkirk."

"And who," Sev inquired sweetly, "will guard Fassa?"

Nancia assaulted his eardrums with a burst of static that attracted the attention of two other visitors. Glancing doubtfully at the artificial Capella fern beside Sev, they moved to the other side of the room and seated themselves well away from the strange, dour young man and his talking plant.

"You're attracting attention," Sev said sweetly. "Better let me handle this in my own way."

"Don't blame *me* if you end up in a recycler," Nancia grumbled in an undertone. "And don't expect me to send Forister to fish you out of trouble, either. After all, as you pointed out, somebody has to guard Fassa."

"I don't," said Sev loudly and clearly, "need anybody to get me out of trouble."

The other visitors whispered among themselves and somebody giggled. Sev felt his face turning red. Two shapes materialized at his elbows, one large and lumbering, one darting in quick as a hummingbird.

"Forgetting your meds again, sonny?" asked the small one in a kindly, concerned voice. He turned towards the other visitors in the room. "Sorry about the disturbance. He hears voices. Should improve with therapeu — ahh!"

Sev drove one fist into the small man's chin and wheeled to confront the big one. A hand like a small boulder descended on his head. The room whirled around him. An old lady screamed. He saw something sharp in the rock-like hand. *Should have guessed. The danger is never where you're looking.* The hand came down for a second time, like an earthquake or an avalanche, vast, implacable, and as Sev twisted away the needle slid into flesh, quiet as a whisper, smooth as sleep.

When she heard the sounds of the fracas in the public waiting rooms, Alpha slipped into the semi-private room she'd assigned to Hopkirk and the snoopy derelict. Damn Baynes and Moss! Couldn't they handle a minor surveillance task without starting a fight? There must be something about Blissto that permanently destroyed the brain cells.

Oh, well, at least the disturbance in the waiting room would draw everybody's attention; there'd be no inconvenient witnesses to her actions here. Not that she expected to be here long enough for any problems to develop. Hopkirk was grinning in his usual loose-lipped, amiable way, and the derelict Benton was limp against her pillow in a Blissto dream. Better take care of her first; she knew Hopkirk was too sedated to give trouble.

As she pushed up the old lush's sleeve to apply the stimpad, Alpha wondered whether Qualia Benton were really a snoop, or just a brain-damaged bag lady who'd had the bad luck to stumble into private places at the wrong time. Not that it made much difference.

She wouldn't be answering any questions now.

The stimpad slapped down on chill, firm flesh. The array of needles clicked but did not sink in. Alpha felt a moment's cold apprehension. *Something is wrong here. Something is very wrong.*

And Qualia Benton's dark eyes were wide open, watching her with amusement.

"The right arm prosthesis is real lifelike," she said cheerfully, "but you won't get stimpad needles through the plastiskin. And now — oh, no, dear. I wouldn't do that. I really wouldn't."

From under the bedclothes she had produced an ugly, snub-nosed needler. *Where did that come from? The old bitch isn't* wearing *anything but a hospital gown.*

"Whatever you had in that stimpad, the charge is wasted now," Qualia Benton informed her in that same cheerful tone. "There should be just enough left for a lab on Central to analyze. Please don't try to throw it away; I'll want to put it in an evidence bag for the trial."

"Trial," Alpha croaked. "Evidence bag." She backed up a step, frozen with horror, while her intended victim swung one real leg and one permalloy prosthesis out of bed, fussily straightened her gown, and produced a plastic bag from under the pillow.

"Just drop it in here, dear, and don't make any sudden moves. You wouldn't want to startle a poor nervous old woman. This needler is set on wide spray, and it's loaded with ParaVen. I don't really *want* to paralyze you," she said thoughtfully, "but if necessary . . ."

Two more backward steps brought Alpha to the door. She dropped and rolled into the corridor, momentarily out of range of the needler. "Baynes! Moss!" she shrieked. "32-A, patient out of control, Code Z, stat!"

Running feet pounded down the corridor and

Alpha closed her eyes in momentary relief. That heavy tread had to belong to Baynes. Let this crazy snoop of a woman waste her needler charge on the aides — then Alpha would spirit her away to the violent ward. She promised herself a long and entertaining series of experiments on the bitch, once they got that damned needler away from her.

"Stop right there," the old woman called in a voice too clear for her apparent age. "I am a legally constituted representative of Central Worlds Internal Investigation. Any attack on my person is treason, punishable by law. You're under arrest."

"The hell I am," countered a voice that most certainly did not belong to the thick-witted Baynes. Alpha looked up and saw that Bryley man, the one she'd sent Baynes and Moss to take care of. "*I'm* the Central Worlds rep here, and *you're* under arrest. What have you done to my witness?"

"The guy in the next bed?" For the first time, the Benton woman sounded uncertain. "He's not going to be a lot of good to you. Too blissed-out to know his own name. But you're welcome to him, if you want him. I expect she was going to kill him next, after she took care of me."

"Kill? You?" Now Bryley sounded equally confused. From her crouching position, Alpha saw the Benton woman bend and fumble along the side of her leg prosthesis. A crack opened and she drew out a thin holographic strip that shimmered with rainbow colors in the hallway lights. *So that's where she hid the needler. . . .*

"General Micaya Questar-Benn," the woman introduced herself. She was standing straighter now, without the hunch and the bent leg that had made her look so small and helpless before. "Undercover assignment for Central, checking out the suspiciously high death rate on the charity side of Summerlands. My colleague Forister Armontillado-y-Medoc should be somewhere around; he can vouch for me. And you?"

"Sevareid Bryley-Sorensen, on temporary assignment to investigate fraud in a Bahati construction company." He looked down at Alpha; she had a dizzying glimpse of blue eyes and an expression as if the cat had dragged in something better left in a back alley. "I think our cases may be connected. I was here to collect Valden Allen Hopkirk, witness to a case of criminal Net interference by one of the del Parma girl's friends. Apparently this 'lady' is another of the gang; she's been concealing the witness and — from what you say — keeping him too doped up to testify. You think she was going to kill him?"

"We'll have to wait until that stimpad in her hand has been analyzed for drug traces," General Questar-Benn said mildly, "but I certainly don't think she was dispensing routine meds. Fortunately, she slapped the stimpad on my upper-arm prosthesis. I think I was supposed to be too drugged to notice her; one of those thugs she uses for aides dosed me with Blissto, or something like it, about an hour ago."

Alpha slowly uncurled herself and stood up. If she was lost, she'd go with that much dignity. She was half a head taller than this Sev Bryley; it helped, a little, to look down on him.

"So what are you," she demanded, "a robot? Nobody's immune to Seduc — Blissto," she caught herself. No reason to give away information.

General Questar-Benn chuckled. "No, dear girl, I'm not quite as badly off as the Tin Woodman. The valves may be helped along by hyperchips, but I still have a heart — something that appears to have been left out of your makeup. But the liver and kidneys are replacements, and last year I had a new hyperchip-enhanced blood filtering function installed so that I could monitor my own internal prostheses. If you'd shown up right after your goon drugged me, I might have been in trouble. But an hour was more than enough time to filter the drug out of my bloodstream."

Alpha glowered at her and Bryley impartially. "And what about you?" she demanded of Bryley. "You looked like a *man*, but I guess you're another fucking cyborg freak."

"I am a man," Bryley said mildly. "I'm also fast — and I learned Capellan hand fighting in the war. Your big thug tripped over his own feet — with a little help — and slapped himself with the stimpad he was aiming at me. I don't know what was in it; perhaps you'd like to tell me whether he'll survive the experience? As for the little one, he collided with one of those big ceramic pots you've got decorating the waiting room. He'll have one hell of a headache when he wakes up, but he'll be in perfectly good shape to testify against you."

"No, he won't," Alpha snapped. "You don't know as much as you think you do! The man's addicted to — something you won't be able to supply. Without his next fix, he'll die in agony before the week's out!"

Bryley raised one eyebrow. "Then," he said cheerfully, "we'd better make sure to get his testimony on datahedron before he dies, hadn't we? Thanks for the warning."

● CHAPTER TWELVE

"Hospitals!" General Questar-Benn made the word sound like an expletive. "No offense, Thalmark, but those damn gowns are just a plot to make patients helpless and submissive. Thanks for bringing my uniform, Bryley."

"I have a feeling it would take more than that to make you submissive, General," Galena Thalmark said with a slight inclination of her head.

Sev and Micaya had met in what used to be Alpha bint Hezra-Fong's office, now occupied by the administrative assistant who'd first alerted Central Worlds to the surprising death rate in Summerlands' charity wards. This morning Galena Thalmark looked ten years younger than the harried, overweight woman who'd greeted Micaya and smuggled her into the wards in the disguise of the alcoholic "Qualia Benton."

"I can't express my thanks to you both," she said, pushing dark curly hair away from her round face, "so I won't try. General Questar-Benn, you have my sincerest apologies for the dangers you experienced."

"Part of the job," said Micaya.

"All the same, we should have been more alert. I should have had staff I could trust watching you at all times," said Galena.

Micaya nodded without further comment. She was favorably impressed by Galena's quick command of the situation, even more impressed by the fact that the young woman had taken full responsibility for problems which were hardly of her making. It wasn't her fault that the aging director of Summerlands had left more and more power in the hands of Dr. Hezra-Fong, allowing the charity side to become disastrously understaffed and letting a deplorable lack of discipline infect the whole clinic.

"Clinic's problems weren't your fault, Thalmark," Micaya said at last, "but they're about to be your problem. The director must have been senile to let all this go on under his nose. High Families, of course, politically unwise to fire him, but I've had one of my aides compose a nice letter of resignation for him. Want the spot? Can't guarantee it, you understand," she added, "but I've some influence at Central."

Galena Thalmark flushed becomingly and murmured her thanks. "Meanwhile," she said, shuffling papers until she'd recovered her composure, "I'm glad to report that Mr. Hopkirk is responding quite well to treatment. Dr. Hezra-Fong has supplied us with full details of the drugs used to keep him sedated. We're steadily lowering the dosage and watching him for seizures, but so far there have been no complications. He should be quite lucid and competent to make a deposition on datahedron within the next forty-eight hours."

"Good work!" Micaya exclaimed.

Galena Thalmark nodded. "Whatever her other failings, Dr. Hezra-Fong is a brilliant biomedical researcher. I feel obliged to tell you that without her full cooperation and guidance, we would not have been able to reverse the effects of the treatment so rapidly." She looked up into Micaya's eyes. "She requested that this fact be formally noted on her dossier."

"It will be," Micaya promised. "But I doubt that it'll bear much weight against the rest of the record."

Galena bit her lip. "All those deaths," she murmured. "If only I'd seen what was going on from the first . . . " Micaya nodded in sympathy.

"Don't torture yourself," she told the younger

woman. "You weren't even at Summerlands when she began. You had every reason to trust your superiors; it's to your credit that you suspected something as soon as you did and called in the proper authorities to put a stop to it. Don't second-guess yourself!"

The last words were barked out in a parade-ground intonation that made Galena's head snap up.

"I mean it," Micaya told her more gently. "My dear, I've commanded soldiers in battle. I've seen brave men and women die because of orders I gave; and sometimes those orders were wrong. You mourn the deaths, you do the best you can, and — you go on. Otherwise, you cannot be of service."

Galena Thalmark looked thoughtfully at the older woman, standing erect and composed in her plain green uniform. Some of her battle wounds were visible, the permalloy arm and leg. Others were buried in the surgical history that Galena had read: the internal replacements for kidneys and liver, the hyperchip implant in one heart valve and the blood-filtering function. And as a doctor, Galena could assess just how many hours of painful surgery and retraining had gone into reconstructing Micaya's body after she sustained each of the original wounds.

"You go on," Micaya repeated softly, "and . . . you serve as best you can. I believe that you will make an excellent director for Summerlands, Dr. Thalmark. Don't let regrets and hindsight cripple you; we need you here and now, not reliving a past that cannot be changed."

"I can see why you're a general," said Sev thoughtfully as they boarded the flyer that was to transport them from Summerlands. "If we'd had a commanding officer like you on Capella Four. . . . "

General Questar-Benn's high cheekbones flushed a shade darker. "Don't delude yourself. Making persuasive speeches is only a small part of the art of war."

"Oh? Seems to me I heard enough of them when I

served on Capella. There may have been more going on in the staff rooms, but I never rose high enough in the army to see the whole picture. That's what I like about P.I. work," Sev added thoughtfully, "now I *am* the whole picture. Or was." He looked directly at Micaya. "I'll consider myself under your command for the rest of this operation."

"The rest — but my assignment's over," protested Micaya.

"Is it?"

It has been a long time since a young man looked at her so intently — and back then, Micaya thought with an amusement that she did not allow her features to reflect, the last man to look at her like that had wanted something quite different. Ah, well. They always wanted something, didn't they?

"Fassa del Parma and Alpha bint Hezra-Fong came out to the Nyota system on the same transport," Sev went on. "So did Darnell Overton-Glaxely. They've all been helping each other get rich by the quickest and dirtiest means they could arrange. There were two others on that transport — Blaize Armontillado-Perez y Medoc, and Polyon de Gras-Waldheim. Fassa's already implicated Blaize — the one who was posted to Angalia. Don't you see? You're holding one thread into this tangle; I'm holding another one."

"You think that together we could unravel it?"

Sev gave her a flashing grin that was all but wasted on his present purpose. "Or take Alexander's solution, and cut the Gordian knot. This corruption ought to be cut off," he argued. "Don't tell me it's just a small part of what 'everybody does.' I don't care. This is the part I can see, that I can do something about. I *have* to see this through!" He stopped, looking momentarily embarrassed by his own intensity. "And I had hoped," he went on in a somewhat quieter voice, "I had hoped that you would want to join us. Lead us."

The flyer skated to a perfect landing just outside Nancia's opened entry bay.

"Come with me?" Sev suggested.

"I've got a scheduled transport to Kailas. Back to my desk job."

"You can change that," he said confidently, and grinned at her as he would at a contemporary. "Come on, Mic! You don't really want to go back to shuffling papers on Kailas, do you?"

Micaya rubbed the back of her neck. She felt generations older than this intense young man: tired, and dirty from the corruption of Summerlands, and not very interested in anything except a long bath and a massage. "Damn it," she said wearily. "You're not bad at persuasive speeches yourself, Bryley-Sorensen. I suppose you think I can get your brainship's orders changed so that we can go on to Angalia, instead of transporting del Parma straight back to Central?"

"It makes sense, doesn't it?"

"Sense," said Micaya, "has never been a compelling argument for any bureaucracy. All right. You win. I'll see what I can do towards persuading Central to reassign both Nancia and me. I must admit, I'd like to see the end of this case." Despite her weariness, she felt a smile beginning deep inside her. "Besides, your ship's brawn owes me a rematch at tri-chess."

"*Caleb?*"

"Forister," Micaya corrected him. "Nancia's been assigned a replacement brawn, remember? Forister Armontillado-y-Medoc. We were working together on this Summerlands business, until Central pulled him off the case to brawn Nancia back to Central." She stopped in the open landing bay. "Wait a minute. What did you say the other boy was called — the one who went to Angalia?"

Sev didn't have time to answer; a second flyer pounced down on the landing strip, and a messenger in the white uniform of Summerlands came running toward them.

"Tried to raise you in the air," he panted. "Your driver's comm unit must have been defective. Hopkirk's testified!"

"The devil he has! Already?"

"He seemed rather eager to do it. Dr. Thalmark thought it would do more harm to restrain him than to let him speak. His deposition's on datahedron — and there are a few honest men left on Bahati, Mr. Bryley; two of them are going to arrest Overton-Glaxely now. Since he'll likely be sent back to Central for trial, they'd like a representative of Central to accompany them now, just to make sure everything's in order."

"You mean, to make sure there's somebody else to blame if his family goes out for revenge," Sev muttered.

"I'll go," Micaya said. "No one will question my word."

"*I'll* go," Sev corrected her. "I've already annoyed so many High Families, one more makes no difference. You go catch up on your tri-chess."

"I always did like subordinates with plenty of initiative," Micaya said wryly. But she was tired, and worried about the possible connection between Blaize and Forister. Well, they'd have some privacy for a little while, with Sev Bryley off to collect his prisoner and Fassa del Parma locked in her cabin. She would have to ask Forister just how close the relationship might be — and whether he really wanted to brawn a ship headed for Angalia to arrest one of his relatives.

Forister was happily unpacking a special order from OG Glimware when Micaya Questar-Benn requested permission to board.

"We've got company coming," Nancia warned him. "And isn't there something unethical about buying something from a firm while you work to arrest its owner?"

"Can't think what," said Forister, whistling under his breath, "but if you find anything in CS regulations, be sure and let me know. Anyway, OG Glimware is the only company this side of Antares that does this particular specialty work." He peeled away the last opaque shrinkwrapping to display his purchase: a foot-high solido of a lovely young woman, every feature sharply delineated in the fragile prismatic carving. Her chin was lifted almost defiantly; she greeted the world with a smile whose reflection danced in her eyes; a short cap of curly hair, so finely carved it seemed the separate strands might lift in any passing breeze, crowned the uplifted head that gazed out at worlds beyond any human vision.

"Ah — very nice," Nancia said slowly, as Forister seemed to be waiting for some reaction. "Relative of yours?" *His records didn't say anything about a girl friend, and isn't he rather old for this one?*

"A very distant connection, like most of the High Families scions. But she may become more than that — my friend, I hope. Perhaps my partner." Forister set the solido on the ledge above the pilot's control panel and turned to smile at Nancia's titanium column. "It's a genetic extrapolation, actually; shows what a certain young woman I know would have looked like if she'd grown up normally, without the one genetic anomaly that made her unable to survive outside a shell. Her name is . . . Nancia Perez y de Gras."

Nancia didn't know how to respond to that revelation. She couldn't respond. *Caleb never wondered what I would have looked like . . . never thought of me as a person.* Even thinking that was disloyal . . . but what *could* she say to Forister?

She was spared the necessity by the opening of the airlock. General Questar-Benn's somber face startled them both. "This part of the mission's completed," she announced. "Hezra-Fong's on her way here — under guard — and Bryley has gone off to arrest Overton-Glaxely. He's suggested that we should request a change in Nancia's orders, to investigate the other two passengers she brought to the Nyota system before returning to Central. Thought I should consult you first, Forister."

Forister's face went gray. "I will accept any orders issued by Courier Service as long as I brawn this ship."

"Know that," Micaya told him. "But I need to know more. Exactly what is the connection between you and this boy on Angalia? Distant relative? How much conflict of interest are we looking at?"

"He's my nephew." Forister dropped into the pilot's seat.

"Can I rely on you?"

Nancia watched and listened without intruding into the conversation. She had liked General Questar-Benn on their previous meeting, but now she felt the general was pushing Forister too hard. For the first time since he'd come on board, he was looking his age; the bristly graying hair lay flat, the sparkle of mischief that had made his face so familiar to Nancia had disappeared. Of course, she realized with a shock of recognition, that was why she felt as though she knew Forister already. It wasn't just his previous trip to Charon. It was the sparkle in his eyes as he hummed and hacked his way into Summerlands' medical records. That redheaded boy Blaize had just the same expression when he was planning mischief.

But Forister had the integrity so disastrously missing from Blaize's makeup. He hadn't tried to argue away Fassa's stories implicating his nephew, and now he would not evade the duty of confirming those stories.

"You don't have to come with us," Micaya told him. "We can get another brawn assigned to this ship.

You're due a real R & R tour after that undercover work at Summerlands — "

Forister lifted his head and gazed at her with flat gray eyes. "You took all the risks at Summerlands," he said in a voice so drained of feeling that it made Nancia distinctly nervous. She increased the magnification of her local sensors until she could see the pulse throbbing in Forister's temple and hear the soft pounding of his heart. The man was under far too much strain.

"I WAS USELESS," his amplified voice crashed upon her, and Nancia hastily retreated to a normal sensor level, nerve endings twitching from the grating sounds. "Couldn't even find computer records to back you up. If anyone deserves a term of rest, Mic, it's you. And if anyone must prove my nephew's dishonor," he finished wearily, "let it be me. We won't be able to keep it in the family — I know that — but I need to know exactly what he's done and how we can make reparation."

"It's not good to be personally involved in your cases," General Micaya Questar-Benn murmured. "First rule of Academy."

Forister's spine straightened. "No. The first rule is . . . to serve. That's all I ask of you. A chance to serve, to make some reparation if any can be made. Besides," he added with just a trace of the old snap in his voice, "you won't find another brawn this side of Bellatrix subspace."

"Oh, come now," Micaya said. "You people with brawn training always overrate yourself. I'll wager there are half a dozen qualified brawns in Vega subspace alone."

Forister straightened another infinitesimal fraction of an inch. "Not qualified for the new hyperchip-enhanced brainships. Our Nancia's got the enhancements, haven't you, my dear?" As always, he turned his head towards the titanium column when addressing her, just as if he were inviting another softshell — soft*person*, Nancia corrected herself — to join in the conversation.

"My lower deck sensors and port side nav controls have the hyperchips," she told him, "and I'm using them in some of the processing banks. I'm on a waiting list for the rest."

"There you are, then," Forister told Micaya. "You need me. And I — need to do this."

"You need this assignment like I need another prosthesis," Micaya muttered, but she sat down again with the air of one who'd given up argument. "And just how do you happen to be qualified for the new chipships, anyway? You've been CenDip for — "

"More years than either of us chooses to specify," Forister interrupted her. "And the term is brainships, Mic, not 'chipships.' Let's not offend our lady."

"It's all right," Nancia cut in. "I'm not offended. Really."

"But I am," said Forister. He took a deep breath and straightened. Nancia could almost see him pushing the pain he felt deep inside, replacing his diplomat's mask. When he turned his head to speak directly to her, he looked almost untroubled — if you didn't focus your sensors on the tiny lines of strain and worry around his eyes. "You are *my* lady now, Nancia, at least for the duration of this mission. And no one speaks casually of my brainship."

Micaya blew out her pursed lips with an exasperated sigh. "You never answered my question. How come you're qualified for the newest models of brainships, when you've been out of the brawn service for . . . years?"

"I read a lot," Forister said with an airy wave of one hand. "Ancient guerrilla wars, new compunav systems, it's all grist to my mill. I'm a twentieth century man at heart," he told Micaya, referring to the Age of the First Information Explosion. "A man of many interests and unguessed-at talents. And I like to keep current in my field — *all* my fields."

"A man of unguessed-at bullshit, anyway," Micaya retorted. "Okay. You're in. At least I'll have someone to beat at tri-chess on the way over to Angalia."

Forister snorted. "You mean someone to beat you. Your ego has increased out of all proportion to your skill, General. Set 'em up!"

Nancia watched with curiosity as General Questar-Benn drew a palm-sized card from her pocket. Forister grinned. "Brought your portable game board, I see."

The general tapped the slight indentations on the surface of the card and it projected a hologram of a partitioned cube, shimmering with rainbow light at the edges. Another series of taps produced the translucent images of playing pieces aligned at two opposing edges of the cube. Nancia twiddled with her sensor magnification and focus until she could make out the details. Yes, those were the standard tri-chess pieces: she recognized the age-old triple ordering. Pawns in the first and lowest rank; above them, the King and Queen with their Bishops and Knights and Castles. Above them the highest rank was poised to swoop down over the gamecube, the Brainship and Brawn with their supporting pieces, the Scouts and Hovercraft and Satellites. The images were blurred and kept flickering in and out, giving Nancia a sensation of tight bands pulled across her sensor connections if she tried to look at them for any length of time.

"Pawn to Brain's Scout 4,2," Forister grunted a standardized opening move.

Nothing happened.

"My portable set isn't equipped with voice recognition," Micaya apologized. "You'll have to tap in the code."

As she indicated the row of fingertip-sized indentations, Nancia hummed softly — her substitute for the rasps and hawks of "throat-clearing" with which softshells began an unscheduled interruption. Both players looked up, and after a startled moment Forister inclined his head to Nancia's titanium column.

"Yes, Nancia?"

"If you'll give me a moment to study the configuration," Nancia suggested, "I believe I can replicate your play-holo with a somewhat clearer display. And I, of course, can supply the voice recognition processing."

Even as she spoke, she assigned a virtual memory space and a graphics co-processor to the problem. Before the sound of her voice had died away, a new and much clearer holographic projection shimmered beside the original one. Forister exclaimed in delight at the perfect detailing of the miniaturized pieces; Micaya put out her hand as if to touch a perfectly shaped little Satellite with its three living and storage globes, complete with tiny access doors and linking spacetubes.

"Beautiful," Forister sighed in delight. "But won't this take too much processing capability, Nancia?"

"Not when we're just sitting dirtside," Nancia told him. "I don't even use that processor when we're doing regular navigation. Might have to shut down briefly when we're in Singularity, that *does* take some concentration, but — "

Forister closed his eyes briefly. "That's perfectly all right, Nancia. To tell you the truth, it never occurred to me to play tri-chess in Singularity anyway."

"Me either," said Micaya, looking slightly green at the very thought. "You don't want to think about spatial relationships at a moment like that."

"*I* do," said Nancia cheerfully.

Less than two Central Standard Hours later, Sev interrupted the first tri-chess game to deliver a subdued Darnell Glaxely-Overton for transport to Central. "He broke when I showed him the hedron of Hopkirk's evidence," he told the others after Darnell had been confined in a cabin. "Funny — almost as if he'd expected somebody to come after him one of these days. Spent most of the flyer trip back telling all he knows about the other three. Here's the recording."

"Four," Nancia corrected Sev as he slid a datacard into her reader.

"Three," Sev said again. "Fassa. Alpha. And . . . Blaize." He carefully avoided looking at Forister as he pronounced the last name.

"Neither of them has said anything implicating Polyon de Gras-Waldheim?" Nancia couldn't believe this.

Sev shrugged. "Who knows? Maybe there isn't anything to say. You never know, there could be one good apple in this barrel of rotten ones."

Not Polyon. But Nancia refrained from voicing her protest. After the conversations she'd heard on her maiden voyage, she was convinced that Polyon de Gras-Waldheim was completely amoral. But would it be ethical to reveal those conversations? Caleb had been so adamantly against anything that even suggested spying, she'd never even thought of telling him.

But that had been five years ago. She had changed; she now saw shades of gray instead of the neat black and white of CS rules. Even Caleb might have changed; after all, he'd consented to this undercover mission.

Under protest.

He might feel doubly betrayed if she chose to violate his ethical code when he wasn't even here to censure her for it.

Perhaps she could put off the decision for a little longer. "It might be worth going by Shemali anyway," Nancia suggested. "You never know. We might find some evidence linking de Gras-Waldheim with the rest of the crew." *We'd have that evidence already, if they weren't all terrified to say a word against him.*

"Possibly," Sev agreed. "Meet me there, after Angalia?"

"I thought you were coming with us!" Micaya Questar-Benn half rose from her seat, putting one hand right through Nancia's tri-chess hologram.

"I was," Sev agreed. "I am. I'll meet you on Shemali. Something's come up."

He was gone before any of them could question him, taking the stairs three at a time and whistling as he went. Nancia briefly considered slamming her lower doors on him and holding him until he explained exactly what he was up to.

She wouldn't do that, of course. It would be an unethical and unconscionable abuse of her abilities, the sort of bullying she'd been warned against in the ethics classes that were part of every shellperson's training.

But it was a sore temptation.

"Something," Micaya said thoughtfully, "has made that young man extremely happy. I wonder what it was. Nancia, is there anything earth-shaking in that datacard of Darnell Overton-Glaxely's testimony?"

Nancia had started scanning just before Micaya spoke. "There isn't even anything interesting," she said, "unless a sordid record of petty bribes and corruption and bullying fascinates you."

"Ah. Overton-Glaxely did strike me as the cheap sort."

"You might want to examine his statement yourself," Nancia suggested. "You may see something I've overlooked."

Micaya nodded. "I'll do that. But I doubt I'll find anything. Bryley said there wasn't any evidence against de Gras-Waldheim, so whatever is taking him to Shemali, it can't be our business. Damn that boy! Oh, well, I suppose we'll find out when we reach Shemali."

"But first," Forister said, "we have a task to complete at Angalia." His face was gray and still again; the momentary animation brought on by the tri-chess game had vanished. *He looks like a man with a deadly disease. Is family honor so important to him?* Nancia wondered how she'd feel if her sister Jinevra were found to have corrupted her branch of PTA and embezzled the department's funds.

Impossible even to imagine such a thing. Well, then, what if Flix — she couldn't think what Flix might do, either, but what if he had got in with the wrong crowd — like Blaize — and had done something that would force her to hunt him down, arrest him, send him to Central for years of prison without his beloved music?

The pain of that thought shook Nancia so deeply that for a moment the even hum of the air stabilizers was broken and the co-processor handling the tri-chess hologram faltered. The gamecube image shivered, broke apart in rainbow fractures, then solidified again as Nancia gained control of herself and her systems.

If even imagining Flix in trouble hurt her so deeply, how could Forister face the reality of Blaize's crime? He couldn't, she decided, and it was up to her and Micaya to distract him whenever possible.

"General Questar-Benn, it's your move," she said.

"What? Oh — Scout to Queen's Bishop 3,3," Micaya said. The move took one of Forister's Satellites and left a probability path to his Brainship. Nancia calculated the possible moves without conscious effort.

"You have only two moves that will not put your Brainship in check within the next five-move sequence," she warned Forister.

"Two?" Forister's eyebrows shot up and he bent over the gamecube. "I saw only one."

"Foul!" Micaya complained. "I challenged the brawn, not the brain."

"We work as a team," Nancia told her.

She certainly hoped that was true. For Forister's sake — for both their sakes. He didn't need to get through this grief alone; she was there to steady him.

"Ah. I see what you mean." Forister bent over the board and surprised Nancia with a third move, one so apparently disastrous that she had not even considered it in her initial calculations.

With a subdued whoop of glee, Micaya Questar-Benn took Forister's second Satellite — and watched dumbfounded as he proceeded to shift an unconsidered knight from the second rank and place her Brainship in check.

"Thank you for the hint, Nancia," Forister said. "Until you forced me to consider the alternative move, I hadn't even thought of using the Jigo Kanaka advance in this situation."

"I . . . ah . . . you're quite welcome," Nancia managed to tell him between the three subsequent moves that brought the game to its slashing conclusion, with Micaya's forces immobilized, her Brawn taken and her Brainship checkmated.

Perhaps Forister didn't need quite so much help as she'd anticipated.

● CHAPTER THIRTEEN

Nancia's landing on Angalia was one of the worst she'd ever executed. The planet took her completely by surprise.

Initial navigation maneuvers went normally. It wasn't until she was in visual range of the landing field that she became confused. The green terraced cliffs behind the mesa and the grassy basin surrounding it looked nothing at all like her memories of the landing five years ago. Could she possibly have miscalculated, come down in some hitherto unknown section of the planet?

Nancia called up her files from that first landing and superimposed the stored images on the green paradise below her. Yes, this had to be the Angalia landing field. The topographical features were a perfect match with her internal map. And there, at the edge of the mesa, was the plastifilm prefab hut with its sagging awning of woven grass, looking if anything slightly more derelict and tottering than it had appeared five years ago.

Intent on her image comparison, Nancia drained computing power from the navigation processor, forgot to monitor the approach, and came embarrassingly close to making a new crater on Angalia's landing field. She corrected the descent, hopped into mid-air, and came down more slowly the second time. Her auditory sensors picked up a variety of crashes, groans, and complaints from the cabins where Micaya and the three prisoners were housed.

"Apologies for the rough landing," she began, but

Forister cut off her speakers for a moment and over-rode her. "Local turbulence," he said. "Nancia recovered superbly, but even a brainship can't compensate for all the freak conditions on Angalia."

He swept his open hand over the palmpad with a caressing gesture, restoring speaker control to Nancia, and smiled at her benignly.

"I didn't need you to cover for me," Nancia transmitted a vibrant whisper through the main cabin speakers.

"Didn't you? I thought we were a team. If you can help me play tri-chess, I certainly have the right to preserve you from apologizing to those overindulged brats."

"I — well, thank you," Nancia conceded.

"Think nothing of it. By the way, what *did* happen just now?"

"I was distracted. This place doesn't look the way it did last time I landed." Nancia switched all her screens to external mode. Forister gazed appreciatively at the triple-screen display of a grassy paradise ringed by flowering terraces.

"What on earth is *that*?" Fassa cried from her cabin. Darnell and Alpha joined her exclamations of surprise.

Nancia was gratified by this response. The screens in the passenger cabins weren't as dramatic as her central cabin's display walls, but at least they showed enough of Angalia to confirm that she wasn't losing her mind — or if she was, she wasn't alone. None of the prisoners had been expecting Angalia to look like the Garden of Eden.

"Do I take it," she asked mildly, "that the planet has changed since your last visit?"

"It certainly has," Fassa said. "Are you sure it's the same place? Only last year — oh, I see."

A prolonged silence followed. For once in her life Nancia longed for a softperson's physical extrusions.

It would be enormously satisfying to take Fassa by the shoulders and shake her out of the trance in which she had fallen. *Why* couldn't softpersons keep transmitting datastreams while they were processing?

She had to content herself with blinking Fassa's cabin lights and assaulting her with raucous bursts of music from Flix's latest sonohedron.

"Do I take it," she inquired when satisfied that she had the girl's attention, "that you recognize some salient features?"

"Yes . . . I think so, anyway." Of course, Fassa would have no control over the visual detail, not to mention the accuracy, of whatever images she'd stored from her previous visit. She would be dependent on whatever her non-enhanced biological memory could provide. Recognizing this, Nancia didn't count on learning much.

"Those gardens on the side of the mountain," Fassa said. "He had the terraces in place a year ago, but nothing was planted. I thought it was something to do with the mine."

Nancia switched the signals going to Fassa's display screen to show the mine entrance. Blue-uniformed figures moved in and out, pushing wagons on railings that curved around the side of the mountain. A magnified display showed that the figures were shambling Angalia natives, neatly dressed in blue shorts and shirts and working together with the precision of a choreographed dance. One native heaved a sack from the mine entrance and tossed it over his head; another casually moved into place just in time to catch it; by the time he'd turned, a third native had backed his wagon down the rail system and into place to receive the load.

"Amazing," Nancia commented. "I thought the Angalians couldn't be trained."

"Blaize," Forister said hollowly, "has certainly been a busy little boy."

"It doesn't look all that bad so far," Nancia pointed out. "Fassa, do you — or the others — recognize anything else?"

She let the display screens sweep over a panoramic view of the mesa and the surrounding countryside. Suddenly Fassa gave a cry of recognition. "Oh, God, he's left the volcano!"

Nancia halted the display and studied it. An evil-looking bubble of brown and green mud heaved and burst and formed again, roiling continuously in the midst of the tall grass covering the rest of the basin.

"I don't suppose planting flowers would do much to disguise it," she agreed.

"You don't understand." Fassa sounded close to tears. "That's how he controls them — how he makes them do things for them. If the Loosies don't please him, he *cooks* them alive in that boiling mud! I saw it done last time — I'll never forget those screams."

"Alpha? Darnell?" Nancia queried the other two.

"That's right," Darnell told her. "Revolting."

Alpha nodded silently, the movement barely visible to Nancia's visual sensors.

She could think of no more encouraging words for Forister.

Micaya persuaded Forister to let her confront Blaize initially. "I'll wear a contact button," she promised him. "You and Nancia can see and hear everything that goes on."

"It's my duty — " Forister began.

"Mine too," Micaya interrupted him. "The young man is more likely to confess if he doesn't think he can bring family influence to bear."

"He can't," Forister said grimly. "I'm not here to intercede for him."

"Yes, but he doesn't know that," Micaya pointed out.

Nancia kept all her external sensors trained on

Micaya as the general picked her way along a path of rounded volcanic stones to the door of the permalloy hut. On both sides of the path, feathery grasses and blazing tropical flowers grew in exuberant, uncontrolled patterning, throwing up their seed-heads and blooms above Micaya's crisp silver-sprinkled hair. Nancia recognized Old Earth species mixed with Denebian starflowers and the singing grasses of Fomalhaut II, a joyous blaze of pink and orange and purple flowers.

Micaya entered the hut and Nancia's field of vision contracted to the half-circle covered by the contact button. In the shadowy hut, stacked high with papers and bits of machinery, Blaize's red head glowed like a burning ember before the computer screen that held his attention.

"Blaize Armontillado-Perez y Medoc," Micaya said formally.

"Um. PTA shipment? I'll sign for it in a minute. Just got to finish this one thing. . . ."

The contact button's resolution wasn't enough for Nancia to read the words on the computer screen, but she recognized the seven-tone response code that chimed out when Blaize slapped his open hand on the palmpad. An interplanetary transmission — no, intersubspace; he had just sent something to . . . Nancia rummaged through her files and identified the code. To *Central Diplomatic* headquarters? What could they have to do with Angalia, a planet where no intelligent sentients existed? Had Blaize's net of corruption drawn in some of her father's and Forister's own colleagues?

"There!" As the last notes of the code chimed out, Blaize swung round, a seraphic smile on his freckled face. "And what — "

His expression changed rapidly and almost comically at the sight of Micaya Questar-Benn in full uniform. "You," he said slowly, "are not PTA."

"Quite correct," said Micaya. "Your activities have attracted some attention in other quarters."

Blaize's jaw thrust out and his freckles seemed to take on a glowing life of their own. "Well, it's too late. You can't stop me now!"

"Can't I?" Micaya's tone was deceptively mild.

"I've sent a full report to CenDip. I don't care who your friends in PTA may be, they'll have to leave Angalia alone now."

"My dear boy," said Micaya, "haven't you got it backwards? *You're* the one employed by Planetary Technical Aid. Or rather, you were."

Nancia had been so caught up in the dialogue, she never noticed when Forister slipped out of her central cabin and made his way down the stairs. She was as startled as Blaize when Forister appeared in the doorway of the hut, just on the periphery of her view from the contact button.

"Uncle Forister!" Blaize exclaimed. "What's going on here? Can you help —"

"Don't call *me* uncle," Forister said between his teeth. "I'm here with General Questar-Benn to stop you, boy, not to help you!"

Blaize went green between the spattering of freckles. He closed his eyes for a moment and looked as if he wanted to be sick. "Not you too?"

"You didn't think family feeling would extend so far as helping you exploit and torture these innocents?"

"Torture? Exploit?" Blaize gasped. "I — oh, no. Uncle Forister, *have* you by any chance been talking to a girl named Fassa del Parma y Polo? Or Alpha bint Hezra-Fong? Or Darnell —"

"All three of them," Forister confirmed, "and — what the devil is so funny about that?"

For Blaize had all but doubled up, snorting with repressed laughter. "My sins come back to haunt me," he gasped between snorts.

"I don't see what's so funny about it." Forister's own face had gone white and there was a pinched look about the corners of his mouth.

"You wouldn't. Not yet. But when I — *Oh*, Lord! This is one complication I never — " Blaize sputtered into hysterical laughter that ended only when Forister slammed a fist into his belly. Blaize was still crowing and wheezing for breath when a second blow to the jaw knocked his head back and flung him in an undignified collapse against the rickety table where his computing equipment had been stacked. Blaize's legs folded under him and he slid gently to the floor. Behind him, the table rocked and wobbled dangerously. The palmpad skated to one corner of the table top and hung on a splinter. A shower of flimsy blue hardcopies fluttered down over Blaize in a gentle, rustling rain of reports and accounting figures and PTA instructions.

Forister snatched one sheet as it drifted down and studied the column of figures for a moment, brows raised. When his eyes reached the bottom of the page, he looked tired and gray and showed every year of his age.

"Proof positive," he commented as he passed the paper to Micaya, "if any was needed."

Micaya held the paper where Nancia could focus on it through the contact button. The figures wobbled and danced in Micaya's hand; grimly Nancia compensated for movement and enlarged the blurred letters and numbers until she too could read the flimsy.

It was a statement of Blaize's Net account balance for the previous month. The pattern of deposits and withdrawals of large sums made no immediate sense to Nancia, but one thing was clear: any single figure was considerably larger than Blaize's PTA salary, and the total at the bottom was damning — more than thirty times as much credit as he could have accumulated if he'd saved every penny of his legitimate pay.

"Uncle Forister," said Blaize from the floor, tenderly

massaging his aching jaw, "you have got it all wrong. Trust me."

"After the evidence before my eyes," Forister spat out, "what could you possibly say that would incline me to trust you?"

Blaize grinned up at him. His lip was bleeding and one front tooth wobbled alarmingly. "You'd be surprised."

"If you were thinking of a small bribe out of your ill-gotten gains," Micaya told him, "you can think again." She lowered her head to speak directly into the contact button and Nancia hastily reduced the amplification. Softshells never could quite understand that they didn't need to shout at a conduct button; the speaker might be tinny, but the input lines were as powerful as any of a brainship's on-board sensors. "Nancia, please enter the Net with my personal ID code. That's Q-B76, JPJ, 450, MIC. Under that code you will be authorized to freeze all credit accounts under the personal code of, let me see. . . . " She squinted at the top of the flimsy, peering to make out a code sequence that Nancia could read perfectly well with the vision correctors damping down movement and enhancing blurred letters. "Oh, never mind, I guess you can read it," Micaya recalled a moment later.

"Correct," Nancia sent a vocal signal over the contact link.

"Don't do that!" Blaize scrambled to his feet, swaying slightly. "You don't understand — "

Forister moved to one side more rapidly than Nancia had ever seen him step, a blur of motion that placed him between Blaize and Micaya with her copy of the account balance. "I understand that you've been exploiting nonintelligent sentients to enrich yourself," he said. "You can make your explanation to the authorities. Nancia, I want you to file a formal record of the charges now, just in case anything goes wrong here."

"Done," Nancia replied.

Blaize shook his head and winced at the motion. "Ow. No. Uncle Forister, you really have got the wrong end of the story. And there's no way you can have me up on charges of — what did you say? — exploiting nonintelligent sentients. On the contrary. The Loosies are entitled to Intelligent Sentient Status and I can prove it — and nobody can stop me now; I've just sent the final documentation to CenDip. Even if you silence me, there'll be an independent CenDip investigation now."

"Silence you, *silence* you?" Forister looked at Micaya. His gray eyebrows shot up. "No question of that. We don't deal in coverups. You'll have the opportunity to say anything you like at your trial. And so will I, God help me," he murmured, so low that only Nancia's contact button picked up the words. "So will I."

"If you people would just *listen*," said Blaize, exasperated, "there wouldn't *be* any need for a trial. Didn't you hear what I said about the Loosies being intelligent?"

Micaya shook her head. "You've been here too long if you've started to cherish that illusion. Face the facts. On the way here I downloaded the survey reports off the Net. The native species don't exhibit any of the key signs of intelligence — no language, no clothing, no agriculture, no political organization."

"They've always had language," Blaize insisted. "They've got clothing and agriculture now. As for a political organization, just think about PTA for a minute and then ask yourself if that's any proof of intelligence."

Micaya laughed in spite of herself. "You have a point. But we didn't come here to argue ISS certification standards — "

"Maybe not," said Blaize, "but since you *are* here, and — " He looked suspicious for a moment. "You're not working with Harmon, are you?"

"Who?"

Micaya must have looked surprised enough to convince Blaize.

"My predecessor here — my supervisor now. Crooked enough to hide behind a spiral staircase," Blaize explained briefly. "He's the reason — well, one of the reasons — I had to do things in this way. Although even an honest PTA supervisor probably wouldn't have approved. I have bent a few regulations," he admitted. "But just do me the favor of taking a brief tour of the settlement. I think you'll understand a lot better after I show you a few things."

Micaya looked at Forister and shrugged. "I don't see any harm in it."

"I suppose if we don't go along, you'll apply for a mistrial on the grounds that you weren't allowed to show evidence in your defense?" Forister inquired.

Blaize's face turned almost as red as his hair. "Look. You're in contact with your brainship via that button. If it's inactivated, or if she sees anything she doesn't like, the full recording can go over the Net to Central at once. What will it cost you to listen to me for once in your life, Uncle Forister? God knows nobody else in our family ever bothered," he added, "but I used to think you were different."

Forister sighed. "I'm listening. I'm listening."

"Good! Just come this way, please." Blaize pushed between Forister and Micaya and flung the door of the hut open. Sunlight and gaudy flowers and a thousand shades of green danced before them, all the brighter for the contrast with the shabby interior of the hut. Blaize started down the path, talking a mile a minute over his shoulder as the other two followed him. Nancia activated the failsafe double recording system that would transmit every word and image directly to Vega Base as well as to her own storage centers.

"The Loosies never developed spoken language because they're telepaths," Blaize explained. "I know, I know, that's hard to prove directly, but just wait till you watch them work together! When the CenDip team gets here, they should bring some top Psych staff. Open-minded ones, who'll arrange tests without assuming from the start that I'm lying. Mind you, it took me a while to figure out myself," he babbled cheerfully, turning from the main path to a secondary one that wound through head-high reeds, "especially at the beginning, when they all looked alike to me. I was so damn bored, and those croaking noises they make got on my nerves, so I started trying to teach a couple of them ASL."

"What?" Micaya interrupted.

"It's an antique hand-speech, used for the incurably deaf back before we learned how to direct-install auditory synapses on metachip and hook them into the appropriate brain centers," Forister told her. "Blaize always did have strange hobbies. But teaching the Loosies a few signals in sign language doesn't prove they're intelligent, boy. A couple of twentieth-century researchers did that much with chimpanzees."

"Yeah, well, that's all I hoped to achieve in the beginning," Blaize said. "Believe me, after a couple of months on Angalia, a signing chimp would have seemed like real good company! But they picked it up like — like a brainship picks up Singularity math. That was the first surprise. I was teaching three of them who sort of hung around — Humdrum and Bobolin and Gargle." He flushed briefly. "Yeah, I know they're damn silly names, but I didn't know they were *people* then. I was just copying some of the strangled noises they made when I would talk to them and they'd try to talk back, before I realized they'd never developed the vocal equipment for true speech — that was when I started on the sign language — sorry, I'm getting mixed up. Where was I?"

"Teaching Humdrum to sign 'Where ration bar?' "
Forister told him.

Blaize laughed. "Not bloody likely. His first sentence
was more like, 'Why did Paunch Man throw ration
bars in mud and treat us like animals, and why do you
make stacks and hand them to us one at a time with
proper respect?'"

He stopped and turned to face them, his freckled
face dead serious for once. "Can you imagine how it
felt to hear a question like that coming from somebody
I'd been thinking of as — oh, like a trained spider to
while away the hours of my prison sentence? I knew
then that the Loosies weren't animals. Figuring out
what to do about it," he said, resuming his progress
through the reeds, "took a little longer."

"I deduced the telepathy when I noticed that a week
after Humdrum caught on to ASL, *every* Loosie who
showed up for rations was signing to me. Fluently. He
couldn't have taught them the rudiments that fast;
they had to have been picking the signs and the language structure out of his mind as the lessons
progressed. In fact, they told me as much when I asked
about it. Which wasn't all that easy. ASL doesn't *have* a
sign for 'telepathy,' and since they don't know English,
I couldn't spell it out. But eventually we got our signals
straight."

"If they were as intelligent as you claim, and had a
system of communication, they should have advanced
beyond their primitive level without intervention,"
Micaya objected.

"Easy for *you* to say," Blaize told her. "I wonder how
well you or any of us would do if we had evolved on a
planet where the only surface fit for farming is
rearranged by violent floods once a week, where the
caves we used for shelter crumbled and were shattered
by periodic quakes? They had a hunter-gatherer culture until a few generations ago — a small population,

not more than the planet could support, ranging through the semi-stable marshlands on the far side of this continent."

"Then what?"

"Then," Blaize said, "they were discovered. The first survey thought they might be intelligent and re-quested Planetary Technical Aid support. By the time the second survey team came along, this PTA station had been handing out unlimited supplies of ration bricks for three generations, and the culture was effec-tively destroyed. Instead of small bands of hunter-gatherers, you had one large colony with no food-gathering skill. There were far too many for the existing marshlands to support, with nothing to do and no hope of survival except to collect the ration bricks. The second survey, not unnaturally, decided they weren't intelligent. After all, nobody on the sur-vey team was stuck here long enough and lonely enough to try signing to them. But they recom-mended on humanitarian grounds, or kindness to animals, or whatever, that we not discontinue PTA shipments and starve them to death."

"But if they're intelligent—" Forister objected again.

"They are. And they can build for themselves. They just needed a—a place to start." Blaize pushed the last of the feathery reeds aside with both arms and stepped to one side, inviting Forister and Micaya to admire the view of the mine. "This was the first step."

From this vantage point, Nancia observed, they could see far more of the mine's operations than had been visible from the landing field. Teams of blue-uniformed workers were scattered across the hillside and grouped under the roofs of the unwalled process-ing sheds — twenty, forty, more than fifty of them, divided into groups of four or five individuals who worked at their chosen tasks with perfect unanimity and wordless efficiency.

"Could you train chimps to do *that*?" Blaize demanded.

Forister shook his head slowly. "And I suppose the mine is the source of your prodigious wealth?"

"It's certainly the source of the credits in that Net account," Blaize agreed.

"Exploiting intelligent sentients isn't any better than exploiting dumb animals."

Blaize ground his teeth; Nancia could pick up the clicks and grinding sounds through the contact button. "I. Am. Not. Exploiting. Anybody," he said. "Look, Uncle Forister. When I got here, the Loosies didn't have ISS. They couldn't be owners of record for the mine, they couldn't have Net accounts, they couldn't palmprint official documents. Of course my code is on everything! Who else could front for them?"

"And your code is also," Micaya pointed out, "associated with the illegal resale of PTA ration shipments that were supposed to be distributed to the natives."

Blaize nodded wearily. "Needed money to get the mine started again. I tried to get a loan, but the banks wanted to know what I was going to do with it. When I told them I was going to revive the Angalia mines they told me I couldn't do that because there was no source of labor on the planet, because the CenDip report said Angalia had no intelligent sentients. Without credits, I couldn't start the mine. And without the credits for the mine, I couldn't — well, we'll get to that in a while. Look, I falsified a few PTA reports. Said the population had tripled. Ration bars aren't exactly a hot item in international trade," he said dryly. "I had to have a *large* surplus to bargain with. Fortunately, I had an outlet right at hand. That bastard Harmon was keeping the Loosies at semi-starvation level so he could trade some of their ration bars for liquor. I had to have a little talk with the black market trader to convince him I wanted hard credits instead of hard liquor, but eventually he ... um ... came around to my way of thinking."

"Don't tell me how you persuaded him," Forister said quickly. "I don't want to know."

Blaize grinned. "Okay. Anyway, you've seen the mine; now I want to take you on a tour of Project Two. We'll have to go up the mountain for that, I'm afraid; I want you to get the long view."

The path up beside the mine was steep, but switchbacks and steps made it easier than it looked from a distance. As they passed the mine door, several Loosies looked up from their work to smile at Blaize. Their loose-skinned, grayish hands moved rapidly back and forth in flickering gestures that Nancia captured as imageflashes for later interpretation. For now, she was willing to accept Blaize's translation.

"They're asking who my mentally handicapped friends are, and whether you'd like a ride down to the processing sheds," he explained.

As he spoke, the team working at the mine's mouth filled a wagon with chunks of ore and poised it at the head of the rails swooping down into the valley. The three workers perched on top of the ore, hands gripping the sides of the wagon, and a member of the next team gave them a shove that started them off on a roller-coaster glide down the hill, swerving around rocks and dipping into hollows.

"Lost a few that way, at the start," Blaize commented, "before I remodeled the rail track so that the dips wouldn't throw anybody off."

The vegetation thinned out above the mine, giving them a view of the terraced gardens that replaced cliffs and rocks wherever a shovelful of soil could find a place. Micaya sniffed appreciatively and commented on the pungent aroma of the herbs growing in the mini-gardens.

At the top of the mountain they enjoyed a

panoramic view of what had been the Great Angalia Mud Basin, now a grassland in which fields of grain shared space with brightly colored blossoms.

"This'll be our first year's crop," Blaize said. "I'd just finished the necessary preparations for planting last year, when those nitwits I came out with were here for the meeting. None of *them* noticed anything different, of course. But if your brainship can call up files of the first survey—"

"She can do better than that," Forister told him. "She's been here herself. Nancia, do you observe any changes here? Apart from the growing things, that is?"

Blaize paled between his freckles. "*Nancia?*"

"You have some problem with my brainship?" Forister inquired mildly.

"We . . . didn't part on the best of terms," Blaize confessed in a strangled voice.

Nancia was feeling rather more kindly towards Blaize now, but she wasn't quite ready to admit that to him. "Horizon shows changes between all major peaks," she reported in the neutral, tinny voice forced on her by the contact button's limitations. "Magnification of one area of variation shows new construction of rammed earth and boulders blocking a system of gullies that appears now to be under 17.35 meters of water. . . ."

"Lake Humdrum," Blaize said. "My first terraforming effort. Trouble was, I had to block *all* the outlets, and build up reservoir walls, before I could guarantee the floods wouldn't crash through the mud basin. Then we needed irrigation ditches down into the basin. And silt collection systems, so that the soil the floods used to carry down here would still reach the basin and renew its topsoil. You want to come back down now? I want to show you the grain samples and the test results. It's not quite ripe yet, of course," he chattered as he led the way down the path, "but it's going to be a prime crop. Amaranth-19-hyper-J Rev 2, if that means anything to you. High in protein, loaded with natural nutrients, super yield from that rich top-soil. We should be able to feed ourselves and have a surplus to sell. That's why I waited until now to claim Intelligent Sentient Status for the Loosies; I wanted to be sure we would be self-sufficient in case PTA decided to curtail the ration shipments. And I didn't dare start planting until the whole flood control system had been put in place and tested. The Loosies would never have trusted me again if they'd put in a crop and seen it washed away. We needed a lot of heavy-duty ter-raforming equipment; sucked up all the mine's profits for the first three years."

They reached the bottom of the mountain and Blaize set off at a brisk walk towards the hut. Forister took his arm and gently urged him away from the hut, towards the edge of the mesa. "I'd like to get a closer look at this grain crop of yours before we go inside," he suggested.

But they didn't wind up standing in the best place to assess the grain; they came to the edge of the mesa just above the ugly volcanic mud hole that disfigured the basin, with its lazy bubbles roiling and tumbling just before the sticky surface of the mud.

Forister eyed Blaize warily. "You've been forcing the natives to work in a corycium mine owned by you."

"Persuading," Blaize corrected.

"They believed your promises to use the profits for their own good?"

Blaize flushed. "I don't think they fully understood what I had in mind at the beginning. Most of them, anyway. Humdrum and Gargle got the idea, but they never believed it would work."

"Then . . . ?" Forister left the question dangling.

"I think," Blaize said almost inaudibly, "I think they did it because they like me a little."

"Other reasons have been suggested," said Forister.

Blaize looked blank for a moment, then noticed the direction of Forister's gaze. He was staring down at the volcanic mud bubble.

"Oh. Fassa del Parma again?"

"And Dr. Hezra-Fong," said Micaya, "and Darnell Overton-Glaxely. You've still to clear up their allegations of torture."

"I — I see." With a sudden leap, Blaize jumped away from Forister and Micaya to perch on a boulder sticking halfway out from the side of the mesa. "You want proof that I didn't torture Humdrum?"

"It won't do any good to produce some other native and claim he was the one you tortured publicly, and that he recovered," Micaya told him, "just in case you were thinking of that. You've no way to prove you didn't murder and bury the one witnesses saw you torturing."

"Well, it was Humdrum, all right, and he'll tell you so, but I see your point," Blaize agreed. He fumbled at the front of his tunic; the synthofilm sides parted and he folded the garment neatly. "My best tunic," he explained politely, "you'll understand I don't want to ruin it."

"What are you doing? Come back, boy!" Forister called, just too late; Blaize had skidded down a couple of feet and was clinging to a rock ledge barely out of reach.

"Just a minute," Blaize panted in between some strange contortions. His synthofilm trousers collapsed in a shining heap around his ankles; he kicked them upwards and they snagged on a thorn bush.

"Blaize, *don't do this*." Micaya spoke in tones of quiet authority that seemed for a moment to weaken Blaize's will. He paused on the ledge, his milk-white skin almost glowing against the dull hues of the volcanic pool beneath him.

"I have to," he said calmly. "It's the only way."

Before either of them could argue further, he leapt from the ledge in a spiraling, awkward dive that ended with a resounding smack in the center of the heaving mud. White arms and legs splayed out, red head still, for a moment he seemed to have been stunned or killed outright by the fall. Then he kicked and wriggled vigorously, sinking deeper into the bubbling glop with each movement.

"Hold still," Forister called, "we'll get a rope to you — we'll do something — "

Blaize turned over onto his back. A thick layer of mud coated his body, barely preserving the decencies. He thrashed around in what Nancia belatedly recognized as an attempt at the backstroke.

"Come on in, Uncle Forister," he called up. "The mud's fine today!"

"Are you all right?" Micaya shouted while Forister, for once, struggled to find his voice.

"Couldn't be better. Mud's just at sauna heat today." Blaize stretched and wriggled luxuriously and grinned up at them through mud-spattered cheeks. "I don't usually dive from that high up — knocked the breath out of me for a minute — but I thought you needed the demonstration. Care to join me?"

Micaya looked quizzically at Forister. The brawn kicked off his shoes and rolled his trouser legs up. "Oh, I'm going down, all right," he said between clenched teeth. "It's the quickest way to get my hands on that boy. And then I'm going to — to — " Words failed him.

"Torture him in a boiling mud hole?" Micaya suggested.

• CHAPTER FOURTEEN

Nancia deliberately slowed her speed for the short hop from Angalia to Shemali. She needed time to check her records, time to access the Net and look for evidence of Polyon's scam. Somewhere in all the past five years' records of metachip and hyperchip transactions there must be some clue to his criminal activities — for she could not believe he had totally given up on the plans he'd announced during her maiden voyage. Not Polyon de Gras-Waldheim.

Even Net access was not always instantaneous, particularly when one was gathering and collating all the public records on sale, transfer or use of hyperchips in the known galaxy. Nancia idled and hoped that her passengers would not notice how long the voyage was taking.

Fortunately, they all seemed wrapped up in their own concerns. Fassa, Alpha and Darnell were all being held in separate cabins, dealing with the long spells of solitary imprisonment in their own ways. Alpha requested medical and surgical journals from Net libraries and studied the technical material Nancia downloaded for her with intense concentration, just as if she thought she would be permitted to practice her chosen profession again. *Not if I have anything to say about it,* Nancia vowed silently. But the truth was, she didn't have much to say. She could record her testimony and the images she'd received via contact buttons, and those depositions would go into evidence at Alpha's trial. But after that, all would be up to those softpersons who controlled the high courts on Central.

Most of them were High Families; half of them had some connection, kinship or financial, with the Hezra-Fong clan. Alpha might very well be free — not immediately, but in five years or ten or twenty, a mere blip in the life of a High Families girl with fewer than thirty chronological years behind her and access to the best rejuv technology to expand her life span close to two hundred years.

Not for me to decide, Nancia reminded herself, and turned her attention to the other two. As a safety precaution she kept sensors in all their cabins active at all times, but she tried not to pay too much attention unless the sensor receptors flashed to indicate unusual activity.

Darnell's activities were usual enough, Nancia supposed, for someone enslaved to a softperson's pitifully limited array of sense-receptors. He had requested Stemerald, Rigellian smokefowl and an array of Dorg Jesen's feelieporn hedra; Nancia had supplied nonalcoholic nearbeer, synthobird slices, and the hedra which Forister told her were the nearest things to porn in her library. Darnell spent most of his time reclining on his bunk, washing down synthobird and candied brancake with the nearbeer and watching a remake of an Old Earth novel over and over again. Nancia couldn't understand what he saw in the datacorded adventures of this Tom Jones, but then, it was none of her business.

Blaize was confined in the cabin opposite Darnell's. After half an hour's furious argument about who would look after "his" Loosies while he was being shipped back to Central, he'd accepted Nancia's promise to see that her sister Jinevra personally oversaw whoever was sent to replace him on Angalia. "One thing about the Perez line, they're hopelessly honest," he said in resignation. "Jinevra may not be creative, but at least she won't let that swine Harmon get his hooks into them again. You do realize that if this year's harvest fails, all my work will be wasted?"

"I realize, I realize," Nancia told him patiently. "Trust Jinevra." And as she sent out a general Net call to Jinevra and explained the situation to her sister, she wondered guiltily just how different she was from the rest of the High Families brats. Daddy had pulled strings to get her sent on this assignment. Now she was calling in favors owed her in Courier Service, and making her sister feel guilty, so that she could interfere in what should have been left to the normal channels of PTA administration.

But "normal channels" left the Loosies without the kind of aid they needed. Nancia sighed.

"Will there never be a bureaucracy that does what it's supposed to without sinking into corruption and inefficiency?" she asked Forister.

"Probably not," he replied.

"You sound like Simeon — advising me to accept corruption because it's everywhere!"

Forister shook his head. "Not in the least. I'm advising you not to waste energy being surprised and shocked about the predictable. No system, anywhere, is proof against human failings. If it were — " he forced a tired smile — "we'd be computers. Your hyperchips may be foolproof, Nancia, but the human part of you makes mistakes — and so do all of us. Fortunately," he added, "humans can also recognize and correct mistakes — unlike computers, which just go on until they crash. Now if you'll excuse me, I'd like access to your comm system for a while. I want to see what I can do to prevent Blaize from crashing."

While Blaize's explanations had satisfied all of them on an emotional level, he still had some legal problems to face. No matter how excellent his motivation, the fact remained that he had falsified PTA reports, sold PTA shipments on the black market, and transferred the profits into his personal Net account. To leave him on Angalia while the others were shipped back for trial would have seemed like the worst kind of favoritism. All Forister could do was to make sure that *all* the facts were on record for the trial — not just how Blaize had obtained the money, but what he had done with it and how he had improved the lives of the people he was sent to aid.

"They *are* people," Forister reported to Blaize with satisfaction.

"Of course they are! Couldn't you tell that?"

"What I thought, or what you thought, is beside the point," Forister told him. "What counts is CenDip's decision. And there must be at least one intelligent man in CenDip, because your report has already been received and acted on. The Loosies have ISS as of yesterday. And the decision's palmprinted by no less a person than the CenDip Secretary-Universal, Javier Perez y de Gras."

Nancia heard that with great satisfaction and turned her attention to her last prisoner. Fassa was spending most of this voyage just as she had spent the trip from Bahati to Angalia, crouched on her cabin floor, arms around her knees, staring at nothing and ignoring the food trays Nancia extruded at the dining slot. Untouched bowls of soup, baskets of sliced sweet bread, tempting fruit purees and sliced synthobird in glow-sauce went back into the recycling bins to be synthesized into new combinations of proteins and carbohydrates and fats. To all Nancia's gentle suggestions of food or entertainment Fassa replied with a dull "No, thank you," or "It doesn't matter."

"You must eat something," Nancia told her.

"Must I?" Fassa seemed obscurely amused. "No, thank you. I've had enough of men telling me what I must do and what I must be. Who cares if I get too skinny to appeal to anybody?"

"I'm not a man," Nancia pointed out. "I'm not even a softperson. And my only interest in your body is that I don't want you to get sick before . . . "

"Before my trial," Fassa finished calmly. "It's all right. You needn't be tactful. I'm going to prison for a long time. Maybe forever. As long as they don't put me on Shemali, I don't care."

"What's the matter with Shemali?" Nancia asked.

Fassa clamped her lips together and stared at the cabin wall. Her creamy skin was a little paler than usual, tinged with green shadows. "Nothing. I don't know anything about Shemali. I didn't say anything about Shemali."

Nancia gave up on Fassa for the moment. After all, there were other ways to find out what was up on Shemali. Reports on hyperchip production and sales should soon be coming in over the Net. A few invigorating hours of compiling evidence against Polyon would calm her and leave her better able to cheer up Fassa.

She felt a sneaking sympathy for the girl after reading her records. Growing up in the shadow of Faul del Parma couldn't have been easy. Losing her mother at thirteen, spending the next five years in a boarding school with not a single visit from her father, then sent out to Bahati to prove herself. . . . Nancia thought she understood how Fassa might feel. *But I didn't turn criminal to impress my family*, she argued with herself.

Your family, she replied, *wouldn't have been impressed.* Besides, she'd had it better than Fassa. Daddy and Jinevra and Flix had dropped in regularly during the eighteen years Nancia spent at Laboratory Schools. It was only after graduation that Daddy had lost interest in her progress. . . .

Softpersons could cry, and it was said that tears were a natural release of tension. Nancia looked up the biomed reports on the chemical components of tears, adjusted her nutrient tubes to remove those chemicals from her system, and concentrated on the Net records of hyperchip sales and transfer.

There was absolutely nothing there to incriminate Polyon. Two years after his arrival at Shemali, his new metachip design had been approved for production and christened the "hyperchip" in tribute to its improved speed and greater complexity. Since then, production of hyperchips had increased rapidly in each accounting quarter, so rapidly that Nancia couldn't believe Polyon was siphoning off any of the supply for his personal use. The manufactured hyperchips were subjected to especially stringent QA testing, but no more than the expected ratio failed the test . . . and all the failures were accounted for; they were sent off-planet for disposal and destroyed by an independent recycling company that had, so far as Nancia could discover, no links whatsoever with Polyon, the de Gras or Waldheim lines, or any other High Families. The hyperchips that passed QA were installed as fast as they were released, and every sale passed through the rationing board. Nancia knew from personal experience how difficult it was to get them; ever since her lower deck sensors and graphics coprocessors had been enhanced with hyperchips, she'd been pushing without success to get the hyperchips installed in the rest of her system. Micaya Questar-Benn, when questioned, told Nancia that her liver and heart-valve filter and kidneys all ran on hyperchips, installed when the metachip-controlled organs began to fail. But she, too, had been unable to get hyperchips to replace the smart chips in her external prostheses; that wasn't an emergency situation, and the ration board had refused to approve the surgery or the supplies.

Polyon had been nominated twice for the Galactic Service Award for the contributions his hyperchip design had made in areas as diverse as Fleet brainroom control, molecular surgery, and information systems. Even the Net, that ponderous, conservative communications system that linked the galaxy with news and information and records of everything ever done via computer — even the managers of the Net were slowly, conservatively augmenting key communications functions with hyperchip managers that had significantly speeded Net retrievals. The gossipbyters speculated openly that Polyon would receive the coveted GSA this year, the youngest man — and the handsomest, said Cornelia NetLink coyly — ever to hold one of the corycium statuettes. Speculation also ran rampant on which distinguished post he would surely accept after the presentation of the GSA. It seemed such a waste for such a talented young man — and so *handsome*, Cornelia inevitably added — to be stuck out at the back of beyond running a prison chip manufacturing plant. Yet so far, Polyon had refused with becoming modesty even to discuss offers of other positions.

"StarFleet assigned me to this post, and my honor is in serving where I am assigned," he declared whenever asked.

Nancia resisted the temptation to imitate a softperson raspberry at the files. Shellpersons, with near-total control over their auditory/speaker systems, didn't need to sink to such childish levels. . . .

"Thpfffft," she declared. There was *something* wrong on Shemali; she knew it, even if she couldn't prove it.

Perhaps their unannounced visit would give her the data she needed.

Despite her slowdown to cruising speeds, Nancia reached Shemali while she was still mulling over how to identify herself to the spaceport crew. Arrival of a Courier Service brainship was an unusual event on these remote planets; she didn't want to alert Polyon, give him a chance to cover up — whatever there was to cover up, and there must be *something*! Nancia thought.

In the event, the decision was made for her.

"OG-48, cleared for landing from orbit," the bored voice of a spaceport controller crackled over her comm link while Nancia hovered and wondered how to introduce herself without alarming anybody.

She quickly scanned her external sensor views. There were no other ships visible in orbit around Shemali, and any OG ship on the far side of the planet should have been out of commlink range. They must be speaking to her — oh, of course! Nancia chuckled to herself. Since the sting operation off Bahati, she'd been far too busy to demand a new paint job. The mauve-and-puce pseudowalls of an OG Shipping drone still cluttered her interior; the OG stencil was presumably still prominently displayed on her external skin. Darnell Overton-Glaxely had a reputation for picking up and retrofitting ships from any possible source. Her sleek CS shape would be unusual for a shipping line's vessel, but apparently not unusual enough to rouse any suspicion in the spaceport controller. As he droned on with landing instructions, Nancia thought she recognized the calm, level, uninflected voice. Not that voice specifically, but the feeling of detachment from worldly cares. *Since when do Blissto addicts hold responsible spaceport positions? I* knew *something was very wrong here. And we — Forister and Micaya and I — are going to find out what!*

She settled on the landing pad with a sense of exultation and adventure. Then, as she took in her surroundings, the bubbles of joyous feelings went as flat as long-opened Stemerald.

"Ugh! What *happened* to this place?" Forister exclaimed as soon as Nancia cleared her display screens to give him a view of Shemali from the spaceport.

The permacrete of the landing pads was cracked and stained, and the edge of the 'crete had a ragged hole eaten into it, as though somebody had spilled a drum of industrial biocleaners and hadn't bothered to clean up the results before the microscopic biocleaners ate themselves to death on permacrete and paint. The spaceport building was a windowless permacrete block, grim and forbidding as any maximum-security prison — which, of course, described the whole planet.

Beyond the spaceport, clouds of green and purple smoke billowed into the air. Presumably they were the source of the greenish-black ashes which had drifted over every surface visible to Nancia.

While they waited for the spaceport controller to identify himself and welcome them to Shemali, a blast of wind shrieked across the open landing field, catching the ashes and tossing them into whirling columns of pollution that collapsed as rapidly as they had arisen.

Nancia's external monitors recorded the wind temperature at 5 degrees Centigrade.

"Shemali deserves its name," she murmured.

"What's that?"

"North Wind," Nancia said. "Alpha knows the language from which all the Nyota system names come. She mentioned the translations once . . . a long time ago."

"Is the rest of the planet like this?"

Nancia briefly replaced the view of the outside with magnified displays of the images she'd taken in while descending from orbit. At the time she'd been too exercised over the problem of an appropriate greeting formula to worry much about the surface problems of the planet. Now she and Forister gazed in horrified silence at stagnant pools in which no living thing stirred, valleys eroded from the brutal road cuts leading to new hyperchip plants, swirling clouds of dust and ash blanketing woods in which the trees died and no birds sang.

"I didn't know that one factory could do so much damage to a planet," Forister said slowly.

"Looks as if there are several factories operating now," Micaya pointed out. "All running at top capacity, I'd guess, with no concern for damage to the environment . . . and Shemali's winds will have distributed the polluting waste products planet-wide."

"Did nobody *visit* Shemali before recommending Polyon for a GSA? Probably not," Forister answered his own question. "Who wants to come to a prison planet in a minor star system? And his records are good, you said, Nancia?"

"The public records are excellent," Nancia replied. "It appears that Polyon de Gras-Waldheim has truly been making every effort to see that the maximum quantity of hyperchips is manufactured and that they are distributed as widely as possible." *At incalculable cost to the environment. But that's not a crime....not legally, not here anyway. If Central cared about Shemali, they wouldn't have located the prison metachip factory here to begin with.*

A pounding on the lower doors reverberated through Nancia's outer skin. She switched back to external auditory and visual sensors. The ones on her landing braces gave her a narrow view of whoever was making this commotion . . . a gaunt man wrapped in tattered rags that looked like the remnants of a prison uniform, gray smock and loose trousers, and with more rags draped over his head and bound about his fists.

He was calling her name. "Nancia! Nancia, let me in, quickly!"

On the edge of the landing field, two bulky figures in gleaming silvercloth protective suits moved slowly forward, awkward and menacing. The silver hoods covered their faces like helmets, the silver suits glittered around them like armor. But the weapons in their raised hands were not knightly lances, but nerve disruptors, bulky squat shapes more menacing than any iron lance point.

Nancia slid open the lower doors. The fugitive collapsed against the opening doors and fell into the cargo bay. As one of the silver-suited figures raised its nerve disruptor, Nancia slammed the doors shut again. The rays bounced harmlessly against her outer shell; she absorbed the energy without conscious thought. All her attention was on the ragged prisoner who was now pushing himself to his knees, slowly and painfully unwinding the rags from around his face.

"That may not have been a wise decision," Forister commented mildly. "We don't wish to become embroiled with the local authorities. Prison disputes aren't part of our mission."

"This man is," Nancia replied. She switched the display screens to show what her sensors were picking up in the cargo bay. Micaya Questar-Benn was the first to gasp in recognition.

"Young Bryley-Sorensen! How did he get into Shemali prison . . . and out again . . . and in such condition?"

"That," said Nancia grimly, "I should very much like to know."

Sev pulled himself upright by one of the support struts that crisscrossed the cargo bay. "Nancia, don't let anybody else in. There's — you don't know — terrible things on Shemali. Terrible," he repeated. His eyes rolled up and he slid to the floor again.

"Forister, Micaya, get him out of the cargo bay before those two guards or whatever come knocking on my doors," Nancia snapped. "No, wait. I have an idea. Take his clothes off first and leave them there."

"Why?"

"Don't have time to explain. Just do it!" She set her kitchen synthesizers to work and turned on the incinerator. What she had in mind would never work if

Shemali were a decently run prison. But what she'd seen of the ravages wreaked on the planet matched what she remembered of young Polyon de Gras-Waldheim's ruthless personality, and Sev's last gasped words were all the confirmation she needed.

While Forister and Micaya stripped the unconscious Sev and manhandled him into the lift, Nancia expanded her sensor reception to examine him more closely. She recorded everything for future analysis, taking particular note of the horrible skin lesions that disfigured both Sev's arms and one leg. Dark bruises flowered in purple and blue and green on his ribs and stomach, and his back was crisscrossed with swollen weals that oozed red as the other two softpersons moved him. His breathing was shallow and irregular and he showed no sign of regaining consciousness while they dragged him to the lift.

What had they done to him on Shemali? Nancia knew how to treat the surface injuries; but this was a planet of nerve gas and acids. The lesions on his arms and legs frightened her. So did his desperate, ragged breath pattern. This went beyond the superficial injuries and known diseases she was qualified to treat. What they wanted was a doctor . . . and there happened to be one on board.

Nancia flashed her images of Sev to Alpha's cabin. There was a cry of dismay, then a strangled sob. Fassa's voice, not Alpha's. Nancia realized that in her hurry, she'd transmitted the same display to all the passenger cabins. Already Darnell was cursing about the interruption of his vid. She switched off the receptors from his cabin and displayed images of the other three prisoners so that she could watch their faces while she consulted with Alpha.

"Dr. Hezra-Fong," Nancia said formally, "we have just brought aboard a prisoner with the severe injuries you see. I fear Ganglicide poisoning. Can you treat him?"

"That's not Ganglicide," Alpha said confidently. "Minor acid burns, that's all. But there may be some lung damage. I can't be sure from these vids. And with the location of those bruises, I'm worried about kidney damage and internal bleeding. Transport him to the medtech center. I'll have a look."

She was cool and quick and competent; Nancia admired those qualities unwillingly. But could she be trusted with Sev's health?

Alpha pushed on the closed cabin door and turned back to the sensor port. Her fine, sharp-featured face was pinched with annoyance. "FN-935, I cannot diagnose and treat this man by remote control! If you're interested in his health, I strongly suggest you open this door and allow me to do my job!"

But what else would she do? Nancia wondered.

"Let me go with her," Blaize suggested.

"And me." Fassa's large eyes were filled with tears. Acting, or desperation? There was scant time to decide.

Nancia instinctively trusted Blaize, but she wasn't sure how reliable he might be. He tended to go along with the majority. And if she let both Fassa and Blaize out with Alpha, the prisoners would be the majority among the softpersons.

And whatever Fassa's crimes, Nancia somehow doubted that she would do anything to hurt Sev Bryley-Sorensen. Not after the scenes she had witnessed between them. Not after she'd watched Fassa sink into a depression between Bahati and Shemali, convinced that Sev had deserted her and that she would never see him again.

"Fassa del Parma y Polo will accompany and assist Dr. Hezra-Fong," Nancia announced with a mental prayer that she was making the right decision.

While the two women raced down the corridor to meet Forister and Micaya at the lift, Nancia slowly opened her lower cargo doors six inches. The silver-suited guard who stood outside had his fist raised to bang on the door; he lowered it now, but aimed his nerve disruptor into what he could see of the cargo bay.

"And what can I do for *you*?" Nancia asked icily.

"Drone OG-48, you are harboring an escaped prisoner," the guard said. "Return him to our custody now, or it'll be the worse for you. Your owner won't approve this, you know."

Nancia managed an icy laugh that chilled her own sensors. "This is not a drone. You'll meet us in good time. As for that diseased bundle of rags that begged entrance, it has been disposed of appropriately. It looked as if it had Capellan jungle rot and Altair plague — not to mention Old Earth lice. Did you think we'd leave something like that cluttering up this nice clean ship?"

"Don't try to lie to me," the guard warned. "This ship has been under surveillance from the moment of landing. The prisoner has not left the ship."

"Who said anything about leaving? There are its clothes — if you can call those rags clothes," Nancia added disparagingly. She slid the cargo doors open another ten inches, just enough to let the guard squeeze in edgewise. "And here's the rest of your fugitive." She opened the disposal slot and extruded the contents. A pitiful little heap of organic ash, partially burnt protein, and charred bone fragments spilled out onto the tray. The guard stepped back, every line of his body expressing horror. Nancia wished she could see his face behind the silver permafilm and the finely woven breath mesh.

"What's the matter?" she inquired. "He was dying anyway, you know."

The guard stumbled towards the doors, making retching sounds behind his mask. "I thought de Gras-Waldheim was a cold one," he said between gagging noises, "but you OG Shipping types are worse yet."

Nancia's last and most spine-chilling laugh followed him out onto the landing pad.

"Don't you want to take the remains back?" she called after him.

She slammed the cargo doors shut before he could answer, just in case he overcame his distaste and came back for the "remains." It would never do to let a lab get hold of the synthesized "bone" and algal-protein "flesh" that she had first created, then charred in the incinerator.

● CHAPTER FIFTEEN

"Stimpad! Drug stores!" Alpha snapped over her shoulder. Nancia silently extruded the required equipment from her medtech drawers. Alpha's slim dark fingers darted among the ampules supplied and loaded the pad with a combination of drugs. Nancia recognized a general nervous stimulant, a breathing regulator, and at least two kinds of anesthetic.

"Er — are you sure those will work all right in combination?" she asked apologetically. Alpha was the doctor. But Nancia had been rigorously trained in the minor first aid and holding techniques she might expect to need until she could get an ailing brawn or passenger to a clinic; and one thing her instructor had been very, very firm about was the danger of unexpected side-effects from mixing two or more drugs.

"You wanted an expert," Alpha snapped, "you got one. I've got to stabilize his condition before I can treat the superficial lesions and check for internal damage. This should keep him breathing . . . if anything will. We haven't a lot of time to waste, you know."

Quietly, Fassa del Parma slid between Alpha and Sev's unconscious body, now prone on the padded examining bench that slid out of one wall in the narrow medtech chamber. "If the combination is harmless," she said, "try it on me first."

"Don't be silly," Alpha sneered, "you've less than half his body mass. You'll be out of it for two days if I give you the same dose I've prepared for Bryley!"

"Then just use half the stimpad," Fassa suggested. She pulled one sleeve down over her shoulder, exposing an expanse of creamy white skin, naked and vulnerable. "Here. I won't move. But I want to see a demonstration before you stick anything into . . . Sev." She gulped on his name, but otherwise her composure was unbroken.

Nancia, who alone had the luxury of viewing the scene from several angles, thought she saw Sev's eyelids flutter at the sound of Fassa's voice. Neither of the young women noticed; they were too intent on one another. From the door, Micaya Questar-Benn watched in concern. Behind her, Forister glanced up at one of Nancia's hall sensors. "Time to intervene?" he mouthed soundlessly.

"Wait a minute," Nancia whispered back, the merest thread of sound.

Alpha stared at Fassa's calm face and the exposed shoulder she was offering. Her own face worked angrily. "I ought to take you up on it," she said, "you interfering dolt. Always were soft on men, weren't you? All right, then!" She tossed the loaded stimpad in the general direction of a disposal chute; Nancia extended the chute's wing-edges and caught the thing before it slid down into the recycling chamber. She wanted to have an independent lab analyze the first mix when they got to a civilized planet.

Alpha prepared a second stimpad loaded with nothing more than a common stimulant. "Happier with this?" she asked the air, brows raised sarcastically.

"Yes, thank you," said Nancia and Fassa simultaneously. But Fassa still insisted that Alpha inject her with a sample of each medication she used to treat Sev.

"You're a fool," Alpha muttered, too low for General Questar-Benn to hear; Nancia had to amplify her audio sensors to catch the thread of speech. Alpha bent over Sev as she spoke, swabbing with short vicious strokes at the acid sores on his arms and legs. "He was in bad enough shape . . . if he'd never waked up, there'd be that much less evidence against you and me both. Do you feel that grateful to him for doing his best to put you in prison?"

"I've already killed once," Fassa said. "That's enough for me. *What's that?*"

"Antibiotic spray. Relax," Alpha told her. "We had our chance to get rid of some evidence, you blew it, it's too late now. Got that freak of a general and the old fart brawn peering over our shoulders, ready to slap me with a malpractice suit on top of everything else. I'll do my best to patch your detective up for you — and my best," she added with simple pride that was quite undiminished by her criminal record, "my best, Fassa dear, is very good indeed."

It was, too. Within the hour Sev was reclining on pillows, sipping camtea loaded with so much sugar and chalker that it was hardly recognizable, and explaining to Forister and Micaya the extent of what he'd uncovered on Shemali and why he'd been in such desperate straits when Nancia landed.

"I made a few mistakes," he admitted with a grimace. "Disguising myself as a prisoner on an incoming transport seemed like the only way to slip onto Shemali unnoticed. It worked, too. But there were a few things I hadn't counted on after that."

Sev had expected his faked "prison" records, showing expertise in metachip mathematics and computer network operation, to earn him a prison job somewhere in the administration, where he'd have a chance to poke around in Polyon's records and find what he was looking for. The position he was assigned to looked promising — but as soon as he started his search, everything had gone wrong.

"Ah — you didn't say exactly what you were looking for on Shemali," Forister hinted courteously.

Sev took a long gulp of his scalding camtea, coughed, gasped, and lay back looking a little weaker. "Not important. Important thing is, more going on than you can guess from outside. Don't have it all myself . . . but enough. . . . "

Polyon's entire computer system was laced with coded traps and alarms; the first time Sev tried to access secure data, Polyon and his trusties were alerted and caught him in the act before he'd more than downloaded a handful of innocuous records. Sev then showed them his Central Worlds pass and explained that he was on an investigative mission having nothing to do with Polyon or Shemali.

"They didn't believe me," he sighed. "Even though it happened to be true."

"Then what *were* you doing?" Micaya Questar-Benn demanded.

"Later." Sev went on with his story. The trusties had beaten him up, stripped him, located and disabled the thin sliver of spyderplate which he'd meant to use as a distress beacon to Nancia in case he got into trouble. "Those things are supposed to start emitting an all-frequencies distress signal hooking into the Net if they're damaged," Sev complained. "So at first I wasn't too worried. But then when you didn't come, and it got to be two days, I thought I might be on my own."

"De Gras-Waldheim must know some way to disable them," Forister nodded.

"Reasonable," Nancia put in from the speaker. "He invented them. They're essentially single-purpose hyperchips — and nobody knows more about hyperchips than Polyon."

Sev's next discovery was that Polyon had stepped up the new plants' production of hyperchips by ignoring all safety precautions. Sent to the hyperchip burnoff lines, where prisoners' life expectancy amid the clouds of nerve-destroying gas could be measured in days rather than years, Sev had resolved to make a break for freedom when the first ship touched down on Shemali — especially when he recognized the slim lines of Nancia's

Courier Service hull behind the disguising frieze of OG Shipping logos and mauve stripes. The escape hadn't been too difficult; all the other prisoners had been terrorized out of even thinking about escape, and the guards were lazy and careless and unwilling to spend much time in the burnoff rooms.

"And besides," finished Forister with a grin, "nobody would expect a prisoner on the run to go to an OG Shipping drone for help. Nancia, your paint job has served us well. I don't suppose you'd consider keeping it after this is over?"

"Most certainly not!" Nancia told him. "And it wouldn't work, anyway. When we've finished in the Nyota system, there won't be any more OG Shipping. But — what do we do now?"

Sev's story had demonstrated enough irregularities to justify arresting Polyon twice over. But he was just one man, with no datacordings or computer records to exhibit in proof of his story. If they took Polyon away now without making sure of their evidence, Sev predicted that Shemali would be cleaned up by the time they got back.

"Impossible," said Forister with feeling.

Sev nodded weakly. "Not the planet's surface, I grant you. But you can be sure there'll be nothing inside the factories for an investigative committee to quarrel with. It'll all be clean assembly lines, strict safety features."

"And the prisoners who've already been damaged by exposure to acids and gases?"

"I don't think," said Sev somberly, "that any of them will be able to testify by that time."

"Then we'll have to go down now and get the evidence," Forister said.

Sev shook his head. "Won't work. He's clever — there's a VIP tour arranged — the disfigured prisoners and the dangerous work lines are all kept well out of sight. Mostly at the secondary plants hidden backplanet. I know how to find one of the worst plants. I was there. But without me, he'll whisk you from one end of the central prison factory to the other, and you won't see anything, and every time you try to turn around there'll be six guards in your way. I'll have to go with you." He tried to raise himself from the pillows, started coughing and fell back again.

"You can't!" Fassa exclaimed.

"May have to," said Micaya Questar-Benn. "Duty." She and Sev nodded at one another. "You two," she jerked her head at Fassa and Alpha — back to your cabins now. Nothing to do with you — shouldn't have let you hear this much."

"Wait!" Fassa cried as Forister took her by the arm. "There has to be another way. It won't work, taking Sev with you, can't you see that? Even if he were stronger, the sight of his face will warn Polyon at once that there's something wrong. None of you — none of us will get away alive."

"Oh, come now," said Forister gently. "Your friend can't be that dangerous."

Fassa's face hardened. "If you don't believe me, ask the others. Alpha?"

Alpha bint Hezra-Fong nodded once, reluctantly.

Fassa looked up at the room sensor. "Nancia, can you connect us with Blaize and Darnell? Just for a moment?"

Both men agreed with Fassa's assessment of the situation.

"Then what *can* we do?" Forister demanded. "Damn it, I'm not going to turn tail and run off-planet for fear of some spoiled High Families brat who's got hold of some dangerous toys!"

"I think," Fassa said slowly, "that you're going to use me." She was very pale. "Take Alpha back to her cabin, and I'll explain what I think we can do." She looked apologetically at Alpha.

"Traitor! When Polyon finds out—"

Fassa's lips were pinched. She was not pretty at all, now. But she was almost beautiful, in a cold remote way. "I'll have to take that chance, won't I?"

"Better you than me," Alpha said. She turned to go. "All right. Lock me up. I don't even want to hear this plan. Maybe he won't hold it against me, if I'm not even here when you discuss it." She didn't sound too hopeful of that.

When Fassa explained her plan, there was a brief silence while Forister, Nancia and Micaya all thought it over.

"You think he'll fall for it?" Forister queried.

"He thinks Nancia is an OG drone," Fassa pointed out. "He believes her passengers cremated Sev for being a nuisance; if he hadn't swallowed that story, believe me, we'd be hearing from him by now." She gave them a strained smile. "Murderers in the escort of OG shipping — what better credentials could you have? And with me to front the introductions—"

"I won't let you!" Sev said hoarsely.

"Fassa stays on board Nancia," Micaya interrupted. "That's understood." She looked at the girl. "No offense, Fassa. But from the ship, we can monitor what you say. And I think you'd better wear these." She bent over briefly, fiddled with the prosthesis replacing her left leg, and straightened with two lengths of shining, thread-fine wire. "Hold out your wrists."

Fassa obeyed and Micaya encircled each wrist with a length of the wire. Where she twisted the ends shut, the wires seemed to collapse and seal invisibly upon themselves.

"Tanglefield? Is that really necessary?"

Micaya nodded. "Security measure, no more. Field won't be activated unless we run into trouble on Shemali. Clear, Nancia?"

"Affirmed."

Micaya touched her synthetic arm. "I've got a portable tanglefield generator built in here," she told Forister. "Might come in handy on Shemali. Want some wires?"

Forister took a handful of the gleaming wires and regarded them dubiously. "I prefer to solve my problems more elegantly than this."

"Me, too." Micaya tugged her dark green pants leg down over the prosthesis. "Isn't always possible, though. Everybody tells me there'll be terrible political complications if we harm a hair on the head of this High Families brat. So . . . " She patted her prosthetic leg again and straightened. "I've stashed the needler. Agree with you, taking him out straightaway would be simpler, but you insisted on doing this by the book."

"That wasn't," Forister said, "quite what I meant by an elegant solution."

Micaya regarded him with a hint of amusement on her solemn, dark face. "Know it. Usually is the most 'elegant' way, though. Leave little tyrants to run loose, they grow up into big tyrants. Then you get the Capellan mess, or something like. Wars," she pointed out, "aren't elegant." She nodded once to Fassa, by way of apology. "Understand, not accusing you of treachery, just not taking chances. Want you to be warned — "

"That a secret signal to Polyon will do me more harm than good," Fassa finished calmly. "You don't trust me. That's all right. I wouldn't trust me, either."

She was white to the lips now, and her hands were shaking, but she led the way from the medtech room without pausing.

Nancia could see that Sev was fretting enough to damage himself by trying to go after them, so she switched displays to give him visual and auditory sensor taps to the main cabin.

Fassa was still pale when Nancia initiated the signal sequence that would open a comm link with planetside authorities, but she managed the promised introductions with perfect composure. For Polyon's benefit Forister and Micaya became Forrest Perez and Qualia Benton, a pair of potential hyperchip customers with cash to invest in the operation. She hinted delicately that "Qualia Benton" was really a high-ranking general from Central, and Micaya started forward to stop her. Forister laid one hand on Micaya's arm. "Trust the young lady, Mic," he murmured. "She has — er — more experience in this sort of thing than you or I."

So it proved. Far from being alarmed by Micaya's military standing, Polyon accepted her presence with Fassa, on an OG ship, as proof that she was as corrupt as his friends. And he was clearly delighted to have made the contact. Within minutes he was arranging to meet Fassa's "friends" and give them a tour of the newest hyperchip plant.

"I don't know why, but Polyon's always been eager to get more hyperchips sold to the military," Fassa told the others after she cut the contact. "It's not the money, either; he offered Space Academy a cut rate once, but the Ration Board stopped him. I knew your rank would be the thing to draw him in, Micaya. A back door into the military supply system is Polyon's dream."

"I suppose he wants to impress his old teachers and classmates by making sure they all use his inventions," Forister surmised.

Nancia was confused. "But surely he doesn't imagine that selling hyperchips on the black market is the way to high standing in the Academy?"

All three softpersons laughed tolerantly, and Nancia heard a weak chuckle from the sensor link to the med-tech cabin where Sev rested. "Investigate the sources of a few High Families fortunes some time, Nancia," Sev recommended to her. "Money washes clean of most any taint — and more rapidly than you'd believe possible."

"Not," Nancia said, "in the Academy. And not in House Perez y de Gras, either."

Nancia fussed over Forister and Micaya until the last minute, fitting them out with contact buttons, spyderplates, and every other remote protection device she could think of. "I don't know what good you think this will do," Forister complained. "De Gras-Waldheim disabled Sev's spyderplate without alerting anybody, didn't he?"

"Sev didn't have me monitoring him," Nancia pointed out.

She should have confined Fassa to her cabin before the other two left, but she didn't have the heart to. "Somebody should stay with Sev," Fassa pleaded.

"Oh, let the child stay with him," Forister put in unexpectedly. "She's not worth much as a hostage anyway. If even half of what Sev told us about the hyperchip factory conditions is true, Polyon de Gras-Waldheim is a murderer a dozen times over who'd think nothing of sacrificing a ship full of his former friends."

Fassa nodded. "Yes, that's about right. Except — I wouldn't say he'd 'think nothing of it.' He'd probably enjoy it."

"Why didn't any of you tell us about Polyon before this?" Nancia demanded. "You were all babbling your stupid heads off, pointing the finger at one another to get some credit for your own plea bargains, and you never warned us about Polyon."

"Afraid to," Fassa said sadly.

"So afraid that you let Sev go off to Shemali without a word of warning? I'd never have let him go unmonitored if I'd guessed."

"I didn't know Sev had gone to Shemali," Fassa defended herself. "Nobody told me anything. I didn't even know he wasn't on board when we left Bahati. All I knew was that he didn't come to see me again, and I thought, I thought . . . and quite right, too; why should he bother with someone like me?" Tears filled her eyes; Nancia thought that for once they were genuine.

"Fassa del Parma, you are a prime idiot!" Sev's weary, hoarse whisper startled all of them; Nancia had forgotten that she'd left the connections between the main cabin and the medtech room wide open. "Get in here and hold my hand and smooth my fevered brow. I'm an injured man. I need attention."

"Call Alpha. She's a doctor," Fassa gulped.

"I want *you*. Now are you coming, or do I have to get up and get you?"

Fassa fled. And Nancia watched, satisfied, and feeling only a little bit like an eavesdropper, as she burst through the door of the medtech room. Hadn't Sev given her explicit instructions to keep full sensors open whenever he was with Fassa del Parma?

Those two were too wrapped up in each other for Fassa to pose any danger to anybody. All the same, Nancia kept those sensors open while she concentrated most of her attention on the images and sounds coming in from Forister's and Micaya's contact buttons. Polyon was losing no time; he'd met them on the landing field in a flyer that swooped directly to the newest hyperchip production facility, a squat featureless building set in a valley that might have been beautiful before Polyon's construction teams sliced through the earth and the waste products from his factory killed off the trees. Now the building stood alone at the top of a sloping hill ringed round by stagnant, poisonous-looking waters and the broken stumps of dead trees. Nancia felt her sensors contracting in repulsion at the image.

"General, can you handle this flyer?" she murmured through Micaya's contact button.

"I'm glad to see you have such up-to-date equipment, de Gras," Micaya said loudly for Nancia's benefit. "I tested the prototype versions of this flyer recently, but I had no idea the model was in general distribution already."

Good. Micaya would be able to bring the three of

them back. Nancia listened in on Sev's and Fassa's conversation while Polyon landed the flyer and took Forister and Micaya into the factory.

"You think too much," Sev was saying firmly to Fassa. "I meant what I told you before, and I still mean it. You idiot, I went to Shemali on your account!"

"On my account?" Fassa echoed, sounding as if she was unable to think at all.

Sev nodded. "Here I'd been pacing Nancia's corridors every night, trying to think out a way to save you, and then Darnell gave me a clue. He said you'd contracted to build a hyperchip factory for Polyon, and that when the original building collapsed you replaced it free of charge. I thought if I could prove that, your lawyer might argue that you never intended to do substandard work — that any problems with your buildings were the result of incompetence, of sending a young girl to manage a business she was unfamiliar with — and that he could prove it by demonstrating how willingly you'd made restitution when a problem was brought to your attention."

Fassa smiled through her tears. "It's a lovely, lovely argument, Sev. Unfortunately, not a word of that is true. I am," said Fassa, "or rather, I was an extremely competent contractor." She sniffed. "Damn Daddy. He accidentally sent me into a business I had a real talent for."

"That being the case," said Sev softly, "why the hell couldn't you just *be* a contractor, instead of slinking around in those dresses that kept falling off your shoulders and driving middle-aged men crazy?"

Fassa's face hardened. "Ask Daddy." She tried to turn away, but Sev had hold of both her hands.

"I guessed some time ago," he said. "And . . . I've been checking old gossipbytes. Was that why your mother killed herself?"

Fassa nodded. Tears were streaming down her face unchecked. "Well, then. You won't want to have anything more to do with me. I understand. I'm not, I'm not . . . it's not just Daddy, you know. There've been all those other men. . . . " She gulped down a sob.

For a man who'd been on the verge of collapse a few hours earlier, Sev demonstrated remarkable powers of recovery. Nancia was impressed by the strength with which he drew Fassa into his arms against her resistance. "You," he said deliberately, "are the woman I love, and nothing that happened before today matters in the slightest to me." He paused for a moment and Nancia blacked out her visual sensors. She didn't really think that the requirements of surveillance on Fassa included watching Sev Bryley-Sorenson kiss her as desperately as a man in vacuum gasping for oxygen.

On Shemali, Micaya Questar-Benn had finally persuaded Polyon to drop the sanitized V.I.P. tour of his factory. She didn't believe he could produce enough hyperchips to satisfy her requirements, she told him, and what was more, she didn't believe he would be able to extend the factory's production fast enough for her. The safety requirements mandated by the Trade Commission simply took too long to set up and maintain.

Polyon suggested that the Trade Commission could, collectively, do something anatomically impossible for the individual members. And if the General wanted to see just how fast he could turn out hyperchips, he added, she and her friend could just follow him. They'd have to wear protective gear, though, he said, struggling into a silvercloth suit himself as he spoke.

While Micaya and Forister put on the suits provided for guests, Micaya commented innocently that the cost of suiting up an entire production line of prisoners must be prohibitive, and that she didn't see how they maintained the dexterity necessary for the assembly process while working from inside the bulky silvercloth gloves.

Polyon chuckled and agreed that the difficulties posed were enormous.

* * *

On board, Sev and Fassa were talking again; Nancia discreetly tuned in to their conversation, but there wasn't much in it to require her attention. Fassa was gloomy about the prospect of years in prison. Sev wasn't any too cheerful about it himself, but he assured Fassa that he'd wait for her.

"I don't think they let murderers out," Fassa said. "Unless they decide to mindwipe me."

"Fassa, you are not a murderer. Caleb isn't dead."

Fassa's slender body became quite still. "He isn't?"

"You were right," Sev said. "Nobody tells you anything. He isn't dead. He isn't even seriously ill; he was in therapy for nerve damage when I left Bahati."

"Latest bulletins from Summerlands say that he should recover full function quite soon and will probably be restored to active brawn status within the next few weeks," Nancia confirmed.

Sev and Fassa broke apart and looked up at the overhead speaker.

"Nancia!" Sev exclaimed. "I didn't know you were listening."

"You gave me the orders yourself," Nancia reminded him.

"Oh. Well." Sev thought. "Can I cancel the orders? Will you obey me if I do?"

"I really shouldn't."

"Lock the door on us both," Sev suggested. "I don't mind. But please, could we have some privacy now? This voyage back to Central is likely to be my last chance to be alone with my girl for a long, long time."

Fassa looked ridiculously happy for someone facing trial and a stiff prison sentence. Nancia left them to it.

She didn't have much to occupy her on Shemali, either. Micaya and Forister hadn't waited to take the full tour of the hyperchip assembly line; a few images of prisoners working unshielded with skin-destroying acids, in rooms that leaked poisonous gas, were all the evidence they needed to bolster Sev's detailed eyewitness testimony. The datacordings were particularly damning when accompanied, as they were, by Polyon's pleasant, cultured voice explaining just how he had cut costs and speeded up production by condemning the prisoners in his care to lingering, painful deaths by industrial poisoning. By the time Nancia had scanned those images, Micaya had already slapped tanglewires around Polyon's wrists, ankles, and even his neck. With the ankle field activated, she read him the formal statement of arrest.

"You can't do this!" Polyon protested. "Do you know who I am? I'm a de Gras-Waldheim. And I have Governor Lyautey's approval for everything I've done here!"

"My brainship has already transmitted a request for drug testing on Lyautey and all other civilian personnel," Forister told him. "I suspected Blissto when I heard your spaceport controller talking. What did you do, make addicts of anybody who could blow the whistle on you?"

"You can't arrest *me*," Polyon repeated as though he hadn't understood a word.

Micaya Questar-Benn had a smile that would have chilled steel to the snapping point. "Want to bet, son? Walk in front of me. Slowly, now. Wouldn't want the tanglefield to think you're trying to escape and cut off your feet; it's too quick and easy a death for your sort." And when Polyon opened his mouth again, she activated the extended tanglefield from the neck wire to keep him from flapping his tongue about any more.

As they left the assembly lines, a ragged cheer went up from the prisoners behind them.

CHAPTER SIXTEEN

To Polyon's shock and amazement, the cyborg freak and her partner actually managed to convince Governor Lyautey that they were entitled to arrest a de Gras-Waldheim and take him away. "Convince" was probably too strong a word. Polyon recognized with rueful amusement that he'd been caught in his own trap. The governor, like all the civilians left on Shemali, was constantly dosed with Alpha bint Hezra-Fong's Seductron. Since Lyautey was in a nonessential job, Polyon kept his maintenance level of Seductron so high that the governor did little but nod amiably and agree with whoever spoke to him last.

Somebody must have figured that out and thought of this way to use it against him. With his mouth covered by tanglefield, Polyon could do nothing but listen while this Micaya Questar-Benn and her partner rattled off official-sounding words, flourished their forged credentials — they had to be forged — and took him away in the very flyer he himself had sent to pick them up at the spaceport.

They considerately removed the tanglefield from his mouth as soon as the flyer took off. Polyon maintained a dignified silence during the short flyer hop back to the spaceport, but his brain was working furiously. He refused to believe that this "arrest" was real. Real Central agents had their own transport, they didn't hitch a ride on an OG cruiser or get a conniving little whore like Fassa del Parma to front for them. This had to be some trick cooked up by Darnell and Fassa to get control of the hyperchips. He had no intention of giving them or their friends the amusement of seeing him struggle and protest. Later, when he'd figured out their game, he would turn the tables and make them squirm. Darnell would be easy to break, but Fassa . . . he smiled unpleasantly at the thought of exactly how he'd take the pride out of her. He'd never yet threatened Fassa physically. Maybe it was time to start.

Then, as the flyer came gently down on the landing pad, he blinked and saw the ship for a moment silhouetted against the bright sky, only sleek lines and smooth design, without the confusing detail of the OG colors and logo, and he knew where he'd seen a ship like that before.

"Courier Service," he groaned, and for the first time he began to believe that he was really under arrest.

"Got it in one," said the spare, quiet man who'd accompanied General Questar-Benn, offering Polyon his hand to help him to the ground. "Time I introduced myself. Forister Armontillado y Medoc, brawn to the FN-935."

"*You* a brawn, old man?" Polyon sneered. "I'll believe that when I see it!" He refused the offer of the steadying hand and swung himself out of the flyer, feet together, hands in front of him, still with athletic grace. Even with his hands and feet constrained in tanglefields, he still had his strength and his natural balance.

"You'll not have to wait long," Forister replied mildly. "I'll introduce you to my Brainship as soon as we're aboard."

Polyon maintained a grim silence while these two escorted him to the ship's lift, up to the passenger level and down a depressing mauve-painted corridor to the cabin where he was to be confined. Once there, he leaned against the wall and waited. The brawn Forister and the cyborg Micaya withdrew, leaving him still confined in the double tanglefield about wrists and ankles. "Wait!" he cried out. "Aren't you going to — "

The door irised shut behind them with a series of clicks along the concentric rings, and a moment later a sweet female voice spoke from the overhead speaker.

"Welcome aboard the FN-935," she — it — said. "I am Nancia, the brainship of this partnering. Your arrest is legal under Central Code — " and she reeled off paragraphs and statute references that meant nothing to Polyon. "As a prisoner awaiting trial on capital crimes, you may legally be confined by tanglefield for the duration of the voyage, which will be approximately two weeks. General Questar-Benn has transferred the tanglefield control function to my computer; if you will give me your word not to attempt damage to me or to your fellow passengers, I will release the tanglefield now and allow you the freedom of your cabin."

Polyon glanced over the narrow space and laughed sardonically. "You have my word," he said. Words were cheap enough.

As soon as he spoke the electronic field ceased vibrating. His wrists and ankles prickled with returning life; an uncomfortable sensation, but far, far better than being electronically bound hand and foot for the next two weeks.

The brainship blathered on with threats about sleepgas and other restraints that could be applied if he gave it any trouble; Polyon didn't bother to listen. He had too much to think about. Besides, he didn't intend to do anything the brainship could see. He wasn't that stupid.

Unobtrusively, under cover of flexing his wrists to restore full movement, he patted his breast pocket and felt the reassuring lump right where it should be, where he always carried a minihedron with the latest test version of his master program. He *was* clever, Polyon thought. Too clever by half for this pair to master for long.

Oh, he'd make some trouble for this interfering brainship and its doddering brawn, all right, just as soon as he got the chance. But it wasn't trouble that they would be able to see or hear coming, and there wouldn't be a damned thing they could do about it once he'd started. Damn them! He wasn't ready for this; he was still two to three years short of having everything in place. How much would it cost him to make his planned move ahead of schedule?

Impossible to calculate; he'd just have to go ahead and find out later. Whatever the cost, it couldn't be as great as that of going tamely back to Central for trial and imprisonment. It had always been a gamble, Polyon comforted himself. He'd always known that one day somebody might figure out about the hyperchips, and that he'd have to move fast if that occurred.

At least now, even if the move was being forced on him, it was forced by some ignoramuses who didn't even guess how he might retaliate. He would have the advantage of surprise on his side.

If only he'd had time to implement Final Phase! Then he could have started everything right now, with a spoken word of command. As it was, he'd have to get this minihedron into a reader slot before he could make his move.

There weren't any reader slots in this cabin; and he was supposed to be confined here until they reached Central; and if he tried to break out of the cabin, the damned brainship would drop him with sleepgas or a tanglefield before he got to any place with reader slots.

Polyon bared his teeth briefly. He did love a challenge. He still had his voice, and his wits, and his charm, and sensor contact with the brainship and her brawn. He set to work with those tools to dig himself an impalpable tunnel to freedom, placing each word and each request as carefully as a miner shoring up the loose earth in the tunnel roof.

* * *

In the long dragging hours until they reached the Singularity point for transition into Central subspace, there wasn't much to do but play games or read. Forister and Micaya began another tri-chess contest; Nancia obligingly created the holocube for them and maintained a record of the moves, but warned them that some of the game data might be lost if she needed to call on that particular set of coprocessors during Singularity.

"That's all right," Forister said absently. "Mic and I have been interrupted by all sorts of things in our time. Aren't you partnering me, then?"

"I don't think I'd better," Nancia replied with real regret. "I think I should monitor our passengers. They've been allowed a great deal of freedom, you know."

Micaya snorted. "Freedom! They're free to move within their cabins, that's all. Granted, I wouldn't cut 'em that much slack, but —

"That," said Forister, "is why you keep having political problems. You never cut the High Families any slack, and they resent it."

"Shouldn't," said Micaya. "I'm one of them."

"That doesn't help," Forister said, almost sadly. "Anyway, Mic, you're not seriously worried about a ship's mutiny?"

"From those spoiled brats?" Micaya snorted. "Ha! Even that de Gras boy, for all the others were so scared of him, trotted aboard like a little lamb. No, there's not a one of them has the brains — saving your Blaize, maybe — or the guts to try anything, now that we've cut off their special deals."

"Blaize wouldn't try anything," Forister said sharply. "He's a good boy."

Micaya patted Forister's arm. "I know, I know. Convinced me. But he did rip off PTA. And what's worse to my mind — he didn't speak up about the others. Have to answer for that, though it's less, all told, than the rest of this precious crew have to stand trial for."

"I understand," Forister said glumly.

Sev Bryley-Sorenson stretched out his long legs. "Think I'll work out for a while," he announced to no one in particular.

"You'd think it was him going back for trial, to look at the long face on the boy," Micaya commented as Sev whisked himself down the corridor to the exercise room.

"Can't be much fun," Forister said gently, "being in love with a girl who's likely to be unavailable for the next fifty Standard Years. And he doesn't have much to take his mind off it. He's not the type for tri-chess."

"Not bright enough, you mean. True," said Micaya with a trace of complacency. "And too bright for that silly game the prisoners are playing. Doesn't leave him much, you're right."

"Do you *really* have to monitor the prisoners all the time, Nancia?" Forister looked at her column with the smile that always melted her best resolutions. "Surely they'll do no damage while they're all wrapped up in that idiotic game. And if you think it's unfair to Micaya for you to partner me . . . we could play three-handed?"

Nancia had to concentrate a little harder for this display, but after a moment of intense processing the holocube shimmered, twisted, danced around its central core and reformed as a holohex, with three separate triple rows of pieces formed at opposing edges.

And in his cabin, Polyon de Gras-Waldheim stopped listening to the conversation in the central cabin and rejoined the SPACED OUT game that was currently helping his fellow prisoners to forget their troubles. Persuading Nancia to open the comm system so that the five of them could play from their cabins had been his first move. Now, at least, he could talk to the others. But he hadn't dared say anything beyond standard game moves while Nancia was conscientiously monitoring them.

The display screen showed that three of the game characters had managed to lose themselves in the Troll Tunnels. Polyon's own game icon was still at the mouth of the tunnels, awaiting a command from him. "I know how we can get out of the tunnels," he said.

"How? I've tried every exit the system shows. They're all blocked," Alpha complained.

"There's a secret key," Polyon told her. "I have it. But I can't get to the door it unlocks from here."

"I never heard anything about a secret key," Darnell announced. "I think you're bluffing." His game icon bounced angrily back along one of the Troll Tunnels, spitting sparks as it went.

"You wouldn't," Polyon said smoothly. "I'm the game master. This secret key can even override your character, Fassa."

Fassa had taken the Brainship icon for this game.

"I don't see how," Fassa responded. "Show me?"

"I *told* you. I can't get to where I can use it. If any of you can get me out of this blind alley, though — "

"You're not *in* a blind alley!" Darnell interrupted. "You're standing right at the entrance to the Troll Tunnels! Why don't you move your icon on into the tunnels?"

"And get lost like the rest of you? No, thanks." Polyon waved his hand over the palmpad and shut off the bickering voices of the gamesters. He brooded in silence for a while. Why had he ever bothered with such an inept bunch of conspirators? They were too stupid to pick up on his veiled hints. They thought he was interested in playing a *game*!

Blaize, now; Blaize was brighter than the others, and he'd taken no part in the brief exchange. Polyon tapped out a series of commands that would give him a private comm link to Blaize's cabin. At least he could hack into Nancia's system to that extent from the keyboard; though it was nothing to the power that would be his once he'd made his way to a reader slot with his minihedron.

While he thought out his approach to Blaize, he was startled by a crackle of sound. The idiot thought he'd achieved a private channel to the lounge! And what was he planning to do with it? Polyon scowled, then began to listen attentively. It seemed that Blaize was too bright to make a good tool.

But he might still be an excellent pawn, in a game whose moves he'd never see. . . .

"Uncle Forister?" Blaize switched comm channels to the lounge. "I need to talk to you."

"Talk," Forister grunted. He was just putting the final touches to a truly beautiful strategy, designed to pit Micaya's and Nancia's Brainship pieces against one another while he moved unopposed to control all vertices of the holohex.

"Privately."

"Oh, all right." Forister got up and stretched. "Nancia, can you store the holohex until I get back? I wouldn't want to tire you by asking you to maintain the display while we're not actually playing."

Nancia chuckled. "You mean you don't want to leave the holohex set up where we can study the positions and figure out what nasty trap you're getting ready to spring on us this time."

"Well . . ."

The holohex folded in upon itself and became a sheet, a line, a point of dazzling blue light that then winked out of existence. "All right. We're approaching the Singularity point, anyway; I really shouldn't be playing games now. Need to check my math," Nancia said cheerfully. "Be sure and get back in time to strap yourself in. You softpersons get so disoriented in Singularity."

"And you shellpersons get so uppity about it,"
Forister retorted. "All right. You'll warn us in plenty of
time, I assume?"

"*And* monitor you while you're in the cabin," Nancia
said. "Don't look like that; it's for Blaize's protection as
well as yours. If you're left alone with him, the
prosecution might try to discredit your testimony, say
you'd been bribed or suborned."

"They won't have much respect for his uncle's good
word anyway," said Forister gloomily, going on down
the passageway to find out what Blaize had in mind.
Nancia triggered the release mechanism on the door
just long enough for him to slide through.

"I think Polyon's planning something," Blaize said
as soon as Forister entered the cabin. He sat at the
cabin console, one hand quivering over the palmpad
without actually starting a program, all red-headed
intensity like a fox at a rabbit hole.

"What?"

"I don't know. He wants to get out of his cabin. He
keeps telling us that he can fix everything if only he could
get out for a few minutes. Listen!" Blaize ran the heel of
his hand over the palmpad and brought up a datacording of the last few transmissions between the SPACED
OUT gamesters. From the cabin console he couldn't access enough memory to store images as well as voices; the
players' words crackled out through the speaker, disem-
bodied and robbed of half their meaning. Forister
listened to the recorded exchange and shook his head.

"Just sounds like a few more moves in that dumb
game of yours to me, Blaize."

"It's a move in a game, all right," Blaize said grimly,
"but he's not playing the same game as the rest of us.
Damn! I wish I'd been able to capture the images and
the icon moves too. Then you'd see."

"See what?"

"That what Polyon was saying made absolutely no

sense in the context of the actual game moves." Blaize dropped his hands in his lap and looked up at Forister. "Can Nancia keep Polyon under sleepgas until we reach Central?"

"She *can*," Forister replied, "but I've yet to see any reason why she *should*. This case is going to have all the High Families buzzing like uprooted stingherbs as it is; it'll only be worse if we give them some excuse to allege mistreatment of prisoners."

"But you heard him!"

"Didn't make any sense to me," Forister allowed, "but nothing about that silly game makes sense, in my humble opinion. Come on, Blaize. Can you seriously see me explaining to some High Court judge that I kept a prisoner stunned and unconscious for two solid weeks because something he said in the course of a children's game made me nervous?"

"I suppose not," Blaize agreed. "But — you'll be careful?"

"I am always careful," Forister told him.

"And — I don't think you should talk to him. The man's dangerous."

"I know you four are scared of him," Forister agreed, "but I think that's because you've been away from Central too long. He's nothing but an arrogant brat who was given more power than was good for him. Like some other people I could name. Now if you'll excuse me, it's nearly time to strap down for Singularity."

He nodded at the wall sensors and Nancia silently slid the door open for him.

Once he was in the passageway again, she spoke in a low voice.

"Polyon de Gras-Waldheim requests the favor of a private interview."

"He does, does he! And I suppose you think I ought to take Blaize's warning seriously, and insist on having Micaya as a bodyguard before I talk to him?"

"I think you're reasonably able to look after yourself," Nancia said, "especially with me listening in. It's not as if you were piloting a dumbship. But there's not much time; I'll be entering the first decomposition sequence in a few minutes."

"All the better," said Forister. "I won't have to spend too long with him. I'll talk with him until you sound the Singularity warning bell, if that's all right. Can't do much less. Visited Blaize — have to visit any of the others who request it."

When Forister entered, Polyon was lying on his bunk, arms folded behind his head. He turned at the soft sound of the sliding door, jumped to his feet and brought his heels together with a military precision that Forister found almost annoying.

"Sir!"

"I'm not," Forister said mildly, "your superior officer. You needn't click your heels and salute. You wanted to tell me something?"

"I — yes — no — I think not," Polyon said. His blue eyes looked haunted; he pushed a wayward strand of golden hair back from his forehead. "I thought — but he was my friend; I can't do it. Even to shorten my own sentence — no, it's impossible. I'm sorry to have disturbed you for nothing, sir."

"I think," Forister said gently, "you'd better tell me all about it, my boy." It was hard to reconcile the haunted creature before him with the monster who'd made Shemali prison into a living hell. Perhaps Polyon had some explanation he wished to proffer, some story about others who'd conceived the vicious factory system?

It took him a good five minutes of gentling Polyon's overactive sense of honor, all the time listening anxiously for the Singularity warning bell, before he coaxed the boy into letting out a name.

"It's Blaize," Polyon said miserably at last. "Your nephew. I'm so sorry, sir. But — well, while we were playing SPACED OUT he was boasting to me of how he'd pulled the wool over your eyes, convinced you he was innocent of any wrongdoing — "

"Not quite," said Forister. He spoke very evenly to control the twist of pain that squeezed his chest. "He did sell PTA shipments on the black market. That's wrongdoing, in my book, and he'll be tried for it on Central."

Polyon nodded. His look of suffering had not abated. "Yes, he said that was the story he'd given you. Then I thought — if you didn't know — perhaps I could trade the information for a reduction in my own sentence."

"What information?" Forister asked sharply.

Polyon shook his head. "Never mind. It doesn't matter. I've enough on my conscience already," he said, raising his head and staring at the wall with a look of noble resignation that Forister found intensely irritating. "I won't compound my crimes by informing on a friend. It's all on this minihedron — well, never mind."

"What," asked Forister with the last vestiges of his patience, "what exactly is supposed to be on the minihedron?" He stared at the faceted black shape Polyon held in his hand, dark and baleful like the eye of an alien god.

"The true records of how Blaize made his fortune," Polyon said. "It's all there — he thought he'd concealed his tracks, but there were enough Net links for me to find the records. I'm very good with computers, you know," he said with a boy's naive pride. "But when I begged him to tell you the truth, he laughed at me. Said he had you convinced of his innocence and he saw no reason to change the situation. That was when I thought — but no," Polyon said, averting his face as he thrust out the minihedron towards Forister, "I don't want any favors."

Forister felt as queasy as though they had already entered Singularity. Was this why Blaize had tried so hard to keep him from talking to Polyon? He'd wanted to keep Polyon drugged and unconscious until they reached Central; he'd had that silly story about Polyon using the SPACED OUT game as a cover for some kind of plot. But what good would it do to keep Polyon from talking for two weeks, when his evidence — whatever it might be — would come out anyway at the trial?

"Just — you take this. Read it once. Then keep it safe — or wipe it if you want to," Polyon said, "*I* don't care. I just wanted to hand it over to — to somebody honorable." His voice broke slightly on the last word, and Forister thought there was a gleam of moisture in the corners of his eyes. "God knows, I can scarcely claim that for myself. You take it. You'll know what to do with the information."

"What is it?"

Polyon shook his head again. "I don't — I can't tell you. Go and read it in privacy. Just drop it into any of the ship's reader slots and have a look at the information. Then I'll leave it up to you to decide what should be done. And I don't," he said, almost savagely, "I *don't* want to profit from it, do you understand? Say you got it from somebody else. Or don't say where you got it. Or destroy it. Do what you want — it's off my conscience now, at any rate!"

He dropped back onto the bunk and buried his head in his arms. Overhead, the silvery chime of the first warning bell sounded. "Five minutes to Singularity," Nancia announced. "All passengers, please lie down or seat yourselves and secure free-fall straps. Tablets for Singularity sickness are available in all cabins; if you think you may be adversely affected by the transition, please medicate yourself now. Five minutes to Singularity."

Polyon fumbled without looking up, caught his free-fall strap and buckled it around himself. "Singularity," he said bitterly, "doesn't make me sick. But what's on that minihedron does."

Forister left the cabin with a sparkling black mini-hedron clutched in his hand, the facets cutting into his palms, his head awhirl with doubts.

"What a magnificent acting job!" Nancia commented with a low laugh.

"You think Polyon was lying?"

"I'm certain of it," she told him. "You know Polyon. You know Blaize. Is it credible for an instant that Blaize could have committed crimes that would turn Polyon's stomach?"

"I — don't know," Forister groaned. He dropped into the pilot's chair and stared unseeing at the console before him. Micaya Questar-Benn tactfully pretended to polish the gleaming buckle on her uniform belt. "Up to now, I'd have said — but I'm biased, you know."

"Well, I'm not," Nancia said decisively. "I don't know what Polyon's going on about, but whatever it is, I don't believe a word of it."

Forister laughed weakly. "You're biased too, dear Nancia." He stared at the sparkling surface of the minihedron, the polished opaque facets that gave nothing away, and sighed deeply. "I suppose I had better find out what this is."

"Can't it wait until after Singularity?" Nancia said, but too late. Forister had already dropped the datahedron into the reader slot. Automatically, her mind already on the vortex of mathematical transformations ahead, Nancia absorbed the contents of the minihedron into memory. Something strange there, not like ordinary words, more like a tickle at the back of her head or an improperly positioned synaptic connector —

She rode the whirlwind down into Singularity, balancing and coasting along constantly changing equations that defined the collapsing walls of the vortex.

Something was wrong; she sensed it even before she

lost her grasp on the mathematical transformations. She had never experienced a transition like this one. What was happening? Sounds as slimy as decaying weed whispered and snickered in her ears; colors beyond the edges of human perception rasped at her like fingernails being drawn over a blackboard. The balance of salts and fluids surrounding her shrunken human body swirled crazily, and a dozen alarm systems went off at once: *Overload! Overload! Overload!*

She couldn't optimize the path; spaces decomposed around her and shot off in an infinity of different recompositions, expanding in every path to lights and chaos that could tear her apart. The hyperchip-enhanced mathematics coprocessors returned gibberish. Her brain waves were strung out on the grid of a multi-dimensional matrix. Something was trying to invert the matrix. No computations matched previous results, and all directions held danger.

Nancia shut down all processing at once. The grating colors and stinking noises receded. She hung in blackness, refusing her own sensory inputs, balanced on the point of Singularity where decomposing subspaces intersected, with no way forward and no way back.

● CHAPTER SEVENTEEN

Polyon was pacing the narrow space of his cabin, too impatient to strap himself in for Singularity, waiting for some sign that Forister had taken the bait, when the air shimmered and thickened around him.

He opened his mouth to curse his luck. The ship had entered Singularity before that thick-headed brawn ambled to a reader slot.

The air distorted into glassy waves, then became almost too thin to breathe. The cabin walls and furnishings receded to specks in the distance, then swam around him, huge menacing free-flowing shapes. Polyon's curses became a comical growl ending in a squeak.

Damn Singularity! There was no chance that Forister would drop the datahedron into a reader now, he'd be safely strapped into his pilot's chair like a good little brawn. By now, too, the ship's reader slots would probably be shut down for Singularity — and even if by some miracle he could persuade Nancia to accept the hedron, he still would not be able to enter the Net until the transformations were over and they had returned to normal space. No, he would have to wait until after the subspace transformation to implement Final Phase — and this transformation would bring the brainship into Central subspace, close to all the aid that Central Worlds and their innumerable fleets could give.

He reminded himself that this made no difference whatsoever. The basic nature of the gamble remained the same. Either his plan had advanced far enough to succeed despite the way they were forcing his hand, or it hadn't. If it had, then the fleets of Central would be obedient to him and not to their former masters. If it hadn't — well, then, annihilation would be a little quicker than if he'd moved from the remote spaces around Nyota, that was all.

He had only to sit and wait. And waiting out a single transformation through Singularity should be nothing to him. He had already spent patient years waiting on Shemali, planting his seeds, watching them grow, seeding the universe, ever since he had the flash of brilliance which at once conceived the hyperchip design and saw how it could be twisted to his own ends.

But this waiting was harder than all those years in which he had at least been doing *something* to further those ends; and it seemed longer; and there was something disturbing about this particular ship's decomposition. Singularity wasn't supposed to be this bad. Polyon breathed and gagged on a sickly swirl of colors and smells and textures, looked down at the wavering distortions of his own limbs and closed his eyes momentarily. That was a mistake; Singularity sickness heaved through his guts. What was the matter? He'd been through plenty of decompositions during his Academy training, not to mention passing through this very same Singularity point on the way out to Vega subspace. Had he so completely lost conditioning in the five years on Shemali, to be gagging and puking like any new recruit now?

No. Something else was wrong. This decomposition was lasting too long. And some of the visual distortions looked oddly familiar. Polyon fixed his eyes on one small sector of the cabin, where braces supporting an extruded shelf formed a simple closed curve of permalloy and plastifilm. As he watched, the triangle of brace, wall and shelf elongated to a needle-shape with one thin eye, stretched out into an open eye as big as the wall, squeezed into a rotating pinpoint of light with absolute blackness at its center, and opened again into the original triangle. Needle, eye, pinpoint, triangle; needle, eye, pinpoint, triangle. They were caught in a subspace loop, perpetually decomposing and reforming in a sequence which preserved topological properties but which made no progress towards the escape sequence leading to Central subspace.

A loop like that couldn't have happened, shouldn't have happened, unless the ship's processors had shut down. Or — a wild hope tantalized him — unless the ship's processors were too busy with some other problem to navigate them out of Singularity.

A problem like assimilating a worm program which would turn over all control to a single user, effectively cutting the brain off from her own body and its processing.

Polyon swallowed his unspoken curses and plunged across the cabin. He had some trouble locating the palmpad and holding his hand steady over it, but eventually he managed to match his shrinking and bending arm with the erratic loop of the ballooning palmpad. He slapped the surface twice. "Voice control mode!"

His own voice boomed oddly in his ears, the soundwaves distorted by the perpetual twisting of space around him, but evidently there was something unchanging in the voice patterns which his worm program still recognized. "Voice control acknowledged," an undulant voice boomed and twittered from the speakers.

"Unlock this cabin door." The first time the words came out as an unrecognizable squeak; the next, something close to his normal speaking voice emerged and the computer acknowledged the command. But nothing happened. A moment later the quavering vocal signal of the program responded with a shrill squeak that gradually became a groaning boom.

"Unable to identify designated entity."

Polyon was beginning to catch on to the rhythm of the subspace loop. If he kept his eyes fixed on any known point, like the triangle of shelf and wall and brace, he could recognize when they were passing through the decomposition closest to normal space. If he spoke then, residual subspace transformations still distorted his voice, but at least the computer could recognize and accept his orders.

He waited and spoke when the moment was right.

"Identify this cabin."

Lights flashed on the cabin control panel, rose and fluttered like fireflies trailing the liquid surface of the panel, swam into elongated hieroglyphics of an unknown language, and sank back into the panel's surface to become a pattern signaling failure.

"No such routine found."

Polyon cursed under his breath, and the subspace transformation loop twisted his words into a grating snarl. Something was wrong with his worm program. Somehow it had failed to complete its takeover of the ship's computer functions.

"General unlock," he snapped on the next loop through normal space.

His cabin door irised halfway open, then screeched and wobbled back and forth as the smooth internal glides had jammed on something. Polyon dove through, misjudged distances and clearance in the perpetual liquid shifting of the transformations, cracked a solid elbow on the very solid edge of the half-open door, landed on a bed of shifting sand, rolled, and found his feet in what was again, briefly, the solid passageway outside the cabin.

"Out! Everybody out!" The loop stretched his last word into a howl. *At least it got their attention.* A green slug oozed through one of the other doors and became Darnell, vomiting. Farther away, Blaize's red head blazed under lights that kept changing from electric blue to artificial sun to deepest shadow. Fassa was a china doll, white and neat and compact and perfect, but as the loop progressed she grew to her normal stature.

"What's happening?" The loop snatched away her words, but Polyon read her lips before the next phase stretched them into rubber. He waited for the next normal-space pass.

"Get Alpha. Don't want to have to explain twice."

Fassa nodded — Polyon thought it was a nod — and ducked into the cabin nearest hers. Darnell quivered and resumed his form as a giant green slug. The passageway elongated into a tunnel with Blaize at the far end, somehow aloof from the group.

Fassa reappeared, shaking her head. "She won't move. I — " She was bright, Fassa del Parma was; in mid-sentence, as space shifted around her, she waited until the next normspace pass to complete her sentence. " — think she's too frightened. I'm scared too. What's — "

Polyon didn't have time to waste listening to obvious questions. When the next normspace passed through them, he was ready to seize the moment. "I'm taking over the ship, is what's happening," he said over the tail-end of Fassa's question. "Any function on this ship that uses my hyperchips is under my command now. The reason — "

Shift, stretch, contract, waver, back to normal for a few seconds.

" — for this long transition is that the ship's brain is nonfunctional, can't get us out of Singularity."

Darnell wailed and vomited more loudly than before, drowning out Polyon's next words and wasting the rest of that normspace pass. Polyon waited, one booted foot contracting as he tapped it, stretching and looping over itself like a snake, then deflating again into the normal form of a regulation Academy boot.

"I can pilot us out of Singularity," he announced. "But I need to be at the control console. May have some trouble there. You'll have to help me take out the brawn and the cyborg."

"Why should we?" Blaize demanded.

Polyon smiled. "Afterwards," he said gently, "I won't forget who my friends are."

"What good — " Darnell, predictably, wanted to know, but the transformation loop washed away his question. And when normspace came round again, Blaize was closer to the rest of them; close enough to answer for Polyon.

"What good will his favor do? Quite a lot, I should imagine. It's not just the hyperchips on this ship, is it, Polyon? All the hyperchips Shemali has been turning out so fast have the same basic flaw, don't they?"

"I wouldn't," said Polyon, "necessarily define it as a flaw. But you're right. Once we're out of Singularity and ready to access the Net again, this ship's computer will broadcast Final Phase to every hyperchip ever installed. I'll have — "

They'd all caught on to the rhythm of the transformation loop by now; the wait through three distorted subspaces was becoming part of normal conversational style.

" — control of the universe," he finished on the next pass through normspace. Blaize had come closer yet; stupid little runt, trying to move during transformations.

"And we'll be your loyal lieutenants?" Blaize asked.

"I know how to reward service," Polyon said noncommittally. *Into a Ganglicide vat with you, troublemaker, as soon as I have the power.*

"Not if I know it," Blaize mouthed as normspace slid away into the first distortion. He swung a fist at Polyon, but before it landed his hand had shrunk to the size of a walnut, and on the next dip through normspace Polyon was ready for him with a return blow that sent Blaize to the deck. By the time he landed, it was soft as quicksand, a pool in which Blaize swirled, too dizzy to rise immediately.

"Stop me," Polyon said to the other two as normspace passed through, "and you die here, in Singularity, because nobody else can get us out of it. Try to stop me and fail," and he smiled again, very sweetly, "and you'll wish you *had* died here. Are you with me?"

Before they could answer, a new element entered the game; a hissing cloud of gas, invisible in normspace, clearly delineated as a pink-rimmed flood of rosy light in the first transformational space. It engulfed Blaize and he stopped twitching, lay like one dead in the yielding transformations of the deck.

Sleepgas. And he couldn't shout through the loop to warn them. Polyon clapped both hands over his mouth and nose, saw that Fassa did the same, jerked his head towards the central cabin. That door too was half open. He made for it, staggering through mud and quicksand, swimming through air gone thick as water, lungs aching and burning for a breath. Fell through, someone pushing behind him, Fassa, and Darnell after her. Forget Blaize, the traitor, and Alpha, by now sleepgassed in her cabin. Polyon gasped and with his first burning breath called, "General lock!"

The control cabin door irised shut with a strange jerky motion, as if it were fighting its own mechanism, and Polyon found his feet and surveyed his new territory.

Not bad. The only passenger he'd been seriously worried about was Sev Bryley-Sorensen. But Bryley wasn't here. Good. He was locked out, then, with Alpha and Blaize; probably sleepgassed, like them. The other two were bent over their consoles, probably still trying to figure out why doors were opening and closing without their command, trying to flood the passenger areas with sleepgas — well, they'd succeeded there, but much good it would do them now! Through the transitions he saw them turning in their seats, open mouths stretching like taffy in the second subspace, then shrinking to round dots in the third. Normspace showed the cyborg freak making a move that wasn't part of the transformation illusion, right arm darting towards her belt. Polyon snapped out a command and the freak's prosthetic arm and leg danced in their sockets, twisting away from the joining point; her flesh-and-blood torso followed the agonizing pull of the synthetic limbs and she rotated half out of her seat. Another command, and the prostheses dropped lifeless and heavy to the floor, dragging the body down with them. Her head cracked against the support pillar under the seat. Polyon stepped forward to take the needler before she recovered. Space stretched away from him, but his arm stretched with it, and the solid heavy feel of the needler reassured him that his fingers, even if they momentarily resembled tentacles, had firm hold of the weapon.

With the next normspace pass he was erect again, holding the needler on Forister. "Over there." With a jerk of his head he indicated the central column. Somewhere behind there the brain of the ship floated within a titanium shell, a shrunken malformed body kept alive by tubes and wires and nutrient systems. Polyon shuddered at the thought; he'd never understood why Central insisted on keeping these monsters alive, even giving them responsible positions that could have been filled by real people like himself. Well, the brain would be mad by now, between sense deprivation and the stimuli he'd ordered its own hyperchips to throw at it; killing it would be a merciful release. And it would be appropriate to kill the brawn at the foot of the column.

But not yet. Polyon was all too aware that he didn't know everything there was to know about navigating a brainship. He would need full support from both computers and brawn if he was to get them out of this transition loop alive.

He studied the needler controls, spun the wheel with his thumb, glanced at Darnell and Fassa. Which of them dared he trust? Neither, for choice; well, then, which was more afraid of him? Fassa had been showing an uppity streak, asking him questions when she should have been listening. Darnell was still green-faced but appeared to be through vomiting. Polyon tossed him the needler; it floated through normspace and Darnell caught it reflexively just before the transition shrunk it to a gleaming line of permalloy.

"If either of them makes a move," Polyon said pleasantly, "needle them. I've set it to kill . . . slowly." In fact he'd left the needler as Micaya had it, set to deliver a paralyzing but not lethal dose of paravenin; but there was no need to reassure his captives overmuch. "Now . . . " He removed his uniform jacket, draped it neatly over the swivelseat where Micaya had been sitting, and sat down in Forister's chair before the command console. Transitions exaggerated the slight flourish of his wrists into a great ballooning gesture, spun out his sleeves into white clouds of fabric that floated over and dwarfed the other occupants of the cabin.

"What do you think you're doing?" Forister cried. His voice squeaked through the fourth transition space and fell with a thud on the last word.

Polyon smiled. He could see his own teeth and hair gleaming, white and gold, in the mirror-bright panel. "I," he said gently, "am going to get us out of Singularity. Don't you think it's time somebody did it?"

His reflection narrowed, gave him a squashed face like a bug, dulled the bright gold of his hair and turned his teeth to green rotting stumps. The control panel shrank under his hands, then swelled and heaved like a storm-tossed sea. As normspace approached Polyon darted in, tapping out one set of staccato commands with his right hand, passing the left over the palmpad to call up Nancia's mathematics coprocessors, rattling out the verbal commands that would bring the whole ship around, responsive to his commands and ready to sail the subspaces out of this Singularity.

She was sluggish as any water-going vessel lacking a rudder and taking in water, half the engines obeying his commands, the other half canceling them. The mathematics co-processors came online and then disappeared before he'd entered the necessary calculations, shrieking gibberish and sliding away in a jumble of meaningless symbols. The moment of normspace passed and Polyon ground his teeth in frustration. In the second transformation the teeth felt like squishy, rotting vegetables inside his mouth, then in the third they became needles that drew blood, and by the time normspace returned he had learned not to give way to emotion.

He made two more attempts at controlling the ship, waited out three complete transition loops, before he pushed the pilot's chair back from the control panel.

"Your brainship is fighting me," he told Forister on the next pass through normspace.

"Good for her!" Forister raised his voice slightly. "Nancia, girl, can you hear me? Keep it up!"

"Don't be a fool, Forister," Polyon said tiredly. "If your brainship were conscious and coherent, she'd have brought us out of Singularity herself."

He used the remaining seconds in normspace to tap out one more command. The singing tones of Nancia's access code rang through the room. Forister's face went gray. Then the transition spaces whirled about them, monstrously transforming the cabin and everything in it, and Polyon could not tell which of the distorted images before him showed the opening of Nancia's titanium column.

On the next pass through normal space he saw that the column was still closed. Transition must have garbled the last sounds in the access sequence. He typed in the command again; again the musical tones rang out without their accompanying syllables; again nothing happened.

"You'd better tell me the rest of the code," he said to Forister on the next normspace pass.

Forister smiled — briefly; something in the expression reminded Polyon of his own ironic laughter. "What makes you think I have it, boy? The two parts are kept separate. I didn't even know how to access the tone sequence from Nancia's memory banks. The syllables probably aren't encoded in her at all; they'll be on file at Central."

"Brawns are supposed to know the spoken half of the code," Polyon snapped in frustration.

"I asked to have it changed just before this run," Forister claimed. "Security reasons. With so many prisoners on board, I feared a takeover attempt — and with good reason, it seems."

"I do hope you're lying," Polyon said. He clamped his mouth shut and waited through the transition loop, marshaling his arguments. "Because if Central's the only source for the rest of the code, we're all dead. I can't tap the Net and hack into the Courier Service database from Singularity — and I can't get us out of Singularity without neutralizing the brain."

"You mean, without killing Nancia," Forister said in a voice emptied of feeling. His eyes flickered once to the cabin consol. Polyon followed the man's gaze and felt a moment of fear. A delicate solido stood above the control panels, the image of a lovely young woman with an impish smile and clustering curls of red hair.

Polyon had heard of brawns who developed an emotional fixation on their brainship, even to the point of having a solido made from the brainship's genotype that would show how the freakish body might have matured without its fatal defects. He hadn't guessed that Forister was the sentimental type, or that he'd have had time to grow so attached to Nancia. The idiot might actually think that he'd rather die than kill his brainship.

"There's no need to clutter the problem with emotionalism," Polyon told him. How could he jolt Forister out of his sentimental fixation? "With partial control of the ship to me and partial control to Nancia, neither of us can navigate out of Singularity."

Damn the transition loop! Forister had caught on to the rhythm by now; and the necessary wait while three distorted subspaces composed and decomposed around them gave him time to think.

"I've a better suggestion," the brawn said. "You *say* you can navigate us out; well, we all *know* Nancia can. Restore full control to her, and —"

"And what? You'll drop charges, let me go back to running a prison factory? I've got a better career plan than that now."

"I wasn't," said Forister mildly, "planning to make that offer."

The rhythm of collapsing and composing subspaces was becoming natural to them all; the necessary pauses in their conversation no longer bothered Polyon.

"I had something like your own offer in mind," Forister continued at the next opportunity. "Release Nancia's hyperchip-enhanced computer systems, and she'll get us out of Singularity — and you'll live."

"How did you guess?"

Forister looked surprised. "Logical deduction. You designed the hyperchips; you tricked me into running a program that did something peculiar to Nancia's computer systems; the failure reports I read just before you came in showed precisely the areas where she has had hyperchips installed, the lower deck sensors and the navigation system; you've since exercised voice control on Micaya's hyperchip-enhanced prostheses. Clearly your hyperchip design includes a back door by which you can personally control any installation that uses your chips."

"Clever," Polyon said. "But not clever enough to get you out of Singularity. I assure you I'm not going to restore full computing power to a brainship who is probably mad by now."

"What makes you think that?"

Polyon raised his brows. "We all know what sensory deprivation does to shellpersons, Forister. Need I go into the details?"

"Take more than a few minutes in the dark to upset my Nancia," Forister said levelly.

Polyon bared his teeth. "By now, old man, she's had considerably more than that to deal with. The first thing my hyperchip worm does is to strike at any intelligence linked to the computers in which it finds itself. The sensory barrage would make any human break the link at once. I'm afraid that 'your' Nancia, not being able to escape the link that way, will have gone quite mad by now. So — I think — if you want to live — you'll tell me, *now*, the rest of the access code."

"I think not," Forister said calmly. "You've made a fatal error in your calculations."

The transition loop stifled all talk for the endless winding, looping moments of passage through shrinking and distorting spaces. Polyon ignored the sensory tricks of spatial transformations and thought furiously. When normspace returned, he reached up from his chair to grasp the solido of Nancia as a young woman. Deliberately, watching Forister's face, he dropped the solido on the deck and ground the fragile material to shards under his boot-heel.

"*That's* what's left of 'your' Nancia, old man," he said. "Are you going to let your love for a woman who never lived kill us all?"

Forister's face was lined with pain, but he spoke as evenly as always. "My — feelings — for Nancia have nothing to do with the matter. Your error is much more basic. You think I'd rather set you free with the universe in your control than die here in Singularity. This is incorrect."

He spoke so calmly that it took Polyon a moment to understand the words, and in that moment the transition loop warped the room and disguised the movements in it. When they passed through normspace again, Fassa del Parma was standing between Forister and Darnell, as if she thought she could shield the brawn from a direct needler spray.

"He's right," she said. "I didn't have time to think before. You're a monster."

Polyon laughed without humor. "Fassa, dear, to righteous souls like Forister and General Questar-Benn we're all monsters. I should have remembered how you sucked up to them before, helping them trick me. Did you think that would save you? They'll use you and throw you away like your father did."

Fassa went white and still as stone. "We don't all take such a simple-minded view of the universe," Forister said. "But, Fassa, you can't — "

Darnell's fingers were twitching. Polyon nodded. Slowly, too slowly, Darnell raised the needler. He gave Forister ample time to grasp Fassa by the shoulders and spin her out of danger. As Forister moved, the cabin seemed to lurch and the lights dimmed. Gravity fell to half-normal, then to nothing, and as Fassa spun into midair the reaction of Forister's thrust pushed him in the opposite direction. The spray of needles went wide, but one bright line on the far edge of the arc stung through Forister's sleeve and bloodied his wrist. The blood danced out across the cabin in bright droplets that the transition loop pulled out into bloody seas; Polyon watched a bubble the size of a small pond float inexorably toward him, settle around him with a clammy grip, then shrink to a bright button-sized stain on his shirt front.

Fassa floated back to grasp Forister's flaccid body and cry, "Why did you do that? I wanted to save you!"

"Wanted him — to kill me," Forister breathed. The paravenin was fighting the contractions of his chest. "Without me — no way to get Nancia's code. Trapped here, all of us — better than letting him go? Forgive me?"

"Death before dishonor." Polyon put a sneering spin on the words, letting the maudlin pair hear what he thought of such brave slogans. "And it will be death, too. See how the ship's systems are failing? What do you think will go next? Oxygen? Cabin pressure?"

In the absence of direct commands, gravity and lighting should have been controlled by Nancia's autonomic nervous functions. Forister groaned as the meaning of this latest failure came through to him.

"She's dying anyway. With or without your help," Polyon drove the point home. "And *you're* not dead yet. I lied to you. The needler was only set to paralyze. Now let's have the access code before Nancia stops breathing and kills us all."

Forister shook his head with slow, painful twitches.

"Come here, Fassa, dear," Polyon ordered.

"No. I stay with him."

"You don't really mean that," Polyon said pleasantly. "You know you're far too afraid of me. Remember those shoddy buildings you put up on Shemali? You replaced them free of charge, remember, and I didn't even have to do any of the interesting things we discussed. But if I'd threaten you with flaying alive for cheating me over a factory, Fassa, just think for a moment what I'll do to you for interfering with me now."

The transition loop was almost a help; the pauses it forced gave Fassa time to consider her brave stand.

"Go on, Fassa," Forister urged when normal speech was possible again. "You can't help me now, and I've no wish to see you hurt for my sake."

"Thank you for the information," Polyon said with a courteous bow. "Perhaps I'll try that next. But I think we'll begin with an older and dearer friend for quick results. Darnell, bring the freak — no, I'll do it; you keep the needler on Fassa, just in case she gets any silly ideas."

Holding onto the pilot's chair to keep himself in place, Polyon turned and aimed a loose kick at Micaya Questar-Benn. The cessation of ship's gravity had freed her of the artificially weighted prostheses that held her down, but the arm and leg were still flopping loose, free of her control. She was as good as a cripple — she was a cripple, disgusting sight.

"I want Forister to get a good view of this," he told her politely. "Lock prostheses."

This to the computer; a signal to the hyperchips clamped Micaya's artificial arm and leg together.

"Lay a finger on Mic — " Forister threatened, struggling vainly against the effects of the paravenin.

"I won't need to," Polyon said with a brilliant smile. "I can do it all from here."

A series of brisk verbal commands and typed-in codes caused the portion of the ship's computer that Polyon controlled to transmit new, overriding instructions to the hyperchips controlling Micaya's internal organ replacements. The changes had the full duration of a transition loop to take effect. When they returned to normspace, Micaya's face was colorless and beads of sweat dotted her forehead.

"It's amazing how painful a few simple organic changes can be," Polyon commented gaily. "Little things like fiddling with the circulation, for instance. How's that hand, Mic, baby? Bothering you a bit?"

"Come a little closer," Micaya invited him, "and find out." But now Polyon had drawn attention to her one remaining hand; they could all see how it had changed color. The fingernails were almost black, the skin was purplish and swollen.

"Keep it like that for a week," Polyon said, "and she'll have a glorious case of gangrene. Of course, we don't have a week. I could trap even more blood in the hand and burst the veins, but that might kill her too fast. So I'll just leave it like that while you think it over, Forister, and maybe we'll start working on the foot as well. Fortunately, the heart's one of her cyborg replacements, so we don't have to worry about it failing under the increased demands; it'll go on working ... as long as I want it to. Want to hear how well it works now?"

A word of command amplified the sound of Micaya's artificial heart beating vehemently, the pulse rate going up to support the demands Polyon was making on the rest of her system. The desperate, ragged double beat echoed through the cabin, droned and drummed and shrilled through a complete transition loop, and no one spoke or moved.

For a heartbeat, no more, Nancia found silence and darkness a welcome relief from the stabbing pain of the input from her rogue sensors. *Is this what Singularity is like for softpersons?* But no, it was worse than that. In the confused moments before she shut down all conscious functions and disabled her own sensor connections, she had been aware of something much worse than the colorshifts and spatial distortions of Singularity; the malevolence of another mind, intimately entwined with her own, striking at her with deliberate malice.

He means to drive me mad. If I enable my sensors again, he'll do it. And if I stay floating in this darkness, that will do it too. The bleak desperation of the thought came from somewhere far back in her memories. When, how, had she ever felt so utterly abandoned before? Nancia reached out, unthinking, to search her memory banks — then stopped before the connection was complete. If sensors could be turned into weapons to use against her, could not memory, too, be infiltrated? Access the computer's memory banks, and she might find herself "knowing" whatever this other mind wanted her to believe.

Is it another mind? Or a part of myself? Perhaps I'm mad already, and this is the first symptom. The flashing, disorienting lights and garbled sounds, the sickening whirling sensations, even the conviction that she was under attack by another mind — weren't all these symptoms of one of those Old Earth illnesses that had ravaged so many people before modern electrostim and drug therapy restored the balance of their tortured brains? Nancia longed to scan just one of the encyclopedia articles in her memory banks; but that resource was denied her for the moment. Paranoid schizophrenia, that was it; a splitting off of the mind from reality.

Let's see, now — she reasoned. *If I'm mad, then it's safe to look up the symptoms and decide that I'm mad, except that presumably I won't accept the evidence. And if I'm not mad, I daren't check memory to prove it. So we'd better accept the working hypothesis that I am sane, and go on from there.* The dry humor of the syllogism did something to restore her emotional balance. *Although how long I will remain sane, under these circumstances . . .*

Better not to think about that. Better, too, not to remember Caleb's first partner, who had gone into irreversible coma rather than face the emptiness that surrounded him after the synaptic connections between his shell and the outside world had been destroyed. As a matter of sanity, as well as survival, Nancia decided, she would make the assumption that somebody had done this to her, and concentrate on solving the puzzle of who had done it and how they could be stopped.

A natural first step would be to reopen just one sensor, to examine the bursts of energy that had come so close to disrupting her nervous system. . . . *I can't!* the child within her shrieked in near-panic. *You can't make me, I won't, I won't, I'll stay safe in here forever.*

That's not an option, Nancia told herself firmly. She wanted to say it aloud, to reassure herself with the sound of her own voice; but she was mute as well as deaf and blind and without sensation, floating in an absolute blackness. Somehow she had to conquer that panic within herself.

Poetry sometimes helped. That Old Earth dramatist Sev and Fassa were so fond of quoting; she had plenty of his speeches stored in her memory banks. *On such a night as this* . . . Nancia reached unthinking for memory, stopped the impulse just in time. She *didn't* know that speech; she had stored it in memory. Quite a different thing. Try something else, then. *I could be bounded in a nutshell, and count myself king of infinite space, were it not that I have bad dreams.* . . . Not a good choice, under the circumstances. Maybe . . . did she know anything else? What was she, without her memory banks, her sensors, her powerful thrusting engines? Did she even exist at all?

That way lies madness. Of course she existed. Deliberately Nancia filled herself with her own true memories. Scooting around the Laboratory Schools corridors, playing Stall and Power-Seek with her friends. Acing the math finals, from Lobachevski Geometry up through Decomposition Topology, playing again, with all the wonderful space of numbers and planes and points to wander in. Voice training with Ser Vospatrian, the Lab Schools' drama teacher, who'd taught them to modulate their speaker-produced vocalizations through the full range of human speech with all its emotional overtones. That first day they'd all been shy and nervous, hating the recorded playbacks of their own tinny artificial voices;

Vospatrian had made them recite limericks and non-sense poems until they broke down in giggles and forgot to be self-conscious. Goodness, she could still remember those silly poems with which he'd started off every session. . . .

And quite without thinking or calling on her artificially augmented memory banks, Nancia was off.

> *"The farmer's daughter had soft brown hair,*
> *Butter and eggs and a pound of cheese,*
> *And I met with a poem, I can't say where,*
> *Which wholly consisted of lines like these. . . . "*

> *"There was a young brainship of Vega . . . . "*

> *"Fhairson swore a feud against the clan M'Tavish;*
> *Marched into their land to murder and to rafish,*
> *For he did resolve to extirpate the vipers*
> *With four-and-twenty men and five-and-thirty*
> *   thirty pipers . . . "*

Nancia went through Ser Vospatrian's entire reper-toire until she was giggling internally and floating on the natural high of laughter-produced endorphins. Then, floating quite calmly in her blackness, she set about testing her sensor connections one by one.

She got the mental equivalent of burned fingers and light-blinded eyes more than once during the testing process, but it wasn't as bad as she had feared. The lower-deck sensors were completely useless, as were her navigation computer and the new mathematics and graphics co-processors she'd just invested in. *Everything, in fact, that contains hyperchips from Shemali . . .* and with that deduction, Nancia knew just who was striking at her and why.

She opened the upper deck sensors one by one, first taking in the sleeping bodies tumbled in the passageway and cabins. Sev, slumped over the isometric spring set in the exercise room with his hands and feet still in the springholders; Alpha, strapped in her cabin; Blaize, floating just above the passageway deck, with an angelic expression on his sleeping face and a nasty bruise coming up on his chin.

Mutiny. And somebody released sleepgas. But which side? She opened the control cabin sensors slowly, cautiously. The port side sensors wavered and gave an erratic display. Somehow Polyon's hyperchips must be working to contaminate the entire computer system. *I don't have much time. . . .*

Even less time than she'd thought, Nancia realized as she took in the standoff in the control room. General Questar-Benn disabled — *of course, the hyperchips in her prostheses* — and Darnell holding her needler on a defiant Forister while Polyon sat in the pilot's chair and played his commands on the computer console. That, at least, she could do something about. Nancia struck back, sending her own commands to the computer, disabling the console section by section, garbling Polyon's commands as they came in. He tapped out a sequence she did not know; she traced it to its source and with shock recognized her own access code. The musical tones were already sounding in the cabin. But the accompanying syllables weren't stored in the same location. . . . *They have to be somewhere, though. In some part of memory not accessible to my conscious probe. Otherwise my shell wouldn't recognize and open to them.* Nancia felt proud of herself for figuring that out, then cold and sick as she wondered how long it would take Polyon to make the same deduction. *And if the syllables aren't where I can consciously retrieve them, how can I block Polyon against doing so?*

She felt queasy from the repeated looping through four decomposition spaces, but there was no safe way to leave the loop until she regained full computing and navigational facility. *First, let's repair the damage....* Nancia worked furiously, permanently disabling the sections of her computer system that had been contaminated by the Shemali hyperchips, finding alternative routings to access the processors that remained untouched. At the same time the worm program unleashed by Polyon squirmed deeper into her system, changing and mutating code as it went, erasing its own tracks so that she could only tell where it had been by the sudden flares of disorienting sense input or the garbled mathematics where it had been. She had to find and stop that code before she could do anything else.

Deep in the intricacies of her own system, Nancia agonized as Darnell struck down Forister.

Don't listen. Don't think about that. She would need all her concentration to disable Polyon's rogue code, more concentration than she'd ever brought to bear on the comparatively trivial problems of subspace navigation. Nancia remembered Sev Bryley's training in relaxation and deliberately, slowly calmed herself, drawing energy away from her extremities and centering her consciousness on the internal core of light where she existed independent of computer and shell and ship. With some remote part of her awareness she sensed the failure of gravitational systems and the dimming of lights, the shock and concern of her passengers, but she could not afford to divert consciousness to those semi-automatic functions now.

The automatic datacording routines Nancia had set up continued to operate as Polyon began Micaya's torture. Nancia could not counter his commands without breaking her trance; she could not even restore gravity and lights to reassure Forister. Ignoring Micaya's pain was the hardest thing she had ever done. *For the moment, Micaya does not exist. Nothing exists outside this place, this moment, this center.* There was the rogue code; she annihilated it in a blaze of energy, destroying deep memory in the process; like an amputation, she thought, the shaft of pain and the nagging ache afterwards. Now to restore lost functions . . . Ruthlessly she cut back on the frills and luxuries of her programming, reducing the power that normally fed her autonomic functions. Lights dimmed even further in the control cabin, and the softpersons made comments about an acrid smell in the air. They would just have to put up with it; she needed that processing power to restore her crippled nav programs. Three of the four major math coprocessors were lost; the graphics processor could double for one of them. No time to think about the others. Nancia erased unnecessary programs and dumped others to datahedron, making space in what little remained of her memory for the processes she had to have. Would that be enough? No chance for tests, no time for second thoughts. She struck back, once, with everything she had; felt hyperchips shriveling to blank bits of permalloy, felt inactive sensors and processors become dead weights instead of living systems.

Some animals will gnaw off their own limbs to get out of a trap. . . .

No time to mourn, either. With the "death" of the hyperchips within Nancia's system, the transmissions that tortured Micaya's cyborgans ceased. The sound of her amplified heartbeat ended between one drum beat and the next. Forister groaned. *He thinks I'm dead.* He would be reassured in a moment. Nancia activated full artificial gravity; Darnell fell to the deck from his wall perch, Fassa went to her knees. Polyon staggered but remained standing. Nancia beamed commands to the tanglefield wires. Darnell, Polyon and Fassa were frozen in place, nets of moving lights encompassing the tanglefield keys at their wrists and ankles and necks. Finally, Nancia spared a little power to bring up the cabin lights and freshen the air.

"FN-935 reporting for duty," she said. "I apologize for any temporary inconvenience. . . . "

"Nancia!" Forister sounded close to tears.

"General Questar-Benn, can you take the pilot's seat?" Nancia requested. "I may need a little help to navigate us out of Singularity."

"Do my best." Micaya's breathing was still ragged, and she leaned heavily on the chair beside her, but she limped to the pilot's seat without help, the prostheses once again responding to her own brain's electrical impulses. "What can I do?"

"I am operating with only one mathematics coprocessor," Nancia told her, "and my navigation units are nonfunctional. When I start the drives, we will move out of this transition loop and into the expansion of whatever subspace we happen to be in. I'll try to maintain a steady path through the subspace options, but I may need you to aid in the navigation. Since the graphics processor is undamaged, I will throw up images of the approaching subspaces. Rest your hand on the palmpad and give me a direction at each branch."

"Do my best," Micaya said again, but Nancia noticed it was the prosthetic hand she rested on the palmpad; the other hand was still an ugly purple color, with blackened moons on the swollen fingertips. She remembered what Polyon had said about gangrene. How much had his hyperchips accelerated Micaya's metabolic processes? *Get her to a medic . . . but I can't do that unless somebody helps me surf out of Singularity . . . and we daren't wait for the paravenin to wear off Forister. . . .*

Then Nancia had no more energy to spare for worrying about Micaya or anything else but the waves of transformations that broke over her head, tossed and tumbled her gasping through subspaces that deformed her body and everyone within, streams of calculations that escaped her processors. Lost and choking, she sensed a firm hand guiding her upwards . . . out. . . . She crunched the last numbers into a tractable series of equations and broke through the chaos of uncountably infinite subspaces into the blessed normalcy of RealSpace.

Before she had time to thank Micaya, a tightbeam communication assaulted her weakened comm center. "Back so soon, FN? What's the matter? I thought you were headed for Central."

It was Simeon, the Vega Base managing brain. "We had a small virus problem," Nancia beamed back. "Returned for . . . repairs."

The rest of the story could wait until she had absolute privacy. There was no need to alert the galaxy to the fact that an unknown number of their computer systems were contaminated by Shemali hyperchips.

"Is everything under control now?"

"You could say that," Nancia replied dryly, turning up her remaining sensors and looking over her internal condition. Half her processors burned out, sleeping bodies littering the passenger quarters, three High Families brats secured in tanglefield and mad as hell, Forister twitching with the pins-and-needles of paravenin recovery, and a crippled general bringing them safe into RealSpace —

"Yes," she told Simeon. "Everything's under control."

● CHAPTER EIGHTEEN

In the days of repair work that followed, Nancia began to understand just how much Caleb must have hated being grounded on Summerlands while she went on with a new brawn to complete the task they had begun. Now she, too, was "convalescent" and temporarily out of the action. To protect herself from the insidious effects of Polyon's hyperchips she had, in effect, crippled herself, rendering large parts of her own system inoperable; to keep the worm program he had implanted from contacting other hyperchips once they got out of Singularity and could make Net contact again, she had slashed through her own memory, ruthlessly excising whole sections of memory banks and operating code.

"It's a miracle you made it back here in one piece," Simeon of Vega Base told her, "and you're not leaving Base until you've had a very thorough overhaul and repair. Those aren't my orders, they're a beam from CS. So no argument!"

"I wasn't planning to argue," said Nancia with, for her, unaccustomed meekness. Indeed, after the stresses of that prolonged stay in Singularity, followed by the limping return voyage on one-third power, she had very little desire to do anything but park herself in orbit around Vega Base and watch the stars wheel by.

Or so she told herself. She *was* tired and injured; she wasn't up to the stressful task of transporting the prisoners and witnesses back to Central for trial. It was far more sensible to prepare a datahedron of her own testimony, something that could be sent back on the bright new Courier Service ship that came to collect the others.

"I'll miss you," Forister said, "but you'll be back in action soon, Nancia. Why, at the speed Central works, you'll probably be returning before the trial's over! And if you don't" — he hefted the gleaming weight of the megahedron in one hand — "this is as good, for all legal purposes, as having you there. You've transferred datacordings of everything that happened on board or that you perceived through your contact buttons, right? Should be the most complete — and most damning — record we could ask for."

"It — may not be as complete as you expect," Nancia said. "I have some memory gaps, you know."

"Yes, I know. But having you there in person — well, via contact button, I suppose — wouldn't make any difference to that, would it? If something's been lost from your memory banks, it won't come back under cross-examination."

That was true enough, Nancia supposed; and if the damage to her memory banks were the only cause of gaps in the recording, there'd be no reason at all for her to undergo cross-examination. The subject was not one she wished to discuss in any detail. She said good-bye to Forister, tried to control the twinge of loneliness she felt when the new CS ship took off, and went back to her observations of the stars of Vega subspace. Stars were restful; bright and calm, in unchanging patterns as familiar to her as — as —

Nancia discovered that she could no longer "remember" the names of the constellations as they appeared in Vega subspace. She had never spent long enough in this subspace to establish the look of the sky in her own human memory; and the navigational maps that she relied on had been erased. So had her tables of Singularity points and decomposition algorithms, her Capellan music recordings. . . .

"Do you know, I'm sorry I used to laugh at softpersons," she said thoughtfully to Simeon while the techs buzzed about her, removing the melted blobs that had been hyperchips, restoring connections and sensors, building in new blank memory banks to be loaded with whatever information she requested. "I never realized how crippled they are, having to rely on no more skills and information than they can store in an organic brain."

"It's not nice to laugh at the handicapped," Simeon agreed gravely. "I trust this has been a learning experience for you, young FN. Would you like me to help you prepare a list of data requests for your new memories?"

"Yes, please," Nancia said, "and" — this she did remember, the frustration of listening to the medical jargon of the techs at Summerlands working on Caleb — "do you think I can afford a classical education? Latin and Greek vocabularies and syntax?"

"I'll indent for the Loeb Classical Hedron," Simeon said. "That has twenty-six Old Earth languages plus all the major literature."

"And — " she didn't want to go too far into debt — "a medical set? Pharmacology, Internals, and Surgical?"

"Should be standard equipment on any ship gets into as much trouble as you do," Simeon agreed.

"Yes, but can I afford it? I've lost some accounting data; I don't know how my credit stands with Courier Service — "

Simeon came as near to a laugh as Nancia had ever heard from him. "FN, trust me, the bonus for this last job, plus the hazardous service pay, will cover any frills you want to request *and* go a long way towards paying off your debt to Lab Schools. Pull off a couple more like this and you'll be a paid-off shell, your own woman. In fact," he added thoughtfully, "there's no reason why you should pay for the classical and medical hedra. I'll just slip those in as part of the replacement list, which is charged to Central — "

"*No*," Nancia said firmly. "That's how it starts."

"How what starts?"

"You know. Darnell. Polyon. Everything."

"Oh. Well, I see what you mean, but it is a gray area, you know . . ."

"Not," Nancia said, "for House Perez y de Gras. I'll buy the extra skills hedra myself, out of my bonus. From the figures you just beamed up, I'll have more than enough to pay honestly for those 'frills' and any other expenses I may incur during this stay."

But that was before she discovered the item that would strain her budget to its limits.

Nancia's repairs were nearly finished when Caleb, now walking without a stick and looking even more muscular than before, landed at Vega Base and requested permission to come aboard. Nancia exclaimed in delight at the bronzed, fit young man she saw stepping out of the airlock.

"My goodness, Caleb, you look as if you'd never been ill a day in your life."

"There wasn't much to do at Summerlands," Caleb said dismissively. "It's a sin to waste time; I worked out in the physical therapy rooms most of the time while they were fussing over final tests and declaring me fit for duty again. What's our next assignment?"

"*Our?*"

"You didn't think I'd desert you? You made some errors of judgment while I was away, Nancia, but nothing that can't be repaired. In fact," Caleb added, looking around the gleaming interior from which all traces of OG Shipping's mauve and puce had finally been removed, "it looks as if the repairs are just about finished."

"They are, but Caleb, I — I'm partnered with Forister now," Nancia said. She felt guilty as she said the words; suppose Caleb felt that she was rejecting him? But it was the simple truth. Her call sign was FN-935 now, not CN.

"Temporary assignment," Caleb brushed that aside. "Now I've been pronounced fit again, Forister can go back into comfortable retirement. No need for him to continue straining himself in tasks he's really not up to. Take this last debacle. You're not to blame, Nancia, being young and inexperienced, but you must see that it was handled all wrong. If . . . "

While Caleb blithely explained the mistakes Forister had made and how he, with the benefit of hindsight, could have done so much better, Nancia attempted to control some new and unfamiliar sensations.

Simeon, she tightbeamed to the managing brain, *is there a malfunction in my repaired circuits? My sensors show a temperature rise and high conductivity, and I'm picking up a strange buzzing in some of the audio circuits.*

The Vega manager's reply was a few seconds delayed. *Fascinating,* he beamed back while Caleb continued his speech. *Your synaptic connectors are picking up direct emotional signals. What an unusual coupling — that's not supposed to happen. You must have done something to your connections while you were fighting the hyperchip attack.*

What are you talking about? Is it dangerous? Fix it! Nancia demanded.

Simeon transmitted a chuckle over the audio circuit, stopping Caleb in mid-peroration.

"What was that? Is Central trying to contact us?"

"No, just a — a message from one of the repair techs," Nancia improvised. "You were saying?"

"Well, try not to let it happen again," Caleb said irritably. "We've got to get our future relationship straight, Nancia; surely that's more important than some last-minute twiddling with your repairs? Now listen. I don't want you to feel guilty over what's past."

"Why should I?" Nancia asked, startled. "Oh, because I didn't report the conversations I heard on my first voyage, and stop those young criminals before they got properly started? Well, I do feel guilty. That was a bad mistake." But one Caleb had encouraged her to make.

"I don't mean that at all!" Caleb said. "You acted with perfect propriety in keeping those conversations private. I mean the way you've been rocketing around the Nyota system, bearing false witness, pretending to be something you're not, encouraging breaches of PTA regulations on Angalia, getting involved in all sorts of violence and mixing with very questionable people indeed —"

Simeon, I know I'm overheating. Can't you send a tech out to fix my circuits?

There's nothing to fix, Nancia, but Lab Schools will want to study just how you achieved it. Briefly, you've created a mind-body feedback loop between your cortex and the ship — one that carries emotional as well as intellectual and motor impulses.

You mean — ?

You're a little more like a softperson than the rest of us, Nancia — or, you might say, a little more human. You're angry, my dear, and your connections are showing it. Flushed, ears buzzing, breathing faster, higher fuel consumption — yes, I'd say you're in a roaring snit. And not without cause. You've outgrown that righteous little snip, Nancia. When are you going to shut him up and kick him off you?

" — but you were misled, and I myself bear some of the fault, having allowed you to persuade me against my better judgment into the first false step on the downward path of deception," Caleb finished his sentence without being aware of the split-second exchange between Nancia and Simeon. "Now that you've seen what such things can lead to, I'm sure you'll repent of your errors. And I want you to know that I freely and completely forgive you. We'll never speak of this again —"

"You're darned right, we won't!" Nancia interrupted. "Go find yourself a ship to match your morals, Caleb!"

"What do you mean?"

To calm herself down, Nancia took a moment to convert her entire Vega subspace map to Old Earth linear measurements and back. By multiple precision arithmetic routines. In surface-level code. She was on the verge of hurting Caleb's feelings. And she wasn't quite angry enough to do that. The inexperienced young brainship who'd teamed with Caleb five years ago would have accepted his self-righteous lecture as if he were laying down Courier Service regulations. It wasn't Caleb's fault, or her fault either, that she'd outgrown his narrow black-and-white view of the world. Forister had taught her the value of shades of gray and the duty of perceiving them. And if now she felt more truly partnered with that spare, sardonic, aging brawn than with the young man who'd shared her first adventures — well, there was no reason Caleb should suffer unnecessarily on that account.

Her overheating circuits cooled down and the buzzing in her ears stopped as she calmed herself with tranquil, fixed equations.

"It wouldn't work, Caleb," she said at last. "You may forgive me, but the past would always be between us. You'd do better to find another brainship, one that has never betrayed your high ideals." *Preferably one that hasn't been commissioned for more than ten minutes.*

"For myself—" Nancia sighed, "sadder but wiser," *that's true, anyway,* "I think it is more appropriate for me to petition Central that my temporary partnership with Forister be made permanent, or to find another brawn if Forister chooses to retire now." *Please, please, don't let him do that.*

"Well." At least Caleb's speech-making impulses had been knocked out temporarily. "If you really think . . ."

"I do," said Nancia, "and," she added firmly, "I will pay the penalty fee for requesting a brawn reassignment. It's not fair that you should bear any part of that burden."

But it was a little disappointing to see how quickly Caleb accepted the offer. . . .

* * *

The trial of the Nyota Five, as the gossipbyters had dubbed Nancia's first passengers, was still in progress when she landed at Central Base some weeks later.

The solitary journey back, with no brawn or passengers to distract her, had given Nancia plenty of time to think . . . perhaps too much. She had no way of knowing how the trial was progressing or how the court had reacted to the testimony presented; in deference to High Families sensibilities, newsbeamers were not permitted in the courtroom and the gossipbyters had nothing but speculations to report. She didn't even know if the court would wish her cross-examined on the deposition she'd sent back on datahedron. Well, if they did, she was available now. And there'd be no new assignment until Forister was released from testifying and free to brawn her again. *If* he still wanted to, once he'd heard what was on her deposition . . . and what wasn't.

Nancia didn't have much time to brood over that possibility; she had hardly touched down at Base when a visitor was announced.

"Perez y de Gras requesting permission to board," the Central Base managing brain warned her in advance.

That was a welcome surprise! The last Nancia had heard from Flix was a bitstream packet from Kailas, mostly consisting of pictures of the seedy cafe where he'd found a synthocomming gig. He must have quit — or been fired. . . . Well, she wouldn't ask him about that. Nancia opened her outer doors and set the wall-sized display screens in the lounge to show the surprise she'd been preparing for him.

"Flix, how lovely, I didn't know you were . . . " she began joyfully as the airlock slid open. The words died away to a faint hiss from her port speaker as she took in the sight of the trim, gray-haired man who stood in the open airlock, surveying her interior with cool gray eyes. Nancia hastily blanked out the moving displays of her new, holo-enhanced, super-detailed SPACED OUT and replaced them with some quiet, correct images of still life paintings by Old Masters.

"As far as I know," said Javier Perez y de Gras, "he isn't. Although doubtless, now that I've been reassigned to Central, your little brother will find another squalid position on this planet from which to annoy me with the sight of his failure."

"Oh." Nancia hadn't previously compared the pattern of Flix's jauntings from gig to gig with her father's diplomatic assignments. Now she made a hasty scan of her restored memory banks and found a surprising number of correspondences. That was something she'd have to ask Flix about. Just now she really didn't feel up to discussing it with Daddy.

"I don't suppose," she said carefully, "that was what you came to see me about? Flix's career, I mean?"

Her father sniffed. "I don't consider that a career. *You* have a career, Nancia my dear, and by all accounts you've done quite well to date — a few errors in judgment, perhaps, but nothing that maturity and experience won't—"

This time Nancia knew what caused the flush of heat that swamped her upper deck circuits and the red haze that trembled in her visual sensors. For a moment she didn't speak, fearing that she would be unable to control her voice; she could not look at Daddy without seeing Caleb and, shadowy in her imagination, Faul del Parma y Polo. Just another man, seeing in her nothing but a tool to serve his plans, coming to give her a rating on how well or ill she'd done for him. Were all men like that?

"Exactly what errors of judgment were you thinking of?" she inquired when she had her vocal circuits under control again. Not that she hadn't made plenty of mistakes for Daddy to pick at. . . .

But what he complained of was the last thing she'd been worried about.

"At least, fortuitously, some other ship performed the service of transporting them back to Central," Daddy said. "But from what I've heard at the trial, you were quite prepared to perform that service yourself. You shouldn't lower yourself that way, Nancia. A Perez y de Gras shouldn't be used as a prison ship to transport common criminals."

"In case you've forgotten, Daddy," Nancia replied, "those 'common criminals' are the very same people I transported to the Nyota system on my maiden voyage . . . and didn't you pull a few strings to arrange that assignment for me?"

Javier Perez y de Gras sat down heavily in one of the comfortably padded cabin chairs. "I did that," he said. "I thought it would be nice for you to have some young company . . . young people of your own class and background . . . for your first voyage. An easy assignment, I thought."

"So did I," Nancia said. Some of the sadness she felt crept into her voice; whatever she'd done to her feedback loops, it seemed to work both ways. She could no longer maintain the perfectly controlled, emotionally uninflected vocal tones she had prided herself on producing before the hyperchip disaster. "So did I. But it turned out . . . rather more complicated than that. And I didn't know what to do. Maybe I did make some 'errors in judgment.' I didn't have a lot of advice, if you recall." *Just a taped good-luck message from a man too busy and important to come to my graduation.*

"I recall," her father said. "Call that *my* error, if you like. Once you'd made it through Lab Schools to graduation and commissioning, you seemed to be doing so well, and I was worried about Flix. Still am, for that matter." He sighed. "Anyway, there you were, off to the start of a glorious career, and my other two children had problems aplenty."

"Not Jinevra!" Nancia exclaimed. "I always thought

she was the perfect example of what you wanted us to become."

"I wanted you to become yourselves," her father said. "Apparently I didn't communicate that to you. Jinevra's a paper-doll cutout of the ideal PTA administrator, and I don't know how to talk to her any more. And as for Flix — well, you know about Flix. I thought he needed attention more than you. Thought a few suggestions, maybe an entry-level position in some branch of Central where he could work himself up and someday amount to something . . . of course he'd have to give up fooling around with the synthcom. . . . " Javier Perez y de Gras sighed. "Flix never has straightened out. I don't know, perhaps he feels neglected on account of all those years when I took every free moment to visit you at Lab Schools. I didn't have that much time for him then. Even the day he was born, I was at Lab Schools, watching you be fitted for your first mobile shell. Seemed he needed me more than you. . . . I thought it was time to redress the balance."

Nancia absorbed the impact of this speech quietly. For the first time, looking at her father's worn face, she began to comprehend how much time and effort he must have really given to his family over the years. Since their mother had quietly retired to the haven of Blissto addiction in a hush-hush, genteel clinic, he had tried to be both father and mother to three obstreperous, brilliant, demanding High Families brats. Another man might have leaned too hard on his children for emotional comfort; another career diplomat might have shunted the children into exclusive boarding schools and forgotten about them. But Daddy was no Faul del Parma, to use and abuse and forget his children. He'd done the best he could for them . . . within his limitations . . . snatching moments between meetings, suffering long tiring reroutings between assignments to spend a day or two on their planets, juggling a diplomat's unforgiving schedule to work in graduations and school plays.

"An error of judgment, perhaps," Javier Perez y de Gras said when the silence had lasted too long, "but never . . . please believe me . . . an error of love. You're my daughter. I only wanted the best for you." And rising from his padded chair, he laid one hand briefly on the titanium column that enclosed and protected Nancia's shell.

"Requesting permission to come aboard!"

There was no identification this time, but Nancia recognized Forister's voice, even though there was something unfamiliar about the way he drew the words out. She activated her external sensors and saw not only Forister but General Questar-Benn standing on the landing pad.

"Request permission to come aboard," Forister repeated. He was pronouncing his words very carefully. And Micaya Questar-Benn was standing very properly, stiff as if she were on a parade-ground. A suspicion began to grow in Nancia's mind.

She slid open the lower doors and waited. A moment later the airlock door opened and Micaya Questar-Benn stepped into the lounge. Very slowly and carefully.

Forister followed. He was holding an open bottle in one hand.

"You *are* drunk," Nancia said severely.

Forister looked wounded. "Not yet. Wouldn't get drunk before I came back to share the news with you. Just . . . happy. Very happy," he expatiated. "Very, very, very . . . where was I?"

"Looking at the bottom of a bottle of Sparkling Heorot, I suspect," Nancia told him.

Forister's wounded expression intensified. "Please!

Do you think I'd toast the best brainship on Central in that cheap stuff? It's only fit for, for . . . "

"Starving musicians?" Nancia suggested. Some day she would have to have a serious talk with Daddy about Flix; suggest that he stop finding Flix promising career openings and just let the boy be a synthocommer. But this latest visit of Daddy's hadn't seemed the right time to bring the subject up. And she couldn't beam him now; Forister had other things on his mind. What there was left of his mind, she corrected with a shade of envy.

"I'll have you know," Forister announced with a flourish, "this is genuine Old Earth wine! Badacsonyi Keknyelu, no less!"

Nancia's new language module included not only Latin and Greek but a sprinkling of less well-known Old Earth tongues. She skimmed the Hungarian dictionary. "Blue-Tongue Lake Badacsony? Are you sure?"

"Believe him," Micaya Questar-Benn chimed in. Like Forister, she was taking great care with her consonants. "If it's as good as the red stuff, it's worth every credit he paid for it. What was the red stuff called, Forister?"

"Egri Bikaver."

"Bull's Blood from Eger," Nancia translated. "Oh, well. You know, sometimes I don't really mind not being able to share softshell pleasures. Er — what are we celebrating?"

"End of the trial! Don't you follow the newsbytes?"

"Not lately. They never have much to say," Nancia equivocated. *And if there were any questions about my deposition, I don't want to hear them.*

"Well, they do now." Forister pulled himself erect and stood in the center of the lounge swaying slightly. "Sentencing was this morning. Alpha bint Hezra-Fong and Darnell Overton-Glaxely got twenty-five years each. They'll do community service on a newly colonized planet — under strict guard."

"Alpha may be some use to the colonists," Nancia

commented, "but I don't know what a bunch of poor innocent colonists have done that they should be saddled with Darnell."

"Farming world," Forister said cheerfully. "They need a lot of stoop labor. As for the rest — " He sobered briefly. "Polyon's back to Shemali."

"*What?*"

"Working the hyperchip burnoff lines," Forister said. "The new manager's worked out a failsafe way to disable the virus Polyon built into his hyperchip design. So the factories are to continue production . . . under somewhat more responsible management. I'm afraid the supply of hyperchips is going to dip for a while; you probably won't be able to replace the ones you burned out for some time, Nancia."

"I can deal with that," Nancia said dryly. It would be a long time indeed before she let any chip designed by Polyon de Gras-Waldheim within connecting distance of *her* motherboards!

Forister still hadn't mentioned the two people whose fate concerned her most. "And Blaize?" It couldn't be too bad, or Forister wouldn't be celebrating like that.

"Five years' community service," Forister told her. "Could be worse. They've dug up a planet in Deneb subspace — sort of like Angalia, only worse, and the only sentient life form resembles giant spiders, and nobody's ever been able to communicate with them. Blaize was moaning and groaning, but I suspect he can't wait to start teaching the spiders ASL. We'll have to drop by after the next assignment and see how he's doing."

"Next assignment?"

"Here's the datacording." Forister dropped a hedron into Nancia's reader slot. She scanned the instructions while he and Micaya broke open the bottle of Badacsonyi Keknyelu. The three of them had been assigned as a team to Theta Szentmari . . . a very, very long way from Central, through three separate Sin-

gularity points. One Singularity transition brought
them briefly into Deneb subspace.

"And what," she inquired, "do we do when we get
there?" *Assuming they still want me as a brainship . . . I suppose
they do. But why hasn't anybody said a word about Fassa?*

"Sealed orders." Forister tossed a second hedron
into the reader; Nancia found to her chagrin that she
could not decrypt the information on this one. "Supposed to be self-decrypting when we pass through the
third Singularity," Forister explained. "Apparently
whatever's going on there is too hot to explain on
Central . . . they're that worried about leaks. They've
been discussing the possibility of making the three of
us a permanent investigative team for hot little scandals like whatever is wrong on Theta Szentmari."

"And what," Nancia asked carefully, "do the two of
you think about that? Now that the trial's over?
And . . . you never did tell me about Fassa."

"Ah, yes. Fassa." Forister's merry twinkle diminished
slightly. "Sev's going out to Rigel IV with her, did you
know that? He says he'll try to pick up P.I. or security
work there, wait out her term."

"Twenty-five years?"

"Ten. They recommended clemency in view of her
apparent rehabilitation . . . helping us trap Polyon,
and that very moving attempt to defend me when
Polyon was holding us all hostage inside Singularity.
Most of which came through brilliantly in your image
datacordings, Nancia." Forister smiled benignly.
"There were a few gaps, though."

Here it comes. She'd been trying not to think about
that aspect of the trial. "I did tell you I'd suffered some
memory loss," Nancia reminded him.

"So you did, so you did. . . . Anyway. The court wasn't
sure what to make of all that; she'd already been arrested,
after all, and she could just have been trying to put herself
in the best possible light for the trial. But there was one

thing from earlier, well before she was arrested, that convinced them she wasn't quite as self-centeredly fraudulent as her partners in crime." Forister twinkled. "It seems that when a factory she built on Shemali collapsed, she put up the new building free of charge. Sev Bryley brought that into evidence. Now, it seems to me that I heard Polyon saying he'd terrorized her into that replacement. But Polyon's trial was over before Sev brought out the story of the Shemali buildings, so he couldn't be recalled for cross-examination. And one of those little blips in your datacording happened just at the moment when Polyon was explaining that little matter to us."

Nancia felt a glowing heat from all her upper-deck circuits. "I *did* tell you I'd suffered some memory loss," she repeated.

"Very conveniently arranged, though."

"All right. I canceled that part of the datacording. I — Fassa's had problems to deal with worse than anything you or I ever faced," Nancia said. "From what I overheard, keeping watch on her and Sev — you don't know what her father did to her."

"I can guess," Forister said.

"Well, then. It doesn't excuse what *she* did, I know that. And it would kill her to have all that brought out in court. But — she hasn't had many breaks," Nancia said. "She never knew what it was to have a loving family behind her." *I've been so much luckier — even if I didn't know it for a little while.* "I thought she deserved that much of a second chance."

Silence followed this statement.

"I — it was dishonest," Nancia admitted. "And I know that. And if you two don't want to be partnered with me any more . . . "

"Knew about the buildings already," Micaya pointed out. "We were there too, if you recall. *I* didn't see any need to stand up in court and contradict Sev's rather touching evidence. Neither did your brawn here." She threw her head back and drained her glass of imported wine in one gulp. Forister winced.

"Then —" Nancia was confused.

Forister patted her titanium column. "It was . . . in the nature of a test, you might say," he told her. "Mic, here, thought you'd been with Caleb too long, absorbed too much of his black-and-white attitude to be as flexible as a good investigative team needs to be. We may be facing some delicate assignments. Need to make some judgment calls — can't rely on CS regulations to answer every question. Now *I* thought you had the maturity to make your own moral judgments — including knowing when to keep silent. After all, you didn't lie about any of Fassa's wrongdoing; all that evidence is clear in your deposition. You just — balanced — what you couldn't say about her tragic childhood, against what you didn't have to say about her work on Shemali."

"You don't despise me for it?"

"I did the same thing," Forister pointed out, "and without benefit of your inside information on Fassa's childhood."

"Then — it wasn't wrong?"

"You're an adult now, Nancia. You use your own judgment. What do *you* think?" Forister asked.

Nancia was still thinking when they reached the first Singularity point on the run to Theta Szentmari. With Forister and Micaya strapped down in their cabins, she arced through the collapsing spaces in an effortless flashing dive. Space and time twisted and reformed about her as she chose their path through continually changing matrices of transformations. For the few seconds of perfect, gliding, dangerous transition she danced and swam in her own element, making her own decisions.

As she continued to do for the rest of her career.

— *THE END* —

THE SHIP WHO SEARCHED

Anne McCaffrey and
Mercedes Lackey

Tia, a bright and precocious seven-year-old, becomes afflicted by a paralysing alien virus while accompanying her archeologist parents on a dig. Too proud to bother them, she hides the progressing symptoms until it is too late – until she can be given no life at all outside a mechanical support system.

But Tia won't be satisfied to glide through life like a ghost in a glorified wheelchair. She would rather strap on a *spaceship*. And Tia has a special mission: to seek out whatever it was that laid her low, to understand and then eliminate it, to make sure that no other young girl will suffer the fate of
The Ship Who Searched.

Set in the same universe as *The Ship Who Sang* and *Partnership*, *The Ship Who Searched* is a tale of courage and adventure from one of the best-loved and most inspirational writers of science fiction today.

THE CITY WHO FOUGHT

Anne McCaffrey and
S. M. Stirling

Simeon was bored with his life. It wasn't being a shellperson that bothered him – he rather pitied the 'softshells' with their short lives and their laughably limited senses – but the routine of running the mining and processing station that made up his 'body' was getting him down. So the excitement generated by the arrival of an out-of-control refugee ship was more than welcome – even if it did interrupt his latest wargame.

The refugees told of an attack by space barbarians who were headed Simeon's way and it soon became apparent that, if anyone was to survive, Simeon had to translate his skills at wargaming into the real thing and become *The City Who Fought.*

CRISIS ON DOONA

Anne McCaffrey and
Jody Lynn Nye

RETURN TO DOONA

More than twenty-five years ago, the first Humans had
set foot on Doona and had found a beautiful, unspoilt
planet. But they had also found that they were not alone.

Their early survey had completely ignored or missed the
fact that the planet was already settled – by the alien,
feline Hrrubans. The ensuing conflict led to the historic
Decision at Doona – a social experiment in living together
that was to last for a quarter of a century.

Now that contract has run out and is up for renewal.
Everything that Human and Hrruban has worked for –
particularly the delicate alliance itself – is in peril and
could be destroyed utterly . . .

TREATY PLANET

Anne McCaffrey and
Jody Lynn Nye

The compelling story of Doona continues . . .

The huge, black spaceship in orbit around Doonarrala is apparently unarmed and seems to present no immediate threat. And yet its very presence and size are menacing to some. A classified tape, seen only by the military, shows that it bears a strong resemblance to another ship found derelict and looming over a planet devastated by war.

For Todd Reeve, leader of the Human colony on Doonarrala, and for his Hrruban friend, Hrriss, the ship represents an opportunity for their two species to extend the hand of friendship to another.

For others, from both Earth and Hrruba, the ship and its inhabitants are a threat of such magnitude that they will stop at nothing to sabotage Todd's efforts at communication, waiting only until their own forces are in place before acting.

DINOSAUR PLANET

Anne McCaffrey

On Earth they had died out 70 million years ago but on Ireta the dinosaurs ruled in all their bizarre splendour, roaming a planet as mystifying as any in the galaxy. And the expedition sent to explore it was trapped within its coils when their relief ship disappeared. Soon the Heavyworlders reverted to type, and as predatory carnivores hunted down their colleagues, only the frozen sleep of cryogenics offered an escape – but for how long?

A superb piece of science fiction by the Hugo and Nebula winning creator of the *Dragon* books.

SURVIVORS
Dinosaur Planet II

Anne McCaffrey

To escape extermination by their heavyworld colleagues, Kai, Varian and their companions sought refuge in the suspended animation of cryogenic sleep. Now time has elapsed – how much is hard to tell, but at least two generations – and THE SURVIVORS emerge from their hibernation.

Ireta, the Dinosaur Planet, is much changed. The heavyworlders have regressed to primitive barbarity. Much necessary life-support equipment has malfunctioned or disappeared. The very face of Ireta has altered.

But help is at hand – a rescue ship is on its way. Even as hope begins to spring, however, new problems arise. What are the motives of the mysterious Theks? Why are the intelligent Giffs – pterodactyls locked in an evolutionary blind alley – acting so strangely? Above all, what possibly could be the cause of the mindless hostility of the heavyworlders?

SURVIVORS – the magnificent successor to DINOSAUR PLANET.

SASSINAK
Anne McCaffrey and
Elizabeth Moon

Volume One of THE PLANET PIRATES

Sassinak was twelve when the raiders came. Old enough
to be used, young enough to be broken – or so they
thought. But they reckoned without the girl's will, forged
into a steely resolve to avenge herself on the pirates who
had killed her parents and friends.

When the chance comes to escape, Sassinak grabs it,
thanks to the help of a captured Fleet crewman.
Returned to the Federation of Sentient Planets, she
initiates her revenge by joining Fleet as a raw recruit
surprising everyone by her rapid rise to senior rank. And
then her vengeance begins in earnest.

Anne McCaffrey and Elizabeth Moon have woven a story
worthy of Robert A. Heinlein in its tough-mindedness,
reminiscent of Larry Niven and David Brin in its
description of human and alien races coming together
both as friends and enemies.

Little, Brown and Company Order Form

Little, Brown and Company, PO Box 50, Harlow, Essex CM17 0DZ
Tel: 01279 438150   Fax: 01279 439376

☐ The Ship Who Searched	Anne McCaffrey and Mercedes Lackey	£5.99
☐ The City Who Fought	Anne McCaffrey and S.M. Stirling	£5.99
☐ Crisis on Doona	Anne McCaffrey and Jody Lynn Nye	£4.99
☐ Treaty Planet	Anne McCaffrey and Jody Lynn Nye	£5.99
☐ Sassinak	Anne McCaffrey and Elizabeth Moon	£5.99
☐ The Death of Sleep	Anne McCaffrey and Jody Lynn Nye	£5.99
☐ Generation Warriors	Anne McCaffrey and Elizabeth Moon	£5.99
☐ Dinosaur Planet	Anne McCaffrey	£4.99
☐ Survivors	Anne McCaffrey	£4.99

Payments can be made as follows: cheque, postal order (payable to Little,
Brown and Company) or by credit cards, Visa/Access/Amex. Do not send
cash or currency. UK customers and BFPO please allow £1.00 for postage
and packing for the first book, plus 50p for the second book, plus 30p for
each additional book up to a maximum charge of £3.00 (7 books plus).
Overseas customers including Ireland, please allow £2.00 for the first
book plus £1.00 for the second book plus 50p for each additional book.

NAME (CAPITALS) _____

ADDRESS _____

_____

_____

☐ I enclose a cheque/postal order made payable to Little, Brown and
Company for £ _____
or
☐ I wish to pay by Access/Visa/Amex* Card (*delete as appropriate)

Number | | | | | | | | | | | | | | | | | |

Card Expiry Date_____ Signature _____